Eileen MacDonald is a freelance journalist and writer and has worked for a variety of national newspapers and magazines, including the *Observer, Independent* and *GQ Magazine*. She is the author of *The Keeper* and *The Infiltrator* as well as two works of non-fiction *Shoot the Women First* and *Brides for Sale*.

Also by Eileen MacDonald

Fiction:
The Sleeper
The Infiltrator

Non-Fiction:
Shoot the Women First
Brides For Sale

First published in Great Britain by Simon & Schuster UK Ltd, 2000
A Viacom company

1 3 5 7 9 10 8 6 4 2

Simon & Schuster UK Ltd
Africa House
64-78 Kingsway
London WC2B 6AH

Simon & Schuster Australia
Sydney

A CIP catalogue record for this book is available from the British Library

Hardback ISBN: ISBN 0-684-84053-7
Trade Paperback ISBN: 0-684-84054-5

Printed and bound in Great Britain by
Butler & Tanner Ltd, Frome and London

For Toby, but with heaps of gratitude to Paul

ACKNOWLEDGEMENTS

I wish to acknowledge the invaluable assistance given to me in researching this book from the following: Terry Taylor, former UN inspector to Iraq and assistant director of the International Institute for Strategic Studies, London; Dr David Kelly, Senior Advisor to the MOD on Biological Defence and also UN inspector to Iraq; Dr Rick Titball, Technical Manager of Microbiology at the MOD's Chemical and Biological Defence Establishment at Porton Down in Wiltshire. I also owe thanks to the epidemiologists at the Communicable Disease Surveillance Centre at Colindale. Any errors are mine and any lapses of security described in the text are purely fictional.

PROLOGUE
December 1988

The parchment lay under glass in the middle of the room. There was no other furniture, no cameras, no sign of an alarm system. On the far wall, a window was open to admit the sounds of the city and a cool breeze.

The woman hidden in the alcove behind the door shivered. She hadn't anticipated the coldness of the Holy Land at this time of year. She had been standing still for over an hour – had many more to go – but she dared not move in case the creaking floor of the old house gave her away.

Time passed with numbing slowness. Down below, she heard the last visitor leave, the curator moving about, his feet slip-slapping on the stairs, doors being closed. He entered the room, and she shrank back into her alcove; he didn't see her. He crossed to the window and, with a grunt of effort, closed it, then went out and shut the door behind him. She heard the front doors being bolted and peace descended.

She stretched her aching body and tried to rub warmth into her cold arms. She checked yet again that her rucksack was at her feet, but she didn't move from her hiding-place. It wasn't yet time.

The noise of the city gradually diminished. The light in the room turned from golden to indigo to inky black. The woman strained her eyes. She could still see the display-case.

One o'clock chimed distantly on a church bell. When the sound had died away, she moved softly towards the case.

As she reached it, it rocked on its spindly legs. She held her breath, waiting for an alarm-bell to ring, for someone to come, but nothing happened. No one came.

Working quickly, she unscrewed the four metal bolts that held the glass in place. As she lifted it, she paused again, dreading the wail of an alarm, but all was quiet.

She set the glass aside and picked up the Eighth Scroll. Her hands trembled. She brought it to her lips, kissed it once, then put it quickly but with utmost care in her rucksack.

She crossed to the window and opened it. Down below, her accomplice waited. She dropped into his arms.

Newswire. 11.12.88. 07.45. Jerusalem, Israel:

The notorious Eighth Scroll, whose discovery four years ago was greeted with intense excitement in religious circles until its denunciation as a fake, was stolen from a museum here last night.

The Scroll, unearthed during an archaeological dig in Jerusalem, contained prophecies about the end of the world and claimed to be the 'secret Scroll' referred to in Revelation, the last, apocalyptic book of the Bible.

It caught the public imagination and was sold in numerous languages around the world. Church authorities were in the process of seeing how to include it in Revelation when, nine months after its discovery, the Scroll was revealed to be a clever fake: written not by the author of Revelation in the first century, as it claimed, but by an unknown nineteenth-century hand.

Professor Daniel Zive, its discoverer, always believed in its authenticity. When it was removed without ceremony from its climate-controlled, state-of-the-art showcase in the prestigious Krier Museum in Jerusalem, he immediately claimed it, and until last night it was exhibited in the tiny Zive Collection near Jaffa Gate.

Professor Zive died three years ago. A friend of the family said this morning: 'The controversy over the Scroll killed Daniel. I think the family will be glad it's gone.'

Police say there was no evidence of a break-in. It is thought that a visitor may have removed the document during opening-hours yesterday, 'although for what purpose, one cannot think', said a spokesman.

Police are asking witnesses to come forward.

Ends.

Notes to Editors:

The Scroll reads:

From John of Patmos, a servant of God and of the Lord Jesus Christ.

May the Lord forgive me for recording these secrets, but I have been driven by torments, led by angelic dreams. Therefore now, in holy awe, I take up my pen to record what the seven thunders uttered, in this, the last of my writings: the Eighth Scroll.

They spoke of ten signs that shall take place before the Lord comes again.

The first: In the Last Days, the two sons of the infidel lord of the desert shall be struck down.

The second: False peace-makers shall be put to death: in their safest places, in their most secret council chambers, God shall cause them to be cut down.

The third: The Great Traitor shall be assassinated.

The fourth: The food that we eat and the water that we drink shall become bitter in our mouths, and many shall suffer, particularly little children and pregnant women.

The fifth: The people shall starve rather than eat.

The sixth: The people shall live in fear of the elements: of fire, sky, earth and water.

The seventh: The proudest of man's works, those things by which he seeks to make himself a god, shall be destroyed.

The eighth: Warm places shall become icy wildernesses: cool oases shall turn to desert.

The ninth: Great stones shall strike the earth with fire; death shall fall from the sky.

The tenth: Christ's covering shall be removed from those who have wrongly taken it. The keeper shall keep it holy. And then the End, the Awful Horror of the Ungodly, shall come.

Let the finder of these words, him whose eyes have been opened by the Lord, be the keeper.

Chapter One

It was nearly midnight, but the sky was as light as a misty day. The snow-smooth mountains glistened in the distance; near to, the figure of a man could clearly be seen, the steel of his shovel glinting as he swung it high above his head and then down deep into the earth below.

He had been digging for many hours, throwing the earth over his shoulder where it fell in soft mounds. He worked steadily, for time was short and he couldn't risk being seen, couldn't rely on the remoteness of that tiny, deserted Arctic island to shield him. A ship or a small aircraft might pass by, might spot his boat moored below in the bay.

He paused for breath. At first he had been cold but he was sweating now. The narrow trench, measuring seven feet by two and a half, was entirely exposed. Ross Edgecombe judged that he was three feet down. At any moment, his shovel would hit the hard-packed ice that marked the start of the permafrost.

Others preparing to rob a grave might have felt qualms, but not he. He was a scientist, engaged on a mission of enormous import. Below him, Edgecombe believed, in the body of a young Norwegian fisherman frozen since his burial in the permafrost, lay the answer to an eighty-year-old medical enigma: the key to a disease that had killed millions upon millions before vanishing as mysteriously as it had arisen.

The fisherman had been washed up on the island, the only survivor from a wrecked fishing-boat, and been cared for by the villagers. A few days later he had succumbed in agony to a disease the villagers had never seen before. He was laid in a hole dynamited deep into the permafrost so that his body would not resurface in a thaw, and so that the germs of the dreadful disease could not crawl up out of the earth to infect the living once again. But it was already too late: within two months, the whole village had been wiped out.

The modern fear of that disease's reoccurrence, the knowledge that even now, in 1999, the newest treatments would be powerless against it, had driven scientists from many nations to do what Edgecombe was doing now: search out the deep-frozen bodies of victims, in the hope of finding the germ still alive in the blood or tissue. Its genetic code could then be mapped and a vaccine made. So far the scientists had failed. The bodies they had unearthed in Alaska and Iceland hadn't been buried deep enough. Coffin lids had been raised to reveal only bones and dead germs.

If they had listened to him, Edgecombe thought bitterly, if they had appreciated the quality of his information, instead of treating him with disdain, what he was doing now, every heave of his shovel, would be being filmed by television crews and recorded for posterity.

No, it wouldn't, he corrected himself reluctantly. If he'd been with the British team, he'd probably have been on wheelbarrow detail again, out of sight of the cameras – he, who knew more than the rest of them put together – and one of the team-leaders would have been claiming the glory. The way it was, he was his own master. Well, almost. On site, he made the rules. He had sought permission from no one, neither the Norwegian authorities nor the relatives of the dead man – let others waste their time doing that, he thought contemptuously. No one knew what he was doing and it was crucial that no one found out. He didn't share those other scientists' aims: his goal was different. He dwelt on that difference for a moment. He wasn't, for instance, interested in a vaccine.

His shovel shuddered in the earth. Staring down, he saw ice spears winking up at him like diamonds. The permafrost.

He knew that the fisherman's coffin might be another seven feet down. To dynamite the frozen ground would be to risk destroying the body; risk too (although the risk was very small) the chance of dispersing the live germ so that he caught it. If the village had still existed on the island, Edgecombe could have used power-tools. As it was, his only way through the solid frozen mass was with hard manual labour.

Over the course of the next thirty-six hours, he worked doggedly with pickaxe and spade. Blisters swelled on his hands. He slept twice, and the second time awoke to feel soft snow falling on his face. It was early May but spring came late in the Arctic Circle.

He renewed his attack on the ground. Early in the morning of the second day, when he was eight feet below the surface of the earth, his spade hit wood. He scraped away the covering soil and saw it: the coffin-lid.

Although he'd expected it, his heart turned in his mouth. He had made such promises to the others about what that coffin would contain. He hauled himself out of the grave and went down to his boat to collect his gear: the modified drill, the sample tubes, the flasks of liquid nitrogen, the biological-hazard suit. He'd bragged that he wouldn't wear a protective suit, had said scornfully that it wasn't necessary. But he put it on nevertheless – the others weren't there to see, after all.

Back at the grave, he pulled on the respiratory helmet, which transformed him at once into a spaceman, and tightened the straps of the oxygen cylinder on his back. Cautiously, he lowered himself back into the pit. His breathing echoed in his ears, an eerie sensation, one that had always troubled him. He used a chisel to prise open the coffin.

The fisherman had been twenty-six when he died. His hair was still blond, his flesh, although marble-white, had not fallen away, and his black suit, though now tinged with green, was undamaged. A Bible lay on his chest, and his arms were crossed over his crotch. Despite his agonizing death, his face looked peaceful. Edgecombe beheld him greedily. If the germ flourished anywhere on Earth, it was within that corpse.

He pushed the Bible off, and slowly, clumsily because of the gloves of his protective suit, removed the man's jacket and pulled up the undershirt. He saw a letter there, resting above the heart, probably from a loved one. It joined the Bible in the grave. Then he picked up the drill and attached a sample-tube to the end.

To defrost the corpse to reach the lungs would have risked destroying the germs. Removing frozen core samples from the lungs was the best way to ensure their survival. Edgecombe began drilling into the skin above the man's chest. His breathing grew stertorous with his own lungs' effort. When the sample-tube was full, he placed it in a flask of liquid nitrogen and resumed his drilling.

When he had eight samples, he stopped. The corpse was riddled now, the peaceful face at odds with the wounds in the body, but Edgecombe didn't care – he'd got what he wanted.

He was in a hurry now to get back to England and the laboratory he had prepared in hope. In certainty, the others had reproved, but they weren't scientists. He knew that only by culturing samples from the frozen tissue would it be possible to see if the germ was indeed still alive. But he felt it was; he had – he smiled sardonically at himself – faith.

Not troubling to replace the Bible, and leaving the man as he had made him, Edgecombe hammered back the lid of the coffin. Once out of the grave, he carried his precious specimens down to his boat, then took off his protective suit and returned to the grave to fling back the earth he'd removed.

He did not set back in the ground the small cross that had marked the grave, indeed, he'd forgotten about it. As his dinghy puttered out into the Arctic Sea, heading back to the main island of the archipelago, the sun shone down upon that desecrated spot, upon that white cross, erected only recently by the fisherman's descendants, shamed that his grave had been so long neglected.

Three days later, Edgecombe arrived back in England. Although his colleagues urged him to rest – he looked exhausted – he retreated at once to his laboratory and set to work. He had to find out whether the organism was still alive. He defrosted the frozen tissue and 'pulverized' it until it was pliable. He took a sample and filtered it to remove any bacteria, then injected it into the amniotic fluid of a fertilized chicken egg. He did that eight times, then put the eggs in an incubator. Over the next three days, he kept anxious watch, turning the eggs at intervals to ensure that the embryos remained alive.

On the fourth day, he took one egg out of the incubator, cracked off the top and emptied out its contents. In this liquid, either the germ lived and multiplied, or it did not. If he had been a religious man, he would have prayed.

He sucked up some of the fluid in a pipette and squeezed it out into a Petri dish prepared with culture. He slid the dish under his microscope. Almost, he couldn't bear to look, and then he did. He saw the telltale pin-pricks in the culture.

He sat back for a moment, trying to absorb it. Then he rose and walked steadily down the narrow hallway to the room where the others waited.

CHAPTER TWO

The success of the 'Foodie Lanes' in London's Covent Garden had brought a new cachet and plenty of extra visitors to the area. Sundays were especially popular, when for a minimal sum, one could stroll amongst the stalls, feasting on exquisite canapés, little cups of soup, miniature Yorkshire puddings in which nestled strips of rare roast organic beef – or, for the vegetarian, red pepper.

The Lanes had started the previous November with mulled wine and mince pies in front of the Christmas trees on the piazzas. Someone had started selling tiny Christmas puddings, someone else offered hot turkey sandwiches the size of a credit-card, and the idea of 'small but beautiful' began. People expected it only to last until Christmas, but by May 2000 the Lanes were an established part of the market.

The stall-holders themselves tended to be aspiring young chefs or middle-class women who hoped to make money by selling larger versions of their 'tasters' or who simply thought it was fun. And it was fun: there was a spirit of bonhomie, and of helping each other out.

Early one Sunday morning in late May, Ruth Grant arrived in the market bearing several large baker's trays covered with greaseproof paper. She'd heard, she said falteringly, that one could set up anywhere, as long as one wasn't treading on any one else's toes, which of course she didn't want to do.

She'd chosen her adviser well. He was a hearty young man from the country, offering venison sausages on sticks, and her frail prettiness and fluttering anxiety appealed to him. He found her a pitch in 'Puddings', borrowed a barrow so that she wouldn't have to rent one, and helped her unload the rest of the trays from her van. When the greaseproof paper was removed, fruit tartlets and rows of dancing gingerbread boys and girls were revealed. They looked wonderful.

'Fantastic,' said the young man. 'May I?'

'Oh do! Please.'

His eyes lit up as he chewed. 'Melt in the mouth.'

'Really?'

He smiled. 'You'll be sold out before you know it.'

An hour later, when the Lanes began to fill, Ruth's stall was one of the most popular. Children clamoured for the gingerbread and their parents, with little reluctance, took the tarts. By one o'clock, the last of her wares had gone.

'See you next week?' the young man called out as she passed. But Ruth, walking quickly away with her empty trays, gave no sign of having heard him. She rounded the corner into Floral Street and was lost to view.

The clock on the canteen wall read fourteen minutes to eight. The break ended at eight; Liam had to do it now.

He shivered with a mixture of excitement and fear. Two minutes' work, he told himself, and then it would be done. He could go home, back to the others, he could be himself again.

Around him, his co-workers chatted and laughed as they drank their coffee.

'I'm off for a pee,' he said and scrapped back his chair. They carried on talking.

Liam made for the double doors and the corridor leading to the Gents. No one else was around. He slipped through the door that led into the production area.

At first when he'd been told what his mission was to be – getting a job in the Yummy Tummy baby-food factory on the outskirts of Rotterdam – he'd been disappointed. All that build-up, he'd thought, all that 'You're so special' treatment, for something so mundane.

Actually the beginning of the mission had proved quite exciting enough, because halfway through the interview, he'd suddenly been terrified about not getting the job when at home, they were depending on him so much.

He had got it, of course. Yummy Tummy were experiencing a desperate staff shortage after two of their rival companies had been forced to suspend production when puncture marks were found in their dried milk packaging. 'Yummy Tummy' had been inundated with extra orders and had stepped up its production to twenty-four hours. Staff had been offered overtime, and there was a recruitment drive locally, extended to the Internet where advertisements were placed for young people willing to work on short contracts for good wages; accommodation and meals included.

The next tricky part had been fitting in. Everyone was around Liam's age and they were friendly. After work, they wanted to enjoy themselves. They went out drinking, but Liam couldn't risk that, in case he said something incriminating, gave himself away, so he made up a story about having an obscure medical condition. They accepted that, as they accepted that this was his gap-year. They accepted every lie he told them, and he felt badly about that, but it couldn't be helped: his mission was what mattered, following the orders the man had given him.

He'd done what he'd been told to do. He'd asked no obvious questions; instead he'd watched and listened and after six weeks, he'd seen the opportunity.

In order to safeguard against infection, the dried formula milk that 'Yummy Tummy' produced was pasteurized. Any contaminant added beforehand would therefore be destroyed. However, post-pasteurization, and just prior to packaging, additives were intro-duced to the formula for the purpose of making it more like breast milk. Those additives were manufactured elsewhere and as they had already been sample-checked, were not checked again on their arrival at Yummy Tummy's premises. In appearance, the substance was very similar to the formula-milk: a fine, dry powder, creamy white in colour.

Inside his pocket, Liam's hand closed around the sachet the man had given him. It looked just like a sachet of coffee-creamer; it felt like that too.

Over to his right now, he could see the post-pasteurization vats. He made his way over, ducking down behind the line of machinery so that he wouldn't be seen from the supervisor's glass-walled office. At the vats, it took only seconds to remove the safety caps on the nozzles of three of them. He pulled the sachet from his pocket, tore it open and emptied a little into each vat. He replaced the safety caps and ran back out into me corridor.

Beside the Gents was a pay phone. Liam dialled the number the man had made him memorize.

Someone picked up at the other end but didn't speak.

'I've fed the cat,' said Liam breathlessly.

'Good,' said the man. 'I'll pick you up later as arranged. Goodbye now,' and he hung up.

Liam ducked into the Gents to flush the empty sachet down one of the lavatories. When he joined the others in the canteen, no one had even noticed his absence. He was shivering again, this time with relief. It had been so easy! Yummy Tummy were almost neurotic about safety, and took painstaking precautions. But no company, Liam told himself with satisfaction, could safeguard against the efforts of a determined saboteur.

A minute later, a bell rang for the end of the break, and everyone headed back to work. The rest of the shift passed so quickly that almost before he knew it. Liam had finished and the bus was carrying him through heavy rain to the place where the man would pick him up.

It was nearly one in the morning, and the rain made the streets seem darker. When Liam got off the bus on the outskirts of the city, he had some way still to go, but he walked lightly. His mission was completed, the tension was over.

Half an hour later, he paused by a lamppost to check his map. Not much further now, and he was grateful for that, because he was cold and tired, almost drained, and the rain was heavier.

He hurried on until he found the narrow, rutted cul-de-sac that was the meeting place. His instructions were to go to the end and wait; the man would come for him. There were no street-lights there and the buildings looked derelict. Liam hoped that he would not have to wait long.

As if on cue, a car turned in at the top of the road, and dipped its headlights twice: the man's signal.

Liam grinned. He was looking forward to bragging to the man about how well everything had gone. He started towards the car. Soon he'd be in it, in the warm, out of this pissing rain, on his way home. They were going to be so proud of him.

The car was coming towards him, its headlights bouncing like flashlights over the ruts. Suddenly it speeded up. Liam was blinded by the glare of the lights and raised a hand to shield his eyes.

The engine-note rose to a scream. In panic, Liam turned and ran, but there was nowhere to go. The car smashed into him, crushing him against the end wall of the cul-de-sac, ramming his body against the brick-work, until the man was sure that his job was done.

CHAPTER THREE

Jane Carlucci hurried back along the path from the faculty-building postbox to the postgraduates' hall of residence. It was nine o'clock on Friday morning. By now, Paul Ryder would be on his way from London. In a little over an hour, he would be sitting in Professor Eccles's study, waiting to listen to her paper, and she still hadn't decided what to wear. She wanted to strike the right note: earnest but not stuffy; and definitely not studenty.

If Ryder took her seriously, if he liked her and admired her work, new horizons might open up, and at twenty-seven, stuck in what had turned out to be a dead-end job, Jane would welcome just about any new horizon. She wasn't sure precisely what Ryder did, but he was from the Home Office and therefore technically superior to Eccles. He might commission her to do special projects for him and if he did, she'd jump at the chance, no matter what it was. Anything so as not to have to waste more time kow-towing to Professor Nigel bloody Eccles.

She smiled sourly. She'd been so pleased, the previous autumn, to get the job as his assistant. Within the little world of religious academics, Eccles was a bright, shining star, the most authoritative voice in Britain (perhaps among the top three in the world) on the fast-growing phenomenon of New Religious Movements, or cults, as most people called them.

Globally, there were tens of thousands of 'non-traditional religions' – in Japan alone there were nearly 200,000 registered groups. Their numbers had increased particularly in the Nineties, and now, five months into the new millennium, that expansion showed no sign of slowing down. In Britain, seventeen new groups had formed since the start of the year. They were mainly Christian or New Age in origin, their births inspired by the year 2000, their creeds announcing a new age of enlightenment or, in some cases, the end of the world.

Jane knew that most of the groups would flourish and die away within the year. Most, too, would have little long-term or detrimental effect upon their followers. For many, it would be no more than a rite of passage into adulthood. But there were a few groups whose philosophies or lifestyles were more sinister. There was the sect in Worcester, for example, whose charismatic leader had been found to be sexually abusing the children of sect members, with, it later transpired, their parents' consent. Or the house church in Wales, whose members had been persuaded to sell all their worldly goods, even their homes, as evidence of 'Faith Alone Living', and whose leader had subsequently absconded with their money.

There were allegations of brain-washing, of personality changes; of members not being allowed out of the cult to visit parents or friends. When their parents went to the authorities for help, they were told there was little that could legally be done if someone aged eighteen or over decided to pursue an alternative lifestyle. It wasn't illegal to state that the world was a wicked, sinful place and that one's parents and friends were going to hell or that their lifestyles were Satanic. On the other hand, it was illegal for parents to arrange for their children to be kidnapped from a cult.

Five years before, the desperate parents of some cult-members had got together and set up a pressure-group which lobbied MPs to 'do something' about the cults. They'd demanded that the cults be outlawed, but had been informed that in a democracy religious freedom was a right. To placate them, they'd been offered GUIDE, a Home Office-funded information centre, and in the absence of anything else they'd had to accept it. Over the years it had accumulated a wealth of data on NRMs, and it also provided a loose network of support for worried relatives.

Professor Eccles, possessor of boyish charm and good on

television, had been asked to chair GUIDE, and the appointment had made his reputation. He now travelled extensively, lecturing and appearing ever more often in the media. So time-consuming had his extra-curricular activities become, that he'd found it necessary to appoint a full-time assistant.

At her interview he'd informed Jane, with his practised warm smile, that the assistant's duties would be to keep abreast of developments within the country's NRMs, to deal with callers, to 'share the burden of all these media appearances and writing for the newspapers', to help him with his research, and to keep an eye on 'my GUIDE girlies'.

Jane's flesh had crawled at the phrase. 'I'm sorry?' she had queried as pleasantly as she could.

'My volunteers. First- and second-year undergrads from my department. They tend to be girls.' He'd given a little laugh. 'Well, it's more of a girlie thing, isn't it, answering phones?'

If she'd been made of sterner stuff, Jane had told herself both then and later, she'd have walked out at that juncture. But she badly needed full-time work – all she'd had in the two years since completing her postgraduate course in the States was a couple of temporary research assignments – so when he offered her the job she took it.

She spent her first weeks sorting out the administrative mess that GUIDE had become. Eccles hardly ever praised her efficiency, or thanked her for working late into the night on his research, but she didn't let her resentment show. Jane was small, dark-haired and pretty in an unobtrusive way. She was also fiercely determined, but he didn't yet know that: she didn't look like a troublemaker and, besides, as the youngest of four children and the only girl, she was accustomed to keeping her feelings to herself.

Eccles's way of thanking her – or, she rapidly learned, any woman – was to admire her appearance, or to make personal remarks. 'You're looking foxy today, Janey,' he'd say, picking up the work she'd done for him. Or 'Sexy, isn't she?' he'd say as he escorted a film crew into the now well-organized GUIDE office, and asked her to 'arrange coffees' while he rehearsed the interview. Jane would mentally inflict on him one of the many tortures she had devised specifically for him, though outwardly she remained calm.

At times, the urge to walk out was almost irresistible. The

television appearances Eccles had promised her never materialized, nor did the radio interviews or the newspaper articles. Those he kept for himself; any media inquiries had to be routed straight through to him. Jane was his dogsbody and, when he could get away with it, whipping-girl.

She knew no outsider would believe how ghastly Eccles was to work for, and even telling people might be damaging. The sociology/religious studies world was tiny and she could easily find herself blackballed. She would have to stay until the end of that year, at the very least, before moving on.

On bleak days, she told herself that it wasn't entirely bad. At least she had a job. At least she was able to help people, if only, for the most part, by listening.

Sometimes the callers sounded desperate. The mother whose son had told her that, as a punishment for talking to the local newspaper about her fears of the movement he'd joined, he wouldn't be coming home for Christmas; in fact he was going to another country . . . Or the father whose brilliant daughter had dropped out of medical school after joining a group calling themselves the Chosen. They believed extra-terrestrial spirits had warned them the Chosen had less than a year in which to prepare for the arrival of a space-ship which would transport them to the planet Sirius.

Jane listened to the parents' stories, and tried to comfort and soothe them when they cried. But sometimes that didn't seem enough.

Which was why, she told herself, as she pushed open the main door of the hall of residence, it was vital that she impress Paul Ryder. It was the reason she had stayed up half the night perfecting her paper on 'End-time documents and their relevance today, with particular reference to New Religious Movements'.

The subject had grown out of a phone call from a woman whose daughter had got involved in a cult that followed the prophecies of Nostradamus. Jane had dug around in a few databases, and come up with five 'alternative' documents prophesying the end of the world. Some of them had been, or still were, taken seriously by NRMs.

Another of Eccles's promises had been that he would help her publish anything she wrote. He'd grunted when she'd told him about her paper, which she'd taken as encouragement, and so she'd worked hard on it, largely in her own time and at home. But when she'd finished, and she asked Eccles to read it, he reacted as if he'd never heard of it.

She doubted that it would have ever have been read by anyone but herself, if Dr Angela Fraser, the Scottish GUIDE representative, hadn't visited Eccles the week before. Eccles resented the mere fact of another GUIDE office (even if it was in Edinburgh) and he let Dr Fraser languish in his room while he had coffee with a student.

While she waited, she had read Jane's paper, then inquired as to the author's whereabouts and come looking for her. It ought to be published, Dr Fraser said. Had Professor Eccles mentioned to Jane, for instance, that the Home Office department responsible for GUIDE, published an annual review, which always included a few papers?

Of course, he hadn't.

Dr Fraser didn't want to step on her colleague's toes, she continued, but she was due to attend a briefing meeting at the department the following week, and if Jane liked she could mention her paper to someone there.

She had obviously been as good as her word, because Paul Ryder had phoned Jane the previous day. He was going to be 'down her way' that morning, and wondered if he might drop in to hear what she had to say on 'this interesting-sounding subject'.

Jane had had to tell Eccles. She'd seen his eyes darken, and had wondered whether her departure from the university was rather more imminent than she'd thought.

Then he'd smiled – not his pleasant camera-smile, but the one where his lips made one tight line. 'You're a dark horse, aren't you, Janey? What else have you been plotting behind my back?'

'I haven't been plotting, Nigel, I—'

'If Mr Ryder wants to meet you,' he cut in, 'I'd better be there, too, hadn't I? To hold your hand, you understand?'

Jane did. The Home Office paid a good portion of his salary as well as hers. He'd want to make sure she didn't tell the visitor who really ran GUIDE. She would have given a lot for Eccles not to have been there, but . . .

She reached her fourth-floor flat and went to run her bath. Once she was out of Eccles's clutches, there would only be her mother left to please. The acquiring-of-a-boyfriend-with-a-view-to-marriage.

Jane smiled ruefully at herself in the mirror: one couldn't please everyone all of the time.

The baby was five months old. His parents shakily reported that he'd started being unwell the day before. He was a particularly hungry infant, which was why his mother supplemented her breast-milk with dried formula milk. But it was of the very finest quality, she had tearfully assured the emergency-room intern at the Milan hospital. Organic, the advertising had boasted, second only to mother's own. Special ingredients had been added to make it more like real breast milk. One simply added water.

The baby had been sick and very miserable. He'd had similar symptoms once before, and on that occasion his parents had called out the doctor, only to be informed with some stiffness that mild stomach upsets were very common in young babies, and that first-time parents tended to over-react.

This time, therefore, they'd told each other not to worry, that the symptoms would pass as they had before. Their baby had eventually fallen asleep. His mother had gone to check him at four o'clock that morning, and had been unable to rouse him fully. His eyes were sunken, his mouth dry. They'd rushed him to the hospital, where he was found to be severely dehydrated. If they'd left it much longer, the intern snapped, he might have died.

As it was, by nine o'clock that Friday morning, the baby was making good progress. According to the ward sister, he'd probably be allowed to go home on Sunday.

That news calmed his parents sufficiently for them to be able to answer a few questions from a health-care worker. They described the pains they always took to ensure their bottle-feeding equipment was sterile. They were meticulous about measuring and mixing. They never added an extra scoop to make it more 'nourishing' or stored made-up formula in the fridge, or reheated old feeds.

The health worker assured them that she wasn't accusing them of anything. She simply wanted to know what their son had been fed, apart from breast-milk, in the previous twenty-four hours.

That was easy, the father answered. Yummy Tummy baby formula, the best on the market.

She wrote it down. There was silence in the room, save for her pen scratching.

'Why?' the father asked suddenly.

It was all right, the health worker said reassuringly.

'Is there something wrong with it?' he demanded, his voice rising.

The health worker did her best. Quietly, she explained that in the previous twenty-four hours, there had been three other reported cases of salmonella in bottle-fed babies in Milan.

'Salmonella?' he shouted, while his wife, white-faced, tried to shush him. 'That can kill babies, can't it?'

But their son was going to be fine, the woman soothed. If he had been infected by the organism – and it was not yet conclusive; his specimen was still being analysed – it had passed from him by now. She cleared her throat. 'Salmonella can be caused by a host of factors and babies are highly susceptible to even a very low dose. It's far too early to start apportioning blame—'

'I'm going to sue the bastards!' the father yelled.

The health worker waited until the worst of his rage had passed, then headed down the corridor to her own office. She called the public-health laboratory in the city and reported another case of suspected salmonella poisoning.

'That's four confirmed, three suspected,' the case officer told her.

'All Yummy Tummy?'

'Yup.'

'We're talking product recall, then,' the health worker said matter-of-factly.

'I think we are.'

The manufacturers had been informed. It was their nightmare come true, but they were well prepared for it. They were even now trying to trace the source of infection by identifying the batch of contaminated milk powder; that would give them the date and place of its manufacture and enable their investigators to trace its distribution. Yummy Tummy was sold throughout Europe and had just extended into Turkey and the Middle East. They could only pray that there was no more than one contaminated batch, and that it had been caught early, in northern Italy.

Even so, Yummy Tummy was all too gravely aware how much damage had been done. Supermarkets were clearing their shelves of the milk-powder; the company's help-line was jammed with calls. Unless parents were reassured, the company might face ruin. Damage-limitation was essential. A press statement was being prepared and would be released within the hour. It would state that until the source of contamination had been found parents should not buy or use Yummy Tummy baby-formula, but should rely on other brands.

At the same time, a Salmonella Alert Notice was being flashed to every Communicable Disease Surveillance Centre across Europe. It arrived in Britain at a modern, brown-brick building in Colindale, on the northern edge of London, at 10.15 on that Friday morning. Its arrival was preceded by a Department of Health notification that Yummy Tummy products were not sold in the UK, and therefore no action was required by Colindale's epidemiologists.

Had action in fact been required, Colindale would have found it very difficult to supply. Their gastro-intestinal laboratory was already fully occupied with an outbreak of botulism, not seen in Britain for eleven years.

Because of its rarity, the botulism's symptoms hadn't been recognized in the first victim, a young man brought into the Casualty Department of Salisbury Hospital on Wednesday night. His legs were already paralysed (during the night the paralysis spread). His mother told the doctors that he had apparently started feeling unwell that morning: he'd vomited and had had diarrhoea too. She went round to his flat in the evening and found him semi-consciousness.

'He is going to be all right, isn't he?' she had begged.

Her son had died on Thursday morning of respiratory failure. By then, several other hospitals in and around London were beginning to admit patients, mostly young children, with similar symptoms. At noon a six-year-old boy died, at 4.15 in the afternoon an eight-year-old girl. In the latter case, the consultant paediatrician ordered gastro-intestinal tests on the contents of the child's gut. At seven o'clock on Friday morning, the culture revealed the presence of the *Clostridium botulinum* organism – and the cause of the child's death.

News of the disease was instantly dispatched, with a reminder of its symptoms and treatment (with an intravenous dose of anti-toxins), to every hospital in London and the south-east. At nine o'clock, Colindale had been notified that thirty-seven cases of botulism had been identified, including that first death in Salisbury.

The chief concern now was to locate the source of the contamination and to stop more people eating it. It was also imperative to find those people who had consumed the product but who had not yet shown the symptoms of the disease – incubation could take eight days – and get them quick and early treatment.

To achieve those ends, epidemiologists at Colindale's main-site laboratory were conducting 'trawling' interviews, by phone and in person, with the patients' relatives and if possible with the patients themselves, to determine what they had eaten in the previous week. It was difficult. People, particularly when shocked and frightened, found it difficult to remember what they had eaten so long before, and no direct questions could be asked – the interviewer must not 'lead' the subject in any way. The task was made no easier by the knowledge that sooner or later – and one always had to assume that it would be sooner – the media would get hold of the story, perhaps before Colindale had been able to tell the Department of Health the source of the outbreak. The prospect of the public in panic over yet another food-scare, this time already with corpses to show for itself, was a nightmare no one at Colindale would have wished to dwell upon, even had there been time to do so.

At 10.36, one of the three epidemiologists conducting the telephone interviews slammed down her receiver, and shouted, 'Yes!'

The woman she'd just spoken to, the mother of a nine-year-old girl currently on a respirator in Kingston-on-Thames, had said that the previous Sunday she and her husband had taken their daughter to the Foodie Lanes in Covent Garden.

'The first guy,' the epidemiologist demanded of the colleague next to her, 'the Salisbury one. He ran a stall in Covent Garden, didn't he?'

Now they had a pointer. It wasn't proof but it was a start. They still had to identify the stall and the 'guilty' product – quite possibly, the epidemiologist suggested, the Salisbury man's wares? But at least they were on the trail. Without leading their interviewees, they could inquire if the victims had eaten out at the weekend. The net could be cast in the right waters.

The first disappointment was Paul Ryder's appearance. He was a big, untidy man with a large nose and short grey hair. His dark suit looked too small for him; in fact, Jane thought, he looked as if he'd slept in it. When he sat down and crossed his legs, brown socks showed, and above them a few inches of white leg.

'Jane, if you'd like to start?' Eccles prompted with a big, TV-smile. Jane collected herself and began.

For the first few phrases, she was too nervous to look up from her paper, but when she did, she saw that Ryder wasn't looking at her. His long legs were stretched out before him and he was studying his shoes intently. So much for her agonizing over her own appearance, Jane thought: the black skirt or the green, the careful application of not too much make-up.

But she knew from the way Eccles was watching her, with a mixture of dislike and wariness, that her paper was good. Her confidence grew. She told herself that Ryder must be listening – people concentrated in different ways – and turned the page.

'The final document to which I refer is the Eighth Scroll.'

A movement caught her eye. Ryder was looking at her at last.

'Although it was, of course, proven to be a fake, I include it here because it demonstrates the potential power of end-time documents to alter received Christian belief, even after two thousand years. One recalls that the Greek Orthodox and Roman Catholic churches were examining the possibility of including the Scroll in an addendum to the Bible, or even of rewriting the book of Revelation itself . . .'

Ryder's eyes were a piercing and rather unsettling blue. He didn't look in the least dozy any more, she thought. In fact, he looked decidedly sharp.

She returned quickly to her text: 'I believe that the Scroll owed its potential power to the specific nature of the some of the ten "end-time" signs it describes. Rather than the vague "wars and rumours of wars", false prophets, et cetera, of the New Testament, the Scroll states categorically that certain things will come to pass in the Last Days.

'For example, the first sign tells us that the two sons of the infidel lord of the desert shall be struck down; the second, that false peace-makers shall be put to death in their safest places; the tenth, that Christ's covering shall be removed from those who have wrongly taken it, and that the keeper shall keep it holy.'

She glanced up. Ryder was still staring unnervingly at her.

She resumed her reading, and didn't look up again until she had finished. When she did, he was studying his shoes again.

'Thank you very much, Jane. That was an excellent paper,' said Eccles fulsomely, and it was only because she knew him so well that Jane detected the insincerity in his voice. 'I'm sure Paul will want a copy to take away with him for the annual review. Am I right, Paul?'

Jane looked hopefully across. Ryder took his time to sit up, pulling one long leg after the other in under his chair. At last he met her gaze and smiled.

'Unfortunately I don't think it's the sort of thing we're looking for. Not this year,' he said.

Jane went cold.

'It was a very good paper,' Ryder went on, and the kindness in his voice got to Jane and made her feel the way she had when, aged twelve, she'd been rejected for the school play because of the braces on her teeth. 'You've obviously put a great deal of research into it . . .'

Disappointment gave way to anger. She knew the paper was good; she'd poured her heart and soul into it, and it was being damned with faint praise by a shabby, patronizing civil servant.

'. . . not really germane to GUIDE's work—'

'Absolutely. My own concern exactly,' Eccles chimed in. 'I did say something of the sort to you yesterday, Jane, if you remember.'

Jane felt her face burn. If only she had another job to go to, she swore, she'd get up and walk out.

The conversation moved on. Eccles suggested that his own most recent paper, on 'The greater acceptance of NRMs into mainstream Christianity' (for which Jane had done all the research) might be substituted for Jane's 'effort' in the annual report. He went to fetch a copy from his secretary.

An awkward silence fell. Jane could think of no suitable subject for conversation. Desperate pleading, she thought grimly, wasn't her style. She got up to leave.

'I meant it when I said it's a good paper,' Ryder said abruptly.

'Oh,' she said, taken aback.

'It was excellent. There wasn't any more information that you didn't mention?' he asked casually.

'No,' she said, wondering lay behind his question, what he thought she'd left out.

'Right. It's just that sometimes people feel they don't want to cram too much in, so they'll save the rest for another paper.'

'It was all there,' she said, unable to keep an edge out of her voice.

He smiled again. 'The annual report's a dreary publication. You don't want to be published in it.'

Oh yes I do, she wanted to tell him. To get on in the academic world, that was exactly what she wanted.

He held out his hand and after a moment's hesitation she shook it. Then he gave her his card. 'If you come across anything interesting,' he said, 'let me know.'

Sure, she thought.

Eccles re-entered and frowned at her. She recognised dismissal, and left the room.

She was still seething when she reached her own office a few doors down. A good paper, she thought, dropping it on to her desk, but not good enough for Paul Ryder. He'd known the title. What had he expected? Why had he bothered to come and see her, thus fuelling her hopes, only to dash them in front of Eccles? She shuddered. She faced another six months of Eccles, with his sexist insults and bullying, which, after Ryder's rejection, were bound to get worse.

She could ring a few friends and see if there was any temporary work available, but that would be back to square one, negating all she had achieved at GUIDE. Eccles would do everything in his power to hurt her, but she was young, she told herself, she could take it, she could start again.

Her eyes fell upon the notebook she had left on her desk. It contained details of an NRM in Colchester that a nineteen-year-old boy had joined. His father had rung last night, crying, desperate, at his wits' end, and she'd promised to help him in any way she could.

That memory cooled her anger. It wasn't simply a career decision that had made her take her present job. She had another, quite separate, agenda.

Her mind filled with almost unbearably vivid memories. She and Sarah making friends on their first day at kindergarten . . . Sarah the bright, conscientious, popular schoolgirl and student . . . then Sarah the NRM member, withdrawn and hostile . . . the rescue-kidnap attempt, using Jane as bait, which had failed when one of the men moved too soon and Sarah saw him and ran . . . that last glimpse of her face, full of shock and betrayal . . . and then, two weeks later, the news that she had been found dead, drowned. Even now, ten years on, and even with regular counselling, part of Jane still felt responsible for the death of the best friend she'd ever had.

She would do anything in her power to prevent other such tragedies, even if it meant working for Eccles at his worst. The job allowed her access to people she knew she could help, and often her advice worked. She told parents to stop criticizing the NRM; if the child was overseas, let them know that an air ticket home was waiting for them at the airport; endeavour by any and every means to keep open a channel of communication. Whenever she heard that a child had left the cult and come home, working for Eccles didn't seem so unbearable. She could survive another six months, at least.

Jane opened her desk drawer and dropped her paper into it.

Her telephone rang.

'Jane? My dear, I had to call you. Danny's written back to us! The first time in two years . . .'

CHAPTER FOUR

The inquest was held on Monday morning in a single-storey, Victorian red-brick building. The family of Prince Harry George Abdul and Prince Michael William Salim al-Amlah had been advised by their Special Branch minders not to attend. In their place, to the right of the court, taking up an entire row of the slatted wooden chairs, sat a group of lawyers.

The man in the witness-box was sombre in a dark suit and black tie. He identified himself as Khalil al-Safr, a Saudi banker based in London. He was present in a dual capacity, as the al-Amlah family's representative and as a close friend of the boys' father, Prince Ibrahim. He began his evidence by describing the boys' lives and background.

'Yes,' he said, 'I have known the two Princes ever since they were born . . . nine years ago. I was with their father at the hospital that night. There was much rejoicing. Identical twin boys, the first-born, born within a month of the end of the Gulf war. It was another of Allah's blessings upon the family. Prince Ibrahim's only regret was that they were born in Rome, not in the palace outside Jeddah where he and his father and his father's father had been born.'

He was asked why the boys had been sent to school in England, rather than in their homeland.

'Prince Ibrahim wished them to learn Western ways and to become truly bilingual, to be able to think in English as well as speak it. As I am based in this country, he asked me to find a suitable school, where they would mix with pupils of their own rank. I recommended Moreton Villiers Preparatory School, which has been attended by children of the British royal family, and the Princes began there a year ago. Their father also asked me to be their legal guardian in Britain, and I gladly agreed. So when the boys went missing, it was I whom the headmaster contacted.'

'What did he tell you?'

The man paused.

'That they had gone gone . . . "AWOL", I believe he said. They had gone on an outing that afternoon to Bodiam Castle, and he believed they had probably wandered off and got lost. Or they might have been hiding in the woods as a prank – he said that Prince Harry had become very adventurous this term.'

'What did you do?'

'I waited. I did not wish to alarm their father unnecessarily, for there was nothing he could do from so far away. So I waited. And then the police came.' Al-Safr's face grew haggard as he remembered that moment and the later one, yet worse, when he'd had to telephone the Prince and break the news. He'd tried to spare his friend, had offered to identify the bodies, but Prince Ibrahim had been adamant: 'No. They are my sons. I will see them. But, my friend, will you bear me company?' And of course al-Safr had said he would.

Never would he forget. The boys looked so perfect lying there. There was no sign of violence: it was as if they merely slept. But the stillness in that small room, the unnatural silence. The Prince had bent and kissed his sons and left, his eyes staring blindly ahead like a sleepwalker's.

Al-Safr's own grief, on top of the strain of his friend's, had made him very tired. He was glad to finish giving evidence and step down from the witness-box. He wished he was anywhere but in court being closely watched by the pack of journalists across the aisle. He turned his head, caught one of them, an untidy individual, staring at him – 'Jackal!' he cursed him – and was grateful when everyone's attention turned back to the witness-box, where the pathologist was preparing to give evidence.

*

The chairs were too close together, Paul Ryder noted despondently. He was already in discomfort, and by the time the inquest was over the discomfort would be acute. He was six feet three inches tall. He wasn't made to sit squashed up.

He took another sideways look at Khalil al-Safr. In the aftermath of the boys' deaths, everyone associated with the family in Britain had been checked out. As well as being undeniably tragic, their deaths were a source of some embarrassment to the authorities. It had transpired that, when considering England for their education, their father – descended from one of the more important branches of the Saudi royal family and notorious in his home country for his secular views – had asked if Special Branch protection was necessary and had been assured that it wasn't. Britain was not a hotbed of political violence, and British intelligence prided itself on knowing the comings and goings of its less desirable foreign guests: the boys would be perfectly safe at their boarding school.

Someone had killed those boys very neatly – very professionally, Ryder and others agreed – with a sharp blow to the back of their necks. There had been no sexual motive; it did not appear to have been a kidnapping gone wrong. So either the father was concealing something – blackmail, drugs, bloody family feud? – or, Special Branch speculated, there was a religious motive.

Which of course was where his, Ryder's, interest lay in the proceedings. As part of his duties within the British security service, he was the country's 'groom', one of the sixty-eight members worldwide of Bridegroom.

Bridegroom took its name from the Parable of the Ten Virgins in the gospel of St Matthew, in which the five wise virgins, unlike the five foolish, stayed awake for the arrival of the bridegroom, Christ. (Having read the parable, Ryder reckoned that it would be more accurate to call them 'virgins', but he kept that thought to himself).

The organization had been formed six years before. The grooms' task was to monitor the activities of cults within their own countries, in case any of them, intentionally or otherwise, triggered catastrophe on a global scale.

'I didn't think we had any cults like that,' Ryder had remarked to his superior, Antony Beck.

'Precisely so. This Bridegroom business is an American idea. They're badly spooked since Waco.'

The previous year, eighty members of a Christian fundamentalist sect, the Branch Davidians, had been killed in a fire at their headquarters in Waco, Texas. The fire was started after a siege by US government authorities, who had since faced criticism for mishandling the affair.

'The Americans,' Beck continued, 'have convinced themselves that next time one of those groups could take the rest of us with them.'

Ryder raised an eyebrow.

'If a sect got hold of nuclear or chemical weapons and decided to go out with a bang, light the fuse for the Almighty . . . See the point?'

Ryder did. He saw the birth of a whole new area of terrorism – as if there wasn't enough of it already, as if he and his small team weren't already fully occupied monitoring the so-called 'legitimate' branches of foreign terrorist groups in Britain.

Beck said he had chosen Ryder as the British groom because in his current field he was frequently involved in the monitoring of religious fundamentalists. 'You can bolt this Bridegroom business on. Shouldn't be too onerous.'

That had proved largely true for Ryder. Other grooms had had very different experiences. Not long after the organization was formed, the Aum Shinrikyo cult in Japan released sarin gas into the Underground system in Tokyo. Twelve people died and 5,500 needed hospital treatment. The group became known as an 'Armageddon cult'.

Bridegroom's founders were vindicated. In the aftermath of the attack, when the risk of a copycat incident was thought to be high, the organization was granted extraordinary emergency powers. These included, in 'time of global danger', unfettered and immediate access to police, government, and intelligence files on suspects; the suspension of privacy laws protecting suspects' computerized data, or telephone or fax communications; and, most extraordinary of all, the right for Bridegroom, if the majority of its members were in agreement, to enforce a further package of powers called the Silent Alert.

The Alert ultimately entailed the suspension of national laws and their replacement by the most draconian of measures. Suspects could be detained and interrogated without trial or legal representation; 'necessary force' could and should, the memorandum stated bleakly, be used to acquire the necessary information; no notes in written or aural form would be taken. The suspect's home – and the homes of his followers, if appropriate – could be searched without warrant. There would be a complete media ban; journalists detained, if necessary; the Internet blocked; prominent persons evacuated to places of safety.

Such drastic steps had not been necessary in the three Silent Alerts called in Bridgeroom's six years of existence: in South Korea, France and Australia. The last had been only the previous year, had been badly mishandled, resulting in unnecessary deaths, and would sooner or later, Ryder and others felt, be exposed in the Australian media.

He was glad that things were run discreetly at his own end.

Professor Eccles of North Downs University near Guildford had no idea, for instance, that his salary, and that of his assistant's, was partly paid for by MI5. Getting a couple of university departments to do his legwork for him – an idea one of Ryder's people had come up with – had struck Ryder as an excellent solution to the unwanted burden.

The GUIDE offices covered the whole of the UK and Ryder's team had access to their databases. Additionally, if GUIDE came across anything untoward, they knew to notify him on the number which was answered authentically by a secretary. So far, very little of interest had arisen. There were nine 'problem' cults in the country but none of them showed genuine Armageddon leanings. Each had been visited by a member of Ryder's team, and in one case a 'mole' had been briefly placed. Their telephones were sporadically bugged and ex-members circumspectly interviewed.

All reports came back to Ryder. In spite of his heavy workload on other matters, if he felt something should be followed up, he moved quickly and mostly in person – as he had the previous week, regarding Jane Carlucci's paper. It was just possible, he'd thought, she had stumbled on something, and if she had, he wanted to be there in person to hear what she had to say. She hadn't written the paper on the GUIDE computer – he'd checked immediately – and he didn't want it relayed to him by a third party or even on the internal web. Crucial information had a habit of leaking out to the wrong ears.

If she had found something, he'd have had to bring her in, and Eccles too, for a thorough debriefing, and perhaps have kept them under wraps until the clean-up operation was complete. Fortunately, his alarm had been unfounded. She had only mentioned the Eighth Scroll; she hadn't unearthed a British NRM that was fulfilling the signs, nor had she referred to recent events as being enactments of those signs. On both counts, he was heartily thankful.

It was the reference to the Scroll in her paper, as relayed to him by Dr Fraser, that had unnerved him, largely because of the timing. Earlier the same week, the Scroll had been mentioned to him – the first time it had come up – by the French groom, Yves Brennard, in connection with the murder of the Saudi Princes.

Yves had phoned from his office in Lyons. 'You know your murders fulfil the first sign of the Eighth Scroll, don't you?'

Ryder only vaguely remembered the Scroll. 'It was a fake, wasn't it?' he asked.

'Yes, but a cult might not see it that way.'

Agreed, Ryder thought.

'And some of the other grooms have mentioned it to me,' went on Yves.

Ryder groaned. Certain members of the organization were apt to see prophecy fulfilments around every corner. He didn't want their attention turned to Britain simply because of the children's murders.

After he'd rung off, he obtained a copy of the Scroll and looked at the first sign: 'In the Last Days, the two sons of the infidel lord of the desert shall be struck down.'

Instantly he saw what Yves meant. The Prince's secularism had angered some of his countrymen, and a quick check on the database revealed that he had been described in the Islamic fundamentalist press as an 'infidel'. Ryder had had a most uncomfortable feeling at the pit of his stomach. The children had been killed by a blow to the back of the neck. But over the centuries, he'd argued with himself, hundreds if not thousands of such sons must surely have been struck down – metaphorically speaking – in war, by pestilence and murder, or even thunderbolts.

The boys' murder did fulfil the sign, he admitted, but there were thousands of signs and prophecies in the world. If one wanted, one could a great deal of time linking current events to prophecies.

He'd put the Scroll at the back of a desk drawer and tried to put it at the back of his mind as well. Then had come Jane's paper; then, on his return from seeing her, an urgent message was waiting for him to call the Italian groom.

The man was close to panic. There had been several cases of baby-formula contamination in his country.

'I see.' Ryder sought for a diplomatic response. 'But why is that of particular concern?'

'The Eighth Scroll,' the Italian hissed, and the uncomfortable feeling had returned in a rush to Ryder's stomach. 'The fourth sign talks about babies suffering from food-poisoning.'

'One moment.' Ryder dug the Scroll out of its drawer and reread the fourth sign: 'The food that we eat and the water that we drink shall become bitter in our mouths, and many shall suffer, particularly little children and pregnant women.'

He understood the Italian's concern. But didn't baby-food regularly get contaminated? He remembered a scare when his own daughter, now nineteen, was a baby.

'And there's the German food-poisoning as well . . .'

Ryder frowned. Several hundred people in Germany had been taken ill with the *E. coli* 0157 bug that week. Was the Italian hijacking every catastrophe, or was he on to something?

'. . . on top of the Princes' murder.'

It was too much, thought Ryder. To suggest that one group was responsible for food-poisoning in two separate countries, while at the same time killing two children in a third. Armageddon groups were simply not that well organized – at least none of the ones he'd come across was. If they became violent, the violence was usually internal, or certainly within their own countries.

He'd been noncommittal with the Italian, had tried again to forget about the Scroll, but over the weekend the story of the botulism outbreak in Britain had broken. One adult and four children dead; twenty-nine more people seriously ill. The Sunday papers had been full of it, and of other food-poisoning stories. Across Europe, in Italy, Germany, Holland and France, there were hundreds of reported cases of salmonella among babies who'd been fed Yummy Tummy milk. In the United States, a brand of cheese had been removed from sale after listeria had been detected in one batch.

In a way, the American contamination eased Ryder's mind: there was obviously an international wave of food-poisoning, he reasoned – such blips did occur. But the British outbreak bothered him. Four children had died. It was as if children were being deliberately targeted. If he'd been given to seeing signs, he'd think two Scroll prophecies had been fulfilled in a shortish time in England.

He'd had the duty officer run a check on the botulism cases. Another child had died on Sunday. Coincidence, Ryder had thought. Or was the unthinkable happening in Britain? And in America, Germany, Italy, Holland and France?

How big was this group? How well organized?

At midnight the previous night, he'd still been working, in his study at home, rereading the Scroll on his database, telling himself that the other signs hadn't been 'fulfilled' yet, and that in any case they were open to a hundred different interpretations; that there was no group out there.

Nevertheless, he could no longer dismiss the Scroll theory out of hand. He just hoped, devoutly, that it wasn't happening, particularly not on his home ground.

That thought brought him back to earth and to his surroundings. Immediately after the inquest, he was flying to Bordeaux for a regular Bridegroom meeting. He knew the sort of interrogation he'd be subjected to as the sole groom present at that inquest.

He studied the burly figure of the pathologist in the witness-box. Part of him wished someone would say something to discredit the Scroll theory. To attest to the fact that the original Special Branch suggestion – that the children had been killed by an Iraqi hit-squad for some undisclosed reason – was correct. Then not only could he himself stop worrying but he could tell the other grooms to do likewise.

He stretched his aching legs and looked down at his reporter's notebook. He saw that, in his usual zombie style, he'd scribbled down the odd indecipherable note. He possessed the ability to function partly in the real world while being mostly elsewhere.

The pathologist was trying to describe the murder blow. He had a predilection for lengthy medical terms. The coroner asked if he could explain what he had just said.

The pathologist looked stony. 'They were killed, sir,' he paused dramatically, 'by a karate chop to the neck. They were, if you like, almost literally "struck down".'

Ryder cursed the man silently. Why choose that particular phrase? Why echo the exact words of the sign?

He felt someone watching him and turned his head. A journalist sitting in the row behind looked away. He had to remember who he was supposed to be, Ryder told himself: a journalist reporting an inquest, not a frightened spook muttering to himself.

The pathologist was winding up at last, Sam Ferryman thought in relief. That meant that as long as the police witness kept his report brief, and the Princes' solicitors didn't cross-question him for too long, there was a good chance the inquest would be over by twelve-thirty.

Sam reckoned that, by working fast, he could cobble together the required six hundred words and get the story over to the newsdesk by one o'clock. If he was lucky – and if he put his foot down – he'd be back to London in time for his three o'clock meeting.

He glanced again at the man in the row in front. Sam didn't know him – he wasn't one of the regular pack – so he guessed he was a freelance or a local man. Sam judged him to be in his fifties. There was a calm about him, as if he'd got where he wanted to be. He didn't look as if he was chewing his finger-nails about deadlines or racing back to London. He didn't look as if he worried about anything much.

Sam had been at the *Correspondent* newspaper for three years. He'd been taken on as Chief Investigative reporter, but over the last few months he'd been asked to carry out extra duties. These involved supervising large breaking stories; covering major court-cases and conducting some celebrity interviews. It left him precious little time to pursue the in-depth stories he loved.

'Superintendent Brian Tiney, please,' the coroner's clerk called out.

The superintendent took the stand. He described, with frequent references to his notebook, the scene of the boys' deaths.

Sam had covered the case from the first. He was hardened to most things but the boys' murder had upset him. Hearing the details again, including how nine-year-old Harry had put up a fight, sickened him.

The coroner asked whether it had been possible to identify any person, or persons, from the fragments of flesh found under Prince Harry's fingernails?

Sam awaited the answer without much interest. For weeks now, there had been no new developments in the murder hunt. Although nothing official had been said, there were rumours of a diplomatic rift brewing between the British and Saudi authorities.

'I'm afraid our inquiries are at a delicate stage in that respect,' answered Superintendent Tiney.

'I see.' The coroner turned to the lawyers who sat on the family's side.

Their spokesman rose. 'How long, Superintendent, does it normally take for fragments of flesh to be identified?'

The policeman paused. 'It can vary.'

'Clearly. It's been six weeks since the death of the Princes, and yet no arrests have been made – or indeed seem imminent?'

'May I remind you,' the coroner said curtly, 'that we are here to establish cause of death only?'

The lawyer subsided.

After a brief recess the coroner delivered his verdict: that the Princes had been unlawfully killed by person or persons unknown.

He turned a kind eye on Khalil al-Safr. 'I should like to send my deepest condolences to the parents, relatives and friends of these two young boys, so cruelly struck down at the very beginning of their lives.'

Sam saw the reporter in front of him start, as if alarmed or surprised at the words. Why? he wondered. They were commonplace at inquests. But he had no time to dwell on others' eccentricities; a press conference was being held outside. He followed the other journalists outside into the weak early-afternoon sunshine.

Al-Safr was reading a formal statement; his hands shook as he read out the words. Sam edged in closer to hear.

'. . . that their father wishes it to be known that, with or without the assistance of the British constabulary, he will avenge the murders of his sons. For the killer, there will be no hiding-place; our vengeance will hunt him down.'

Good, blood-curdling stuff, Sam thought, scribbling fast. He saw that the local freelance was standing nearby but not taking notes, which again struck Sam as odd.

The banker was still talking, but Sam felt he had enough, and he was in danger of being late back to London.

He edged his way to the back of the crowd and returned to his car to write his story. Twenty minutes later, having sent it over, he set out for London. It would be his third meeting with Kirsten Cooper. If she came up with the goods she had promised last time, he could foresee an excellent article for the paper, and for himself, perhaps, more time 'off-rota' in future to pursue his own stories.

She'd phoned him, out of the blue, two weeks before, introduced herself as a trainee journalist, with a 'hot tip' – which made Sam smile – and said she was calling from the lobby downstairs and had a story about a Kent-based cult called the Fellowship, which she believed was targeting wealthy youngsters for the sole purpose of getting its hands on their trust funds. As soon as she said 'cult', he was interested but on guard. Cult stories could be dynamite, but they were also very time-consuming and frequently produced little material that could safely be used. So many cults were litigation-happy, and sometimes their members' parents were, too.

'I've got this brilliant idea of how to get the story,' she rushed on. 'Won't you please see me?'

She'd sounded so desperate and young. He'd remembered how it had felt to be a trainee, so he'd gone down and taken her out to a nearby café.

She had eye-catching red hair and blue eyes. She was very serious.

What she'd heard about the cult was deeply worrying, she told Sam. But she'd give him no names until she'd verified them for herself, in person: she was going to go into the Fellowship 'under cover'. She didn't expect him to commission an article, she assured him; she was merely looking for interest from a national paper, so that if the story worked out – as she knew it would – she wouldn't have to waste time hawking it around.

Sam thought quickly. If the story worked out, it could be a good one. If not, he'd lose nothing. He'd given her a little money for expenses, along with a warning that there would be no more unless she came up with something, and had gone back to his office, wondering if he'd ever hear from her again.

She'd phoned three times and met him once more, the previous Thursday. She had been in the Fellowship for eight days by then and it occurred to him that she looked thin. But his attention had been taken up with the names she had given him, the daughters of two very wealthy men, one in the rock business and the other who owned an airline.

'They're having to hand over their money?' he'd asked.

'That's right.'

For the first time, he'd seen real potential in the story. The following day, he'd made a few discreet enquiries himself about the two girls. He was still waiting to hear back about the airline owner's daughter, but had had it confirmed that the rock star's was pursuing an 'alternative life-style' in the countryside. Her parents were not concerned – although they might be, Sam thought, if they knew their wealth was now in the hands of a weird cult that subjected its members to all-night prayer-meetings and brainwashing.

He still needed more details on the cult, and more information too, on the 'Trust Fund Babes', but if Kirsten was as dedicated as she seemed, Sam suspected she would have it all for him that afternoon.

He joined the motorway and put his foot down for London.

CHAPTER FIVE

T o soften the stark white cubicle that was her office, Jane had brought in a few things of her own. A blue vase currently filled with bluebells, a silver-framed photograph of her parents when they were still together, and a pocket-sized floppy giraffe, which sat on top of her computer monitor.

She was scrolling down the screen, resentfully doing research for Eccles's forthcoming speech to the Women's Institute millennial celebration.

'I want you to find me a list of what NRM leaders call themselves these days. An alphabetical list. E-mail it to me tonight.' And he was gone, slamming the door behind him.

Bastard, Jane thought again. He hadn't missed a single opportunity to remind her, or anyone else, of her humiliation in front of Ryder. That morning she'd overheard him talking to the department secretaries: 'Poor Janey. Did you see how dressed up she was? She'd pinned all her hopes on Mr Ryder and I'm afraid he just wasn't interested. No wonder the poor little thing was on the verge of tears. Be sure you're nice to her now, girls.'

Jane ground her teeth. She mustn't let Eccles get to her. In the academic world, it was too easy to cut oneself off, to think that the likes of Eccles – even the publication of her paper – were the only things that mattered.

Making a resolution over the weekend that she would be more immersed in the 'real' world, she'd bought a Sunday paper and read it while eating cornflakes. Her eye was caught by a photograph on an inside page. It showed a golden-haired little boy with a mischievous grin, the latest fatality in the botulism outbreak. Jane was shocked. He looked so full of life. She read that he was the fourth child to have died. She hadn't realized that any children had died; the latest she had heard, on the news last week, was that a man in his thirties had died, and she hadn't paid that much heed. The odd person was always dying of food-poisoning, and botulism, she'd thought, was just another variation on the *E. coli* theme. She herself sporadically stopped eating red meat, shellfish or broccoli in response to the latest scare, whatever it was. Her hand, en route to her mouth with a clutch of cornflakes, stopped. Were these safe? Or had someone forgotten to zap the bugs that could cause – she glanced back at the article – paralysis and then death?

She shook herself. She was getting as bad as those people who complained that eating food was like playing Russian roulette; that nothing was safe to eat; that every processed food was stuffed with harmful additives.

That morning, as she ate her breakfast, the radio news had reported that in connection with the botulism outbreak, the authorities were looking for a woman who'd sold gingerbread from a stall in the Foodie Lanes at Covent Garden. Most of the sick people had visited her stall.

'Gingerbread,' she murmured aloud as she read a paragraph on her screen. She was browsing through the database, letting her curiosity guide her. Her current stop was the home-page of the Universal Fairie Ring, to which she'd been drawn by their leader's name, Queen Maya of the Highest Sphere. The Ring believed that good and bad fairies existed and directed the affairs of mortal men. Queen Maya claimed that she was the reincarnation of the original Good Fairie Sprite of the Northern Universe and had been chosen to send messages to lost mortals.

On the home-page, her followers were encouraged to send details of their visions for her interpretation (for which there was a hefty fee) and reminded about the forthcoming Grand Ring event at which photographic records of her fairy visitors would be on sale.

In comparison with some of the other NRMs, the Faerie Ring sounded childishly innocent, Jane thought. But then, who would have thought that a man who called himself and his co-leader by names like Tiddly and Wink, Bo and Peep, Nincom and Poop, would have persuaded his thirty-eight followers to kill themselves? Yet Marshall Herff Applewhite, leader of the Heaven's Gate sect in San Diego, had done just that. Then there was the Australian Earthbound movement, whose members had solemnly met in the desert each month to play out episodes from the *Star-Voyager* TV series – and then one day shot one another dead, believing their bodies would be 'beamed up' into a spaceship.

The more she learnt about what people – many of them intelligent and well-educated – were prepared to believe, the more Jane marvelled. It had to be a matter of one person's needs matching another's aspirations, of the disciple finding his master. Even before Sarah joined the NRM, she'd never felt the need to find God, and after that . . .

She had prayed for something twice in her life: first, that Sarah would come home, and, second, that her parents wouldn't split up. God had refused both requests, which made him either a bastard or simply not real. Jane preferred the latter option: she didn't like how hatred made her feel.

She saw the time. She'd worked through her lunch-hour.

Cursing, she returned to her list. It contained six names: Captain, Dearest, Guardian, Keeper, O and Zulu. She added Queen Maya. Being conscientious, she hated to leave a task unfinished, but Eccles's request was impossible. He could pepper his speech with a few names, couldn't he? He didn't need the entire alphabet. She was sure, the more she thought about it, that he'd known what a miserable task it was, and that's why he'd told her to do it.

She heard the distinctive, heavy tread of Miles Riordan, her postgraduate volunteer, as he passed her door on his way to GUIDE. It was nearly time for the answerphone to be switched off and for the phone-lines to go 'live' for callers. Jane was on duty that afternoon. But first, in keeping with her new resolution, she was going to find out what else was going on in the world.

She went into Newsfile. The top two items were highlighted, which meant they were very recent news. She clicked on to the first. It was another story on food-poisoning, about salmonella in

American baby-milk formula. Jane went to the next item, which was headlined: 'Inquest Verdict on Saudi Princes' Deaths'.

She remembered that story breaking. She'd been watching the television news and a story on the economy was interrupted: the newsreader announced that the children had been found dead.

She read the item, noting with a shudder that one of the boys had tried to put up a fight but had, like his brother, Prince Michael, been overcome. Could there have been a ritualistic element to the boys' deaths? the police inspector had been asked after the inquest, and he had said the possibility could not be ruled out.

There was a quote from Khalil al-Safr, described as a lifelong friend of the boys' father: 'The deaths of the twin sons of Prince Waled al-Amlah, struck down before they had grown, will be avenged.'

Those words sounded like an Old Testament vow, Jane thought. She frowned: something in them struck a chord, as if she'd heard them before. The memory escaped her. She hit the key to exit from Newsfile.

'Jane?'

She jumped.

Miles's head was poked apologetically round her door. 'I'm sorry. I did knock . . .'

'It's OK. I'm just coming.'

'There's a woman on the phone asking for you – her daughter's with the Icarus group. She says she spoke to you last week.'

Jane remembered. The mother had been hysterical: unwilling, or unable, to believe that Icarus wasn't a problem. Jane suspected that her daughter saw the cult as a means of escape from a suffocating home life.

She picked up her list and followed Miles out. 'D'you think the name "Walter" is amusing?' she asked. 'As the name of an NRM leader, for example?'

'Um,' he said.

'No. Perhaps not, then.' She went into the GUIDE office. As always, the poster of a woman in silhouette listening to a telephone, met her gaze. 'GUIDE', it said in black capitals along the top. 'Is your child in a New Religious Movement? Let us be your GUIDE'. Every time that Jane saw it, she hated it more.

She picked up her telephone.

'Hullo, Jane? Jane, is that you? Claudia's sent me a postcard from Athens! She says she's not coming back! Can you believe it? She's been brainwashed! I told you it was going to happen . . .'

In the woods the trees met overhead and blocked out the sunlight. On the dry ground, things fell, twigs snapped, wood splintered – sharp cracks of sound for which there was no reason.

Unless, Kirsten thought uneasily, there was someone there. A man watching her, following her at a distance, hiding, anticipating when next she'd turn her head – she whipped round: there was no one there. She was imagining things, she knew she was. She'd hated woods since childhood. They were dark places where witches hid. But these woods cut ten off minutes from the walk to the railway station, and meant that she didn't have to go through the village where people always stared, and sometimes made stupid remarks, because she was from the Fellowship. She went on.

The path plunged downhill, taking her past clumps of bluebells, but she kept her eyes fixed ahead so that they passed on the edge of her vision as a soft violet fuzz. A bird flew up suddenly, making her jump, but she was determined not to give in again to foolish fears.

She began to chant softly: 'Yea, though I walk through the valley of the shadow of death, I will fear no evil.' It was a Bible verse which David had taught them and which Kirsten had learned with fervour, repeating it whenever she was afraid. Not that she had anything to be afraid of, she told herself. It was merely her guilty conscience making her nervous. David said that when God couldn't get through on an open channel, He used the conscience to stir the human soul. That when He was drawing a lost child to him, He stirred that child's innermost being with the breath of the Holy Spirit.

A breeze came out of nowhere, brushing against her cheek. She shivered: was that God speaking to her, through the wind? Shakily she put her hand to her face. Was David right? Was God using nature to bring her to Him?

There was no getting away from God if He was after you – that was what David had said at the previous night's service. Kirsten felt her face grow hot at the memory. She'd been with Mary, her 'discipler', sitting halfway back in the nave of the old church. David was at the front, standing on the shallow stone steps, with his arms outstretched, and that warm, loving smile directed straight at her.

'Come to me, little one, and I shall give you rest.'

How she longed to rest! To set down the weary burden of deceiving the most caring, genuinely good people she'd ever met. When she'd first heard of them from a friend, she'd thought only of herself, of her precious career: if she could infiltrate the Fellowship, she'd be able to sell the story to a national paper, earning lots of money, making her reputation, perhaps even being taken on by the paper, thus cutting short her dreary time at journalism training college.

As soon as her friend had mentioned the cult, Kirsten was on the alert; in media terms, cults were sexy. Her friend's experience sounded a bit dull: at Waterloo Station, she'd met some people who'd invited her to a Christian meeting. She'd gone, hadn't liked it, and had left. But she'd mentioned two very wealthy young women who were members of the cult – 'Probably being fleeced,' she said.

'Probably,' Kirsten replied thoughtfully.

She checked the college library database for national media mentions of the Fellowship. There weren't any, but she found plenty of other material on cults. She noted the common denominators: money, sex and corruption. The Fellowship, she reckoned, would be like all the others. It just needed someone like herself to ferret it all out, and her friend had given her an excellent lead.

She began her tour of the national papers that lunch-time. Sam Ferryman was her fourth call.

At first she'd been euphoric at how easy it was to get in to the Fellowship (one quick call to the number on the card her friend had given her, and they'd arranged to pick her up at the local railway station). She hadn't spared a thought for what it might be like to live an undercover life: to lie for days on end to people she was coming to like; to withstand their love for her, their desire for her to become truly one of them. Kirsten had thought only of the glamour, of finding the story she was sure would be there – which was, she acknowledged drearily, her other problem.

Nothing wicked was happening at the Fellowship. It was true that two 'Trust Fund Babes' had been members (although one had left some time before) but there was no question of them being coerced into handing over their money. Indeed, the remaining girl, the daughter of a Seventies rock star, had confided to Kirsten that when there'd been concerns about the church roof she had gone to David offering him her money and been turned down.

'He told me I was very sweet, but not to worry, the Fellowship had "more than enough" cash. I can't tell you how lovely it is, Kirsten, to know that no one here is after my money!'

If ever a quote was designed to sink a story, Kirsten thought gloomily, that was it. She didn't know where the money came from – certainly not from the proceeds of the coffee-shop in Hastings or the four farm-shops – but there was obviously plenty. The Fellowship owned every dwelling in the Moor, which was sixteen houses, an old school, the church, and there were three minibuses and several cars. There were also one hundred and two members to feed and clothe. According to Mary, David had once been an estate agent. Kirsten had never realized before that they made that sort of money. 'There's nothing sinister about it,' Mary said with a smile, and Kirsten knew by then that Mary didn't lie.

As far as Kirsten could tell, there was no sex going on at the Fellowship either. The men and women lived in separate houses; Kirsten lived with four other women in Laurel Cottage. David taught that sex was a holy thing, to be enjoyed only within the confines of marriage – and there were no married couples at the Fellowship.

David himself was celibate, 'married to God', he said. There were a few boy-and-girlfriend couples (Kirsten hadn't noticed any homosexuals) but their meetings were always chaperoned by their 'disciplers' and only 'holy kisses' (chaste pecks on the cheek) were permitted. Most Fellowshippers seemed content to follow David's lead, in sexual desires as well as in everything else, which might seem peculiar but wasn't exactly newspaper splash material. People wanted to do what David did.

Apparently he hadn't intended that there should be a uniform but everyone wanted to wear what he did. That was true also of the food that was served three times daily in the old schoolroom. David was a vegetarian so, although there was usually a meat course on the menu, not many people chose it. And Kirsten had noticed that lots of the older members had the same mannerisms as David – a tilt of the head to the right as they listened (Mary did that); a rocking back and forth, hands clasped under armpits, during prayers; a closing-of-the-eyes and a murmured 'Yes, Jesus' when particularly spiritually moved, as when a newly converted member gave his or her testimony.

Kirsten had heard such testimonies, night after night in the church while candles threw their shadow-light against the yellow stone walls. Members' life histories, stories of real abuse, sexual and physical, made Kirsten's own fictional account – that she had run away from home following years of abuse by her step-father – sound cheap in her ears. People talked of resorting to drugs and crime and prostitution because they hurt so much, because they felt guilty and hated themselves enough in some cases to attempt suicide. Their lives had been turned round there at the Fellowship. Each one had been led through David to Jesus, and given a new life: one that would conquer death, that would last forever. Each one now had eyes that shone with a special light, an inner light of hope and assurance. Join us, those eyes begged silently. Be like us.

'Lay down your heavy burden, take my gentle one instead.'

Kirsten felt her throat constrict. Last night she'd been on the point of getting to her feet – she'd seen David's eyes rest upon her, and hadn't they held a look of special delight? – when in the pew in front, a tall girl had stood up. Her discipler had led her up, and she, not Kirsten, had stumbled into David's outstretched arms, and sobbed out her need for Jesus. David had cried as he always did when someone converted – they were tears of joy, he explained, of holy happiness – and Kirsten had cried too, not because everyone else was but because she so badly wanted David to hold her like that, his arm round her shoulders, his face alight with love as he praised God for another miracle.

'I am the Beloved's and He is mine and His banner over me is love.' David had led the singing of the 'New Birth Hymn'. It had gone on until after midnight.

Tonight, Kirsten promised herself: she would go up to the altar. She glanced at her watch. She reckoned that she ought to be back from London by seven-thirty, so long as Sam was at the café on time – *Sam*, she thought, and froze there on the path. What was she thinking of? Being converted and staying forever in the Fellowship? What was happening to her? She whimpered. Sam had warned her, at their last meeting, not to let herself get brainwashed. Was that what was happening? She felt automatically in her jeans pocket for her cigarettes.

Before she'd joined the Fellowship, she had only really smoked for show, but during her first few days there she'd started smoking in earnest, out of nerves.

She wouldn't, she promised herself, lighting up, think about David any more. She'd concentrate on what mattered so much to her: journalism; her brilliant contact, Sam; her passport to a national. She swallowed nervously and almost choked on the cigarette smoke.

In her phone calls, she'd managed to fob off his inquiries about the trust-fund scandal but at their last meeting, she'd seen he was losing interest so she'd given him the names, and then had had to lie in detail. This afternoon, he was expecting further details on the 'Babes': when and why they'd joined; if possible, how much money they'd already paid over; whether they'd been allowed out to see their families; details, too, on life at the Fellowship.

She bit her lip. How was he going to react when she told him she'd lied, and that there was no brainwashing, sleep-deprivation or starvation? No all-night prayer-meetings, or Fellowshippers being forced to work unpaid in the farm-shops, fed only on carrots and potatoes, and made to wear the same clothes to encourage loss of identity. That there was as little financial as physical coercion. People were free to come and go, especially the 'not yet committed' like herself. All she'd had to do that morning was to tell Mary that she needed to visit her friend in London again. No problem. She'd even been given money for her ticket.

Sam, she thought, with another drag on her cigarette, was going to kill her, was going to make sure she never worked on a national paper, or anywhere else, unless she delivered the promised goods. She couldn't give him the 'Trust-Fund Babes' – but she could spice up the lies she'd already told him.

She knew how to make things sound bad. She knew what papers liked. Why, she'd probably get a whole page devoted to her 'near escape' from a dangerous cult! The Fellowship would deny every-thing of course, but one would expect them to.

An enormous weight lifted from her. She stubbed out the cigarette and set off up the hill.

Very soon she'd be out of the hateful woods and back in the sunlight. Then it was a two-minute run down the lane to the station and less than ten minutes until her train left for London. In fifty minutes she'd be with Sam. She remembered how much weight she'd lost through nervousness – that tied in with the starvation theory, she thought exultantly. She'd make it so good that Sam would forget all about the Trust-Fund Babes.

There was a thud behind her but she hardly noticed it. She could see the leafy poles of the hop-field ahead, the sun dappling the plants. She stepped sideways to avoid a fallen branch, heard something behind her, turned, but a hand was wrapped across her mouth, an arm seized her round the waist and she was lifted off her feet. She saw the branches sway above her, tried to scream, but she couldn't breathe. Other hands grabbed her at her feet; two men were running with her. Then nothing, just a rush of hot darkness as she fainted.

The second Bridegroom meeting of the year was to be held in the vast dining-hall of a small château overlooking a vineyard, forty minutes' drive from Bordeaux. It was rumoured that once Toulouse-Lautrec had stayed there, and on one wall was a bar-scene mural reminiscent of the artist's work.

Paul Ryder, regarding it and the room in general through the open doors, while he waited for Yves Brennard, wondered how the French groom had managed it. When the grooms had met in London, the British government had provided an overheated boardroom in Queen Anne's Gate for their deliberations and a Holiday Inn in Swiss Cottage for the night.

A message to call Yves had been waiting for him on his arrival and they had agreed to meet outside the dining-hall.

When Yves arrived, they adjourned to the library. The Frenchman looked grave, and warned that the mood of the grooms was swinging in favour of drastic action.

'Meaning?' Ryder asked cautiously.

'A Global Alert.'

'*Global?*' Ryder repeated.

There had never been a Global before, although its use was sanctioned in the Bridegroom charter. In times of perceived extreme risk, when neither the identity nor the country of the NRM was known, all signatories to the Bridegroom convention agreed to implement a full Silent Alert within their own countries.

Ryder had never given serious thought to the impact of a Global. Faced with it now, he recoiled. 'It won't be possible to keep it quiet,' he said, 'not if over half the countries in the world start hitting on their cults. Isn't it more likely to start something, than stop it?'

Yves nodded. 'My own feeling. But I think we may find ourselves in the minority.'

Ryder felt dazed. 'But why? Has anything else happened? Any more signs?'

Yves shrugged. 'There seems to be an epidemic of food-poisoning.'

'I know, but—'

'Targeting young children.'

Ryder was silent.

'In addition, there've been terrible fires in California and here in France. The Scroll's sixth sign talks of people living in fear of fire.'

'Yves, for God's sake! There have always been fires!'

'I know, I know.' The Frenchman held up his hands. 'It's easy to say, "Ah, another sign fulfilled." But I can see where some of the other grooms are coming from. Especially since the murder of the Princes.'

That silenced them both.

The meeting started soon afterward. As he'd expected, Ryder was questioned about the inquest.

He was unable to set his colleagues' minds at ease. The manner of the boys' deaths, it was generally agreed, couldn't have been a clearer fulfilment of the first sign.

The New Zealand groom was speaking via a live satellite link-up. Her face and upper body filled one of the screens on the wall opposite Ryder.

'I share the general concern,' she said. 'I cannot help but think that, if there's a possibility that one or several groups may be fulfilling the Eighth Scroll, we must act, and act decisively.'

Ryder studied the whorled grain of the wood on the table in front of him. He had no wish to expose the world's population to danger, but surely a Global, at that stage, was going too far? He had meant it when he had told Yves that such a step might prove catastrophic.

He knew, as surely everyone round that table did, how the worst cults operated. They were paranoid; they would perceive an attack as the work of the Devil; they would press their button, whatever it was.

'We don't know how many signs have been fulfilled,' the New

Zealander went on. 'It could be two or three, it could be nine.'

Ryder silently concurred. He gazed down at his own copy of the Scroll.

The first sign, like an echo in his head: 'In the Last Days, the two sons of the infidel lord of the desert shall be struck down.'

The second: 'False peace-makers shall be put to death; in their safest places, in their most secret council chambers, God shall cause them to be cut down.'

The third: 'The Great Traitor shall be assassinated.'

The fourth: 'The food that we eat and the water that we drink shall become bitter in our mouths, and many shall suffer, particularly little children and pregnant women.'

The fifth: 'The people shall starve rather than eat'.

The sixth: 'The people shall live in fear of the elements: of fire, sky, earth and water.'

The seventh: 'The proudest of man's works, those things by which he seeks to make himself a god, shall be destroyed.'

The eighth: 'Warm places shall become icy wildernesses; cool oases shall turn to desert.'

The ninth: 'Great stones shall strike the earth with fire; death shall fall from the sky.'

The tenth: 'Christ's covering shall be removed from those who have wrongly taken it. The keeper shall keep it holy. And then the End, the Awful Horror of the Ungodly, shall come.'

The New Zealander was following roughly the same script as the other speakers: the first and fourth signs appeared to have recently been fulfilled; the fifth – and in part the sixth – was coming true because of the fourth. In fact, the sixth had been true for some time: the modern world lived in a state of fear.

Five of the other signs could be said to have been fulfilled, the groom went on. Or not: it depended on one's interpretation.

Exactly, thought Ryder.

'The only sign which we can be certain remains unfulfilled is, in my opinion, the tenth, about Christ's clothing,' the New Zealander concluded.

A light came on inside Ryder's head. He caught Yves's eye and the Frenchman invited him to speak.

He dispensed with the formality of introducing himself. 'We all know that these groups are tunnel-visioned, to the exclusion of all else, you might say.' He saw that he had everyone's attention. 'As my colleague has just reminded us, the tenth sign has not yet been completed.'

The Italian groom, who had originally proposed the Global, snorted impatiently.

'Are we agreed that "Christ's covering" refers to the Turin Shroud?' Ryder asked.

No one disagreed.

'So why don't we arrange for the Turin Shroud to be placed under lock and key, so that it can't be "taken"? If a cult is carrying out these attacks, they'll be stopped in their tracks. If they can't join up all the dots, they won't play.' He paused for breath.

'I'd vote for it,' said the Australian groom immediately.

'And I.'

'And me,' the Brazilian groom echoed from one of the satellite screens. 'Much better than the Global.'

The Italian glared.

On the other side of the table, Yves raised an eyebrow at Ryder. 'Shall we take a vote?'

It was almost unanimous – just four abstentions, from the Italian, the German, the Austrian and one of the two Americans.

It was agreed that the Shroud should immediately be removed from public view, and that the media should be alerted as soon as possible. Then, it being nearly nine o'clock, the meeting adjourned for dinner.

Yves came over to Ryder. 'Well done, my friend,' he said under his breath.

Ryder nodded. He felt only enormous relief.

CHAPTER SIX

The view from the landing window that morning pleased Ross Edgecombe very much. One field was yellow with rape and another one green with . . . cabbages, he supposed; he wasn't knowledgeable about such things. And the sky was perfectly blue, as a sky in late May should be. He guessed that he must have looked at that same scene dozens of times without properly appreciating its loveliness.

He leant on the window-sill and steepled his fingers. He thought of himself as a particular man, who liked things done properly: a new white coat every day even when he had to launder them himself; hands thoroughly washed and dried; septic procedures followed at all times; the machinery kept clean and in perfect working order, observation notes meticulously kept up to date. Such things were essential to the smooth running of any scientific endeavour, in Ross's opinion.

And they had reaped success. It had taken him a year to conduct his experiments, to transform the bug he had dug out of the permafrost into what was required of it. Having tested it, and found it remarkably effective – its manifestations, particularly in its last stages, at least as dramatic as those described in the medical literature – a brief stumbling-block had arisen: the container. Whatever was used had to look innocuous, and yet do its job. Eventually, as so often before, Ross's previous experience had been invaluable. There was nothing to suggest that the four canisters nestling in their travelling-case downstairs contained anything unusual.

Soon, after the final clean-up, there would be no tell-tale signs left at the Lodge to reveal what had been done there. His laboratories, where once he had been so busy, were empty. His assistant, whose stupidity and carelessness had at times driven him to distraction, had gone.

Only he and Ruth were left. That, Ross acknowledged with a smile, was the real source of his good feeling, the reason why he saw colours these days, and why he liked to see the sun shining. Ruth had been with him for most of the previous year, but there'd always been his assistant around, and the volunteers, and a few others. Now, at last, they were on their own.

He almost didn't mind not sleeping with her any more – although when she'd told him, a month before, that that was how it must be in future, he'd been so upset that he'd begged her, he'd even cried. It was enough that she was there with him, alone; that night after night she slept in the bedroom next to his; that they ate together each day; that they talked, with no interruptions from others. And there was still their work together, of course.

This morning, they'd been up since dawn, cooking.

Ruth was bringing the van round, and soon she'd be gone for the day. His stomach tightened as he saw her below, parking on the forecourt.

When the small white Bedford van wasn't in use, it was kept out of sight, in one of the garages behind the main building. The Lodge, in the heart of the Welsh countryside, was isolated, but they agreed it was foolish to take unnecessary risks. The van's number plates had been changed as soon as it returned from its first outing to Covent Garden, but even so . . .

He smiled as she got out of the van. She had short, blond hair and today she was wearing a floaty, long-sleeved dress and rope sandals. She was small-boned and very slight. He thought she looked like a piece of thistledown being sped along the path by the breeze. He heard her open the front door, and hurried downstairs.

'I'll help you load,' he offered.

She nodded. She was fastidious in her speech too, another quality he loved. They walked side by side through the echoing, slate-tiled hall towards the kitchen. Formerly, the building had been a centre for outdoor activities and its dormitories, the estate agent had informed them, could sleep a hundred and twenty adults.

'You're thinking of opening it as an outdoor centre yourselves, then?'

'Eventually, yes.' Ruth said. It had been agreed that she should do most of the talking.

'You'll have no problems getting your spaces filled. The old boy who had it before had let things slide.'

Ross and Ruth made suitable noises. They'd been playing man and wife that day: she wore a gold wedding-ring.

'The nearest village is quite a way off,' she murmured.

The agent nodded. 'It is, but you can be in Hereford in a couple of hours, do a big shop there, stick it in the freezer.'

Food hadn't been a problem. Ruth scarcely ate a thing and Ross was perfectly satisfied with reheated, pre-packed meals and long-life milk. His assistant had whined occasionally, as had the volunteers, for the short time they had been there, but they were ignored. The important thing had been to attract no attention, to provoke no questions from curious locals, and in that they had been entirely successful.

When they moved in, the Lodge had stood empty for three years and that, plus its location, had guaranteed no casual visitors. The postman was a necessary evil, but he wasn't the old gossip on a bicycle whom Ruth had feared. He came and went in a quick red van, depositing the mail in a box. Apart from that, they'd been cut off from the rest of the world, apart from the telephone, of course, and the Internet. But Ross hadn't felt lonely, except for Ruth's brief stays away; he had had plenty to keep him occupied.

Six months into the project, when things were going very well, Ruth had paid a fleeting visit to David Norton, and on her return had asked if Ross could do something 'extra'.

She'd been apologetic, and very sweet as she always was, explaining that they'd hoped it wouldn't be necessary to burden him when he was so busy, but unfortunately 'full completion' had not yet occurred.

When she had described what she wanted – food-poisoning – he'd thought it a wide brief, and an easy one. There were a score of different bugs he could acquire: salmonella, *Bacillus cereus*, *E. coli* 0157 . . .

She got down to specifics. She wanted fatalities. *E. coli* was a killer, Ross said, especially among the elderly; there'd been that recent outbreak at the old people's home in Dublin . . .

'No. It has to be children. And babies.'

The brief had been abruptly narrowed. 'Babies aren't difficult,' he'd said thoughtfully. 'But children as well?'

She'd nodded emphatically. 'Young ones.'

'I don't think there's anything that specially targets young children.'

Silence fell. Ross had been desperate to fill the void, but it was Ruth who had suddenly said: 'What about something made specifically for young children to eat? Couldn't we put something in that?'

Which was how, ultimately, by a long and at times arduous process, they had arrived at the idea of the gingerbread men for the Foodie Lanes.

Once they'd decided on that, the next step had been the acquisition of a suitable bug. Ross had plumped for *Clostridium botulinum* and, having described what sort of person he needed, Ruth had found someone suitable.

The boy was about twenty, Ross judged; the right age and, with his slouch and dull stare, the right temperament too. He was a drop-out from a biology course at one of the northern universities. Ross and Ruth had coached him in what to say – he was looking for lab work . . . anything would do, really . . . it didn't matter where the job was . . . he had a relative who lived locally – and had sat opposite him listening on the extension phone while he made the calls.

Halfway through the list of hospitals, university departments and public and private laboratories, the boy got lucky: the Public Health Laboratories at Colindale in north London were looking for a 'washer-upper'. The pay was dismal, but the hours were good, and he could play music all day long if he wanted.

'Take it,' Ruth had mouthed.

'I'll 'ave it,' the boy said. 'I've got a sister that lives local.'

Ruth had arranged a flat and had taken the boy there, and stayed with him for the duration of his employment. On his second Friday, he had walked out of the Colindale complex, under the red steel archway, with four Petri dishes in his pockets. Two contained the *botulinum* culture, one held a salmonella culture, and the last was

Listeria monocytogenes. He'd obeyed Ross's instructions: that while he was there, virtually unseen by nature of his lowly position, he should bring home whatever he could safely lay hands on. It was dead easy, the boy had boasted.

The salmonella had been used to great effect in the baby-milk formulations. The gingerbread men had produced similarly excellent results.

'Are they set?' Ruth said, bringing him back to the present with a start. They had reached the kitchen.

'I'm sorry?' he said.

'The apples. D'you think they look set?'

Ross shook himself. He gazed down at the five trays of toffee-apples they'd made that dawn, taking it in turns to dip apples into the pot. To ensure that the faint, almondy smell of *botulinum* couldn't be detected, Ruth had added some cinnamon – the smell was wonderful. He'd injected the toxin when the toffee casing had cooled, pushing the needle deep into the flesh, near where the sticks jutted out. The needle-marks were tiny, only evident if one knew they were there.

'They look fine.' Ross tapped one gently. 'Perfect.' He opened a drawer, pulled out a roll of grease-proof paper, and cut it neatly into shape, to cover each tray. He'd inoculated Ruth and himself with the anti-toxin serum; although the paper was hardly a hermetic seal, at least it gave some extra protection.

He took the trays out to the van, loaded them on to lockable shelves and shut the doors.

'Well.' Ross hated saying goodbye to her. Sitting in the driver's seat, she looked so fragile. He wished he could go with her, or take the things himself. He hated the thought of exposing her to danger, and he knew, from his news-monitoring, that they were looking for 'the gingerbread lady' from the Foodie Lanes. But she insisted.

'Take care,' he said bleakly.

'I'll be back by this evening.'

It was not yet eight o'clock. Her destination was two hours away, in Birmingham. It had been her idea again, and as ever, he considered, a good one. At least, he comforted himself, it wasn't London, and she wasn't dark-haired any more.

She started the engine, then looked up at him and, uncharact-

eristically, smiled. 'God bless,' she said gently, and she gave a little
wave as she drove away.

After the traffic news, the radio promised, Professor Nigel Eccles
would be in the studio to discuss the implications of cult members
taking their parents to court.

Jane glowered at the machine. It was just after eight in the
morning. As if it wasn't bad enough working for the man, she
thought, now she had to set her alarm to make sure she listened to
him. He'd called at ten o'clock the night before. It didn't look as if
he'd be getting home, he had said, so he wanted Jane to monitor the
programme for him.

Her mother had telephoned not long after that, 'just to see how
she was', but Jane knew a call at that time of night meant she was
feeling miserable. For as long as she could remember, and
particularly since the divorce, Jane had felt it her duty to cheer up
her mother. This call was no exception. To hear herself talk, Jane
had thought, it sounded as if her own life was one long swirl of
parties and encounters with fascinating, witty people. Now her
mother was coming for lunch on Thursday.

Jane took a stoical bite of toast. On the radio, the rush-hour report
ended with a jingle. She imagined Eccles licking his lips, and leaning
forward in his chair – the way he always did before the start of an
interview.

The female presenter welcomed him and he purred back his
pleasure at being there.

How, Jane wondered, did such an unpleasant man manage to
sound so cuddly?

The presenter explained that later that morning the parents of a
twenty-three-year-old man would be standing in the dock at
Knightsbridge Crown Court, accused of stealing money from their
son, a member of the New Disciple Community. It was understood
that the parents feared their son was about to give the group a large
amount of money, inherited from his grandmother, and so had
allegedly removed it themselves. What advice, the interviewer asked,
would Professor Eccles, eminent authority on cults, have given those
parents?

'My first piece of advice would have been not to call the Disciple
Community a cult; it's actually a new religious movement.'

Jane clenched her jaw.

'So it would be the New Disciple Community New Religious Movement. Rather a mouthful, Professor Eccles.'

Jane grinned but Eccles didn't rise to the bait. He never did on air. Instead he launched into his oft-repeated speech about history turning many NRMs into mainstream religions.

'Look at the Methodist movement,' Jane murmured, in almost perfect synchronization with his words.

Eccles moved on to address the main issues. He spoke touchingly of the tragedy of parents who refused to let go; his voice became firmer, but still properly concerned, when he turned to the rights of the adult child. By the time he had finished, when he asked rhetorically what else, given the circumstances, the son could have done but report his parents to the police, Jane nearly found herself agreeing with him.

There was no doubt about it, she thought. Put the man in front of a microphone or a camera, and he was a professional. She could tell by the way the interviewer thanked him that she was pleased with him too.

Jane looked down at the notes she had made. Not having done it before, she wasn't sure what Eccles expected of her. Marks out of ten, or a proper critique? She knew how badly he received criticism.

She took her plate to the sink. The news headlines came on: more on the European baby-formula scare; unrest in China; at home, a rise in the mortgage rate.

'Because of fears that lights are damaging its fabric, the Turin Shroud is to be temporarily removed from display. The papal authorities say that the Shroud, still believed by many to bear the image of Christ, will be expertly examined and if necessary repaired before being replaced in Turin Cathedral.'

It was remarkable, Jane thought, that even though twenty years ago scientists had proved that the Shroud was a fake, it still attracted such attention. What was it about religion that made people go on believing in artefacts even after they were exposed as fakes?

The phone rang. No one ever called her at that time in the morning. She picked up the receiver.

'Well?' demanded a man's voice.

'I'm sorry, who is this?'

'My piece,' Eccles hissed.

'Oh.' For one glorious moment, she considered her options. 'You were very good, Nigel,' she said.

One of the advantages to being the *Correspondent*'s chief investigative reporter, Sam considered, was being allocated his own space in the car-park beneath the building. It meant he could guarantee being in the office twenty minutes after leaving his flat.

He eased the Saab into its slot. He was feeling particularly content with life. That morning he had the front-page lead – and the story had been handed to him on a plate. Having been asked late the previous afternoon, to do a 'follow-up' on the latest food-poisoning cases both at home and abroad, he'd put in a call to the Surveillance Centre at Colindale.

The young woman he spoke to had been very excited. She had just found out that a British supermarket chain had been selling as own-brand powdered baby-milk what was in fact Yummy Tummy, and, although well aware of the product-recall in Europe, had continued to do so. No other paper had got the story; it was a good, old-fashioned scoop.

Both at home and on the car radio, Sam had heard his story mentioned and followed up on the news. It was deeply satisfying, and he rather thought there might be a follow-up from his Colindale source. Right at the end of their conversation, when he had made a derogatory remark about Yummy Tummy's hygiene standards, she'd hinted that it wasn't necessarily the company's fault. She'd refused to say more but perhaps now, Sam wondered, having seen and heard the coverage the story had had, she'd be willing to go a bit further, especially if he offered to take her out to lunch.

The elevator halted at his floor. He said 'Hullo' to a couple of people on his way over to his desk. He saw that he had a heap of mail and several telephone messages already: the top one was from Colindale.

'Ah, there you are, Sam.'

He looked up: it was Monica Fowler, his news editor and she had brought Frank Delany, the specials editor with her. How nice, he thought. They'd come in person to congratulate him on his story.

'I think I might be able to get another follow-up out of Colindale,' he said eagerly.

'Oh good.' Monica frowned. 'It won't take long, will it? I mean, you'll be able to do it over the phone?'

'I . . . er . . . Yes, probably.'

'Good.' Monica pulled up a chair. She beamed at him. 'Because I want to take you off-rota so you'll have all the time you need for your cult investigation.'

'My cult investigation,' Sam repeated.

Kirsten Cooper hadn't shown up for their meeting. He'd felt first peeved – he'd hared back from the inquest, breaking the speed limit more than once – and then worried. He remembered how nervous she'd been last time, and that he'd warned her, only half jokingly, to make sure she didn't get brainwashed herself. Suppose she'd 'gone over' to the cult? Suppose they'd found her out? Ought he to call the police?

Then he'd calmed down. He was prone, he knew, to imagining the worst. She'd probably only been unable to escape from her 'discipler', the minder-girl she'd told him about. She'd call him when she got the chance and arrange another meeting.

Then his mobile had rung: Monica, summoning him back to the office for the Yummy Tummy story. In the rush, all thoughts of Kirsten had fled. He'd been remiss, he thought now.

Sam glanced at his pile of messages. One was probably from Kirsten, explaining her no-show.

Monica said, 'Frank told me all about it . . .'

Sam looked at the specials editor. He'd asked him to say nothing until Kirsten brought in more.

'. . . in conference this morning. The editor's keen to do a really good backgrounder on the cult kid who's shopped his parents. Frank says you've already been looking at a group that steals kids' trust funds? You've got a contact in there?'

'Er, yes.'

'Great!' She clapped him on the shoulder. 'Very finger-on-the-pulse, you know? How about "Inside the World of the Trust-Fund Fundies"? They are fundamentalists, aren't they?'

He nodded. He was longing to look through his messages.

'D'you think I should meet your contact?'

'She's quite shy, actually.'

'OK, run your own show. But keep me informed. When d'you think you'll have enough to start writing it up?'

Sam smiled nervously. 'In a day or two?' he suggested.

'Fine! Terrific!' She leant forward conspiratorially. 'Never let it be said that I don't let my journalists do investigations. Just as long as I know the editor wants them, so no one's wasting time.' She winked, and she and Frank wandered off.

Sam leafed through his messages. Nothing from Kirsten. She ought to have called him by now, he thought. He was worried again, and his worry was magnified by the pressure of getting the story. Had something happened to her? Ought he to drive down there and look for her? But if he did, and she was perfectly fine, in 'deep cover', unable to break away to call him, he might blow everything – her cover, his story – by appearing out of the blue.

He ought to have agreed with her a cover-story for himself in case of emergencies. But he hadn't imagined it would be necessary. He'd thought he'd had all the time in the world, that no one else knew about it, and Kirsten could go at her own pace. He'd been sloppy, and now he just hoped she wasn't paying for it.

She might still call. It was less than twenty-four hours since her no-show. Suppose she'd been in one of the marathon prayer-meetings she'd told him about? And then frog-marched off to work in a farm-shop? It might be that evening before she called. He would have to wait at least until then before doing anything drastic.

Over at the newsdesk he saw Monica and Frank in animated debate with the picture editor. Probably arguing for a photographer to be assigned to the 'cult-special', he thought uneasily. If he didn't produce the goods on this one, he could kiss goodbye to investigations, at least in the immediate future.

His eyes fell upon the message to call his Colindale contact, which was marked 'Urgent'. He could maintain his current high standing in Monica's eyes by producing an excellent follow-up.

He dialled the number, and enthusiastically announced himself.

'You bastard.' She sounded as if she'd been crying.

He reeled. 'What? What's wrong?'

'You've probably only gone and got me the sack!'

'But how?'

'I didn't know you were going to use SuperSave's name!'

'But I didn't name you as the source,' Sam protested.

'They guessed! Someone told them I've been talking to you!'

'Oh God, I'm so sorry. Is there anything I can do?'

'No! Haven't you done enough?' The line went dead.

Sam put his head in his hands. The last thing he'd wanted to do was harm her. There were days when he hated being a journalist.

He caught Monica's eye. She gave him a thumbs-up.

If Kirsten failed to contact him, he told himself, he was sunk. He couldn't write the story on what she had given him thus far. He'd better start looking for an alternative.

He went to see the religious/gardening correspondent, a nice man who was ignored by Monica. Without even asking why Sam wanted it, he supplied a list of cult-specialists in Britain.

CHAPTER SEVEN

The signs for the Third European Fruit Fest began as Ruth left the motorway. She saw the fields of yellow-and-white-striped marquees, their pennants whipping in the breeze. It was a lovely morning and already quite hot.

She drove into the vendors' car-park, being careful to avoid any ruts. She knew that the apples were packed tightly, and that the trays were fixed firmly in their brackets, and Ross had assured her that the toxin couldn't be dislodged. Nevertheless, she had a vision of the apples rolling about and their poison escaping.

A man wearing a curved banana hat guided her to a space. The objective of the day was to celebrate fruit, in all its manifestations, and thus to improve public consumption. There were to be competitions for the best cherry pie, banana split and fruit trifle, and, more earnestly, trade exhibitions, orchard auctions and produce stalls. Next to Ruth, a man and woman were unloading wooden melon wedges from the back of their car. The man held one up for her. 'Make great door-stops,' he grinned.

She smiled and shook her head. She checked her appearance in the rear-view mirror: long, flaxen plaits, blue eye-shadow, lips a rich ruby-red. She had disguised herself in a deserted layby on route. Now she got out of the van and slipped over her gypsy-style dress an ankle-length ruffled white apron.

'Maid Marian?' asked the melon man.

'You guessed!'

She took out a large wooden tray, which she had decorated with brightly coloured felt, and hung it around her neck. She went round to the back of the van, and holding her breath, inserted the first metal tray. It fitted snugly. She straightened up and removed the grease-proof paper. The toffee-apples glinted temptingly in the sunlight.

She went towards the main field. With quiet satisfaction, she noted the arrival of school coaches in the visitors' car-park. From her telephone inquiries, she had been expecting them: children were always welcome at the festival; there were special educational activities for them, even a fruit-themed funfair.

Ruth had thirty-six apples on her tray, and four refills in the back of the van. She was glad now that she had come herself, in spite of the slight risk of identification. It had been suggested that one of the girls do it but Ruth would have worried terribly, waiting – it had been bad enough with Liam – and anyway the risk, she told herself, was minimal: she looked quite different from 'Helen', the woman selling gingerbread at Covent Garden.

Directly ahead was the tail-end of an untidy crocodile of children. Ruth estimated they were aged eight or nine. How sweetly they were dressed, she thought, and how bright and clear their voices! If things had been different, it might have been nice to have had a child like that. She bore down upon them with her tray.

'Oh, Miss, Miss! Can we have a toffee-apple? Please, Miss?'

The teacher turned. 'They do look nice,' she said. 'How much are they?'

Ruth named a reasonable price, adding that the apples were sweet-tasting and organic.

'OK, kids. But remember there are lots of other things to eat, and we've only just got here.'

Her warning was drowned out as Ruth was besieged by small, eager hands.

Throughout her phone conversation with Sam Ferryman, Jane was aware that she shouldn't be having it; that if Eccles found out, she would be fired. But he was unlikely to find out, and, besides, she was enjoying herself.

Sam had come through to her asking for Eccles, but the line was engaged and they had started talking. He said he was from the *Correspondent*, and he seemed interested in everything she had to say and impressed by her knowledge. Which was quite a change, Jane thought wryly, and very flattering.

'So, of the couple of hundred cults in the UK—'

'New Religious Movements, or NRMs,' she corrected him automatically.

'God, what a mouthful! D'you have to say that every time?'

She smiled, remembering that she had thought exactly that the first time that she heard the title.

'OK then, NRMs,' he went on. 'How many would you say are dangerous?'

She knew the Eccles response to that one: that 'dangerous' was not a helpful term. 'Problematic' was both less emotive and closer to the mark, especially when one considered that some of the problems arose from members' parents, rather than from the NRMs themselves.

'About nine,' she said calmly.

'Really?' He sounded excited.

It was a heady thing, she realized, talking to journalists. No wonder Eccles didn't want to share it.

'Is the Fellowship one of the dangerous ones?' Sam asked.

'The Fellowship?' she echoed. The Fellowship, she nearly told him, was so far off any 'danger list' that it wasn't even called an NRM – it fell within the New Age Church of England category – and it did a lot of 'good works' with drug addicts. Jane had only heard of it because Freddy, a friend of hers, who'd gone cherry-picking years before on a farm near the commune, had mentioned it. Fellow-shippers wore blue clothes, Jane remembered, and the leader had at one stage called himself 'the Keeper', although he later dropped the title. For some reason, though, it had stuck in Jane's mind, and when she went through the alphabet to make Eccles's list it had seemed worth using.

How strange, she thought now, that Sam should ask her about the Fellowship. Her mother would call it a sign.

'Are they on the list?' he prompted.

'No. No, I'm sorry, they're not. In fact, they're not on any list that I know of. We've never had a call about them before. You're the first.'

'Oh.' He paused, then said carefully: 'Can I speak to you in complete confidence?'

She smiled. 'Most of our callers do.'

'Have you heard a rumour about a trust-fund scandal at the Fellowship?'

'No,' she said simply. 'But if that's what you're interested in, there's a court case going on at the moment—'

'I know. Look, I hope I don't sound rude, but GUIDE would know if there was anything dodgy going on at the Fellowship, wouldn't they? There isn't anyone else who might have . . . er . . . sort of a closer ear to the ground whom I should talk to?'

Jane knew Eccles would have taken serious umbrage at that. 'We hear most things,' she said evenly. 'We are the central agency.'

He gave two women's names, one of which Jane recognized, and asked 'Did you know they're both members?

'I didn't,' she admitted, 'but then I wouldn't expect to. We have no interest in the Fellowship.'

There was a pause. Then, 'I've offended you,' he said humbly.

'No, you haven't.'

'It's just that I've got myself into a bit of a hole, you see, about the Fellowship. I've got someone working there under cover.'

She listened until he had finished his tale, hearing in his voice his concern about Kirsten, and liking him for it.

'How old is she?' she asked.

'About nineteen.'

'Even if you told the police, it's highly unlikely they'd do anything,' Jane said. 'She's an adult in the eyes of the law, and you're not even a relative. Besides, from everything I've heard about the Fellowship, it's very tame.'

'Kirsten said there were all-night prayer meetings,' Sam protested.

'Tame,' said Jane. She heard a page being turned at the other end of the phone.

'Weird diet restrictions.'

'Like what?'

'Lots of potatoes.'

Jane smiled. 'Chips?'

'She wasn't specific,' Ferryman said defensively. 'She was supposed to be telling me more at our meeting.'

'I'd do what you suggested,' Jane suggested diplomatically. 'Leave it another twenty-four hours before doing anything.'

He sighed. 'Thank you,' he said. 'Sorry if I've wasted your time.'

'You haven't.' Although actually, she remembered, she had promised to get a letter in the post to worried parents in Bath. 'I do think if your interest is NRMs with trust-fund ambitions, you should be looking elsewhere.'

'Oh yes?' His enthusiasm rushed back.

Fleetingly, she considered what she was about to do. Occasionally Eccles's ambiguous attitude towards the NRMs tipped over into positive liking for one of them. Currently he was attached to 'Hampstead for Jesus', a popular charismatic NRM with a growing number of very wealthy young members. Jane had heard him on the telephone to the group's financial adviser, warning him to make sure that members were over the age of consent before they transferred their trust funds, because 'You don't want any unwelcome press attention.'

Jane took a deep breath and told Sam the name of the group.

'You're an angel,' he breathed.

'Mm. I'm not sure about that.' She heard Eccles out in the corridor and felt herself go hot and cold. It would be unbearably humiliating to be sacked, ordered off the campus. 'What I've just told you is completely off the record,' she said swiftly.

'Don't worry, I never reveal my sources.'

Jane laughed, then realized how rude it sounded. 'Sorry. It's just that I didn't think journalists said that in real life.'

'Oh, that and much more.' He sounded amused, too. 'Look, d'you have files on this Hampstead mob? Would it be all right if I came down there to have a look?'

'No! I mean, yes, of course you can come as a journalist, but if you start asking questions about Hampstead Eccles might get suspicious.'

'Ah.'

'And fire me.'

'It's all right, don't worry,' he said hastily. 'I won't come. But maybe we could meet for a talk? I needn't come to the campus. I could meet you in Guildford.'

'Well, OK.' She thought she'd like to meet him.

'Oh, good. Great. Can I give you my direct line in case there's anything else you remember?'

She wrote it down and they said goodbye. She heard Eccles haranguing the secretary for no good reason, turned back to her computer, pulled out the standard 'Parents' letter and began work on personalizing it.

Most of the houses that made up the Moor were grouped round the village green, and four were close to the church. The most imposing by far was an enormous manor house, said to date from Elizabethan times; it even had a minstrels' gallery. Newcomers and visitors to the Fellowship assumed that David Norton lived there, but they were wrong. Eighteen male Fellowshippers occupied the twelve bed-rooms. David lived in far less splendour, in the old doctor's house, a large but rather rambling residence that backed on to woodland. Set a little apart from the other houses, it was approached by its own short drive bordered by cedars and shrubs. The house was painted white but the greenery overshadowed and tended to darken it, making it look slightly sinister.

No Fellowshipper felt that way about the house. It was where David lived, where they came if they had a problem; to his ground-floor study, a pleasant, high-ceilinged room which had formerly been a library.

David never hurried them or made them feel foolish, and although it wasn't quite an 'open door' policy – everyone had to have an appointment – people felt supremely comfortable there. It was as if Love lived in that house.

In the mornings, two Fellowshippers came in to run the administration side of things from the office opposite his study. Others tended to the cleaning, devoting special care to the sitting-room at the front of the house which had most light and was set aside for visitors. They polished industriously and always made sure there were fresh flowers in the vases, that there wasn't a speck of dust anywhere.

As for the rest of the house, David was a very tidy man. And he liked a little privacy. When he couldn't be found in the village, when he wasn't in the church or his study, the office staff knew where he would be: behind the green baize door that led to the back of the house and his private rooms.

Behind it, the polished wooden floorboards gave way to stone slabs; the back of the house was much older than the front. The passageway was narrow and quite dark. At the very end was a door which opened on to the stable-block, but which was kept bolted top and bottom. On the left was a small, windowless room containing a computer, a television and two telephones. There was another room beyond it, then a passage branched off to the left, towards other parts of the house.

On the right was another room. There was one small window, but it was high up and now so overgrown with ivy that hardly any light penetrated, even during the day. At night the room was pitch black.

It was almost midnight now and the candles were lit on the simple altar at the front. David knelt before it, his white hair gleaming in the soft light, his blue eyes reflecting two tiny flames as he gazed up at the altar, at the wooden cross and the oak box that lay open before it.

He felt so close to the Lord tonight! Tears coursed down his cheeks. He could feel himself changing, his earthly body preparing to fall away, his spiritual one taking over.

'Thank you, oh thank you, my heavenly Father!'

He had so much to thank Him for: first, the revelation that the Scroll was truly the word of God. Then the calling of him – him, David Norton – to His Holy purpose, that he might be the Chosen One talked of in the last of the ten signs, the Keeper of those signs.

At first, after he and Ruth had brought the Scroll back to England twelve years before, they had waited for the Lord to fulfil the signs Himself. They'd eagerly watched the news; they'd squeezed and manipulated facts like Cinderella's slipper to make them fit. But then had come stalemate. No matter how hard they had prayed, how absolute their faith, there were no more fulfilments. A year passed, then another. They had been puzzled, they had begun to doubt.

And then, on 20 December 1990, in a dream like those of the prophets of old, the Lord had spoken: His wishes lay in the final sentence of the Eighth Scroll, 'Let the finder of these words, him whose eyes have been opened by the Lord, be the keeper.'

David, by God's grace, had 'found' the Scroll; David was to carry out the Signs; he and Ruth and, later, Ross. The Lord had unfurled His purpose; there was to be a fellowship of believers led by David, providing cover and willing hands.

Having shown what He wanted, the Lord had not been slow to act. By His grace, in the New Year, David's estate agency business had been sold for a considerable sum to a building society, and the Moor acquired.

Then the children had started to arrive. From the streets and from the gutters had come the lost souls: drug addicts, alcoholics, runaways, ex-prisoners, children whom the world despised but whom the Lord and David wanted – oh, so much! They had qualities that others lacked: a yawning gap in their lives; a need to love and be loved, and, when they had experienced that love first hand, in the person of one man – utter adoration of him, unswerving obedience.

The only criterion was spiritual innocence, judged right at the start. The Lord didn't want those who had been corrupted by a previous faith, who knew too much of others' interpretation of His scriptures, who might know of the Second Coming and the ending of the world, who might, therefore, cause problems. The Lord wanted fresh hearts for the Last Days: good, obedient, loving children to do David's bidding; faithfully doing whatever he asked of them.

Some had become Shepherds, guarding the flock; others, such as Liam, and the children Ross had needed in Wales, were Volunteers for the signs; still others were to be his Missionaries for the Great Release.

David's eyes blurred. The hour was nearly upon them. In four days, the Awful Horror would begin.

At times, he admitted now, he had doubted whether some of the signs would ever come to pass.

'The food that we eat and the water that we drink shall become bitter in our mouths, and many shall suffer, particularly little children and pregnant women'. 'Bitter' had posed a problem, because if something was bitter, people wouldn't eat it. David had fretted over 'many', too – exactly how many? Thousands? Thousands would be too difficult, the source of the contamination would be traced before thousands could be infected. But would a mere hundred be enough?

'Be still and know Thy God,' the Lord had said, and David had obeyed: he fell silent. Then God showed him the true meaning of those words: that 'bitter' was to be understood in the figurative sense, and that in a spiritual context 'many' didn't necessarily refer to huge numbers – after all, the Lord himself said in the Bible, that where two or three were gathered together in His name, He would be there among them.

David, through Jesus, had come to see that the beloved apostle John, author of Revelation and the Scroll, had had some problems with the interpretation of God's word. So it didn't matter how many young children became ill – five dead at the last count, but probably more to come – it was the intention that counted; what was in David's and Ruth's and the others' hearts. Even if they failed – and they had failed to contaminate Scotland's water supply, and to introduce a new strain of *E. coli* in Switzerland – it was the fact that they had tried that mattered.

It had become a sort of game between David and the Lord. The Lord did the difficult bits, leaving David with some meaty problems, but always being there in the background to come to his aid. They had more or less split the signs between them: God had provided the meteors which had been striking the earth in ever-growing numbers over the past few years (Sign Nine); He'd brought tidal waves and droughts, fires and global warming (Signs Six and Eight); He'd destroyed many works of which man was proud – starting with the Temple in Jerusalem in AD 70 – (Sign Seven). He'd even dealt with Sign Three Himself: the assassination of the Great Traitor, Yitzhak Rabin, the Israeli prime minister who'd treacherously sought to do a deal with the Palestinians. David had wanted to do that Sign himself, and his plan had been half-formed when the Lord struck. He'd felt childishly put out until he'd realized that the Lord had known David's plan wouldn't work, and had acted quickly to prevent the earthly authorities from discovering him.

David's misty blue eyes shone. The Lord had been more than generous to him. He'd let David have the first Sign (the two Princes); Sign Two, about the peace-makers, was also his, as was Sign Four, which led on to people being afraid to eat (Sign Five), and Sign Ten was to be David's too.

Four days from the Release, two of David's signs remained unfulfilled. One was to be carried out that night.

David felt a twinge of anxiety which he quickly crushed. Nothing would go wrong. Nothing and no one would stand in the Lord's way now. He would make seeing eyes blind, as He had blinded the world to what was happening there at the Fellowship.

'A bit bland' was the local churches' view of his sermons; 'a saint' was what most in the main village thought of him.

David smiled. Did he not have earthly as well as heavenly protection? Who, then, could go against him?

The candles on the altar flickered and he was reminded of his duties. He had someone to see, a lost little one, a child who might have jeopardized everything if the Lord hadn't shown David in time what she was up to.

Now, he rather thought there might be a special role for her. Not needed in this world, but needed very much by himself and the Lord.

He closed the lid of the oak box on the altar, and went out into the passageway that led to the sound-proofed rooms.

CHAPTER EIGHT

Afterwards, Paul Ryder was to remember it as being his last good night's sleep. He was dreaming of a tiny tower in Tuscany where he and his wife had stayed on their honeymoon. They'd had it to themselves, and every night they dined on the roof-terrace under the stars, their solitude interrupted only by the ringing of bells from the nearby monastery.

'Paul,' his wife said.

Still in his dream, Ryder reached out and stroked her face.

'Will you wake up?'

His eyes snapped open at her tone. She was angry; he always slept through night-calls. She thrust the telephone into his hand.

'Who is it?'

'Yves,' she said.

'I'll take it in the study.'

'Yves,' he repeated aloud as, still half-asleep, he stumbled down the stairs. Why was Yves calling him at quarter to six in the morning? He'd left him in Bordeaux only the day before, after a very fine lunch on the Frenchman's expense account. He picked up the phone in his study and upstairs his wife put down the extension with a clatter.

'Yves?'

'Paul. It's not good news, I'm afraid.'

Ryder tried to make his mind work. 'What?'

'Jesus' swaddling-clothes. They've been stolen.'

'His *what?*'

'Swaddling—'

'OK, OK.' Ryder felt sick. He sank down on to a chair. 'Christ's covering shall be removed'. The words of the Tenth Sign echoed in his head. He had never for one moment imagined they referred to anything but the Turin Shroud.

The 'swaddling-clothes' were a pile of dirty bandages 'discovered' by a nineteenth-century monk in Bethlehem and exhibited in one of the town's dubious tourist shrines. But everyone knew they were a fake, Ryder told himself. Just as everyone knew, jeered a voice at the back of his mind, that the Eighth Scroll was a fake, too.

It made perfect, awful sense. Anyone who believed in the Eighth Scroll – especially anyone deranged enough to carry out its signs – would believe the swaddling-clothes were genuine too. Why hadn't he thought of that when he'd felt so inspired at the Bordeaux conference?

'Jesus Christ,' he whispered.

Yves sighed. The swaddling-clothes, he went on, had been stolen from the Baby Jesus Holy Sanctuary at about midnight. Nothing else had been taken. The Israeli groom had notified Yves thirty minutes before – after he'd called the Italian and German grooms.

Ryder cleared his throat. 'It'll be the Global, then?'

'Yes. It can't be a coincidence, Paul' – Yves's voice held a note of pleading – 'not after the Saudi Princes.'

'No, I know.' Ryder shut his eyes. If only he could wake up, he thought dully. He opened one eye: the room was as it had been; if anything, with the lightening of the sky, it was in sharper focus. He found that he could not imagine what the day held in store. Doubtless, it was his mind trying to protect itself. He knew he had to notify Antony Beck, his superior.

Yves said, 'The Israelis are trying to keep the theft quiet.'

'They'll be lucky.'

'They've detained the caretaker at the shrine. They've put out a media ban. The Israelis do these things quite well.'

'So perhaps they will be lucky.' But Ryder didn't believe that.

'Look, Paul, I've got to go.'

'Sure. Thanks for the call.'

After he had replaced the receiver, he remounted the stairs as quietly as he could, went into the spare bedroom and put on his jogging-trousers and T-shirt. He didn't want to be standing in his pyjama bottoms when he notified Beck. Afterwards he'd change into the suit he always kept in the spare room for such contingencies, and go to work. He passed his wife's door. He was glad they had had such a pleasant evening together. He'd leave her a note. He guessed it could be some time before he saw her again.

For the second morning in a row, Jane's phone rang at eight-fifteen. It couldn't be Eccles again, she thought, and, suddenly worried, she snatched it up.

'Jane? Hi, it's Rudi. Rudi Highmountain.'

For a moment, she couldn't place him – they usually communicated by e-mail. He was an American (he'd changed his surname from Hoffberg) who held a similar position to her own at a university in Tel Aviv, except that his professor, in her opinion, was a darling. Jane had met them at a conference in London before Christmas. She'd had high hopes of that conference, of meeting interesting international academics, or at least hearing them speak, but Eccles hadn't got her full accreditation – he'd wanted her there solely as his bag-carrier. She'd met Rudi at a reception that Eccles hadn't wanted to attend.

Rudi had been outrageously camp, very charming and full of gossip. They'd exchanged numbers and, since then, fairly frequent e-mails.

'Something terribly exciting has happened,' he said breathlessly. 'Nobody's supposed to know. I only know because my friend in the police called me at home this morning and told me.'

'Oh?' Jane said with a smile. He sounded like a little boy.

'Yes. It's about Jesus' swaddling-clothes.'

'His what? Oh yes.' The swaddling-clothes were, to her mind on a par with weeping statues of the Virgin Mary. 'What about them?'

At first, as she listened she felt inclined to scoff: the theft had to be a publicity stunt. Then he said something truly bizarre.

'What d'you mean, the caretaker's been taken away?' she exclaimed.

'It's true, I tell you! They've hauled him off to a compound where they hold political prisoners. Anyone who starts asking questions is going to get shipped off there too, including journalists, my friend says.'

'Rudi, this sounds a bit . . .'

'They're talking about it being a fulfilment of an old prophecy.'

Jane caught her breath. The previous night, she had watched a current-affairs programme in which an expert on ancient cloth had been interviewed about the Turin Shroud. He had been involved in designing the exhibition case for the cloth, and it was 'preposterous', he declared, that anyone should now say that the material could possibly have been damaged by the lights.

'But why else should the authorities wish to remove Christ's alleged covering?' the interviewer had asked boredly, and Jane, also tiring of the subject, had gone to bed. She'd woken not long after, a string of words running in her head. It had taken her a few minutes to put them in sequence: 'Christ's covering shall be removed . . .' There was more, but the rest had escaped her, as had the words' provenance, and she'd soon fallen asleep again.

Now she remembered the sentence in full: 'Christ's covering shall be removed from those who have wrongly taken it.'

She knew, too, its origin. It was from the Eighth Scroll, one of the signs foretelling the end of the world. In preparing her paper for publication, she had industriously typed out those signs, along with other relevant passages from the end-time documents to which she'd referred.

If what Rudi said was true, one of the Scroll signs had just been fulfilled. She felt a cold thrill – half excitement, half fear. In spite of her work, or possibly because of it, she had never seriously entertained the idea of an NRM, or anyone else, actually fulfilling Apocalyptic prophecies.

'Jane, are you there?' asked Rudi.

'What? Yes, sorry. Rudi . . . Jesus' swaddling-clothes,' she said carefully, 'they could be described as Christ's "covering", couldn't they?'

'Well, yes, if you believe in them.'

Of course, Jane thought, the swaddling clothes were fakes – as was the Eighth Scroll.

'Anyway, the reason I'm phoning you is' – Rudi paused dramatically – 'your secret service people and the FBI are coming over here.'

'Why?'

'Search me. But keep it quiet – and don't write anything down. I'm serious. That's why I didn't e-mail you. I'm not supposed to know, am I? I'm only telling you and my friend in Washington. He won't be awake yet. See if you can find out anything from your end, about why your secret service are coming. But Jane?'

'What?' Her head was reeling.

'Don't tell anyone else – anyone at all.'

For a full minute after he'd gone, she sat staring at nothing in particular. Whether she believed in their authenticity or not, within a few hours two sets of Christ's coverings had been removed. It could be said that the Scroll sign had been fulfilled twice over. If Rudi was right, the British security service was interested. Her mind spun. Did they genuinely believe someone was fulfilling the signs?

She tried to remember more of them but couldn't, nor could she think about anything else.

She quickly finished getting ready, let herself out of the flat and crossed the campus to her department. She wanted to read the Scroll again. She wanted to find out what else might have already happened.

It was a little after nine o'clock, but there were few people about: most of the lectures did not start until ten. The air felt heavy and sticky.

On her floor, the secretaries had not yet arrived. She closed her office door and pulled out her copy of the Eighth Scroll. The slim volume contained both the original Greek and the English translation. She read the last sign. She had remembered it perfectly.

Her eyes ran up the page, to the first: 'In the Last Days the two sons of the infidel lord of the desert shall be struck down.'

She thought suddenly of the two young Princes. The day before, when she was reading about the inquest, a memory had half-surfaced. She went into Newsfile and found the story. She found the quote from al-Safr's about the boys' father vowing vengeance on the killer of his sons, and there just above it were the pathologist's words: 'They were killed by a karate chop to the neck. They were, if you like, almost literally "struck down".'

Her stomach seized. Could it really be happening?

In the NRM academic world, there was quiet but fierce competition to find the next Apocalyptic NRM before its actions brought it worldwide notoriety. Jane, knowing Eccles would never let her be involved, had always privately likened it to the hunt for a new galaxy, but now she could see the attraction: excitement was coursing through her.

She turned to the rest of the Scroll. She didn't know about the second and third signs, but the fourth, about food-poisoning, was currently being fulfilled in Britain and half the rest of Europe, even down to the detail of young children. She frowned: was somebody actually crazy enough to be poisoning children in the name of their brand of Christianity? At least only part of the sign had been fulfilled: no pregnant women had been harmed.

She pondered the fifth, about people starving rather eating. If the contaminations continued, that would probably come true soon too. The sixth and seventh were pretty vague but the eighth, about warm places becoming icy wildernesses, could well be a reference to global warming. The fiery stones in the ninth must be meteors, a number of which had indeed fallen in the last few years, and the tenth was the swaddling-clothes/Turin Shroud.

She estimated that perhaps six out of the ten signs had been fully or partly fulfilled. That, taken in conjunction with what Rudi had said about the British security service . . .

Her heart thumped. She needed to find out more; their conversation had been too brief. She called his number in Tel Aviv.

There was a click at the other end of the line and then a man's voice.

'Rudi? It's Jane. You know the old prophecy your friend was talking about?'

Silence.

'Rudi?'

'I'm afraid Rudi isn't in today,' the man said, pleasantly and in good English.

Jane frowned. 'Oh? But I've just spoken to him.'

'And you are . . . ?'

Something stopped her giving her name. 'Just a friend. It doesn't matter,' she said swiftly.

'Wait,' the man commanded. 'Tell me who—'

She hung up. Her hand was trembling. She didn't know if she'd imagined it, but it seemed the man had caught his breath when she mentioned the 'old prophecy'. And when Rudi had phoned her, she'd had the impression that he was in his office. She rang his home number but there was no reply. Did it mean, she wondered, that he'd been taken away like the shrine janitor? How serious was this thing?

She glanced down at the Scroll again. The Princes had been murdered in Sussex, and Rudi had said the British security service was involved. Was it possible there was a British connection?

She turned to the Scroll's postscript: 'Let the finder of these words, him whose eyes have been opened by the Lord, be the keeper.'

She stopped dead. As she had recalled only the afternoon before when talking to Sam Ferryman, the leader of the Fellowship had once called himself 'the Keeper'.

She blinked. She flipped to the front of the book and the original Greek version of the Scroll. She located the Greek for 'keeper' and then took down her Greek–English dictionary and found its English translation. 'Keeper' she saw and, beside it, 'deliverer'.

The Fellowship? A group so far down the scale of potentially dangerous NRMs that it wasn't even listed? A bit like Britain, she thought, at the bottom of the league of countries most likely to harbour the next Apocalyptic NRM. But David Norton had once called himself 'the Keeper'. And Sam's reporter had failed to make contact.

There was a protocol she was supposed to pursue if she came across anything suspicious in her work. Inform first Eccles and then GUIDE head office. If she told Eccles, he'd take over, cut her out of the chase. She could go straight to GUIDE, of course, perhaps to Paul Ryder, but he was a shambling, dozy civil servant who hadn't listened properly to her paper. He'd probably patronize her again, then file whatever she told him.

What about the security services, then, allegedly already interested?

No, she thought with a shudder. Her postgraduate thesis had been on Waco, where, in her opinion, most of the deaths had been both unnecessary and caused by the forces of law and order. Besides, did she want whatever had happened to Rudi to happen to her? A chill ran through her. Of course, nothing might have happened to him – only where was he? Tell no one, he'd said, and then he'd vanished.

That couldn't happen to her, here in England. Could it?

She set the idea uneasily aside. She wouldn't report the Fellowship to anyone, she decided, not only because she was afraid for herself, but because all she had was one link, and that second-hand: Norton had once called himself 'the Keeper'. She needed to find out much more before she told anyone anything. She might go down there herself, go under cover as Sam's reporter had done.

She experienced a dart of fear, and concern, too, for Kirsten. She'd told Sam not to worry, to give the girl another twenty-four hours. Suppose the result of waiting was that Kirsten had been harmed? She went cold.

She'd probably made contact by now, Jane told herself. She glanced at the time – twenty to ten – and dialled Sam's number. If Kirsten had indeed resurfaced, Jane wanted very much to talk to her. Sam's number rang and rang. She was about to give up when he answered. She introduced herself.

'Oh yes?' He sounded breathless and a little surprised.

'Er, I was just wondering if you'd heard from Kirsten yet?'

'No, not yet. Why?'

'Oh, nothing really.' She wanted to say as little as possible over the phone. 'Would it be at all possible to meet? Today, if possible?'

They arranged to meet at his office at one o'clock.

The hypermarket stood five miles outside the town on the Severn estuary. Its siting, a year before, had been controversial, arousing fears of urban decline amidst the High Street shops and businesses. But an expected ring road had yet to be built, making the vast store difficult to reach. Except at weekends, and when coaches visited, it was often nearly empty.

It was Ruth's first port of call that morning. At a little before eleven o'clock, the automatic doors hissed open to admit her. There was muzak playing: 'The Way We Were'. Except for two lots of shoppers at the check-outs, she could see no other customers, which might or might not be a good thing, she cautioned herself. Fewer eyes to see her but with less to distract them from watching – and everyone was looking for her, she reminded herself. She'd seen the e-fit of 'Helen', her Covent Garden self, on the news. A stall-holder had remembered her name.

But the E-fit was nothing like her, and, besides, today she looked very different. She had on a shoulder-length auburn wig and thick-rimmed glasses, and was dowdily dressed in leggings and a big jumper. No one would recognize her as 'Helen' or 'Maid Marian'.

She took a trolley and advanced up the central aisle, putting goods in her trolley, hesitating over some items as if worrying about the price. A security guard came by, a large, bored-looking young man who scarcely seemed to see her, but whose appearance nevertheless made her tense. She watched him out of the corner of her eye until he was out of sight. She was nervous today, she acknowledged, which was unlike her.

She continued to the end of the aisle. Along the back wall ran refrigerated units containing fresh meat, fish and dairy products. She walked slowly, looking closely at them. The cold air from the cabinets cooled her and she welcomed it, for her clothes felt clammy against her skin. Originally, she had considered adding padding to her slim figure, but Ross had dissuaded her. What if it should fall off? he'd asked, and she'd taken his point. Dear Ross, she thought distractedly, how he worried about her.

She came to the pre-prepared meals and paused. Her eyes ran over the packets, seeking a particular brand. Not every supermarket stocked it, but she'd thought a hypermarket like this one would. Then she saw, over on her left, the whole range: Chicken Paprika, Cod in Tomato and Yoghurt Sauce, Vegetarian Lasagne, and the rest. Ross had read about them on the Internet, and later there had been stories in the media. Great Expectations pre-prepared meals for pregnant women, each meal containing all the proteins, vitamins and minerals necessary for the mother-to-be and her unborn baby. Busy women need no longer worry if they were eating the right things, the advertising copy boasted. Great Expectations took care of that for them, with organic, tasty foods that met all government health-and-safety controls. For extra reassurance, and so that the woman could see what she was buying, the meals were displayed on microwaveable dishes, and sealed with transparent plastic.

Ruth glanced about her. There was another woman down at the other end of the cabinets, but she wasn't close enough to be a problem. There was no sign of the security guard, and no sign, either, of cameras. Ruth knew some supermarkets used them to deter shoplifters, but in that case they tended to be displayed prominently.

She took a deep breath and slipped her hand in to the zipped compartment of her handbag. Her fingers closed gingerly around the rubber ball there and drew it out. It was dark green, about the colour and size of a squash ball. She cupped it in her hand, being careful not to prick herself with the small, thin needle protruding from it. Ross had given her several inoculations as a precaution, but there was no specific vaccine against what the ball contained. It probably wouldn't kill her but it would make her feel very ill, and she couldn't be spared at this stage.

She looked down at her right hand. The short needle now stuck out from between her second and third fingers. It was less than two centimetres long, very discreet. With her left hand, she picked up a Chicken Paprika. The separate sachet of creamy yoghurt sauce lay alongside the chicken. It was into that sauce that the needle had to go. Ruth saw that she was trembling. It was all right, she told herself. No one was watching her. 'Please Jewus, warn me if it's not all right,' she pleaded suddenly. It was the sort of childish prayer David would approve of; the sort that normally she disdained, believing that Jesus didn't want to be constantly bothered with minutiae, that He was too cosmic for that.

One quick squeeze would do it, Ross had said. She stared through the plastic at the sauce. Suppose it oozed out, she wondered? Suppose there was a tell-tale trickle left behind?

'God knows what is in our hearts,' David said. Allowing herself to hesitate no longer, she plunged in the needle and squeezed the ball. She had no way of knowing if enough had gone in, but that part, as David would say, was up to God, and Ross said the ball contained enough for a dozen doses; she didn't want to overdo it. She withdrew the needle. The pinprick was tiny but just in case, she covered it with the cardboard wraparound.

'They're ever so good,' came a voice behind her.

Her hand froze on the packet. She turned to see an obviously pregnant woman standing there. 'Oh?' was all that Ruth could manage.

'They've got all you need, haven't they?' She smiled in a sisterly fashion at Ruth. 'That chicken one's the best.'

'Is it?' Ruth croaked.

'I think so.' The woman stretched in to the cabinet and took out four meals. 'How long?' She said.

'I'm sorry?'

'How many weeks are you?'

'Oh! Um, nine.'

'Thought you weren't showing much.' She smiled again. 'Good luck.'

'Er, thanks. you too.'

Ruth watched her go; she'd been nice. Ruth had never imagined meeting one of her targets. She recalled the toxin's effects on an unborn child and for a moment was filled with terrible doubt. Then she shook herself. She knew what she was doing, and why it had to be that way. If she had only been quicker, she chastised herself, that woman might have taken one of her meals. Swiftly, she dealt with eleven more packets, making sure to replace them at the top of the relevant piles. Ross wasn't sure how long the toxin would survive 'on the shelf'. She didn't know if there was any liquid left for the last two, but she'd done her best. She replaced the ball in her bag, and for authenticity, put one of the meals – an intact one – in her trolley.

She made herself linger in another aisle before heading for the check-out. She had three more little green balls in her van and lots of driving to do. Now that she had started, she was keen to finish.

CHAPTER NINE

Since seven o'clock that morning, Ryder had been in meetings, some conducted face to face, others by telephone.

It was noon now and the Global Alert was due to begin in two hours. Ryder had cult-leaders to interview, a groom team to put together, but he was in another meeting, in a basement room of a building off Whitehall. It was an emergency meeting of ARIC (Assessment and RIsk Control) and the most important meeting of the whole day. It was chaired by a representative from Number 10. Also present were a brigadier who was the Director of Military Operations, several senior police officers, representatives from MI5 and MI6, and a medical adviser. To Ryder's left, sat his assistant, Lucy-Ann Burroughs, who through an earpiece was in constant communication with their office. To Ryder's right, sat his boss, Antony Beck.

The chairwoman asked for the latest from Bridegroom.

Ryder glanced swiftly round the table. He knew what he was about to say wouldn't be popular, and yet he had to get everyone on Bridegroom's side. 'We're being asked to assume the worst: that whoever took the swaddling-clothes is part of an Armageddon cult fulfilling the Eighth Scroll and intent on unspecified aggression against a sizeable part of our population.'

There were some exclamations from round the table, although everyone had been previously briefed.

'We're also being asked to assume that the cult is British,' said Ryder, and the uproar he'd been expecting broke out.

The chairwoman quelled it and asked him to explain.

'We come under the spotlight for two reasons. Firstly, every Bridegroom country is being asked to make the same assumption, namely, and until proved otherwise, that it is harbouring the cult, and—'

'So it's not just us,' interrupted the brigadier.

Ryder didn't comment. He went on: 'Secondly, we are one of two countries, the other being Israel, where a specific sign has been fulfilled: the murders of the Saudi Princes in our case, the swaddling-clothes' theft in Israel's. We're more in the frame than Israel, because, if the group had its eyes on the swaddling-clothes all along, obviously it could steal them only in Israel. Whereas, with the Saudi children, the group didn't have to choose Britain. There are a dozen countries in which they could have assassinated "two sons of the infidel lord of the desert".'

'Doesn't necessarily mean it's a British group,' insisted the brigadier.

'No.' Ryder bowed to him. 'It could be that a foreign group hired a mercenary to carry out the killings here. But it's generally felt—'

'By Bridegroom?' interposed the chairwoman.

'Yes. That the choice of the UK, plus our recent botulism outbreak in which five children died – a fulfilment in large part of the Scroll's fourth sign – indicates we are the cult's likeliest base.'

'But the United States and half of Europe have got food-poisoning outbreaks,' exclaimed the brigadier.

'Yes.' Ryder glanced down at his folder. 'There have been an average number of food-poisonings worldwide in the last four weeks. But in only in the UK and one other country – Holland – does the contamination seem to have been deliberate.'

'Do we know that for sure?' inquired the medical adviser.

'It's looking increasingly likely.' Ryder consulted his file again. 'The botulism was identified last Friday. The source was traced to the Foodie Lanes at Covent Garden that same day, and all stall-holders at the Lanes have now been interviewed. Several remember a woman selling gingerbread, "Helen", a newcomer, who hadn't appeared again. On Monday, efforts to track her down began. Yesterday, she still hasn't come forward and it is therefore being assumed the poisoning was deliberate.'

'The papers are carrying the story today,' said Beck, 'with an e-fit of her, and her name.'

Ryder glanced at him gratefully. Beck hadn't always been supportive during that long morning. 'That's correct. And I understand *Crimewatch* is doing a special on her tonight. With any luck we should get her within the next twenty-four hours.'

'Yes,' interjected the commissioner of the Metropolitan Police. 'Anything that touches on the nation's children is going to arouse huge public concern. We can only be grateful that she hasn't struck again.'

'Perhaps five dead children satisfied her?' suggested the medical adviser drily.

Ryder focused on the chairwoman. 'I believe if we find this woman, and/or the murderer of the Princes, we find the group. Or we rule ourselves out of the frame as the cult's base-country.'

She studied him for a long moment. 'Well then,' she said, 'we'd better find them, hadn't we? It does sound as if the public, through the media, is going to be our best bet for locating this "Helen" woman. I take it there's enough police officers available to follow up *Crimewatch* leads?'

The Met commissioner nodded.

'What about the Princes' killer?' The chairwoman turned to a Special Branch man on her right.

His face was impassive. It had been hoped, he said, that fragments of flesh taken from beneath Prince Harry's fingernails would lead, by means of DNA testing, to the identity of the killer. Unfortunately that had not happened.

'Why not?' asked the chairwoman with a frown.

'In spite of promises given to the contrary on paper, ma'am, several countries, including the USA and a sizeable portion of Europe, are unwilling to check their DNA records for a criminal wanted in another country.'

'For pity's sake!'

'Yes, ma'am. There are fears, apparently, of their nationals not being given a fair trial.' For such reasons, he went on, six weeks into the hunt, no suspect had yet been identified. The killer had left no trail whatsoever. It was assumed he was a professional hitman, hired for the job.

'Aren't there lists of such people?' asked the chairwoman.

'There are,' he admitted. 'All those known to us have naturally been checked, and, I'm afraid, ruled out.'

'I see. I understand a team from Scotland Yard is to lend its expertise?'

The man nodded.

'And that police officers from East Sussex will be conducting fresh door-to-door inquiries in the area where the Princes were found?'

'And in the area immediately around the boarding-school,' said the Special Branch man.

'We must hope, then, that a fresh lead appears; particularly as the rest of the world will now be breathing down our necks to see that it does.' The chairwoman turned, with a tight smile, to Ryder, and asked, 'What about our cults, Mr Ryder? What are we doing about them?'

That morning had been spent checking and rechecking data, Ryder told her. Of the nine 'problem' cults in the UK, only three were thought capable of violence. All the members of those three were being detained, and the leaders were being interrogated.

'Anything?'

Ryder glanced inquiringly at Lucy-Ann, who was listening intently to her radio-earpiece. She shook her head.

'I'm afraid not,' he said, 'but we've only just started. I'll be taking over the interrogations after this meeting. In the next couple of days, all cults will be looked at, by my office and' – he looked across the table – 'Special Branch?'

The Scotland Yard man nodded.

'We've also got two GUIDE offices, in Guildford and Edinburgh, working for us,' added Ryder.

'Right,' said the chairwoman. 'On a point of interest, how are you determining which cults may be dangerous?'

'On their track records,' Ryder said. 'Whether they've been violent before, or threatened to be. Whether they embrace Apocalypticism. Then, personality traits of the members, and particularly the leaders. What they say, do, call themselves. In that connection, Ms Burroughs came up with a suggestion.'

'Yes?'

'The last sentence of the Scroll reads: "May the finder of these words, him whose eyes have been opened by the Lord, be the keeper."' It's possible,' Ryder went on carefully, ' that the cult-leader calls himself "the Keeper".'

'Of course! And does anyone?' demanded the chairwoman.

'Not that we know of. All databases have been checked.'

'That would have been too easy,' put in Beck.

Ryder said nothing.

'Who stole the Scroll in the first place?' the chairwoman asked abruptly.

'No one knows,' he replied. 'But I think it's safe to say that if we can identify that person, or persons, then we'll find the group responsible for completing the signs.'

'Quite. Let's hope the Israelis are on to it.' She frowned for a moment. 'You said at the beginning, we must prepare ourselves for the worst?'

Ryder hadn't said exactly that, but he let it pass.

'How long, worst-case scenario, are we talking about?' she asked bluntly.

Ryder had hoped no one would ask; everyone was watching him intently. He took a deep breath. 'No one knows. We can't get into the mind of whoever's fulfilling the signs, and therefore it's largely guesswork. But the very specific nature of the three signs we've talked about here – the boys' deaths, the swaddling-clothes, the food-poisoning – leads many in Bridegroom to believe that this is the last phase of the plan.'

There was dead silence.

Eventually, the medical adviser said: 'But we can only say with any confidence that three of the signs appear to have been fulfilled. It might take whoever is responsible years to complete the rest.'

'It might,' Ryder agreed. 'But whoever is behind this is probably aware that, in echoing the signs as accurately as he has, he's going to attract exactly the sort of attention we're currently giving him.'

'So he knows he hasn't got long?'

'Precisely. If he's failed to complete the other signs, the chances are that he'll pluck an event from history to fit, so he can quickly move to his end-game.'

Beck coughed softly. 'And we note that the tenth sign, the stealing of the clothes, runs on into the description of the end,' he said. 'As if the two are linked.'

Ryder wished Beck hadn't pointed that out. Panic had a way of seeping out through cracks in the wall.

The meeting studied the last sign. Ryder, too, although he knew the words by heart.

'Christ's covering shall be removed from those who have wrongly taken it. The keeper shall keep it holy. And then the End, the Awful Horror of the Ungodly, shall come."

Beck cracked his knuckles. It was a sound Ryder hated. Caught off guard, he flinched. 'I'd say we're not talking about very long at all,' Beck said – it struck Ryder that, in a macabre way, the man was almost enjoying himself – 'perhaps only days.'

The chairwoman stared at him, then turned back to Ryder. 'What sort of "horror" do you think such a group would envisage?' she asked.

Ryder decided not to share some of the nightmares put forward by other grooms. 'I think they'd like to *envisage* the absolute worst. Nuclear holocaust. A wipeout of mankind. But of course their fantasies will probably have little bearing on what they can actually achieve.'

'We hope,' said Beck.

'Indeed,' agreed the chairwoman.

'Depending on what they've got access to,' Ryder went on carefully, 'they might try to copy Aum Shinrikyo, release deadly chemicals into the Underground. Or, given their recent interest in food contamination, do more of the same, perhaps on a grander scale.'

The chairwoman nodded. 'Hopefully both those scenarios could be detected and great harm averted.'

'Yes.'

She steepled her fingers. 'But the sign describes the "End". Suppose they've got a nuclear bomb?'

Suppose indeed, Ryder thought. He said nothing. Neither did anyone else.

'Or a chemical or biological weapon?' she went on. 'Suppose we don't find them in time? Suppose they release it?' Her eyes lit upon the brigadier. 'How do we protect our population?'

The brigadier squared his shoulders. Ryder knew why: he had seen the latest data. In the event of a biological or chemical attack, there were not nearly enough gas-masks and protective suits (known as NBC kits for nuclear, biological, chemical) for the whole population. It would take weeks, perhaps months, to manufacture the quantity required, and in the current situation there was no likelihood of being able to import any.

The brigadier told the meeting as much.

'I see. How about a vaccination programme?' the chairwoman asked in a leaden voice.

The brigadier looked her in the eye. 'There is a vaccine,' he admitted cautiously, 'which would provide a degree of protection against some of the known biological agents – anthrax, and perhaps the *botulinum* toxin, for instance.'

'Well, that's something,' she said more optimistically.

'Yes. But no one knows how long it's effective for, and again, I'm afraid, there's not a great deal of it. It's rather at the prototype stage.'

'Can't production be speeded up?' she asked impatiently.

'Yes, but to obtain the amount we require would take weeks.'

The chairwoman took a deep breath. 'What about NBC suits? How many of those are there?'

After a moment, the brigadier said, 'About four thousand gas-masks for the general population and perhaps twice that number of NBC suits.' Before she could speak, he hurried on. 'As a precaution, production of both masks and suits has already been stepped up to around the clock.' He glanced over at a colleague. 'I believe equally urgent measures are in hand as regards the vaccine?'

The other man nodded.

The medical adviser cleared her throat. She spoke quietly: 'I've no wish to add to the alarm, but it's my understanding that the vaccine is only definitely effective against anthrax spores?'

The brigadier shot her a look of loathing.

'Suppose the group doesn't use that particular weapon?' she went on.

No one answered.

'There are bunkers, and special places for leading persons, aren't there?' asked the Met commissioner.

The chairwoman eyed him coldly. 'There are. But many of those have been closed down in recent years. The sort of threat we're talking about was thought to have significantly diminished.

Therefore there aren't that many places, even for prominent people. I foresee a nasty rush.'

Again, no one spoke.

She said, 'I think it's fair to say that we can offer our population virtually no effective protection in the event of a biological, chemical or nuclear attack. So we'd better hope that the group has got its eyes on something much smaller – or, even better, that they're in Israel, Japan or the States, not here.'

'But even if the cult turns out to be Japanese,' said the medical adviser, 'if it releases enough of its biological weapon into the atmosphere, or if it targets the UK, the results are going to be same, aren't they?'

'Thank you,' the chairwoman said brittlely.

The doctor opened her mouth to say more, then thought better of it.

The chairwoman looked at her watch and then at a document in front of her. 'In one hour, the Global goes on. We're going to be implementing some pretty draconian measures. People will be detained without trial, and their civil liberties are going to be severely infringed. Airports and ports are going to be swarming with armed police and military personnel. Our seventeen "hotspots" nationwide are going to be sealed; all army and police leave has been cancelled. All members of our most dangerous cults are already in detention.

'Clearly, rumours are going to start. We don't need public panic to add to our problems. We can't obviously, given the scale of the thing, and not knowing how long it may have to last, have a media black-out.

'We're tending towards the idea of issuing a press release about another INSEC.'

An INSEC was an International Security Alert, which was similar in some respects to a Global Alert – there'd be a strong military deterrent at ports and airports, for example. It had been introduced some years before, in response to the ever-increasing number of 'red alerts' in the European Union, and covered emergencies ranging from kidnapped children to possible terrorist attacks.

'There are on average three a year,' the chairwoman continued. 'Ours should go unnoticed. Mr Ryder, how are you going to present your detention of the cults to the media?'

Ryder hadn't thought about it at all. He gave it swift thought now. 'Perhaps something along the lines of child abduction or members being held against their will?'

'Not bad, and you could always resort to D-notices.'

D-notices were issued by the Ministry of Defence on stories which, if published, might damage national security. Ryder used them only sparingly, because, although no media organization could ignore a notice, issuing it tended to increase journalistic curiosity rather than lessen it. If any case, he thought, if all 191 cults had to be detained, there was no way he could have that many notices issued.

He told the chairwoman he'd bear D-notices in mind. She nodded and then, to his relief, gathered up her papers.

She thanked everyone briefly, reminded them that everything discussed was highly confidential, and said there would be another meeting at six o'clock that evening – or sooner if the need arose.

Ryder followed Lucy-Ann out into the corridor. Jack Broughton, his deputy, was leaning against the wall nearby, waiting for them.

Broughton had very large dark eyes which gave him a lugubrious air. The effect when he actually was miserable was quite alarming.

Seeing that expression now, Ryder winced. 'What is it?' he demanded.

'The Israelis called. They lifted a guy who'd been told about the swaddling-clothes, put taps on his phone, someone in his office. A British woman rang. She referred to a conversation she'd just had with the guy, something about an "old prophecy".'

Ryder closed his eyes. The last thing they needed, ARIC had just agreed, was information leaking out.

'We got a name for this woman?' he asked.

'Oh, yes. They traced the call. It was from GUIDE's office at North Downs University.'

Ryder clenched his jaw until it hurt. 'Jane Carlucci?' he said hoarsely.

Broughton nodded.

She knew about the signs, Ryder thought woodenly. Of course she would have made the connection with the swaddling-clothes.

'Right.' He took command. 'She'll have to be detained. Has anyone gone down there yet?'

Broughton shook his head. 'I only took the call twenty minutes ago. I came straight over.'

'Thanks,' Ryder said brusquely, 'but we'd better get someone down there fast.'

Broughton proffered his mobile, but Ryder waved it away: the bunker was full of electronic 'ears', which interfered with mobiles. They set off down the corridor.

'Two-man job?' asked Broughton.

Ryder remembered how small Jane Carlucci was, but there was her tutor to consider, and God knew how many other people she might have told by now – students, her parents, a boyfriend, friends.

'Make it four, just in case. Lucy-Ann, I'd like you to be one of them.

She nodded.

'How long ago did Carlucci get the first call about the swaddling-clothes?' he asked.

Broughton consulted his notes. 'About four hours ago, they think.'

'Oh.' If Jane had talked, Ryder thought, if her story were to reach the ears of the media, there would be mass panic. The cult would be warned. How would they react if they felt cornered?

'She may not have realized the full implications,' Lucy-Ann suggested.

'I wouldn't bank on it.' They reached the lift. 'Where's the nearest SecSite to Guildford?'

There were thirty-seven Security Sites, ranging from one-bedroomed flats to military-style compounds capable of housing several hundred inmates. What they had in common was the fact that, outside a very small circle, nobody knew of their existence.

'There's a house in Godalming,' said Broughton.

Good, Ryder thought. That wasn't far; he'd be able to go and question her himself if necessary.

The lift was too slow arriving. They took the emergency stairs instead.

CHAPTER TEN

For Jane, the morning, which consisted mainly of a tutorial on Roman religions, dragged on and on. In the end, she cut short the tutorial and drove to the station in good time for the London train.

She arrived at the the *Correspondent*'s offices in the Strand just before one o'clock, and asked at reception for Sam Ferryman. She was told he'd be down in a couple of minutes. She sat down to wait for him, and looked around. The ceiling was double-height and the walls marble; in the middle of the floor, in what looked like a glass cage, stood an old printing-press.

On a low table in front of her were several copies of that day's paper. Jane picked one up. ' "HELEN" SOUGHT IN BOTULISM SCARE', ran the front-page headline. Underneath was an artist's impression of a woman with large dark eyes and short hair.

Jane stared at the face. Was she involved? Was she a member of the Fellowship?

'Jane Carlucci?'

A man in his early thirties with dark, curly hair was smiling down at her.

She stood up quickly. He had to be over six feet tall, she estimated, and she was glad she'd worn her Cuban boots: they gave her an extra couple of inches.

'Thanks for seeing me so quickly,' she said.

'Not at all. Shall we go?'

They went through the revolving doors into the street. The day's earlier sultriness had passed without a storm and now it was sunny and pleasantly hot.

They branched off into a cobbled pedestrian precinct with flower-tubs and benches set round a fountain.

'This isn't about the Hampstead NRM, is it?' Sam asked.

She was momentarily taken aback. 'Er, no, sorry, it isn't.'

'I thought not. We're in here,' said Sam, holding open a door for her.

It was an attractive restaurant with pink table-cloths and a lot of glassware. A waiter led them over to a table in the window, brought them drinks and menus, and let them take their time ordering.

'So,' Sam said, offering her a bowl of olives, 'you wanted to see me?'

'Yes.' Now that he was there in front of her, she wasn't sure where to start. 'Did your reporter – Kirsten, isn't she?'

Sam nodded.

'Did she mention what the atmosphere was like at the Fellowship?'

Sam screwed up his eyes. 'Not really. She said there was brain-washing, sleep-deprivation, and each new member had a minder, so it sounds pretty heavy.'

Jane frowned. If all that was true, the Fellowship ought to have attracted GUIDE's attention before now.

'May I ask you something?' said Sam pleasantly.

'Sure.'

'Yesterday you told me I was wasting my time with the Fellow-ship. That they were tame to the point of dullness. Today you phone me up to check on Kirsten, then make a special journey to question me about them. Why?'

She felt herself redden. She had, she realized, been anything but subtle: of course she'd put Sam on his guard. He was a journalist, wasn't he? He was watching her intently now, waiting for her reply.

'If I tell you,' she said, 'it's on the strict understanding that it's completely off the record.'

'Okay,' he said cautiously.

'I mean it.'

'So do I,' he said at once.

Their starters arrived but were left untouched.

'So what've you found out about the Fellowship?' Sam asked.

'I'm not sure. But a whole lot of coincidences have happened since we spoke.'

'Such as?'

Feeling foolish – yet perhaps not so foolish – she looked around. There was no one within earshot, but even so she lowered her voice. 'Someone phoned me this morning. He said I mustn't tell anyone what he was about to say. And when I rang him back, only an hour later, he'd vanished.'

Sam stared at her. 'Okay, you've got me hooked.'

'All I'm saying is, in telling you, I'm taking a risk, and exposing you to it, too.'

'But you're going to tell me all the same, aren't you?'

He was right, Jane thought; she could hardly stop now, having whetted his appetite. Besides, he was the nearest source she had to find out what was really going on at the Fellowship.

She took a deep breath, and began. She told him everything, from Rudi's phone call to her interpretation of the Scroll and Norton calling himself 'the Keeper'.

Sam was a good listener. He didn't interrupt, although his face expressed a whole range of emotions: astonishment, doubt, excitement, worry.

When she finished, he let out a low whistle. 'God, what a story!'

Instantly she stiffened. 'It's not a story,' she said.

'Sorry. No, I know it's not. I promise you, I won't use a word. But my God!' He was still staring at her; his blue eyes had gone indigo. 'If you're right . . . I was at the inquest on the Princes on Monday, you know.'

'Were you?' Her stomach flipped, although she told herself it wasn't such a coincidence: a case like that was bound to have been reported by lots of journalists.

'And you're right about the botulism stuff. The police reckon it was deliberate; they're looking for someone, a woman.'

'I saw the story in your paper.'

'Yes. She's targeting kids. That's what the Scroll says?'

Jane nodded. She saw her own mingled fear and excitement mirrored in Sam's eyes. For a moment, she felt as if they physically touched; a surge of energy went through her.

Sam refocused on her. 'You really think this Fellowship might be responsible? And Kirsten's in there . . . And I was worried about getting a good enough cult-special!'

'What?' Jane said, suddenly realizing what he meant.

'Kirsten's researching an article for me.'

Jane shook her head in despair. 'You mustn't write it,' she said urgently. 'If they're really fulfilling the signs, and they're exposed, you might push them over the edge.'

'I won't,' said Sam. 'Write it,' he added.

'You won't?'

'No, not if they turn out to be maniacs – I'm not utterly irresponsible, you know – and even if I did, I'd undoubtedly get a D-notice slapped on it.'

'What's that?'

He told her. 'So I couldn't write anything until it was over.'

'Oh,' she said, hugely relieved.

'I just wish I knew if Kirsten's still there,' Sam went on.

'You think she might not be?'

'I don't know, but I was wondering about it this morning. She might have found the whole thing too much, don't you think? She might have got scared, especially if you're right. She might have walked out.'

'But wouldn't she have let you know?'

'No. She doesn't work for us; she's freelance. I might never hear from her again.'

Jane absorbed the implications of that.

'But if she *is* still there,' Sam went on, picking up his fork and spearing an asparagus-tip, 'and still intends to do the story, why the hell hasn't she rung me?'

'I don't know.'

'I could ring them,' Sam said. 'They're in the book. I checked last night.'

'But what would you say? Even asking for her might alert them.'

Sam looked worried. 'I know. That's what I thought, too.'

She ate a piece of salmon. 'I'm going in there,' she said. 'I'll soon find out what's happened to Kirsten.'

'*You?*' Sam repeated.

'Yes.'

He frowned. 'D'you think that's wise? What if they really are up to something?'

'That's what I'm going to find out. Don't worry about me. I know how to look after myself.'

'Oh. You do. Good.' He smiled at her, and she thought what an attractive man he was. 'You've done this sort of thing before, then?'

'Not precisely,' she admitted.

They finished their starters. The waiter came and removed the plates.

'I need to know as much as I can about the Fellowship,' Jane said when he'd gone. 'Can you tell me everything Kirsten said?'

'Sure, but it's not much. ' Sam produced a notebook and flicked it open. 'Everyone lives in separate houses. They recruit people at Waterloo and around London or in Hastings. They've got a coffee-shop there called the King's Café.' He turned a page. 'The trust-fund kids have to sign over a third of their money on joining. There's hardly anything to eat but potatoes.' He looked up. 'I'm sorry, this isn't helping you much, is it?'

'Well, I admit I'd hoped for a little bit more.'

Their main courses arrived.

'How many of these Scroll signs d'you think have been fulfilled?' Sam asked.

'About six, maybe more – it's difficult to tell. Why?'

'I was just wondering what sort of time-scale we're working to.'

'Yes.' For the first time, she thought properly about that herself. 'It could be weeks or months,' she said.

'Or days.'

They looked at each other.

'Much as I hate to suggest it, d'you think maybe you should tell the authorities?' Sam asked.

'No,' she said flatly.

'Oh?'

'It's only by hearsay that I know Norton once called himself 'the Keeper".'

'Can you contact the friend who told you?'

She shook her head. Freddy had long ago departed from her life on worldwide travels, she explained, then she briefly touched on her doubts about the authorities' ability to contain an Armageddon group, even if they were told about it.

Sam nodded. 'How does the Scroll describe the world's end?' he asked.

She fished her copy out of her bag. '"And then the End, the Awful Horror of the Ungodly, shall come".'

'"Awful Horror",' Sam said thoughtfully. 'That's conveniently vague, isn't it?'

'It gives them a pretty free hand, yes.' She glanced past him out of the window. People were sitting on the benches, soaking up the sun. Over by the fountain, two young women were playing the oboe and violin to a small, appreciative audience. In the Last Days, according to the book of Revelation, locusts would burst forth from the earth . . .

'Sitting here, Armageddon seems remote, doesn't it?' Sam said.

'Yes.'

'When are you planning to get yourself recruited?' he asked.

'Tomorrow afternoon.' She'd already worked it out. She was reluctant to delay going in, even by a day, but she'd got teaching duties the next morning and she couldn't simply vanish from the campus without explanation. On Fridays, Eccles rarely came in.

'With the weekend and the bank-holiday on Monday, that'll give me five days. It should be enough,' she said.

'Let's hope so. How're you planning to get in, if that's not being too inquisitive?'

'No, not at all. I thought I'd take the train down to Hastings, and go to that coffee shop you mentioned.'

He nodded. 'If you get in, will you tell me what you find out? Whether Kirsten's there?'

'Of course. So long as you don't print it before I get out.'

'I promise.' He paused. 'You don't think I ought to go down there myself? Have a reccy for Kirsten?'

'No, I don't,' Jane said honestly. 'If there is something going on, you might alert them, and make them suspicious of any newcomer – i.e., me. If Kirsten really is in trouble' – Sam's face darkened – 'one more day isn't going to make much difference.'

Sam didn't look convinced.

'NRMs rarely physically hurt people,' Jane went on.

Sam's eyebrows went up. 'We were talking about Armageddon a moment ago,' he exclaimed.

'Yes, but that's a very extreme example.'

'One you suspect the Fellowship may be planning,' he pointed out.

She smiled wrily. 'Touché. But I could well be wrong. A problem group almost always flags itself way before D-Day.'

'And the Fellowship's clean?'

'Squeakily so.'

'Good cover, if they've got everyone believing that.'

'That's one way of looking at it. Look,' she appealed, 'I can't stop you going down there, but I'd really urge you to leave it to me. The worst that's happened to Kirsten, in all likelihood, is that she's been brainwashed, and I'll be able to help her when I get there.'

Sam studied her for a long moment. 'Okay,' he said reluctantly. They exchanged cards.

'I'll call you,' she promised.

He nodded. 'Are you telling your boss what you're doing?'

'Can't be trusted,' she said briefly.

'Uh-huh. Are you going to finish that Caesar Salad?'

She glanced down and saw that she'd hardly touched it. She shook her head.

He called for the bill and paid it, and they went out into the sunlight. Sam said he had to get back to the office, and asked her what she planned to do.

'I don't know.' Jane hadn't thought further than their meeting. After the dramatic events of the morning, tomorrow afternoon seemed a long way off and she was too keyed up to go back to the campus, to sit around waiting.

'I think I'll go for a walk,' she said. 'It's a lovely day.'

'All right for some.' He smiled as they shook hands again. 'It's been good meeting you,' he said. 'And good luck tomorrow. Let me know as soon as you hear anything.'

'I will, and you'll do likewise, won't you?'

He nodded, turned and walked away.

She watched him go, then headed towards Covent Garden.

Ross Edgecombe was a practical man. David called him 'the brainy one', and said it with that soft look on his face which, if Ross hadn't known better, would have made him think David was queer. Nobody expected a practical man to be nervous. And in most things – in his work, in his dealings with people – he wasn't. Where Ruth was concerned, though, it was different.

She'd been gone for seven hours now. All day, he'd watched the TV news and listened to the radio bulletins. The hunt for her was hotting up. 'Botulism Helen', they were calling her, and they kept flashing up the e-fit, though luckily it looked hardly anything like her. But he guessed that by now more witnesses would have come forward. They'd make amendments to the e-fit; it would start to look like her. Someone might recognize her van from the Fruit Fest; it was carrying the same number plate – that was a risk, they'd had agreed, but there were only two plates, and Ruth had already used the other one.

The net was closing in, Ross thought with a gulp, and she was out there – even though she was disguised, she might be in danger.

She'd seen the e-fit before she'd left that morning, but had said nothing. Helping her load, however, he'd thought that for the first time she'd seemed nervous. She'd stalled the van, which she'd never done before. Her expression had been faraway, her 'Goodbye' wooden. Ross didn't like it.

All day long, alone in that vast empty place he had wandered from one room to another, unable to keep still for long, unable to concentrate on anything except those bulletins. He kept imagining things going wrong. Someone recognizing her, or seeing what she was doing, or her hand slipping on to that needle . . .

He gnawed at the knuckle of his thumb. Even if that did happen, he told himself, even if she did prick herself, it would be all right. The listeria bug took forty-eight hours to act, and for months he had been administering vaccines and antibiotics to Ruth; she ought to be immune. Besides that, she was young and, of course, her best defence was that she was not pregnant. She'd be fine, he whispered aloud, just fine.

He turned away from the long hall window though which he'd been staring sightlessly. The storm had at last broken, the rain bringing relief from the heavy sultriness. He wondered where Ruth was now; how far through her assignment. They had agreed that, given the size of area she might have to cover, she probably wouldn't get back until mid-evening, or later. Another seven hours, alone with his fears?

Thunder clapped overhead, making him jump. In his mind's eye, he saw Ruth on the road, the rain lashing down, making it difficult for her to see, a telegraph pole, struck by lightning, falling towards her in slow motion. Ross stuffed his hand in his mouth. If anything happened to her . . .

Lightning flashed in through the window where he'd been standing and he yelped. If he hadn't moved when he did . . . He looked up. No matter what David and Ruth said, to Ross God existed (if He did actually exist) 'up there' in Heaven, as He had in Ross's Sunday-school days. Was God angry with him for his disbelief? he wondered fearfully. Had that near-strike been a warning?

He caught himself. What the hell was he thinking? He wasn't one of David's halfwit Fellowshippers; he knew what caused lightning. He was in danger of losing his mind, interred in this gloomy pile.

He saw his car keys on the window-ledge where he'd left them. For authenticity's sake, the vehicle was registered to the Lodge and was therefore only to be used on strictly 'worldly' business. No mission journeys in it.

Ross pondered what he was about to do, then he snatched up the keys, slammed the door and was outside, running towards the garages before he could change his mind. He'd made the visit once before. It hadn't jeopardized anything then and it wouldn't now.

The storm roared around him, and the rain poured down, but he wasn't afraid any more. In fact, he was enjoying it now.

The car bumped down the track on to the road and turned right. At the next main junction, he joined the main road to Newport. His destination was only thirty minutes away. He switched on the radio and caught the pips, announcing that it was three o'clock.

'Helen' was only the fourth item: the police around the country were 'still looking for a woman believed to have sold poisoned gingerbread to children'. There was nothing new. Nothing about a woman being arrested for contaminating food for pregnant women. Nothing, either, about schoolchildren who'd attended a Fruit Fest the day before suffering from double vision or paralysis. Ross sniffed. In spite of the previous week's botulism outbreak, it seemed as if doctors were still being unbelievably slow to recognize the symptoms. At least some of the children who'd eaten Ruth's toffee-apples ought to be suffering now.

The last news item was a flood in India. In spite of his tension, Ross smiled. Ruth would like that. It was another fulfilment of the sixth sign: 'The people shall live in fear of the elements: fire, sky, earth and water.'

The weather forecast came on. Ross's breathing returned to normal. She hadn't been caught.

The rain was easing. A watery sun peeped out, and then, so quickly that it seemed like magic, the sky was blue again. Ross wound down his window and smelt the freshened air; he filled his lungs with it.

A road-sign flashed by. He was driving steadily, keeping to the speed-limit even when he saw a police car waiting like a crocodile in a lay-by. If he slowed down, he told himself, they'd be after him, thinking he had something to hide. As it was, they vanished to nothingness in his rear-view mirror. The turn-off came up on his right, a red-rimmed sign, and he took it.

The army compound lay two miles down the road. He saw the fencing first, eight-foot-high steel links topped with razor-wire. The fence was backed with sheets of corrugated steel, high enough to shield the compound block from the view of anyone in a car. Ross didn't see why they'd bothered. For the first half-mile, the view was blocked anyway by stands of conifers, and after that all one saw was old-fashioned Nissen huts, humped into the ground like sluggish caterpillars. He didn't care what went on in there – signals, intelligence, it mattered little. He hadn't come to spy.

The road curved round to the left. Up ahead, Ross knew, was the entrance, with the heavy-duty gates and the single bored-looking young sentry. Ross would do as he had before, drive past casually without so much as a glance to his left and then, a bit further on but still in view of the compound, pull in to the layby and get out his road atlas. If anyone asked – and he couldn't imagine who would – he'd merely be a motorist who had lost his way. He wouldn't stay long. He wanted only a few minutes close to the base, within sight of it so that he could close his eyes and picture the scene that would occur there in less than a week. Controlled panic, he thought with a smile, or perhaps not even controlled. The footsoldiers would, as ever, be kept in the dark, but their officers, the lieutenant-colonels and chiefs-of-staff, they would know.

Their inoculations against anthrax and bubonic plague wouldn't help them. There wasn't an antidote for the virus he'd awakened and by the time they found one – if they could – the virus would have done its work. One-third of the world's population, David had said. Ross knew his virus was capable of achieving that, which had satisfied David entirely. Other factors would come into play as well, of course – environmental ones, like the weather on the day of release, and the health of the first-strike populations – but once it was out, it couldn't be reined back in. It would fly on the air, it would be inhaled and exhaled, each infected person passing it on, each becoming a weapon in his or her own right. There was no cure, no treatment. There would be a breakdown of law and order, and the army would be sent out on to the streets, where they too would be infected.

Ross looked at the wire-topped fence. He had come to gloat. Had circumstances been different, he'd have driven down to Salisbury, to the army's chemical and biological defence section at Porton Down. That was where the real action would be, as their microbiologists tried frantically to find an antidote. Ross sighed: but he couldn't go there, it would be too dangerous. As it would be to visit the SAS base in Hereford. No, he'd have to make do with this small military base in Gwent. He remembered one of David's sermons about a woman with a haemorrhage who believed that, if she touched Jesus' cloak, she'd be healed. Seeing this base was enough; he had faith – his mouth turned down – that, as it had last time, it would lift his spirits, renew his dedication to Ruth, his vow to do anything for her, including dying with her.

Until now, he hadn't bothered much about that: the fact that he, too, would die of his virus. It had seemed remote, far in the future, and he'd had Ruth with him to distract him. But now the release was only three days away. It was beginning to dawn on him that his own death would be every bit as agonizing as those of the volunteers he'd monitored: they'd choked, turned black, and suffocated.

Ross shuddered. It was all right for Ruth and David, he thought. They believed in what they were doing. When Ruth had explained what they wanted him to do, he hadn't believed her. He'd scoffed, thought she was joking. Then he had seen the look on her face and been appalled. She was mad, he'd thought, she and the old man, both. But Ruth had started talking to him; she'd soothed and caressed him, she'd pleaded; and, little by little, he'd come round to an acceptance of her and David's way of thinking.

Why not? he'd thought. What did it matter? What did anything matter?

Ross didn't believe in anything, not in God, certainly not in an afterlife. He suspected that Ruth knew that, whereas David simply assumed, with that irritating childlike innocence, that Ross was a believer. Why else, he could imagine David saying, his high forehead wrinkling, would Ross have helped them? But – the forehead smooth again – it was a good thing he had, because without him they couldn't have done even half of it.

Ross grimaced. It never occurred to David that Ross might have his own agenda. There was a short-circuit in David's brain when it came to other people's motives or the way they saw the world. To Ross, that world was a dark place. The only person he cared for was Ruth: she was his raison d'être, or his main one. His other one was getting his own back on the army, on those bastards who'd rejected him.

They'd valued him once, and cherished him. He'd worked on the most sensitive projects, the ones whose very existence the government denied. Ross had been second only to the teamleader, a man who'd pretended to be his friend, although Ross hadn't been fooled. And when things had gone wrong, things that hadn't been his fault, they'd needed a scapegoat and Ross was elected. They'd cast him aside – his 'friend' the team-leader, and all the others – as if he was of no account, as if his life's work didn't matter. They'd insulted him with the offer of an invalidity pension. Ross's breathing quickened; it always did when he thought about that time.

He made himself calm down, take long, deep, soothing breaths, the way the army doctor had taught him. Ruth's arrival in his life had saved him. She had given him hope and if her beliefs meant they'd have only a short time time together, so be it. If those beliefs brought him a hideous death, that didn't matter either. He would live and die with Ruth.

Of course, he'd have preferred David to be out of the picture. At first, Ross had been blackly jealous, until he understood the nature of Ruth's relationship with the man. They had never had sex. When David explained how he hoped Ross would be able to help them, Ross had seen it for what it was – an opportunity to pay the army back for its betrayal, while at the same time pleasing Ruth. David, typically, saw it in terms of a miracle, but that was his affair.

The road straightened. The entrance was just on the left now. Ross looked in. The gates were open, the entrance barrier was raised, there were sandbags heaped up on either side. Beyond in the compound, he saw trucks and soldiers moving about, and unless he was mistaken, the dark uniform of the MOD police. He frowned: this was not the sleepy place he remembered. Where was the dull sentry boy? In his place were two armed sentries, and they were staring at him. He slewed his gaze away, corrected the drift of the car, saw coming towards him an army convoy.

His flesh crawled. If, at this late stage, he were to ruin the years of careful planning, he knew Ruth would never forgive him. David would, though: David would pray for him. He felt his gorge rise. On his right, a Land-Rover passed him. Then a truck. Only when the last vehicle had gone by, did he dare to follow its progress in his rear-view mirror, see it follow the others into the compound. No one was coming after him. The sentries had stared because he had been staring. By now, he assured himself, they would have dismissed him as merely a curious local driver, with good cause to be curious. What, he wondered for the first time, was going on at that place? Why the transformation into a hive of activity? Was it an exercise, or had something happened?

He kept driving. After a while, two more army trucks passed him and then a police car raced round the bend and overtook him. That gave him palpitations, but he quickly realized they weren't interested in him. They went tearing off towards the town. Ross was truly curious now, and a little fearful, without quite knowing why. He went into the town himself.

It looked perfectly normal. People wandered about in the way that people did, looking in shop windows, pushing pushchairs. He saw the police car, or one like it, parked in front of the police station, which should have reassured him but for some obscure reason didn't.

There was a sign for the port and Ross took it, tucking in behind a large container lorry, and lowering his speed accordingly. The lorry's brake-lights came on and it stopped. Ross was so close to its tail that he couldn't tell what the obstruction was. He waited, drumming his fingers on the wheel.

A movement in his rear-view mirror caught his eye and he glanced round. Another army Land-Rover was speeding along the road behind him, its headlights on. His stomach lurched again, but before he had time to feel thoroughly afraid, the Land-Rover swerved to the wrong side of the road and overtook both him and the lorry.

Something was obviously going on at the docks too. Leave now, an inner voice urged, but another lorry came trundling along the road and stopped behind him, effectively blocking him in. Ross was sweating. He took his hands from the wheel and rubbed them on his trousers. He had been mad to come, crazy.

'Know what's going on, mate?' A face came in at his open window. It was the driver from the lorry behind. Ross didn't trust himself to speak. He shook his head.

Another driver came up. He wore a look of bored resignation. 'Delay, isn't there? There's another eight chaps in front of me. God knows when we'll get off.'

The first driver swore loudly.

'It's one of them bloody alerts again,' said the second.

Ross stiffened. 'Alerts?' he repeated.

'Yeah, you know. All-ports alert, like it'll be someone's kidnapped his own kiddy and wants to take him out of the country, or it'll be drugs or something like that.'

'Chemical scare, the dock-master said,' added another driver. 'They're doing a real job of it this time – the army's doing it.'

There were groans all around. Ross didn't join in. His throat had constricted so painfully that he found it difficult to speak. 'I'm going to leave it,' he croaked. No one had heard him and he had to repeat it. The driver of the lorry behind obligingly got back into his cab and backed up. Reversing, Ross shot backwards too fast, making the men on the roadway look round. He must not panic, he told himself firmly. It was imperative that he didn't panic, didn't draw attention to himself.

He had to get back to the Lodge. He had to warn Ruth and David. In times of national crisis, the army took over the ports. That, on top of the activity at the army base . . . Ross bit his lip hard. He slammed the car into first gear and took off, leaving the other drivers staring.

CHAPTER ELEVEN

The lifting team went first to Jane Carlucci's hall of residence. Her flat was empty, but one man was left there, sitting in a car outside. The others went to her departmental building, one stayed in the car; the other two, Jack Broughton and Lucy-Ann Burroughs, mounted the stairs to the Sociology Department.

Professor Eccles's secretary was waiting for them. Before they left London, Ryder had phoned, asking for Jane, and on hearing of her absence had sounded genuinely anxious.

The secretary had met him the week before. She remembered what a nice man he was. Was there anything she could do to help? she had asked him.

It was a very delicate matter, Ryder had confided, concerning the teenage daughter of a Cabinet Minister who had got herself involved with an NRM. Ryder had seen from his records that Jane had done a lot of work on the group, and he was keen to find out all she knew, as soon as possible. The girl's father was becoming extremely agitated; he was demanding that the police burst in and rescue her, but Ryder felt that with sufficient knowledge a more low-key approach would be better.

The secretary, mindful of Eccles's attitude to such raids, readily agreed. Jane didn't have any teaching duties that afternoon, she told

Ryder, but she was often around. The secretary had promised to 'look after' the GUIDE official and senior civil servant Ryder told her were already on their way down.

When Lucy-Ann and Broughton arrived she offered them tea and newspapers, then, because there was nowhere to sit, suggested they might like to wait for Jane – or the Professor, who was expected back shortly – in the GUIDE office? The postgraduates would be in to man the phones later, but for now it was empty.

They accepted gratefully. She took them along the corridor, unlocked the door and, assuring them Eccles wouldn't be long, left them to it.

They saw the Samaritan-style poster on the wall, the two desks with their computers and phones, the shelves stacked with paper-work.

Lucy-Ann locked the door. Broughton lowered the blinds.

They were both skilled searchers. They divided the room in two and worked in silence, methodically, searching among the papers; the data on the computers had already been checked. They found nothing to interest them. Lucy-Ann played back the messages on the answering-machine: again, nothing.

It was five to four. Jane Carlucci or Eccles might walk in at any moment. That wouldn't be a problem, exactly, but it would save time if they were able to confront Jane with evidence of her knowledge.

They went back out into the corridor. Eccles's office was opposite, its name-plate on the door; Jane's a little further down, similarly identified. They paused for a moment to see if the secretary called out, but she didn't. They could hear her on the telephone.

Lucy-Ann went to Eccles's door, Broughton to Jane's. Entry was by card-access but they each carried a swipe-card to unlock such doors.

Inside Jane's room, Broughton ran his eyes along the bookshelf. A copy of the Eighth Scroll which he had rather been expecting was not there.

He opened Jane's desk drawer. Inside was a copy of her paper. It didn't tell him anything new but he put it in his briefcase anyway.

He returned to the GUIDE office. Lucy-Ann was still in Eccles's room. He heard the secretary, still on the telephone. She sounded perfectly relaxed, he thought. If Jane had been frightened by the Scroll, she didn't seem to have shared her fears with the secretary.

The voice changed suddenly. It said nervously, 'Oh, good afternoon, Professor. I'm glad you've come. There are some visitors waiting in the GUIDE office.'

Broughton pressed the emergency button on his bleeper to alert Lucy-Ann. He heard Eccles coming.

He remembered what Ryder had told him about the man, so when Eccles came in Broughton thanked him profusely for agreeing to help them with a very delicate matter. They needed to speak to Jane, but of course the Professor's expertise was also urgently sought. The personal assistant to the Minister – he saw Eccles light up – was out of the room at the moment, Broughton added, but would be with them very shortly.

He gave Eccles a quick version of the cover-story. He wasn't at liberty, he said regretfully, to tell the Professor which Minister was involved, but if he bore in mind that only one had a seventeen-year-old daughter . . .

'I see,' Eccles breathed greedily. 'Which NRM is it?'

Broughton looked at his shoes as he supplied the fictitious name.

'I don't believe I've heard of them before,' said Eccles.

'It's a splinter group from the Sword of the Lord.' That was one of the nine most dangerous NRMs.

Eccles's eyebrows went up. 'I didn't know there'd been a split there. Jane must have forgotten to tell me. She's been working on it, you say, and in communication with yourselves?'

Broughton nodded.

A tic started in Eccles's cheek. 'Well then, her notes should be lying around somewhere,' and he began to search through the paperwork.

Lucy-Ann came in and closed the door behind her; Broughton thought he heard the 'click' of the lock. She was holding a sheet of paper down by her side, and he could tell by the look she gave him that she had found something she thought significant.

Eccles glanced up. 'Nigel Eccles,' he announced expansively, with a smile he clearly expected to be reciprocated.

Lucy-Ann gave her pseudonym. 'Could I just have one moment with my colleague?' she asked charmingly, and, turning her back, gave Broughton the sheet of paper. 'Here,' she said under her breath, pointing to two words. He saw immediately what she meant.

'Is there something I can help you with?' Eccles inquired, bending sideways to see.

Broughton slipped the paper into his briefcase. 'I do believe there is,' he said sombrely.

He glanced at his watch. They had a time problem, he explained. The Minister had just been in touch with his personal assistant, demanding again that someone brief him in person, at once, about the rogue NRM.

'In Jane Carlucci's absence, Professor, we were wondering if you would be so good as to do this for us?'

Lucy-Ann nodded beseechingly.

Eccles turned an unlovely pink. 'Ah, well, of course, yes, delighted, but, er, the problem is, I can't quite seem to put my hand on Janey's notes. They're probably in her office, and I can't get in without her swipe-card.'

That didn't matter a bit, Broughton and Lucy-Ann soothed. The Professor was the country's leading authority on NRMs. If he would just meet the Minister, to speak in general terms about NRMs, the Minister would find it so reassuring. He would be extremely grateful, as would they.

'Well, if you're sure,' said Eccles, drawing himself up to his full height and holding in his stomach.

Quite sure, they said positively. Lucy-Ann would remain behind to meet Jane when she arrived, but if the Professor would accompany her colleague to the Home Office? A car would of course bring him home afterwards.

Eccles let himself be ushered to the door. There he paused. 'I was just thinking,' he said.

The others waited, Broughton beside him, Lucy-Ann over by the desk. If need be, Broughton thought, Eccles could be manhandled out, lifted bodily to the fire-escape and down, but it would be much better if the secretary saw him leave of his own volition.

'There's no need for Jane to meet the Minister as well, is there? I mean, she might be gone for the rest of the day, and I thought I could phone her from the car, or when we get there, before we meet him, and get her to brief me, couldn't I?'

Lucy-Ann stared at him.

Broughton said, 'Absolutely. No need for her to be there at all.'

'Good.' Eccles beamed. 'It's just that she gets rather nervous, you see, poor little thing. Perhaps your boss told you?' Still talking, he preceded Broughton into the corridor and the door shut behind them.

Lucy-Ann spoke quietly into her mobile, alerting the team in the cars to their imminent arrival and requesting a back-up vehicle. That was one away, she thought with satisfaction as she ended the call. She wondered who, besides Eccles, was aware of the list she had found on his desk, with the Keeper's name on it.

Sam had intended, when he got back from lunch, to call up a copy of the Scroll on his database, and go through it thoroughly, trying to match recent events with signs, but the newsdesk had dictated otherwise.

'Whole load of kids with upset tummies in Birmingham for you, Ferryman.'

'But I'm doing the cult-special. Monica's taken me off rota.'

'But it's Monica's day off, isn't it? And I know she'd want me to make use of her best man for a big, breaking news story.'

It crossed Sam's mind to argue, but he forbore; it wasn't worth making an enemy of the deskman and he'd have time later to look at the Scroll.

He began work on the Birmingham schoolchildren.

By three o'clock that afternoon, nineteen children, aged between seven and eleven, had been admitted to four hospitals, suffering from blurred vision, sickness, in some cases diarrhoea, and difficulty swallowing; some of the children had become paralysed. Botulism was immediately suspected, and treatment given, although its presence was not publicly admitted to until five o'clock. Also announced was the fact that all the children had attended the Fruit Fest the previous day. They had eaten a great many things there but a common denominator was emerging: many of them had bought toffee-apples from a woman dressed as Maid Marian.

The media, already running stories on the suspicious 'disappearance' of Botulism Helen, went into a frenzy.

'Woman poisoner targets schoolchildren' screamed the wire services.

'"Botulism Helen" strikes again!'

By then, ninety-eight children were ill, eleven seriously.

Sam was curtly told to hurry up: his story was heading for the front page.

He was having difficulty concentrating. Over lunch, he and Jane had worked out that Botulism Helen's activities fitted in perfectly to the Eighth Scroll. It was one thing, Sam found, to link a recent past event to the Scroll; another entirely to watch it unfold before one's eyes.

Did he have a duty to inform the police?

He made sure no one in the newsroom was watching him – no one was, they were all too busy – then called down the Eighth Scroll from the Internet.

He stared at the words on the screen: 'many shall suffer, particularly little children and pregnant women.' He thought suddenly of his Yummy Tummy story; realized that that could also be said to fulfil the sign, that he ought to have mentioned it to Jane over lunch.

He took out her card and dialled her number. A woman's voice answered promptly; and told him Jane was wasn't in. She asked if she could take a message?

Sam thought quickly. He didn't know who the woman was, and Jane had said her boss could not be trusted. 'It doesn't matter,' he said and rang off.

He sat, thinking more slowly.

If he called the police and mentioned the Eighth Scroll in connection with the botulism poisonings, what good would it do? In all likelihood, they wouldn't believe him; he'd be dismissed as a nutter. He'd no proof that the Fellowship was involved, nor had Jane. That was why she was going down there.

Although, in one way, he wanted her to find evidence linking the group to the Scroll – it would make the most amazing story – in another, away from her infectious enthusiasm, he admitted to entertaining doubts about what she would find there.

The Fellowship, according to Kirsten, lived openly, as part of the wider community. They ran a coffee-shop, and farm-shops; they recruited rock stars' daughters. Admittedly, they liked to sit up all night and pray, but religious groups did that sort of thing. He didn't know whether it was just the journalist in him but he found it much easier to imagine the Fellowship stealing trust funds than being about to start Armageddon.

Jane was an academic. In her ivory-tower world, the fact that

Norton had once called himself the Keeper had assumed huge significance for her. But cult-leaders were by definition weird people; one more or less expected them to use peculiar names – and Jane's information, he reminded himself, was second-hand.

She might be partly right. A group in the UK might be fulfilling the signs. Botulism Helen, Yummy Tummy, the Princes' murders, the theft of the swaddling-clothes might all be connected. But there was a large question mark in Sam's mind as to whether that connection was the Fellowship.

His worries about Kirsten, coupled with Jane's imagination, were a powerful combination. Jane was upset by the disappearance of her Israeli friend. But he, like Kirsten, might not have gone missing at all, Sam thought. Kirsten might simply have left the Fellowship, as he had suggested to Jane, and been too embarrassed to contact him. Or she might have joined it, which to Sam's way of thinking would be regrettable but none of his business. He would not give in to any other more worrying scenarios – kidnap, torture, murder – until Jane had been there and contacted him. If she too disappeared, if she failed to turn up for work next week, he would call the police without delay.

He switched back to his story. He'd only written the first paragraph. On the wires, descriptions were coming in of the Maid Marian who'd sold toffee-apples: blonde, blue-eyed, of medium build.

He called up the Foodie Lanes stories and studied the two descriptions side by side.

Botulism Helen was dark-haired and slender. Because of the new outbreak, more information had come in about her. She'd been driving a white van, witnesses said. Sam checked the Birmingham story. An eye-witness said Maid Marian had been on foot.

On the face of it, Helen and Marian didn't have much in common, but Sam had little doubt that they were the same person and that during the evening the two descriptions would start to merge. There must now be dozens of fresh eye-witnesses coming forward from the Midlands.

He began typing. When he reached a quote from a police spokesman, who said it was likeliest that Botulism Helen was simply a warped individual acting on her own, he paused, thinking about the Scroll again, then he typed in the policeman's words.

He finished the story with a reference to the *Crimewatch Special* due that evening. With the amount of public interest in the story, he thought, Botulism Helen would probably be caught before morning.

If there did turn out to be a Fellowship link, the police or the SAS would raid the place. Kirsten, if she was still there, would be able to write the most terrific piece for the paper. He chastised himself for thinking of the story in such circumstances, but the idea stuck. He could help her write it, he thought, along with an interview of Jane Carlucci talking about the Scroll.

'How's it coming?' asked the deputy news-editor, appearing by his side.

Sam showed him.

'Good stuff,' the man said gruffly.

'Splash?'

'Probably.'

'Only probably?'

The deskman cocked an eye at him. 'Never let it be said that Ferryman's ambition is on the wane.'

'I only meant . . .'

'Worry not, my vaulting friend. There's an INSEC alert going on, that's all.'

'Oh.' Sam knew an international security alert in itself signified little. They were always happening, and often they were no more than exercises. In recent years, they'd become nearly as common-place as national ones. It was the reason behind the alert that mattered; that, in newspaper terms, allocated it a paragraph on an inside page, the front-page lead, or, in exceptional cases, a D-notice.

The news-editor said there'd been reports of increased activity at army bases around the country. Initially, it had sounded interesting. 'But the MOD says it's just part of an exercise.'

'D'you want me to take a look at it?' asked Sam. 'I've got contacts.'

'When didn't you have?'

Despairingly Sam wondered why his deputy news-editor seemed to resent him for doing his job.

The defence correspondent had contacts too, the man reminded him. 'Excellent ones, Ferryman, the type you can only dream of.'

Sam said nothing.

'They've already told him it's not significant, so don't exercise yourself. Why don't you get on with your "special", if you're looking for work to do?'

Sam eyed him thoughtfully as he wandered off. Then he typed 'swaddling-clothes' into his Search box and waited for the computer to find the story.

'Not found' appeared on screen.

He frowned. Had Jane's Israeli friend been right? Was there a media black-out? Had the Israeli been 'taken away'?

Sam knew a good journalist near Jerusalem, but he didn't know him very well. There was no guarantee that the man wouldn't be tempted by the swaddling-clothes' theft and decide to run the story himself. And, if subsequently questioned by the Israeli authorities, he'd probably finger Sam as the source of the story. Sam had no wish to be interrogated by experts. He had a horrible feeling that he might not withstand torture for very long.

He caught himself. Only minutes before, he'd managed to convince himself that Jane had been overreacting. What was he now doing?

He switched off his computer and went home for the night.

Holding the telephone receiver at arm's length, David sighed softly. Ross wasn't listening to him.

He loved Ross but he was concerned about him. At times he seemed too swayed by the events of the world, too eager to be drawn away from the one clear path. Sometimes, secretly, David wondered about the depth of Ross's faith, and whenever he did he asked instantly for Jesus' forgiveness for he knew that each soul's relationship with the Lord was holy in its own right. But, oh, if only Ross would let himself be lifted up, if only he would let his eyes see the Lord's glorious purpose!

The message to call Ross urgently had been flashing on David's pager when he had emerged from his meeting with Kirsten. At the thought of her, David smiled. She had been such a naughty child to begin with, so deceitful with her lies when he had first talked to her last night. He shook his head. But she was all right now. At a little after dawn, through Christ Jesus, he had turned on the light for her, led her to the Lord where no shadows or evil dwelt, and now Kirsten was living in that light. David could tell a believer by the light in their eyes. He told himself that the next time he saw Ross, he must check his eyes.

'Ross,' he said gently. 'Please, don't worry.'

'Don't worry?' Ross snarled. 'It was on the news! There's a security alert on. The army's at the fucking airports' – David closed his eyes; swearing hurt Jesus – 'in case you missed it. Oh, but of course you did miss it, didn't you?' His tone changed to one of dripping sarcasm. 'You were about your "Father's" business, weren't you? What were you doing with Father this time? Praying, or just crying?'

In fact, David had been with Kirsten, marvelling at the difference a few hours had made. The child was a pleasure to be with now. It occurred to David that he would quite like to keep her in his annexe, a pet to visit during the Last Days. But he didn't know how much longer he'd be allowed to keep her. Soon a young woman was going to be needed, and the Lord had already confirmed to him that Kirsten was special. He hadn't yet revealed, however, whether He wanted Kirsten for the mission, or the other girl, the little runaway from Colchester.

'Fuck it! You're not even listening to me, are you?

Ross was still very upset, David reminded himself. At first he'd been almost incoherent: Ruth wasn't back yet; the army was every-where, which could only mean that 'they' had guessed about the Scroll; Ruth had been arrested, was even now being interrogated; to save her, David must implement the emergency procedures at once.

Between Ross's gasps and spurts of information, David had analysed the situation. He'd checked the news-service on his com-puter, and Ross was right: there was an international security alert in progress. It wasn't the lead item, it was near the end, and the story said it was the sixth such alert in two years. He'd also checked for reports on the swaddling-clothes: there were none, which briefly saddened him, made him realize that, as with the Scroll itself, people cared so little about God's holy things, that their disappearance aroused no interest. Nor was there any mention of a woman answering Ruth's description being arrested.

He tried to explain those things to Ross, reasonably, lovingly, to remind him that the camouflage or 'emergency' procedures were already in hand. But Ross remained obdurately, increasingly blind.

But what if, David thought slowly, the Lord was testing him? Was He allowing poor, beloved Ross to be beset by demons of doubt and terror so that David would rescue him? Not with his usual gentle words, but with firm authority? The kind of authority that might well be needed, in the remaining days, to steer his little ark through the last storm to safe haven?

'That's enough.' His voice was rock-steady and barely recognizable as his own.

'What?'

'Pull yourself together. You're going to listen to the voice of Jesus now.'

Ross snorted. 'Like hell I am.'

David's voice dropped half an octave; he could make it go very low, steam-rollering all opposition. 'I'd hate anything to happen to Ruth, wouldn't you?' he asked softly.

'What?' Ross said incredulously.

At last, David thought in triumph, he had Ross's full attention. 'Suppose someone tipped off the authorities,' he went on, 'told them what's she's doing today, the area she's in, the sort of supermarkets she's targeting. Maybe even gave them her registration number?'

'You're fucking mad!'

'Crazy for Jesus,' David chuckled. 'Yes, I am.'

'But you'd ruin everything!'

'Would I? Ruth will probably have done enough by now. Everything else is going perfectly to plan. There's Saturday to think of, of course, but you said yourself that everything's ready, and it's a simple matter of transport.'

'As for Ruth . . .' David paused. 'She's got her cyanide capsule with her, hasn't she?'

Ross was breathing heavily. 'You fucking bastard,' he whispered.

'Mm, but you see, Ruth would agree with me. If she thought the one way to make you see sense was to sacrifice herself, she would do it.'

'No!' Ross whimpered.

'Yes. We can't allow you to ruin everything. To go running around screaming, drawing attention to yourself, to us. Not when we've worked so long and hard – and so have you, Ross, if you think about it.'

Ross made an unintelligible sound.

'You've given us so much help, Ross, haven't you?' David softened his tone. 'What with your superb scientific knowledge and your military contacts? Where would we have been without you? Where would Ruth have got her cyanide pill?'

There was a gurgle, then sweet silence at the other end of the line.

'Anyway, let us not dwell on such matters. Let us lift up our eyes. Remember who is Lord, the Director of our affairs. Are you doing that, Ross?'

Ross made a sound that could have signified anything.

'That's right. Why don't we close our eyes?' He closed his own. Instantly, he saw Jesus on a hillside. There were little children round Him, baby birds sitting on His hands, and furry rabbits by His feet. David laughed softly. 'D'you see Him, Ross?

'Ross?' David repeated more sharply.

'Yes.' Ross's tone was dull.

'It's a sign, you see, that everything's going to be fine. We just have to stick together, to stick to the Lord's blue-print. There's no need to panic. There never was.'

He turned back to the computer screen. 'Do you really think the Lord would let us be stopped by a – what do they call it? – an INSEC?' David chuckled. 'It's laughable isn't it? Let me hear your voice, Ross. "Our Father." Come on,' he jollied him.

'Our Father, who art in Heaven,' mumbled the other voice, like a dead man's, but at least obediently now.

The news about the Birmingham schoolchildren reached Ryder when he arrived in Suffolk to take over the interrogation of a cult-leader.

At first, botulism was only suspected. Then the London groom office told him that it had been confirmed. The news hit him like a blow. Helen was still out there, hurting children. Ninety-eight new victims, and how many more to come? Was it possible that a member of the Angelic Revelation Society was responsible?

There were forty-seven of them. They lived 'out' – that is, in the world. A membership list had been found and with the help of the local police all bar a couple had been detained. None was Botulism Helen, or, when shown the E-fit of her, showed the faintest sign of recognition.

The Angelic Channeller himself was being temporarily housed in a seventeenth-century cottage on the outskirts of the village.

Initially, Ryder had thought the Channeller might be his man. He prophesied Armageddon before the end of the year; he wielded enormous and rather sinister power over his followers (there had been several suicides, and allegations of abuse); he preached exclusively from his terrifying 'Angelic Scriptures', which he claimed to receive from the Archangel Gabriel, and before turning to religion he had been employed as a nuclear engineer at Sizewell on the Suffolk coast.

Additionally, the Society, or certainly the Channeller, had a lot of money. Members paid tithes to him of at least thirty per cent of their wages. More than enough, Ryder thought, to have paid for a hit-man for the Princes, a professional thief for the swaddling-clothes.

But after two hours, Ryder concluded he'd been wrong. The Channeller was too unbalanced to have directed the fulfilment of the Scroll; his followers too frightened of him to do anything of their own volition.

When Ryder inquired as to the Channeller's views on the book of Revelation, the man began to bark like a dog. 'There are no other Scriptures!' he howled.

Ryder excused himself, and let the psychologist take over.

He went into the empty kitchen and made himself a cup of coffee. At the front of the house, the interrogation continued, as it would probably all night, but Ryder didn't intend to stay. He'd shortly be on his way to Scotland, and the second cult worthy of his attention.

What if it, and the third group, proved also to be in the clear? he wondered. What then? The detention of the country's remaining one hundred and eighty eight NRMs? If need be, he thought resolutely. And every religious group, listed or not, in the land, if it came to that. He'd worry about what the press made of it when the crisis was over. His chief fear remained, however: that it might be not a group but one or two determined individuals who'd been meticulously planning the thing for years, who had the funds and the expertise to carry it through to the end, who were, as he'd said to ARIC, willing to take risks now because they were so close to that end.

He pressed a key on his laptop. In the two hours since the public had learned of the Maid Marian attack, there had been over three thousand calls to the police, claiming sightings of her all over the country.

More had come in too on her mode of transport; she'd been not 'on foot', as originally described, but driving a white van, like the one from Covent Garden. Of course, the public was aware of that connection; in their efforts to be helpful, Ryder knew, false claims were probably being made. But several witnesses said they'd seen the number plate and remembered part of the number. The first letter, K, and the last, P, kept coming up. The field was narrowing.

Ryder allowed himself to hope. The public was in lynch-mob mode and *Crimewatch* was still to come. It wouldn't be long before he had Helen he told himself, and then he'd know within a very short time the name of the group she was working with.

He couldn't believe, although a part of him wanted to – the same part that hoped the cult would turn out not to be British – that she was acting on her own. In the current climate, it would be too great a coincidence.

He pressed another series of keys to check up on the hunt for the Princes' murderer. The second house-to-house search of the area immediately around Bodiam Castle was in progress, and the local television station would be running an appeal for new eye-witnesses that night.

Thank God for the media, he thought wryly. He saw the time. He ought to be on his way to Aviemore. He picked up his raincoat, but before he could put it on, his mobile rang. It was Lucy-Ann Burroughs.

'Yes, Burroughs?'

He'd hoped to hear that they had Jane Carlucci, but he learned instead that she hadn't yet returned to her university campus, or to her car, which was parked at the local railway station. The line led up to London or down to Portsmouth. The station was unmanned, so there was no ticket-collector to question about which train she had caught, or where she had gone.

But she hadn't seemed panicky when she left. She'd mentioned nothing to Eccles or anyone, about any specific NRM, or ancient prophecy. Eccles, now at the SecSite, was adamant that he had 'no idea' where Jane had obtained the name 'the Keeper'.

She might have come across it by chance, Ryder conceded, but he thought not. There were too many arrows pointing in Carlucci's direction. He didn't find it helpful to dwell on where she might have been that afternoon – a newspaper office, a television studio. He told himself instead that she'd probably been shopping and would return at any moment. It was only seven-fifteen in the evening.

When she did, she'd find Burroughs waiting for her at the station and another two watchers outside her hall of residence. Having nothing to hide, she'd tell what she knew immediately, and within the hour the Keeper's group would be in detention and, if necessary, rendered harmless.

Two women held the key to the information he wanted. He needed only one of them.

'I'll call you as soon as she arrives, sir,' Burroughs finished.

'Do that.' Ryder ended the call abruptly and shouted through to the helicopter pilot that they were leaving now.

CHAPTER TWELVE

On parting from Sam, Jane had hoped that an afternoon in Covent Garden would divert her attention from the Scroll but she found herself almost constantly reminded of it. She wandered, by chance, not knowing the area, into the Foodie Lanes. The stall-holders's main topic of conversation was, not unnaturally, Jane appreciated, Botulism Helen.

She turned a corner. A man with a billboard round his neck was proclaiming that the end of the world was nigh.

She sought refuge in a second-hand bookshop and there, while she was browsing through a box of books without covers, she suddenly remembered Miles Riordan's thesis. She'd had promised weeks before that she'd read it, but the manuscript was alarmingly weighty and she'd put it off. Now she remembered him saying that he needed it back by the beginning of the next week, but from the following afternoon Jane would be in the Fellowship.

Almost glad of the excuse to get back to Guildford, she caught a bus to Waterloo. Waiting for her train, she saw no Fellowshippers in blue recruiting among the commuters and worried suddenly that they might have ceased recruiting. She might trail down to Hastings, only to find she couldn't get in.

She told herself to stop imagining the worst. In less than twenty-four hours, she'd know one way or the other: whether she could get in; whether anything was really going on at the Fellowship or whether Norton's old title was simply a timely coincidence. She'd also be able to discover what had happened to Kirsten Cooper and set Sam's mind at rest.

As she took her seat on the train, she considered him. In spite of what she'd heard about journalists, she could tell that Sam was truly worried about Kirsten; his professionalism had slipped when he'd asked if he shouldn't go down himself to look for her.

She liked him. She remembered his eyes turning dark with excitement as she told him her story; the spark inside her as she had realized he was fired with it, as well. He was nice-looking, too, but not perfect, which was a good thing – she'd had experience of a very good-looking man before.

She caught herself. What was she doing? she asked herself severely. Day-dreaming about Sam Ferryman when she was about to do the most dangerous thing she'd ever done: join an Apocalyptic NRM, gather evidence to present to the authorities, stop Armageddon and, in the process, make her name. Anyway, Sam was probably married or living with someone.

The man beside her opened his newspaper almost under her nose, slapped it in half, then settled down to read it. Jane took out the novel she was reading and immersed herself in it.

The journey passed quickly. She looked up as the train began to slow down on its approach to her station. She'd be back at the campus within twenty minutes, and, depending on where she had left the manuscript, she would be started on it by eight o'clock at the latest. She ought to be finished by midnight. At that thought, her resolve quailed; she was very tired. But she had promised Miles. She opened the carriage door and set off along the platform.

At the top of the station steps that led down to the covered subway, Lucy-Ann Burroughs waited.

It was 19.22. She had memorized Jane's face from the photographs, memorized, too, that evening's timetable. It took the quickest commuters four minutes after the train had pulled in to emerge from the subway below.

They began coming out. Looking at their grey faces and slumped shoulders, their eyes blinking like moles', Lucy-Ann felt a twinge of pity that was at once tempered with irritation. How could they choose to live that way? she wondered as she searched, moving between the knots of people, pausing, looking for a young woman with dark hair and almond-shaped eyes, olive complexion.

The crowd was dwindling. Lucy-Ann cursed under her breath: where was the wretched girl? She was about to turn away, to go back to the boredom of her parked car, when she heard the click of heels echoing along the subway below. A dark head emerged from the covered walkway and a young woman began mounting the steps quickly, as if in a hurry. Lucy-Ann marshalled her thoughts and stepped forward, smiling in her best, gentle way.

The two men assigned to surveillance duty outside Jane's hall of residence were young and were dressed in T-shirts and jeans. One sat behind the steering-wheel of the department's oldest pool car, the other tinkered with a rear wheel. A couple came out of the building and walked past without even a glance or a pause in their conversation.

The man behind the wheel looked up. A movement in the flats above had caught his eye. The target lived in one of those flats, on the fourth floor, above the entrance. Its living-room window was slightly open and gave directly on the car-park. But it was a man standing at his window on the second floor, and as he looked up at him, the man turned and walked away and was lost from view.

The watcher checked the time, which he had been checking with increasing regularity in the previous hour. He was getting very bored. He could see the job dragging on into the night.

Then a burst of static came from the radio, and Burrough's quiet voice was heard. At last! thought the watcher, snatching up the handset.

The departure board at Waterloo had made up Jane's mind. There was nearly an hour's wait for a train that would stop at the local station, where she'd left her car, and so, mindful of Miles's thesis, she had caught the fast train to the nearest main station, where she knew she could get a minicab. The fare was more than she'd expected, and in the end, she reminded herself as she paid it, she'd probably only saved half an hour. Now her car was stranded at the local station and she'd have to trek down there to fetch it the next morning. Muttering quiet oaths, she set off across the campus.

It was a lovely evening, still hot from the day, and lots of people were about, walking, lying on the grass, talking. A group she recognized hailed her, and she was tempted to join them, to be indolent that evening rather than good. Then she pictured Miles's face the next day, his disappointed realization that she hadn't kept her promise, and with a despairing gesture at her friends she grimly soldiered on. She could always skim Miles's work, she told herself, and join them later.

She went in through the utilities door at the side of her building and up the back stairs rather than traipsing round to the main entrance and risking another encounter with a very dull Canadian who lived on the second floor and who seemed to leave his door permanently ajar.

With a sense of relief, she reached the sanctuary of her flat. It was pleasantly warm, because she'd left the swing-window fractionally open that morning. The sun still shone in, there was no need to put on a light.

The first thing she did was check her papers on the table: the thesis was among them, and not, as she'd feared, in her office. She went through to the bedroom, eased off her boots, wincing at the sight of a blister, and changed into jeans and a sweatshirt. She needed coffee. In the tiny kitchen, while she waited for the kettle to boil, she debated whether or not she was hungry. She decided not and then, telling herself it was ridiculous to delay any further, went back into the sittingroom, picked up the thesis and sat down on the sofa to read it.

It was numbingly dull, too heavy to skim. Miles had taken as his subject 'Christian Attitudes to Non-Christian NRMs'. Clearly not wishing to be considered critical of either side, he had gone to extraordinary lengths to counterpoint each argument he made. The result was a confusing, unwieldy muddle, not helped by the layout, or the sheer size of the manuscript.

Jane put her feet up on the sofa, resting the script on her knees. There was still half of it to go. She suppressed a yawn and went on, dropping each completed page thankfully on the floor beside her. Her pace got slower. Her jaw was aching, her eyes were beginning to smart, both from tiredness and from the gradual dimming of the daylight. She really ought to get up and put on a light, she told herself drowsily.

She felt herself drifting off to sleep. She'd nap for just half an hour, and then she would wake up refreshed. She was tired . . .

She seemed to dream at once and to be aware too that she was dreaming. She knew that she was smiling as she slept.

She was walking down the cobbled street where she had walked that day with Sam, and Sam was beside her, or certainly a man was. She wanted to turn to look at him, to make sure that it was he, but as was the way of dreams she found that she couldn't turn her head. They kept walking, in silence. She wasn't exactly afraid of the man – she knew now that it wasn't Sam. She knew he wouldn't harm her, indeed that he loved her, and yet he was taking her somewhere she didn't want to go.

The man stopped and she stopped too. She saw that she was suddenly much younger, a teenager. She knew then what was coming and tried to wake up, felt herself struggling to do so, and nearly making it, but the dream pulled her back down.

The man bent down to her level. She had to do it, he told her. She was his daughter; she was going to do it for him.

Then she was going forward on her own. They were in a crowded pedestrian precinct but no one else knew what was happening. She stepped slowly between the people. Each step felt as if her feet were glued to the ground, it was an effort to lift them up and set them down again, but she was getting there; she could see now where she had to stop. She saw the two men waiting, they were supposed to be hidden but they weren't, they were in fancy dress, like clowns. She turned away from them and saw Sarah.

Jane moaned in her sleep. She would give anything, she begged, for the dream to stop. No, said the cruel dream-master, there was more. Sarah was as she'd been when Jane last saw her: pale and terribly thin. But her smile was like sunshine when she saw Jane, and they hugged and Jane thought it might be all right: Sarah might want to come home, and they'd be best friends again, together as they always had been. Then the clowns came out and the one with blue hair was carrying a gun. Jane tried to shout, 'Run!' but the word stuck in her throat. The clown took aim at Sarah. He pulled the trigger.

Jane woke with a cry. The room was dark. She sat up and switched on the small table-lamp. She was shivering, although she wasn't really cold. At least she wasn't screaming or wet with sweat as she had been, night after night, for a year after Sarah had died.

The lamp threw out a soft yellow circle of light, enclosing her in it. It was only a dream, she told herself, hugging herself. Only a dream she hadn't had for years. Her counsellor had said it would probably recur throughout her life, particularly in times of stress.

Jane stood up and saw her ghostly reflection in the window. Miles's thesis could wait until morning, she decided. She'd set her alarm early: she was going to bed. She crossed to the window to close it, and as she did so, she heard voices in the car-park. She looked down. A man was leaning in the window of a car where another sat behind the wheel. She heard a burst of static, abruptly cut off.

Instinct made Jane step back out of sight. Her heart was racing. She didn't think they'd seen her. Then she heard one man say quietly, but quite clearly in the still night air, 'OK, flat six, you're sure?'

Jane froze. Who were they and why did they want her? She'd done nothing wrong. Rudi's words came back to her in a rush. They'd traced her. But that was in Israel, she thought wildly, Mossad did that sort of thing . . . The man's steps sounded on the gravel outside, quick, careful steps, lightly planted, doing their best not to be heard. She had to move, she had to get out of there. She heard the footsteps pause, the external door squeak open. She shoved her feet into her trainers, snatched up her bag and ran for the door.

In the corridor the lights were dim, casting an orange glow. Jane glanced towards the stairs. Distantly she could hear the footsteps coming, soft shoe-soles on the stone.

She pulled the door shut behind her, cursing the 'click' it made, and ran. There was carpet on the floor, which she prayed would stop anyone hearing her. She got to the first fire-door, tugged it open, and ran on to the next. She didn't look back until she had reached the end of the building and the flight of stairs there. Through the fire-doors, she couldn't see if anyone was after her. She sped down the stairs and out through the utility door, catching it in her hand so that it wouldn't clang behind her. The night was warm and the moon hazy-bright. She kept to the shadows of the buildings as she ran.

CHAPTER THIRTEEN

Beside her in the narrow bunk bed, Ross slept soundly.

Enough light came in from the landing for Ruth to see his features: the strong, well-defined nose, the deep ridge that ran down to his lips, the dark stubble on his chin that felt so rough and yet good against her own.

She had always been attracted to Ross. She had first met him when she was fifteen and he, the son of a family friend, in his mid-thirties. She had been aware of his interest in her and had flirted with him. When, years later, David had told her that she must do anything to win Ross over to their cause, there were tears in his eyes. 'For Jesus's sake,' he whispered, taking her hands in his own. 'Do it for Jesus, and Jesus will forgive.'

Ruth didn't know about that: she didn't think that Jesus cared if people had sex or not, but David seemed to consider it terribly important, and so she'd let him think that her seduction of Ross had been a shocking ordeal. In fact, she'd enjoyed it a lot. She thought God had invented sex for pleasure, that there would be sex in heaven too – only of a spectacularly better kind.

Once, early in her relationship with David, she had tried explaining her views but he was so dismayed that, at his bidding, she admitted them as sin and hadn't mentioned them again. Ruth loved

David, and she revered him as God's last Prophet on earth, but to her mind his beliefs were sometimes rather alien, of the 'gentle Jesus, meek and mild' school. She didn't see how he equated those with the ruthlessness he'd displayed in fulfilling some of the signs, but she supposed all prophets had their peculiarities: John the Baptist, she remembered, ate locusts.

After Ross had done all that had been asked of him, David said the sex must stop. He had expected her to be glad, but in fact she missed it. And then, when she got back to the Lodge after her foray to the supermarkets, she'd found Ross in a dreadful state.

She'd still been on a high from her mission and, rarely for her, looking forward to talking about it.

Ross, however, had been in no frame of mind to listen. Indeed for the first few minutes, Ruth feared he had lost his mind. He had been sitting in the kitchen, staring vacantly, not appearing even to see her, and chanting aloud the words of what he later informed her was the 'Nunc Dimitis' from the Church of England litany.

Gradually, although only to an extent, he had come out of it. She had managed to extract from him the events of his day and heard about David's refusal to take fright at the INSEC alert. News of that – the first she had heard of it – had initially frightened her too, so much so that she had cut Ross short and rung David. Unlike Ross, she had found David's quiet explanations completely convincing – she knew on a practical level how intent God was on fulfilling His signs, that time after time He had protected her. She had accepted David's implied rebuke that she should have more faith and had promised him that she would look after Ross.

'Give him a hot drink and put him to bed,' David had suggested lovingly.

She had made Ross cocoa, and taking his hand – for he was still dazed, mumbling that David wanted to kill her – had led him upstairs and sat him on his bunk. When she bent down to give him a sisterly kiss (the only kind permitted now) she saw the longing in his eyes. It was the first spark of life he had shown all night.

'Please, Ruth,' he had pleaded like a little boy.

She said nothing, but neither had she moved away and tentatively, not taking his eyes from hers, his fingers had reached for her nipple and started to rub it in the way that she loved.

For comfort then, she had told him, and as a reward for being a good boy, nice and quiet. She'd taken off her clothes, slowly, piece by piece, and lain down beside him.

'Sorry,' he'd kept whimpering, 'I'm sorry, baby,' because he'd thought he was doing it against her will, whereas the feel and smell of him, his riding of her deep inside, his coaxing of her to climax, had been glorious, wonderful.

If that was what it took to keep Ross on an even keel, Ruth thought, she didn't mind a bit. David need never know. A little smile played on her lips. The next day, when she and Ross cleaned out the laboratories, eradicating all traces of what had been there, they could take breaks in her bedroom. A small reward to herself, she thought, for having had such a good day in the supermarkets. All doses successfully delivered with only one near-miss, a hypermarket outside Shrewsbury, when she thought a child had seen her, but clearly not, for no one had come after her, no one had recognized her from the pathetically poor E-fit.

Ross rolled over in his sleep and she slid out from under him, not waking him. She went into her own room, to her own narrow, virginal bed and slipped on the long white cotton nightdress she'd left folded under her pillow. In the morning, she thought, yawning luxuriously, when Ross appeared in the doorway, shame-faced and begging for forgiveness, she would allow him to enter first the room, then her bed and then herself. She closed her eyes. She might as well enjoy the pleasures of her earthly body in the short time that was left to it.

The couple who ran the Pilgrim Community Church in the Scottish Highlands, presented a serene, unified approach in the face of Ryder's questioning.

Yes, they believed that Christ had already returned to earth. Yes, there were great tribulations ahead for unbelievers, culminating, they believed, in the destruction of the world within the next twelve months.

Piles of 'writings', in tiny black lettering, had been found at their headquarters. They were being checked to see if they contained any reference to the Scroll. Meanwhile, every one of the eighty-seven Pilgrims was being detained in a former isolation hospital outside Aviemore.

After over an hour with the leaders, Ryder still hadn't ruled them out as suspects.

He waited until the man finished speaking, then asked conversationally, 'Is either of you known as the Keeper?'

They looked at each other, then back at him, as if he was a particularly slow-witted child. 'We've already told you our names,' the man said patiently. 'Could you please tell us when we can go home?'

There came a discreet tap at the door. 'Sir?' One of the support staff stuck his head in. 'Telephone.'

It must be urgent, Ryder knew, or he wouldn't have been disturbed. He excused himself with alacrity. It would be Burroughs, he thought, at last calling with the news that they had Carlucci. He only wanted one name, then the nightmare would be over.

In the adjoining room, he snatched up the telephone. It was indeed Burroughs, but there was a hint of appeal in her voice that augured ill.

'Well?' he said curtly.

He could hardly believe it when she told him the story.

'For Christ's sake,' he swore.

'She'd only just left, sir,' Burroughs continued hurriedly. 'We're sure of that – the sofa was warm. She can't have gone far. The men are searching the campus now.'

In the corner of his laptop screen, he saw the postbox icon jumping up and down, signifying that he had new e-mail. Crushing the phone into his neck, effectively cutting off Burroughs's voice, he leant forward and pressed the key to receive it.

It was a one-page document with a two-line introduction. Ryder scanned it, then his eyes came to rest on one sentence. Of course, he thought bitterly; he should have guessed.

'Carlucci knows we're after her,' he said into the phone.

'I'm sorry, sir?'

Ryder sighed. 'She was warned this morning that we were interested in the swaddling-clothes. I quote from the transcript of her telephone call from her Israeli friend.' He bent nearer to the computer screen to read the words. '"Your secret service people and the FBI are coming over here." And "anyone who starts asking questions is getting shipped off to a political compound". She was running around with that in her head all day. God knows who she's already told.' He shied away from that thought himself. 'If she heard the team coming . . .'

'I'm sure they were very quiet, sir.'

'Not quiet enough, evidently.' Why was Carlucci running? he wondered. Why hadn't she come straight to him with whatever suspicions she had? Did she – alarming thought – harbour sympathies for the unknown group? No, he was sure that wasn't it. She'd run because she was scared, because she didn't want what had happened to her Israeli friend to happen to her too.

'There is one other thing, sir,' began Burroughs.

'Yes?'

'There was a train to London from the local station at ten to twelve.'

'What?' said Ryder, gripping the handset so hard that it hurt. It was twenty past midnight now.

'I've got someone meeting it.'

Carlucci might still slip through the net, Ryder thought. She'd done so before.

'Did you find an address book?' he demanded.

Eagerly Lucy-Ann said that she had.

'Start going through her contacts,' Ryder ordered. 'Call her parents and tell them she's in trouble, and if she turns up it's important they keep her with them. And set up a telephone tap.' He thought for a moment. 'See if there's any evidence of a boyfriend and do the same with him, with anyone close to her. It's absolutely imperative that she's found, ' he said and ended the call.

He saw he had another e-mail, this time from Yves. 'Any names for me yet, Paul?' it said. 'Sorry to ask, but I'm coming under a lot of pressure. If it helps, the Americans are looking at a group in California, and the Japanese have nominated two potentials.'

Only because they knew they were in the clear, Ryder thought bitterly, because everyone believed the cult was really British. He sent back a noncommittal one-liner.

The Pilgrims were waiting. He knew he ought to go back in, but he couldn't face them right then.

He tapped in to his database. There was nothing new on the murder hunt, merely repetition of what the witnesses had said six weeks ago: the ticket-collector at the castle remembering a gypsy-like man loitering by the castle on the morning of the day the boys were killed, a sightseer noticing the twins going off by themselves into the woods where their bodies were found.

Ryder switched to the *Crimewatch* update. A record number of calls had come in on Botulism Helen, in no small part due, Ryder guessed, to the still deteriorating condition of one of the Birmingham schoolchildren, a seven-year-old girl. There had been scores of alleged sightings of the white van. It seemed it was a Bedford, that the first number of its plate was 2, which with what they already had added up to P2 something, something something K. There were over six hundred such Bedford vans whose plates matched that partial number, and during the night, with the aid of local police, the owner of every single one would be checked out. Ryder couldn't help but feel a revival of hope.

He glanced through the list of *Crimewatch* calls. Helen had been seen in Cornwall, in Birmingham, getting on a bus in Cardiff, in a pub in Leicester, near a school playground in Newcastle, boarding the Eurostar at Waterloo, in Inverness – not far from where Ryder was sitting – buying groceries at a supermarket. He pitied the officers, including four of his own team, screening those calls: the false leads, the sheer waste of time, and yet the knowledge that none could be dismissed; that the crucial clue might be buried in the mass.

They would be working all night, Ryder thought. Well, so would he if need be. He rose and returned to the Pilgrims.

Once she was sure no one was following her, Jane stopped worrying about making a noise. She crashed through the woods away from the campus, her sole intention being to get to her car, fast, and drive – she wasn't certain where, that wasn't important. But when she arrived, winded, at the station, and saw a train coming and her car sitting alone in the moonlight, it struck her that if 'they' were who she thought they were, they'd probably know her car's registration number and be able to trace her through it. On the other hand, in her own car she would be able to go where she wanted, to find somewhere to hide. The train was drawing in to the station. At the last moment, she dashed for it and leapt on board.

It was been a slow one, the last of the night, calling at all stations to London. For most of the journey, her carriage was empty. She had plenty of time to think.

She wasn't a conspiracy theorist but there could be no doubt who her callers were. She'd been on the point of being carted off to the English version of the compound that Rudi had talked about. Thank God, she thought with a shudder, that the dream had woken her.

They'd known her flat number. They'd been waiting for her to come home. They wanted her because of what Rudi had told her, because of what they thought she knew. But what did she know? Only that Norton had once called himself the Keeper – and even that wasn't first-hand.

To be going to such lengths, the authorities must be as deeply concerned as she was that the Scroll prophecies were being fulfilled. Should she tell them her suspicions about the Fellowship?

She gazed out of the train window. In researching her thesis on Waco, she had visited the offices of the federal agencies involved and spoken with survivors of the tragedy, and their lawyers. She'd seen photographs of the blackened, twisted bodies of men, women and children who had perished in the fire. Some said the authorities had started that fire, others that the cultists had set it themselves. To Jane's mind, the crucial issue wasn't who was responsible, it was the way the FBI's had mishandled the siege. They'd treated the Branch Davidians like terrorists, refusing to listen to advice from Apocalyptic experts. Jane believed no one need have died at Mount Carmel, neither the Davidians nor the four FBI officers whose murders by the cultists had started the long siege.

The Davidians believed they were God's faithful living in the End Time; that they were entitled to use force to resist the enemy. When the FBI decided to 'increase the pressure' on the besieged compound, by noise-torture and searchlights, the Davidians saw their tactics as confirmations of End-Time prophecies.

From what Jane understood of her own country's authorities, they were less prepared than the Americans to handle an assault on an End-Time NRM. The Home Office's only indication that it knew there might be an NRM problem was the existence of GUIDE, overseen by the kindly but, Jane considered, rather ineffectual figure of Paul Ryder. The vetting of the country's NRMs was left to herself, a few volunteers and the Scottish GUIDE. In many ways it was laughable – pathetic. It was only by the merest chance that she knew Norton's former title.

A raid on the Fellowship would be carried out by the army, or police, she imagined, possibly with the assistance of the very security services which had so ineptly failed to catch her. What sort of bloodbath would they cause if they raided a nervy, Apocalyptic NRM? If that, indeed was an accurate description of the Fellowship. It had survived for nine years without once attracting adverse attention, without even earning for itself the distinction of being called an NRM. She had no proof that anything worrying was going on there; she was hanging everything on what Freddy had told her, and the disappearance of Sam's undercover reporter, who might not have disappeared at all.

She could not bear the responsibility of wrongly crying wolf. Too many lives were at stake. Admittedly, thousands more would be if the Fellowship really was fulfilling the signs, planning the End, the Awful Horror of the Ungodly . . .

Which was why she was going there later in the day, she told herself resolutely. Before she spoke to anyone in authority, she was going to get some evidence. It might be arrogance, but she reckoned she was one of the very few people with specialist knowledge who could quickly and accurately 'read' an NRM and determine whether it was dangerous.

She'd let herself be lulled that day, she thought. She'd wasted time while all the while the security services had been hunting for her. Soon she would be at Waterloo. She could catch a train straight down to Hastings, be there waiting in the morning when the Fellowship café opened.

But suppose the police were also looking for her? Always supposing there was a train to Hastings at that time in the morning, she'd be arriving in the early hours. Did she want to be caught before she had a chance of getting recruited? If she was, she knew she'd talk. So she mustn't get caught.

Lights of suburban homes flashed by her window. She was in outer London. It was almost one o'clock in the morning, and she needed a bed for the night. She got off at Clapham Junction.

At three o'clock in the morning, local time, in the West Bank town of Ramallah, four Shin Bet men kicked in the apartment door of a young Palestinian journalist and dragged him off down the communal stairs.

Those listening in their beds and at their doors, wondered what he had done now to upset the authorities. He was a well-known documenter of human-rights abuses and had been arrested at such ungodly hours before.

The journalist himself, being bumped backwards down the last flight by his captors, was similarly unclear as to which of his many enterprises – the series of shocking interviews with child-workers; his embryonic investigation into the chemical plant near Haifa – had led to his current predicament. It didn't occur to him that it might have something to do with a phone call he'd received four hours earlier.

The caller was an old woman who worked in the canteen of the Israeli detention centre outside Nazareth. There was something fishy going on, she'd told him. She wanted payment for what she knew. Once before she had been very useful to him; since then not at all. With a sigh, he'd agreed to a moderate sum.

An area of the centre had been sealed off, she told him. 'Unusual prisoners' – not the run-of-the-mill 'politicos' – had been brought in. She'd heard it was to do with the theft of artefacts from the Baby Jesus Sanctuary in Bethlehem.

The journalist knew the Sanctuary by reputation, and reckoned he'd wasted his money, but the old woman was adamant, and mysteriously mentioned 'foreign' police. That was interesting, so he'd scribbled down a few notes and decided that in the morning, if he'd nothing better to do, he'd give the Sanctuary a call.

Those notes were now in the hands of the Shin Bet man who preceded him into the jeep. As he was being hauled up into the back, the journalist remembered to call out into the night the name of his lawyer and the request that he be called, but the jeep's engine was already running and it was doubtful that anyone heard him.

Although the *Crimewatch Special* had ended at midnight, calls were still coming into the studio at two o'clock in the morning.

The police fielding them had the winnowing procedure finely tuned: callers who were too glib, or who merely repeated what had been said or shown on the programme, were politely but speedily got rid of; vehicle registration numbers were gratefully received, as were clairvoyants' claims. All other information was added to the database for cross-checking, and, where necessary, calling back the informant.

One of the team, a police sergeant, was doing that now. He had just spoken at length to an elderly woman who claimed that her neighbour was Helen, and had decided to go with his gut instinct that the informant was merely malicious, when his phone rang again.

A very young voice came on the line.

The sergeant raised an eyebrow. 'How old are you?' he asked.

'Ten,' the child said. 'They said they'd phone me back.'

'Did they? Shouldn't you be in bed?'

'I am,' the boy said firmly. 'I saw that lady doing things in the supermarket.'

'Uh-huh. ' The sergeant decided that the quickest way to get rid of the boy was to let him have his say. 'What sort of things?'

'She was squeezing a green ball into a packet of chicken.'

'What?'

'She was,' insisted the child. 'It looked like a squash ball.'

It was a curious description. Outlandish, the sergeant thought, yet the child was so definite, and too old for pure fantasy. He switched on the tape and said, 'Tell me what you saw. Right from the very beginning.'

The boy made a good, precise witness. He'd been shopping with his mother in Shrewsbury that afternoon. He'd seen a woman pick up food from the chill-counter, and press her ball into it, then slip the cardboard sleeve back over it to hide what she'd done. He'd told his mother, but she paid no attention. He'd watched *Crimewatch* with the babysitter.

The officer asked if he could remember the brand of the food the woman had picked up.

The boy couldn't. He hesitated. 'There was one thing,' he said in a small voice.

'Yes?'

'The lady didn't look much like the picture.'

'Ah.' He wasn't about to divulge to the boy that the consensus reached that night was that a new E-fit would be a good idea. The current one wasn't attracting the leads it should.

'And she had red hair, not fair like in your picture.'

It was known that Helen used wigs. The observation made the boy a stronger witness. The officer briefly consulted a colleague, then asked the boy to wake his mother. They obtained her startled agreement to accompany her son, with two police officers, to the twenty-four-hour supermarket in Shrewsbury.

There, at three-thirty in the morning, the boy unhesitatingly pointed out the meals he'd seen the woman tampering with.

One of the policemen picked up the 'Great Expectation'

container. He slipped back the sleeve and saw a neat puncture mark in the plastic covering.

Five minutes later, that information reached the groom office in London. Jack Broughton called Ryder in Scotland.

Ryder sounded shattered. 'Little children and pregnant women,' he said numbly.

'Yes.'

'I didn't know there were special meals for pregnant women, did you?'

Broughton admitted that he did not.

That was no comfort, Ryder thought. He or someone ought to have known. They had made it too easy for 'Helen'. He felt sick to his stomach. That, on top of Carlucci's non-arrival at Waterloo, after they'd failed to catch her on campus. He wondered what botulism did to pregnant women.

'We'd better get that stuff off the shelves,' he said.

'Yes,' said Broughton.

'How about surveillance cameras at this supermarket?'

'They have them both in store and in the car-park. The footage is being gone through now.'

'Good.' Hopefully, they'd get a clear picture of 'Helen', Ryder thought, rather than the questionable E-fit likeness. He asked Broughton to call him as soon as there was any more news.

The product recall began at four o'clock that morning when most supermarkets were shut anyway.

The vast car-park of the hypermarket outside Bristol was almost empty when Sally Goodall drove in at twenty past four. There were only four other cars there, parked close to the entrance, and they probably belonged to the staff. She would be the only customer, but she didn't care. She parked beside them and looked over at her son, Ned, who grinned gummily back at her.

He was cheerful now, she thought, as always when he was in the car. He'd be fine while she did her shopping, and hopefully by the time they got home he'd be asleep and let her sleep too. Her husband wouldn't get up when Ned cried. He said it was her job, that his was to provide and he needed his eight hours' rest. What about me? she thought. Wasn't looking after a teething baby a full-time job? Especially when she was pregnant again?

She got out of the car, strapped Ned into the seat of a trolley and entered the shop. For her the hypermarket with its twenty-four-hour opening time was a godsend.

At the prepared foods section along the back of the store, she loaded her trolley with sausage and mash, chilli con carne and beef and roast potatoes, the dinners that her husband liked. She came to the end of the unit where the organic produce was displayed. It was always more expensive, and she rarely bought it, but when she saw the new line of products, all that they offered, she smiled and thought, why not? She was forever worrying that she wasn't eating the right things for the new baby. She selected a plastic-covered tray and put it in her trolley.

Ned twisted in his seat, trying to get it.

'Not for you, greedy-guts,' she told him, and then, because he grinned so adorably back at her, she bent down and kissed his downy head.

Forty minutes later, news of the Great Expectations recall reached the hypermarket's night manager. Till records showed that one meal had been recently purchased, but Sally had paid in cash and at that time of night the surveillance cameras weren't on, either in the car-park or in the store. There was no way of tracing her.

CHAPTER FOURTEEN

The friend whose doorbell Jane rang at ten past one in the morning, had sought no explanation beyond the fact that Jane needed help.

'We'll talk in the morning,' she told Jane blearily, showing her to the tiny spare room.

Jane expected to lie awake for hours, and to have a repeat of her nightmare if she slept, but she fell asleep quickly, and when she awoke she remembered nothing of her dreams or even, for a moment, where she was. The thought didn't alarm her. The sun was streaming in through the thin curtains, and she felt warm and relaxed, and imbued with an almost childlike sense of safety.

Then her eyes fell on her trainers on the floor. They were caked in mud from the woods. Everything came back to her. She glanced at the time: it was nine o'clock.

Katie would have gone to work. Jane was partly sorry and partly glad to have missed her. The thought of having to explain everything from the beginning was, at that moment, too much to contemplate. Also Jane didn't know how safe it would be to tell her friend the truth. Katie liked to talk.

Jane went through to the kitchen, and saw Katie's note offering her clothes or anything she needed, and asking her to ring her at work. She went for a shower and under its scalding water came properly awake. Her midnight run through the fields seemed unreal now. Such things didn't happen to her – oh yes, they did, she checked herself, they did now. If she wanted to stay free, and judge for herself whether the Fellowship was guilty or innocent, she'd have to be constantly on the alert. She had no doubt that the police and security services would be hunting for her, but she *had* to get into the Fellowship.

If she found evidence that they were fulfilling the signs, she would, if there was time, notify fellow academics first – there was a monitoring unit at Boston University in the States, and perhaps she'd tell Dr Fraser from Scottish GUIDE. In that way, the experts would know before the authorities; they could present the police with a modus operandi – possibly even withholding the name of the group until fully satisfied that the correct approach was going to be used. Surely, if there were enough experts, from enough countries, the British authorities would have to listen to them, take heed of their advice?

No one but herself, she hoped, knew of the Fellowship connection. It was on no database. But she couldn't foresee all eventualities: she had to get down there fast. And if she felt the group was about to blow, she'd call the police. She wasn't irresponsible.

She dressed quickly. She was scribbling a quick note to Katie, when she remembered what day it was. Her mother was coming to lunch, only Jane wouldn't be there. She dialled her mother's number. It was answered almost at once.

'Mum,' she began, 'it's me. I'm afraid something's come up. I'm in London and—'

'Jane! Oh, darling!'

'What?' Jane gripped the receiver. Her mother sounded distraught.

'The police say there's nothing to be scared about; they only want to talk.'

Suddenly there was too little air in the room.

Down the line, a man's deep voice rumbled, 'Jane, are you there? Please don't be frightened. We just want to ask you a couple of questions.'

She slammed down the receiver, grabbed her bag and ran for the door. The police were in her mother's house. How long before she gave them Katie's name and address – Katie, her best friend in London?

She fled down the stairs to the ground floor. The hallway leading to the street entrance was directly in front of her but instead she followed the signs for the tradesman's entrance at the back of the building. The yard there gave on to a lane and she jogged to the end, looking left and right before emerging. There were parked cars in the street, but she couldn't see anyone in them.

She set off along the pavement, heading away from the main traffic, her eyes watchful.

The call had been brief but the equipment was very good – `vicious', according to its operator. It pinpointed the target's position as south London, then the cursor edged westwards and stopped. Jane's address book, now on the database, gave only one Clapham address. Within five minutes of the call, a two-man team was on the way there, armed with a photo of Jane scanned from her university file.

They didn't have far to go – from Vauxhall – but at that time of the morning, the traffic was awful and even the backroads were clogged. The whole of London seemed to be on the streets. Swearing under his breath, the driver braked as a tide of pedestrians surged across the road in front of them.

By ten o'clock in the morning in Jerusalem, it was obvious to the Israeli groom that the theft of the swaddling-clothes could no longer be kept secret. Either the Nazarene canteen worker had been more talkative than she had so far admitted, or else others also knew of the theft. Already that morning, there had been three inquiries from journalists – and they couldn't be as easily incarcerated as the Ramallah trouble-maker.

The groom decided that brief details of the theft should be released to the media. Further inquiries would be dealt with in such a manner as to deflect curiosity. Lack of interest, rather than denial, was to be the key. With luck, he thought, the story would be stillborn.

He was aware, as he gave his instructions, that he should have warned the other grooms of the problem, then proferred his suggestion and waited for them to vote on it. But that would have meant delay, and possible argument from people on the other side of the globe, when the problem was there on his doorstep. By killing the story in Israel he would be killing it worldwide, thus saving his fellow grooms the problem when their own media got hold of it.

He issued a further instruction that all Bridegroom offices should be advised of his decision. Then he immediately left the building to travel in the back of an armoured car to a prison on the outskirts of the city where an old man, who everyone had assumed was dead, was waiting unwillingly for him in a cell.

There was a vacant seat in Jane's tube carriage, and when the train stopped and fresh people got on, a man gestured to her that she should have it, but she shook her head. Seated, she'd be too easy to spot and also it would be harder for her to get away. She felt safer standing in the squash by the doors, like everyone else not meeting strangers' eyes. The train slowed to a long halt between stations, and around her passengers sighed and tutted, but Jane didn't mind.

The curved wall behind her head was womb-like; no one, she felt, could get to her there. She was tempted to stay there all day, shuttling up and down on the Northern line, hidden in the throng. But the crowds were already beginning to thin. The rush hour was over; it was ten-thirty. Over an hour had passed since her flight from Katie's flat; she had to be on her way. She didn't know for certain which mainline station she needed, but she was intending to get out at Waterloo and find out.

The train eventually restarted. The next station was Kennington, and then she had only one more stop to go. Then, further down the carriage, two uniformed Transport Police officers boarded.

Jane stared at them for a moment, then quickly got off. She was probably being paranoid, she told herself, but she wasn't going to risk it. She walked up the elevators to reach the top more swiftly. Once outside the station, she paused. She didn't know that area of London at all. She started walking. On the other side of the road, she saw a police car coming.

She turned into a side street, hurried to the end, and turned again. She was in a quiet, prosperous square. She consulted her street guide and saw that she was within easy walking distance of Waterloo but now the prospect of entering that vast, international complex seemed unwise. She should have gone the day before, she told herself. She should have found an excuse to take time off, rather than going to meet Sam.

There was a phone booth on the corner. Sam might know, or be able to find out easily, which station she needed for Hastings. Besides, before she disappeared into the Fellowship, she wanted to let him know what was happening.

She stepped into the booth and rang his number. It was engaged. If he didn't answer when she tried again, she decided, she would hire a car and drive down to Hastings.

She dialled again.

'Sam Ferryman.' His voice was clipped.

'Sam, it's Jane Carlucci.'

'For God's sake, Jane,' he muttered. 'Where are you?'

He sounded tense. 'What's wrong?' she asked.

'They're looking for you.'

She knew that but how did he?

'Tell me where you are,' he said, 'and I'll come and get you.'

'I'm still going into the Fellowship,' she protested.

'Fine, okay, but I want to show you what they're saying about you.'

Her head spinning, she gave him the name of the street. He told her he'd be there within ten minutes, and that she should keep out of sight if she could. She replaced the receiver, too dazed to move.

As the helicopter began its descent, it tilted forward to a degree that Ryder, although a veteran of such flights, still found alarming. Another millimetre or two, he felt, and the tilt would go too far: the helicopter would overbalance and plunge them down upon the frantic streets of London.

He gazed down as those streets rushed up to meet him. Carlucci was down there somewhere, running scared. An attractive young woman, from a verifiable academic background. Her claims might sound wild, but they tallied neatly with the alarming events of the day.

At least no newspaper or television station would dare run what she said, he reminded himself grimly. Half an hour earlier, upon hearing that yet again Carlucci had evaded her pursuers, he had ordered that the D-notice, prepared 'just in case', be released. Attached to it was an off-the-record briefing claiming that Carlucci was a high-ranking MOD man's mentally unstable daughter, who confused fact with fiction to a dangerous degree, and also suffered from religious delusions; if she appeared at a newspaper or television centre, she should be detained and the police called at once.

However tempting Jane's story might be, Ryder knew the media would not cross the D-notice line, not with that addendum. If any inquiries were made concerning it, or Jane's allegations, there was an alarm system in place, as there was at her university.

Her description and photograph had been issued to all airports, ports and railway companies, as well as to Special Branch. Her capture was flashed 'Urgent, urgent'. The friend with whom she had stayed the night was being picked up for questioning.

No matter how surveillance-conscious Carlucci was, he thought, she couldn't evade capture very much longer. He frowned: he had envisaged having either her or Helen in custody before now.

The child from the Shrewsbury supermarket, on being shown the surveillance film, had instantly identified the woman he'd seen spiking the food. Unfortunately she was facing away from the camera, so although there was an excellent shot of the boy staring at her, only the back of her red-wigged head showed. All that showed clearly was her left hand – long, slender fingers – replacing one meal in the chiller section, and picking up another.

In the car-park, her white van had been captured on film, the registration number easily legible: P211 SPK. Hearing that, at five o'clock that morning, Ryder had punched the air: they had her.

Except they hadn't. The number was not on the national list of white Bedford vans; the plate was false. Another indicator, Ryder thought, of how much planning had gone into the operation, the determination of Helen and her group not to get caught.

There was still a lot of potentially useful surveillance film to be gone through. Every supermarket that had carried the Great Expectations range should by now have handed its footage to the police. A new, clear picture of Helen might still emerge and lead him to the group.

The Scottish group no longer interested Ryder. At seven that morning, he'd come to the same conclusion as the rest of the interrogation team: the Pilgrims were innocent. Although believing that the world would end violently, they wept, literally, as a group, every day, for its suffering. They prayed that Christ would delay the End until the whole world had been saved.

The last cult Ryder had been due to visit, in London that morning, had been ruled unworthy of his attention. The group was in complete disarray: two days before its leader had run off with a member's wife.

Where do we look now? thought Ryder. The scenario he'd imagined only the night before, of detaining every NRM in the country, was coming closer to reality. He might have to suggest it to the ARIC meeting he was due to attend at noon. They'd be expecting suggestions as to what to do, and all he could give them was reports of failure: failure to capture either woman; the failure of his hastily assembled Bridegroom staff, the GUIDE organization and the national databases to find the group concerned.

Was it British? The thought nagged. He tried to suppress it, but it kept resurfacing. At seven that morning, when he was at his lowest through lack of sleep and bad news – he'd just heard that the little Birmingham girl had died – Yves had rung.

Had he seen the latest E-mail from the Boston groom?

Ryder had not. Not only had he been trying to snatch whatever sleep he could between phone calls but he found monitoring the Bridegroom database, which seemed to consist mainly of e-mails asking him for information, profoundly depressing.

'No? What?' he said blearily.

In Atlanta, Georgia, at midnight the previous night, stores had begun clearing their shelves of It's Good For You, Baby food after the packaging was found to be leaking in one large supermarket.

On closer inspection, needle-marks had been found in the cardboard boxes.

'Are you serious?' Ryder exclaimed.

'Read it for yourself,' retorted Yves.

Ryder had. As he was reading, another e-mail came in from the same source: a second supermarket, within a mile of the first, had found similar puncture-marks on another brand of boxed baby-food.

The American attempts were much clumsier than the British, Ryder thought, but they had given him a glimmer of desperate hope.

He didn't deny that Helen was fulfilling the Scroll sign, but might she not be part of an international group, based in the States? Or Australia?

Looking for more American data, he'd come across an e-mail from the Melbourne groom. Yummy Tummy, the Dutch baby-food manufacturers, who had been so infuriatingly slow and secretive in conducting their investigations into their contaminated feeds, had just announced that they suspected a former temporary employee, Liam Keighly, an Australian, of involvement. He had had access to the additives area. He had gone missing just before the babies became ill. His body had been found in a canal.

He must not give in to doubts that the group was British, Ryder told himself firmly. Nevertheless, the story gave him a little breathing-space, a snippet of good news to present to ARIC: Britain was no longer so firmly centre-stage as it had been.

His stomach lurched as the helicopter dropped like a stone on to the landing pad of the MOD building.

As Sam drove to work, he heard on the car radio the news of the spiked maternity meals, the likelihood that Helen had struck again. He remembered the reference to pregnant women in the Scroll. As soon as he reached his desk, he checked it on the print-out of the Scroll he'd made the night before. He'd been right.

He switched on his computer, and called up the wire services. Although shops had cleared their shelves of Great Expectations meals within hours of the suspected contamination, it was too soon to tell whether anyone had eaten the food. Public warnings were being issued, given added force by the death overnight of one of the Birmingham schoolchildren.

Sam requested all data on spiked maternity/baby foods. He read of the findings in the Shrewsbury supermarket in the early hours of the morning. Even if the police dismissed him as a nutter, he thought, he must tell them of his – or rather Jane's – suspicions about the Scroll and the Fellowship. He couldn't in all conscience do otherwise.

Then he saw the story that followed. 'Atlanta, Georgia: Stores clear It's Good For You, Baby food from sale after holes were found in the cardboard packaging. Detectives say needles had been used to inject . . .'

Was someone in the States was doing exactly the same thing? he wondered. If so, it put Botulism Helen in an entirely different light. Made her part of something much bigger – perhaps an international group of consumer terrorists – and nothing to do with Jane's imaginings.

Then a 'flasher', a message from the Editor to all staff, came up on the screen: 'The MOD issued the following D-notice at 10.22 this morning, concerning information given by a member of the public, Jane Carlucci . . .'

'What the hell?' Sam muttered, reading it. They said Jane was crazy, a danger to the state. What sort of game were they playing? Was she right about the Fellowship? If so, why were they trying to blacken her name?

He picked up his phone to warn her, but stopped himself just in time. If they were issuing D-notices about her, they'd have her line tapped. She couldn't be at GUIDE any more, otherwise they wouldn't be issuing extraordinary orders to journalists to detain her on sight. His head was spinning. Then Jane rang.

Pausing only to print off the stories, and tell Monica he'd just received a brilliant lead on the Hampstead NRM – 'Go to it, Sammy boy' – he dashed down to his car, found Jane's whereabouts on his street-map, and drove off to find her. As he did so, he couldn't stop himself checking in his rear-view mirror to see whether he was being followed. He wasn't. Paranoia was catching, he thought, turning into her street.

He couldn't see her. On either side of the street there were tall, white Regency houses with black railings, pillars by some entrances, but no sign of a small, slim Italian-looking girl with dark hair. Had they found her? Was he too late? He saw the phone booth she must have used to call him, but it was empty. What would they do to her to make her talk? He ought to have got there sooner.

Her head appeared as she looked cautiously round a pillar at the end of the street. Relief rushed through him. He put his foot down and pulled into the kerb alongside her.

She peered at him, then ran to the passenger door and jumped in.

He saw how pale she was. 'Are you okay?'

She nodded. Her eyes were huge in her face. 'What's going on?' she gasped.

'Take a look at this lot,' he said briefly, and thrust the wire stories and the D-notice at her.

There was silence while she read, then she cried, 'But does this mean Helen has got nothing to do with the fellowship?'

'I don't know.' He drew up to traffic lights. Waiting alongside him, on his side, was a police car. Sam leant slightly forward, shielding Jane from the officers' sight.

She gave another cry. 'They can't say this about me!'

'I know. Dirty, isn't it?'

'But anyone wanting to check me out would only have to phone GUIDE,' Jane exclaimed.

'They'll have that covered,' Sam said. 'They'll have someone down there, or an intercept on the line. They'll probably trace our calls from records.'

'Really?' she said weakly.

The lights changed. The police car turned right. Sam kept straight on.

'They came for me last night,' said Jane.

'What?'

She told him what had happened. He was impresssed by how calm she was about it.

'They really mean business, don't they?' he said.

'You don't think I should give myself up, tell them what I know?' she asked.

Sam shot her a quick, hard look. 'D'you want to?'

'No. I want to go down to the Fellowship and get some evidence first. If it hadn't been for the American spiking, I might have felt differently . . .'

'I know. It makes everything less certain doesn't it?'

She nodded.

'If the security services had played it straighter,' Sam said, 'asked you outright what you knew, would you have felt differently?'

'Perhaps.'

He saw how determined she looked. He realized how much he liked her.

'I can only imagine what sort of cock-up they'd make of an assault,' she went on, half to herself.

'You might be right.'

'Where are we going?' she asked.

'Hastings?' he suggested.

'Are you sure?'

'I want to make sure you get there,' he said.

'Thank you. Sorry to have dragged you into this,' she added.

'Don't mention it,' he said with a brief smile. They drove on in silence.

Three supermarkets, besides the one at Shrewsbury, had found pin-prick holes in their Great Expectations meals. Their surveillance films had been sent directly to the Scotland Yard team leading the hunt for Helen, and copies had been despatched from the Yard to the Bridegroom office at Vauxhall.

When Ryder got there, Jack Broughton, who was in overall charge of the Helen case, was waiting for him, armed with three stills from the Shrewsbury film. He followed Ryder into his office and laid them on the desk.

'This is the best there is,' he said flatly.

They showed a woman shopper in a supermarket aisle. She was looking down at the few goods in her trolley. The fringe of her red hair was in sharp focus; her face, apart from a rough outline of her nose and cheeks, was indistinct.

'You're joking!' expostulated Ryder.

'I'm afraid I'm not. It's the way they position the cameras.'

'It's bloody awful!' Ryder picked up the second picture. Most of it was taken up by a large woman bending over a food fridge. In the corner of the frame, a thin left hand with a gold ring on the third finger reached out to pick up a Great Expectations meal.

'You can't tell anything from this,' said Ryder. 'What about the next frame, or the one before it?'

'Random shots,' Broughton said briefly.

The third photograph showed the white Bedford van being driven into a supermarket car-park. It showed merely a figure behind the steering-wheel, too vague to make out whether it was male or female.

'Oh, Jesus,' said Ryder. He'd been relying on that footage more than he had thought.

'Mm, not good, but the police artists have come up with this.' Broughton put a portrait of a woman on the desk. She was small-boned, her cheeks slightly sunken, her eyes rather too large for her face.

'She looks half-starved,' commented Ryder.

'Mmm. The boy at Shrewsbury says it's "quite like her".'

'He can't give us any more?'

'He's done his best. He's ten and hasn't slept all night.'

Ryder grunted. He considered the picture again. The woman looked less hard than the previous E-fit, more like an everyday person, the sort one might see in the street. But perhaps that was wishful thinking: the ARIC meeting was due to start in just over an hour.

'So, they're releasing this, and the false number plate?' he asked.

Broughton nodded.

Together the new face and the registration plate might jog a memory, Ryder thought. Of course, Helen might simply change plates, if she had spares, or change her vehicle, but she might, she just might, be flustered into making a mistake and thus draw attention to herself. He only hoped that the coverage wouldn't light the fuse of her group. But it would have been impossible to have muzzled the media on her activities, and, apart from its chief intention of identifying her, the coverage might stop her future operations, if she had any more planned.

'You've seen they've got a baby-food poisoner in the States?' asked Broughton mildly.

'Yes,' said Ryder.

'There was that group in Oregon, d'you remember, a few years back? They were into contaminating food.'

'Georgia's a long way from Oregon.'

'I know, but—'

'Look, Jack, until proven otherwise, we've got to assume it's us. Otherwise, if we take the heat off, we'll lose support and momentum, and leave the door open for the cult to press their button.'

'So you do think they're ours?'

Ryder was silent for a moment. Then he said, 'I've got to believe that for now. It's the only way I can work.'

There was a tap at the door and Lucy-Ann Burroughs looked in. She wondered if there was time before ARIC to give Ryder an update on the Carlucci situation?

'Well?' he said ungraciously.

She spoke swiftly. The friend with whom Carlucci had stayed the night knew nothing of her whereabouts. Every media organization had been issued with the D-notice. There had been some inquiries from editors, but no question, thus far, of anyone breaking the agreement. Every name in Jane's address book had been checked. She had spoken to no relative or friend before her disappearance; she was at none of the addresses listed.

'So where is she, then?' said Ryder, knowing that he was being unfair.

'We don't know at the moment, sir.'

'She's slipped through your fingers three times now, hasn't she?' He saw Burroughs grit her teeth. 'I want her found,' he said.

'Yes, sir, so do I.'

'What about her phones? Who's she been speaking to in the last few days?'

'The phone records have just come in.' Burroughs indicated a file she was carrying.

'Only just?' snapped Ryder.

She returned his glare steadily. 'I requested them yesterday, as you told me to, as a priority. But there are dozens of other priority commands at the moment, sir, as you're aware.'

Ryder grunted.

His red telephone rang. Broughton answered it, then passed over the receiver. 'The Israeli office, sir.'

A lead on who had stolen the swaddling-clothes, Ryder hoped, taking the receiver.

As he listened to the Israeli groom, he became aware that silence had fallen in the room, that Broughton and Burroughs were watching him.

His mouth felt dry. He heard himself telling the ARIC meeting the day before, that if they found the person who'd stolen the Scroll, they would ultimately find the guilty group. It was his own fault for being unkind to Burroughs, he thought irrationally.

The Israeli groom said that they'd found a witness to the theft who swore the thieves were English.

He'd been right never to succumb to the false hope that the group was foreign, Ryder thought bitterly.

'We can send you a transcript and a translation,' the groom went on.

Ryder wanted to be there in person. He wanted to be sure that the witness had remembered all that he could. 'I'd like to come over,' he said.

The Israeli prevaricated but gave in.

Leaving instructions with Broughton for ARIC, Ryder left by helicopter for a military airfield and a jet bound for Jerusalem.

The pre-dawn trip to the hypermarket had worked – Ned was asleep by the time Sally Goodall got home – but it had exhausted her. She managed to stay awake to make breakfast, but as soon as her husband left for work, she fell deeply asleep and didn't wake until she heard Ned crying.

Shocked, she saw that it was late morning. She'd meant to do a host of things that morning, not least tidy the house and take Ned swimming, and now everything would have to be rushed.

'It's all right,' she cooed, lifting him out of his cot, but his yelling intensified. 'You're hungry, aren't you?'

She took him down to the kitchen. Until recently, feeding him had been a matter of opening a jar and warming the contents, but with the spate of baby-food scares she no longer trusted any brand and puréed his food herself. She thanked heaven that there was some ready in the fridge.

She heated it quickly, got him into his high chair and began spooning it into him. He wanted to do it himself and she knew she ought to let him, but he made such a mess and took so long, and she was ravenously hungry herself.

'There's a good boy.' She got the last mouthful into him and allowed him the spoon as a reward. She turned to the bread-bin, intending to make a sandwich, but then realized she craved something hot.

The tins in the store-cupboard didn't inspire her and she wasn't sure, anyway, that processed macaroni cheese was good for her or the unborn baby. Then, like a godsend, she remembered her early-morning purchase.

She took out the Chicken Paprika. '"All things necessary for the busy mum-to-be",' she read aloud from the label. 'Well, that's me, isn't it, Ned?'

He babbled happily back at her, banging his spoon on his tray.

'Yep. Organic chicken. Organic yoghurt sauce. Only the best, the purest ingredients. "With all the extra vitamins and minerals that you need". And d'you know the best thing about it, Neddy? It only takes three minutes in the microwave.'

She removed the packaging and put it in the oven. Even cold, it looked good, she thought hungrily. She peered through the glass, willing it to hurry up and be done.

Ned's banging stopped. She looked round and saw that he too was intent on her meal's progress. 'Don't think you're having any,' she told him.

Immediately his face crumpled.

'Oh, Ned.' This was a new ploy of his, to get whatever she had. Sensing a momentary weakness, he opened his mouth in a howl.

'For goodness sake,' she said in exasperation. He increased the volume; she saw him watching her, making himself go bright red in the face. She knew she mustn't give in. Behind her, the oven pinged its bell, telling her the meal was ready. She took out the dish, tore open the sachet of sauce and poured it on, all the while trying to ignore the crescendo behind her, but she knew she'd get no peace until he had some.

'All right then.' She snatched his spoon, scooped up some creamy sauce, blew on it to cool it, and raised it to his lips.

'Satisfied?' she asked him crossly.

He gave her a victorious grin.

CHAPTER FIFTEEN

Ross wished he hadn't turned on the radio that morning. But he and Ruth had just finished making love again, and she had wondered aloud what the weather was going to be like.

They had caught the national headlines. Botulism Helen had been seen, the van's number taken, and a new picture of her was due to be released. Ruth sat bolt upright in bed, pushing him off.

She'd been glued to the television screen ever since, brushing aside his attempts to soothe her, to remind her that the plate was false; that they'd never be able to trace her to the Lodge.

After a while the new e-fit was shown.

'It's like me,' she whispered. He followed her eyes to the screen, and saw what she meant.

The new picture did look more like her. It captured her fragility, he thought, and the size and shape of her features really rather well.

'It'll be all right,' he promised. 'We'll be off back to the Fellowship tonight. You'll travel in the back of the van, just as we planned. No one will see you.'

'Leave me alone,' she whispered.

'I don't like to, my darling. Not while you're like this.' Chalk-white and shaky, he meant, curled up on the sofa, so small that she was almost lost in it.

'Why don't I make you some lunch? Some poached chicken, or something?'

'Go and do something useful,' she snapped. 'Go and paint the van.'

Silently, Ross obeyed. He went to the outhouse where the van was kept, removed the number plates, got out the spray-painter and the can of blue paint and began work.

He didn't blame her, he thought sadly, seeing a bit of white that he had missed on an offside wheel-arch. She was frightened; he was too. They mustn't find her. They wouldn't find her: he'd make sure of that.

Ruth was his baby, his precious love. She was so good, she could see no evil in others. The night before when he'd tried to warn her about that madman Norton, about how he'd threatened to turn her in, she'd put her finger on his lips, and said, 'No.' She wouldn't listen.

Tears came to his eyes. He hadn't realized until last night how much he'd missed their love-making; and this morning had been, if anything, better. He was renewed, awakened, whereas he had been dead before. It wasn't simply the love-making, although that was wonderful. It was the knowledge that she felt as he did: that they were one again.

He'd protect her with his life, he resolved: that day, that night, the next day at the Fellowship, and then on Saturday . . . His thoughts swam out of focus. He tried again. On Saturday . . .

He groaned aloud. On Saturday, unless he did something about it, Ruth was going to be exposed to the virus. The virus that he had dug out of the earth, brought back to life and nurtured until it was strong enough to go forth on its last terrible journey. He bit his thumb.

She was already in danger – in danger of being found, in danger from Norton – but he could protect her from both those perils. As for the virus, he could stop that too, if only she'd let him. He had to make her see there was another way. They didn't have to do what David wanted. The aerosols need never leave the Lodge; he could render them harmless. He and Ruth could stay there together, Ruth keeping out of sight until everyone had forgotten about her. There was enough food in the freezer to last them several weeks, and when that ran out he'd go and buy more. Until then, he thought, hugging himself, it would be just the two of them and their love. He'd disconnect the phones in case Norton called. Let the old bastard sweat, he vowed, let him find someone else to carry out his dirty work.

But she hero-worships Norton, warned a voice at the back of his mind. She thinks he's God on earth.

He heard a noise behind him, and whipped round.

Ruth stood in the doorway, a small dark figure against the bright sunlight.

'Angel?' He started towards her in alarm.

'They're saying I'm wicked, Ross! On the television. They're saying I want to hurt pregnant women.'

'Oh, my darling!' He took her in his arms. 'Of course you're not wicked.'

She sobbed into his chest. He felt his heart expand with joy. 'I'm going to look after you,' he promised.

'Are you?' Her voice was muffled.

He kissed the top of her head. He felt inspired.

'Yes, my darling. We're one again, aren't we? One flesh, that's what the Bible says, isn't it? And it says that once two are joined together, let no man tear them asunder, doesn't it?'

'Yes, Ross.' She nestled closer, like a kitten, he thought delightedly. He began to rock her.

'Just the two of us. No room for anyone else. Just you and me and our new life together, for always.'

'Oh yes,' she murmured dreamily.

'We'll stay here all summer and then in the autumn' – her body rocked in rhythm with his – 'we'll go away together, shall we? America, how about that? You've always said how much you loved America. Or Australia? No one would ever find us there. We can put the past behind us.'

'Oh Ross, it would be nice, wouldn't it?' she whispered.

'Not would be, my darling, going to be,' he promised.

He kissed her hair, her forehead, her thin cheek. Under his lips, he felt her grow still, the realization, he thought, of the truth sinking in. He held her tight, telling her with his body, as much as with his words, that it was true.

'I know, it's a lot to take in, darling,' he murmured. 'But we can do it. We've got those other passports, and no one's going to be looking for us by then. We're going to start again.'

'But Ross.' She pulled away. Her face was tear-stained, her eyes anxious. 'We can't.'

'We can,' he said, smiling. 'There's enough money to see us through for quite a while, and then I can get work.' A thought struck him. 'Ruth, if you like, we could have a baby! How about that? I know I'm a bit older than you'd have liked, but—'

'Ross, please don't.'

'Think of it, Ruthie! A little bit of us running around.'

'Ssh.' She put her finger on his lips. Her eyes were wet. 'You mustn't do this.'

'Do what?' he said, looking down at her, still smiling, still telling himself that he could bring her round; but there was fear inside him now, like a ghost, waiting.

'Imagine it can be any other way. It's my fault.'

'No!'

'It is.' Tears began to trickle from her eyes. 'I've been selfish. I thought you understood.'

'I do!' He seized her shoulders. 'I do! I love you!'

'And I love you.'

He released her abruptly, for he knew it was no good.

'I thought we were just having fun, a last fling,' she said.

He shuddered.

'I didn't realize that it would take you like this, knock you off course. Nothing's changed, Ross, don't you see?' She tried to make him look at her but he turned away.

'Oh Jesus,' she whispered, 'help me get through to him.'

Suddenly he knew that he could hate her. Love, he remembered, was close to hate.

'We are going to have a future together, darling, in heaven. We're going to make love together there that's going to make what we've had seem like, ooh I don't know' – she laughed lightly – 'a quick bang.'

He flinched but she didn't seem to notice.

'And I think rather than mess our heads up with any more of this earthly stuff, we'd better put it off for a bit. Just until we get to heaven.'

He did turn now to stare at her. Heaven, he thought: was she crazy? Did she really believe that such a place existed, and that if it did, they, after all they had done, would be allowed in? He'd always assumed that Norton had got her under his spell. Only that morning he'd rejoiced that finally her love for Ross had opened her eyes. Not a bit of it, though. No, what had been to him sublime had been to her no more than a diversion, and a poor, pale one at that.

'It would break David's heart, you see, Ross, if we didn't go ahead with things.'

David's heart. She was telling him she loved David more than him, that she'd toss his love aside in an instant, rather than hurt one of David's precious feelings. The knife twisted inside him. David had warned him of this, he remembered: that Ruth's first allegiance would always be to himself and that he, Ross, came second.

He knew then that he had lost her. But her eyes were shining with tears; her heart was breaking too.

'Oh Ruth,' he cried, bending to embrace her.

Poor, lost little Ruth and poor lost Ross, too, he thought piteously. They were bound together now and would remain so, whether or not they made love again. If she chose to continue on her present path, he would walk with her, unto death. Better death than life without her.

She put her arms his neck, and pressed her cheek to his. 'The Last Days were always going to be the hardest,' she murmured.

The bell buzzed twice in David's office. He had been waiting for that sound; he rose at once and went to open the green baize door. One of the boys stood there.

'Here's your parcel, David.'

It had come at last. He had known that it was only a matter of time; the Lord allowing one more little test, but still, he admitted the long hours of waiting had proved unexpectedly hard. Worldly doubts – what he termed 'Ross-style' fears – had crept in. If the packet didn't arrive; if the authorities had intercepted it; if Ruth had got caught; even, in his darkest hour, had he imagined his special closeness to the Lord all along, including His revelation concerning the Scroll?

He took the parcel reverently. It was professionally wrapped in corrugated brown cardboard and stamped, in red letters, 'Urgent Medical Supplies'.

The boy hesitated. 'You're not ill, are you, David?'

'No, bless you. I'm not ill.'

'Is there anything I can get you? Some tea? Or a sandwich?'

David shook his head. 'You're trying to make me fat!' Still smiling, he closed the door. He resisted the urge to tear open the package there and then. Instead, he took it to the chapel, where the box stood open on the altar, waiting.

. He had brought a pair of scissors. The binding tape was strong, and he had to saw at it rather than cut. The cardboard fell off, revealing a white metal box with a red cross in the centre. He opened the lid.

The contents were those found in any small first-aid kit: plasters, ointments and pain-killers, a sterile syringe, scissors, all neatly fitted into a compartmentalized tray. He lifted it out. Underneath, squashed in, were rolls of bandages, hygienically sealed in white paper. David took a deep breath and picked one up. With the care of a nervous surgeon, he slit open the top. The bandage inside was not hospital white but dirty brown, stained and yellowish. He pulled off the paper and with trembling fingers, unravelled it.

It was not whole. The longest piece was perhaps ten inches long, and it was so thin that through it he could see the flesh of his fingers. He raised the fragment to his nose, closed his eyes, and sniffed.

Beyond a faint mustiness, there was no scent, but David inhaled deeply. Christ the Babe's own body had been wrapped in this! His little arms and legs had been tightly bound to stop Him flailing, to give Him comfort. David touched either cheek with the cloth, then put it to his lips and kissed it. He was the closest man could come on earth to touching the body of God.

He slid to his knees. The Lord God who had made the mighty oceans and placed each star in the firmament, as many stars as there were grains of sand, had brought His own dear son's swaddling-clothes safely home.

The Lord had been watching over them. He had caused the removal to go off smoothly: the janitor to be slow and dull-witted; the thief to be skilful and quick.

'Come quickly, O Lord,' David whispered, his eyes fixed on the cross. 'Make perfect the work that You have started. Overlook my sinful doubts, which I know have caused you pain.'

He felt warmth invade him, a tingling sensation that hit his stomach first, doubling him up, then spread to his limbs, to his finger-tips and toes, washing over him.

'O, Lord!'

The Lord hit him again with love.

David laughed. He couldn't help it, the feeling was so supreme: intoxicating and invigorating, such a reaffirmation of their Oneness. He rolled on the floor, laughing, cradling the Holy cloth to him, holding it against his chest so that it wouldn't come to harm.

'Father, stop it, please!' he pleaded, because the feeling was almost too much, the pleasure too intense for his puny earthly frame to bear.

Fractionally the warmth retreated, although he knew it was still there inside him, the Lord's Holy Spirit kept in reluctant abeyance.

Wiping his eyes, he sat up. It seemed to him that the chapel was filled with special light, that everywhere he looked was brighter. He ran his fingers through his hair. 'Oh, that was good, Lord, ' he breathed. 'The best yet. Forgive me for ever doubting.' He stopped as he felt the Spirit stir again. He understood that he was risking another tickling if he continued on the 'forgiveness line'.

'All right, all right.' He unwrapped the other bandages. If anything, they were in poorer condition than the first but it hardly mattered: their physical existence wasn't going to be required for much longer. David wondered if the Lord would make them whole again, a thing of beauty, a shimmering exhibit in the heavenly museum of Jesus' years on earth, or whether they would simply be destroyed in the tumult of the world's end.

He took them over to the altar. For twelve years now, the box had held only one item, the sacred Scroll. He hoped that the Lord would preserve that, whatever He chose to do about the bandages.

He placed them next to the Scroll. The box was full now, as if it had been designed with its eventual contents in mind. As it probably had, he thought with a smile.

He closed the lid and returned to his office, to the task that had occupied him for most of the night: monitoring the news via computer and television. Most of the time the latter's sound was turned off. Only when there was an item of special interest did David restore the volume or create a still of what was on screen.

Nothing on the previous night's *Crimewatch* had alarmed him, but the 5 a.m. news about the maternity food recall had caught his attention, and the new e-fit of Ruth had given him pause. He'd frozen the image.

Though it was clearly not her, there was now a resemblance. It was a good job that her work in the world was over, he thought, that she'd be coming home tonight. No one at the Fellowship would see her, and even if they did it wouldn't matter. There were no televisions, radios or newspapers there. As for former members, over the last few years, there hadn't been many – he counted them on his fingers – and of them, how many would remember a woman who had rarely ventured outside David's private quarters, rarely even attended services?

Ruth had never liked the idea of the community, would have preferred just himself and her. His barnacle, he'd called her. Still, he thought, studying the face hard. He asked for the Lord's judgement. He felt himself receive it.

The face – Ruth – looked utterly different from the old Ruth. She had been chubby, dark and heavy-browed. Now she was a delicate creature, blonde, eyebrows plucked, big eyes in a sensitive face. She looked years younger, David thought with a smile. She was a different woman. No one would recognize her.

It said on the news that they had the van's registration number. That was all right. It had always been the plan that Ruth and Ross would use the Covent Garden number plates for the journey home. Eleven days on, no one had announced that number, David thought in satisfaction. He had been wrong to fret that a third false plate would have been a good idea – getting false plates wasn't easy; they had to protect their source. As ever, David told himself, the Lord had pre-planned everything.

Channel-hopping, he saw the shelves being cleared of baby food in America; the Americans referring to the similar British incidents and vice versa. That didn't worry him; in fact it was a good thing. Everything was coming together beautifully.

The TV screen showed flames sweeping across a hillside. He turned up the volume, and heard the announcer say that wildfire was continuing to lay waste large tracts of northern California: after four days, the flames were not yet under control, and whole towns were being evacuated.

'The people shall live in fear of the elements: of fire, sky, earth and water,' David murmured aloud.

It wasn't just the fires. The dreadful floods in India in the past week, the food contamination, the swaddling-clothes home at last.

There was no room left for doubt: to every sign that the Fellowship fulfilled, the Lord added of His bounty.

David knew at a deep level that the last sign, due to be carried out that night, would be perfectly fulfilled. As would the three special events planned, with the Lord's guidance, to divert the authorities' attention far from England, away from – the Lord forbid – the Fellowship.

The first of those events – David checked the time, allowing for the five hours' difference, was probably being set in motion even now. The second would follow within twenty-four hours and then the third. About that last event, the Lord still had to show him which of the two girls, Kirsten, or the Colchester runaway, He wanted to carry out the special task. The Lord would tell him in His own good time.

Kissing the air three times, once for the Father, and for the first incident, once for the Son and the second, and once for the Holy Spirit and the third, David let his eyelids close upon the vista of heaven laid out before him.

For a building that contained enough viruses to wipe out most of the population of the eastern seaboard of the United States, Jordan didn't think much of its security. Although there were guards on duty day and night inside the Veerholt Institute in Charleston, South Carolina, the small park right outside was open to the public.

At 6.30 a.m., Eastern time, when it was still not yet fully light, Jordan entered the park and made his way swiftly to the area nearest the side of the building. It was a swing-park, asphalted to cushion children's tumbles, nicely landscaped and planted with bushy shrubs. Under the largest shrub, Jordan left the device. Across the single lane road was the Institute, a mere fifty feet away, Jordan judged, well within range of the bomb's blast.

He had little doubt that it would detonate and wreak the damage required of it. As David had said, Jordan had only to do his best, and the Lord would make it perfect. Jordan smiled. He had ample evidence now of that simple truth.

His handiwork in the grocery stores in Atlanta the day before, jabbing at the packets of baby food with a needle, had been clumsy in the extreme and yet the Lord had protected him from capture.

More than that, He had ensured that several of the packets were sold before the tampering was discovered.

Then there had been the finding of a suitable house, the safe arrival of the others, the acquisition of the chemicals, and the device itself. David had told him before he left England that it was possible to buy anything in America, and although Jordan had privately entertained some doubts, so it had proved. The right-wing militia group whom he had been advised to approach had asked few questions; they presumed he shared their views; they had wanted, ultimately, only his money.

The Lord was with him! Who could go against him? Not the world, not the others, waiting obediently back at the house, praying for his safe return. Although Jordan did not presume for an instant to liken himself to David, he knew that in their eyes, he possessed a little of David's charisma; a little, too, of David's special relationship with the Lord.

He kissed the air in the way that David did, and felt, he was sure, the softest touch of reciprocal air upon his lips. The Lord's kiss that David so often talked about, he thought in wonder. The Lord showing that there was no need to be afraid, it wouldn't hurt.

In his hired car he drove to the airport. In seven hours he'd be reunited with the others in Vermont, and together they could begin the final preparations for taking leave of the Earth: they, his Followers, and he, their Keeper.

Being an old man, retired, a widower and childless, the Rector was used to spending a great deal of time on his own. He filled it doing the *Telegraph* crossword, replaying old bridge hands in his head, dozing and watching game-shows on television.

He woke up in front of it in time for the early-afternoon news. A distraught couple whose little girl had just died were begging a woman to give herself up.

The Rector frowned. There were such wicked people in the world those days, but to think that a woman had killed a child . . .

A face flashed up on the screen. A young woman – to the Rector those days, everyone seemed young – with very large eyes in a rather gaunt face. He stared. The face was vaguely familiar. It reminded him of . . . he struggled to make the match. Got it! She reminded him of his great-niece, Ruth. He stared again at the thin face. Ruth as she had been as a child of twelve, maybe thirteen. A strange, sad child, which was not remarkable, given that her parents had just been killed when their light aircraft crashed, leaving Ruth an orphan and their sole heir. The Rector and his wife had wanted to have her, but the will had dictated otherwise. Ruth had been sent off to boarding-school, becoming an occasional visitor during the holidays, less so as she had got older.

When had he last seen her, the Rector asked himself? Ten, twelve years before? She'd been so happy! A different girl. She'd filled out – rather too much, his wife had privately suggested – but the Rector had simply been glad at the change in her.

She'd become a Christian, she'd told them. A bit too evangelical for his taste, the Rector seemed to remember. She'd been about to go into the mission field. The Australian bush, rang a bell, he thought.

They'd lost touch. When his wife had died two years before, the Rector hadn't known how to contact Ruth.

He looked at the television again. The face had gone. In its place was a scientist standing in a laboratory.

The interviewer was saying: 'So the pre-cooked meals for pregnant women were contaminated not with botulism, as was originally assumed, but with listeria?'

'That is correct,' the scientist responded gravely. 'As I think most people are aware, listeria causes miscarriage in pregnant women.'

The Rector shuddered. It was listeria that had caused the miscarriage in his wife's sole pregnancy. Unwittingly she had eaten spoilt cheese.

'Professor,' the television presenter said to a bald man in glasses, 'what do you think is motivating Helen?'

'It's difficult to say without being able to examine her of course, but she seems to have a homicidal grudge against young children and pregnant women.'

The Rector blinked. They could not be talking of Ruth. Ruth would never do such an evil thing. Ruth had wanted to go forth and save the souls of little children, he recalled her saying so.

A vehicle registration number flashed up on the screen, confusing him, and then the woman's face again.

He stared at it once more, and a wave of relief ran over him. That wasn't Ruth. He couldn't even see the resemblance now. There was nothing similar at all. Helen was a skinny, demented creature; Ruth had been full of light, a big, buxom, lovely girl.

The Rector shook his head. He was being a silly old man, frightening himself like that, imagining things. Perhaps he ought to go to a day centre, as his doctor advised.

Chilled at the thought, he switched channels to a game show, and soon was nodding off again.

Stung by Ryder's bawling-out – in front of Jack Broughton, too – Lucy-Ann had retired to her desk in the main Bridegroom office, and to the study of Carlucci's telephone records for the previous ten days.

There were a lot of them, because Carlucci had access to five lines – four at work, and one at home. Lucy-Ann knew that many of the calls from the work numbers could have been made by other members of the department, so she concentrated first on Carlucci's direct line, immediately identifying Paul Ryder's call the week before. Also listed, as expected, was Carlucci's call to her friend in Tel Aviv. The next one was to a direct line at a newspaper, the *Correspondent*. She looked back to Tuesday's calls. The same number was listed as an incoming call on Tuesday afternoon.

In front of her, Lucy-Ann had the transcript of the call to Tel Aviv. Carlucci had been so spooked that she'd slammed the phone down. And then, four minutes later, at 09.41, she'd called someone on a newspaper?

Lucy-Ann didn't like failure, and she felt it keenly in the matter of Carlucci, with or without Ryder's censure. She called the safe-house where Nigel Eccles was being kept. Eccles knew the religious correspondent on the *Correspondent*, but claimed he had not spoken to him in months.

Another journalist, then, Lucy-Ann mused, with whom Carlucci had been in recent, repeated contact. She flicked back to the top page of the telephone records, and saw the last call made to Carlucci's work number, at 18.06 the previous night.

It was the same number, and she, Lucy-Ann, had taken the call. She remembered the man's voice – pleasant, classless – disappointed that Carlucci wasn't there but unwilling to leave a message.

Suspicious? wondered Lucy-Ann. Her stomach somersaulted.

Composing herself, she rang the number. After a long time, it was answered by an irritated female voice. 'Sam Ferryman's phone.'

Lucy-Ann made note of the name. 'Could I speak to Sam, please?' she asked.

'He's out at the moment.'

'At lunch or . . . ?'

'On a story. I dunno when he's expected back.'

The woman didn't offer to take a message. Lucy-Ann thanked her and rang off, then requested on her database all security service information on Sam Ferryman.

Because of the enormous demands being made on the system, it asked her to wait. A journalist, she thought in quiet satisfaction. Ryder's worst nightmare come true, and she had the power to prevent it.

CHAPTER SIXTEEN

The sky was overcast and the sea a sludgy, slow-moving brown as Sam drove along the front at Hastings.

Now that they were actually there, Jane could feel the nervousness jump inside her. She had never done anything like this before. She didn't know if she could carry it through. She'd said nothing to Sam. In fact, since hearing on the radio news that the pregnancy meals had been spiked with listeria, neither of them had spoken much.

They parked and made for the centre of town. Outside an amusement arcade, a party of bleak-looking tourists was climbing into a coach. Some teenagers hung about smoking, but even they looked dispirited. Jane and Sam emerged from an underpass into a pedestrianized shopping area. She was expecting they would have to ask for directions, but Sam said suddenly, 'There it is, up on the left.'

She saw a blue-painted shop, with large picture windows, and The King's Café inscribed in yellow above the door.

'Can we talk for a minute?' Sam asked.

She nodded.

He led her into a small side-street, into the doorway of a house there. 'Are you sure you want to do this?' he said.

'Please don't ask me that. Not now.'

His voice softened. 'You're scared, aren't you?'

'A bit. But I'm going to do it for all the reasons I've told you about. And I'd better get on with it before I lose my nerve.' She glanced back towards the main concourse.

'Look, you'd better give me my card back – in case you're searched.'

That hit her hard, but she saw the sense in it. She pulled out her wallet, and took from it his card, those of a couple of contacts, and her own small supply.

Sam pocketed them. 'I was thinking, you'd better memorize my direct-line number.'

It was fairly straightforward one. She realized she already knew it. 'Yes?'

'When I'm not at work, I'll hash all incoming calls through to either my mobile or my home. That way, you've only got one number to remember. Okay?'

'Okay.'

Sam was frowning. 'What's your story?'

Succinctly, she told him.

'Fine, keep it simple like that. Say as little as you can, and use your own Christian name. It's always hard to remember to respond to another one.'

She smiled at him. 'Thank you.'

'Oh, that's all right.' He gave a twisted grin. 'The regular good Samaritan, that's me.'

He looked both angry and troubled, she thought. Instinctively, she moved closer to him, raising her mouth to his. His lips were soft and warm, and she felt his arms come round her. She felt safe, cherished. She could stay there forever with him, she thought. She pulled away.

'You'd better go,' Sam said.

'Yes.'

'Ring me as soon as you can.'

'I will.'

'Take care of yourself.'

'Yes. You too.'

She walked away. She didn't look back, although she longed to; she had never felt so lonely in her life. When she reached the café, she saw several people seated at tables with yellow-checked cloths. She opened the door and stepped inside.

*

The high-security prison was less than five minutes' drive from the air-force base near Jerusalem. Ryder, easing himself out of the air-conditioned car that had met him at the airfield, was hit by the intense heat of the Israeli sun. He managed three deep lungfuls of air before being ushered into the cool interior of the building.

The Israeli groom and an interpreter were waiting for him. The groom looked cheerful, Ryder thought. No doubt he was relishing the fact that, with British guilt reaffirmed, Israel was in the clear.

To make the interview easier, the groom said, he was going to go next door so that the witness wouldn't know of his presence.

'How is he?' Ryder asked.

'Querulous,' the groom replied, with a fraction of malice.

Ryder put his file on the table, and sat down beside the interpreter. There was a tape-recorder on the table, an ashtray, three glasses of water. The clock on the wall showed 17.50. Ryder heard a door down the corridor open and shut, and then footsteps, young, brisk, booted ones, and slower, heavier, older ones.

A guard came in. He said something in Hebrew.

'The witness,' said the interpreter.

The janitor came in, shuffling his feet like a captive, although there were no restraints on him. He didn't look up, but when the guard tried to help him into a chair he pushed him away impatiently. He regarded Ryder through small, distrustful eyes. Then he began to speak in a high, complaining voice that almost drowned the interpreter's words.

He was eighty-seven years old. He'd already told them everything he knew. Now he didn't care what they did to him. He was a Palestinian who'd seen his land seized by the Jews, his sons imprisoned . . .

'Can we move this along?' Ryder asked the interpreter. The Israeli shrugged. 'Tell me,' Ryder said, locking eyes with the old man, 'what you saw that night?'

The janitor sighed. Then, staring down at the table-top between them, he began to speak.

Twelve years before, he'd been a night watchman guarding a shoe factory in Jerusalem, opposite a museum. It was cold that night. In his makeshift shelter by the main gate, he'd lit his stove, and the fumes had made him sleepy. At one in the morning, he'd been woken by a sound or a movement in the street. A man had passed by. The janitor hadn't moved. No one who didn't know he was there would have seen him.

The man was slim, of medium height and, he judged, about fifty years old. He was wearing dark clothing and was trying to be very quiet. He crossed the street to the museum and tilted his head back to look up. The janitor followed his line of sight. On the first floor, a window was open. A head emerged. The man in the street called softly – but in the cold, still night air, the janitor heard him clearly.

'It's all right,' the man said. 'Jump.'

'In English?' Ryder interrupted. 'You're sure?'

The old man looked pained. 'Sir, I know some English. He spoke like a British army officer,' he said with emphasis. 'The Queen's English.'

'All right. Thank you.'

The janitor looked thoughtful.

'And did he jump?' Ryder prompted. He wanted to know every detail.

The witness seemed to savour the question. 'That person did,' he agreed ruminatively.

'"That person"?' Ryder raised an eyebrow at the interpreter, who checked the phrase in Arabic.

'That's what I said.' The janitor gave a ghost of a smile. 'It was a woman, you see, sir, in the window.'

'A woman.' Ryder repeated, not betraying any of the emotion he felt. 'What can you remember about her?'

'She was young. Twenty, twenty-two.'

'Her shape? Colour of hair?'

The old man sighed again. 'I told the police years ago. They weren't interested. They didn't even write it down. Now it's so long ago. . .'

Ryder took from his file the latest e-fit of Helen, and slid it across the table. He knew it was a long shot, but he had nothing to lose. 'Did she look anything like this?' he asked.

The janitor frowned down at it in silence.

'All right.' Ryder reached out to retrieve the picture, but the old man wouldn't let go.

'I've got a good memory for faces,' he murmured.

Ryder became very still.

'They came back past me, you see. There was a light above the gates. He was in the shadow, but I saw her. I saw her face.'

'Yes?' asked Ryder, hardly daring to breathe.

The janitor was still staring down at the e-fit. 'She wasn't thin like this one. But there is a likeness. Her eyes were like this: big, wide-set. Dark eyes, just like my daughter's.'

A large woman who had become very thin, Ryder thought. Could the thinness be part of her disguise?

'Is there anything else?' he asked.

The janitor looked up. 'The man called her by her name,' he said softly.

Ryder's heart skipped a beat.

'It was a name from the Bible. Rebecca? Rachel?' The old man frowned with effort. He shook his head. 'I can't remember.'

Ryder knew he'd got everything the janitor knew. He thanked him sincerely and the guard led him away.

The Israeli groom re-entered at once, earnestly protesting that the old man had divulged to him not a tenth of what he'd told Ryder.

'It doesn't matter,' Ryder said sincerely. 'What matters is that we've got it now. Is there a room I can use?'

He was shown into a side-office. He rang Broughton in London and told him to check the cult databases for a woman aged between thirty and forty with a Biblical first name that began with R. Additionally, within the same group, a well-spoken man in his sixties.

'Worth the trip, then?' asked Broughton.

'Let's hope so. Anything interesting come up?'

With the remaining two priority cults under guard, a small team in Vauxhall had been assigned the task of combing all relevant databases for any Scroll indicators within the UK's remaining NRMs.

'Nothing so far. I mean, some of them are pretty weird.'

'Sure,' said Ryder impatiently. He hadn't time to listen to tales about the strangeness of cults. He asked for updates on Carlucci and Helen.

'Burroughs thinks a journalist may be involved with Carlucci,' Broughton said, and Ryder closed his eyes.

'Who?' he asked.

Broughton told him, adding that Ferryman had 'form' – that his work had brought him to the attention of the security services fairly regularly over the past few years.

'Perfect,' said Ryder bitterly. He felt a moment's envy of the Israelis. They could simply lift a journalist from the streets and carry on, unmolested by the rest of the media pack.

'Do we know what he knows?' he asked Broughton.

'No. But apparently he's on a cult-special.'

'Jesus.' Ryder rubbed his head. 'Who have we got on the *Correspondent?*'

'A newsdesk secretary. But that's all she's been able to find out. If he has got a lead from Carlucci,' Broughton went on, 'wouldn't the D-notice cover it?'

'Not if he doesn't admit her as his source,' Ryder retorted.

'Can't we issue another D-notice that would cover it?'

'Exactly how would you word it, Jack?' he asked acidly. '"The MOD requests that there be no coverage of cults in Britain"? If you were planning to flag what we're doing, you couldn't do a better job.'

'Sorry,' said Broughton shortly.

Ryder gave himself a mental shake. If he carried on like this, he told himself, soon none of his staff would be talking to him.

'Burroughs had better have a discreet word with Ferryman, as soon as she can,' he suggested in a more conciliatory tone. 'And we'd better get taps on his lines.'

'We might have a problem there,' Broughton said. 'He's got a loop on his work number.'

Ryder grimaced. Of course a journalist like that would have such a device installed, he thought. Loops were ultra-sensitive electronic ears, available from some of the London spy-shops, which could be fitted to any telephone line. They gave warning by a series of clicks if there was a listener on the line.

'His home number, then,' Ryder said heavily.

'Will do.' Regarding Helen, Broughton said, there'd been a record number of calls – twenty-four thousand – to the police and *Crimewatch*. Among those that might be of genuine interest was one from a landlady in Colindale, north London, who was sure that a woman answering Helen's description had rented two rooms from her in March, one for herself, and one for her brother, who had worked at the nearby Public Health Laboratories.

'That's them,' exclaimed Ryder. 'That's where they got their bugs!'

Broughton agreed that it seemed likely. Colindale had been approached. They admitted that a washer-upper had walked out after two weeks, but said there was nothing unusual in that. Such people were always leaving, and nothing had been taken.

'I bet,' said Ryder. 'What about the landlady?'

'Says she hardly saw the boy, and the woman only a couple of times. Said she was weird, stayed in her room all day, didn't use the kitchen. They only stayed two weeks. Left one Saturday morning.'

'They paid cash, I presume,' said Ryder.

'Correct. She, Helen, also paid cash at a petrol station on the M6 just north of Birmingham on Tuesday evening.'

When she was on her way home from the Fruit Fest, Ryder realized. 'Any picture of her?'

'Sorry. A good one of the van, though. That's how they knew it was her.'

They didn't need a picture of the bloody van, Ryder thought. 'Which way was she heading?'

'North.'

That led them nowhere. She could have been on her way to Wales, or the next junction, or off to the north on the M1. He asked about her victims.

There was better news on the botulism children, Broughton told him. All but six had now been released from hospital. But four pregnant women were in hospital with suspected listeria poisoning. It was too soon to know if they would lose their babies.

What a sick-minded, callous bitch Helen was, Ryder said to himself. 'The Saudi murder hunt?' he asked aloud.

'Nothing new.'

No, Ryder thought. If there had been going to be a break on that, it would have come weeks before. He ended the call.

Within a minute, the Israeli groom came back into the room, making Ryder wonder if he'd been listening – not that Ryder cared if he had.

'I thought perhaps you'd like to go to the Baby Jesus Sanctuary in Bethlehem,' the groom suggested, 'where the swaddling-clothes were kept before they were stolen.'

He didn't have time for sightseeing, Ryder thought. Thanking the groom for his help and hospitality, he returned to the air base, where his jet was waiting, to take him back to London.

*

From his pushchair, Ned energetically hurled the last of the breadcrumbs in the general direction of the ducks. Not much reached them, but they didn't seem to mind. In a flurry of quacking, they raced after the specks on the pond's surface.

Sally looked regretfully at her watch. It was four o'clock.

'Time to be getting back to the grindstone?' her friend, also with pushchair, asked.

'You said it.'

Together, they wheeled their children back through the park; Sally, aware of how much awaited her to do at home, kept the pace brisk. At the gates they parted and she was able to speed up until, coming into her road, she was almost trotting.

Once inside the house, she got Ned out of his buggy and into his swing-chair in the kitchen before he had a chance to escape. He gave her a hurt glance – clearly he'd been intending to go crawling – but she hardened her heart.

'You stay here and talk to me,' she told him and began stacking dishes in the sink. While she waited for the sink to fill, she raced around putting things away. Ned, prepared to be entertained, watched her as he swung to and fro.

'Your daddy,' she informed him, 'thinks I've got it easy. That he's the one hard at work all day.'

Ned caught her eye. He waved his hands about and chuckled.

'Mm, you think it's funny, do you?'

She switched on the radio and began to sweep the kitchen floor. She saw that Ned was beginning to be lulled to sleep by the swing, and moved out quietly into the hall.

The news came on: she heard it in fits and starts as she moved about the sitting-room, picking up Ned's toys. A name she recognized caught her attention and she went back into the kitchen to listen.

'A spokeswoman for the company said that, as a precaution, all Great Expectations products were being recalled.'

A coldness seized her. In slow motion, she went over to the bin, bent down and rummaged in it.

The presenter said, 'Although there have so far been no confirmed cases of listeria poisoning, the company is urging anyone who has eaten their pre-packed meals for pregnant women in the last few days to seek medical attention at once.'

The cardboard sleeve from her lunch was at the very bottom of the bin. She withdrew it. The name was emblazoned clearly on the front. She could feel her eyes sticking wide open in shock.

The room swayed before her, there was a booming echo in her ears, but she told herself that she mustn't faint, that she had to look after Ned. She put out a hand to steady herself and lurched over to the phone.

The surgery number was continually engaged, although she tried it again and again. Her whimpering woke Ned. He gazed up at her disapprovingly, and when she bent to touch his forehead, he felt hot. She'd poisoned him, she thought. Her hand slid down to her stomach: both her babies.

She dialled 999, and screamed that she needed an ambulance. Then, with the phone still in her hand, she slid down the wall because, quite suddenly, her legs would no longer support her.

Jane bought herself a cup of coffee and took it to a small table close to the back of the café.

There were two Fellowshippers – easily identifiable in their blue denim – a man and a women, behind the counter. They obviously had good relationships with their regular customers, exchanging pleasant banter with some of them.

There was no attempt at conversion, no mention of God or Christianity that Jane could hear. Even the posters on the walls were of the 'Tomorrow is the first day of the rest of your life' variety, and not overtly religious. The Fellowship clearly played it very low-key. An hour passed. Jane sat, waiting. She could not make an approach.

Eventually the woman behind the counter came over. 'Can we get you anything to eat?' she asked with a smile. She had an Australian accent.

Jane had never felt less like eating in her life. But recalling to mind her persona: a young woman in despair, on the run from a wretched home-life, she asked what there was.

'Well, we've still got some of today's special left from lunchtime, cauliflower cheese and sweet potato. Or there's salmon?'

Jane tried to look as if she was pondering the choice.

'We knock the prices down now it's five o'clock,' the woman cajoled. 'We could do you the special for a pound.'

They thought she was short of money, Jane realized, which was good, in keeping with her role. 'All right then,' she conceded.

'I'll bring it over to you.'

While she waited, Jane prepared for the approach she felt sure would come with the food. She remembered Sam's advice to keep her story simple.

'Here you are, and I brought you a knife and fork myself, seeing you're our last customer.'

Jane saw that that was true. Only one other table was occupied, and the couple there were on the point of leaving. The Fellow-shipper must have been waiting for the café to clear, she thought.

'Eat it while it's hot,' the woman advised, before retreating behind the counter again.

Nervously, Jane put a forkful into her mouth. In her current state, it tasted like cardboard, but she realized suddenly that she was hungry. She finished the food. The couple at the other table had left the shop some time ago, but no one came near her.

Behind her, in the kitchen, she heard washing-up in progress: hot water hissing and the clatter of cutlery. She could leave, she thought, and the Fellowshippers wouldn't see her go. Perhaps that was their intention, to give her a free meal without being seen to do so, as might be expected of genuinely good Christians? Would she have to return many times before they made an approach? How long would that take?

Or perhaps they didn't recruit there, although Kirsten had told Sam they did. Or was it Jane herself? she wondered. Did she look so obviously a fake?

'Stay as long as you like,' the Australian woman said, reappearing from behind the counter and making Jane jump.

'Sorry, I didn't mean to startle you. What a nice clean plate.'

'I was hungry,' Jane said.

'Oh?'

The first indication of concern, Jane thought in relief.

'Let me take your plate.'

'Thank you. Here's the pound.' Jane proffered a coin.

'Oh, thanks. Would you like another coffee?'

Jane shook her head.

'Is there anything else I can get you?'

'No, thanks.'

The woman bore off her plate, then came back out with the man who had been behind the counter. They began washing the tables. The man turned the 'Open' sign on the door to 'Closed'.

'I'd better go,' Jane suggested, taking a risk.

'Don't if you don't want to. If you need to sit, sit,' said the woman, and the man turned to smile at her.

Jane fiddled with her ring. It was one that her mother had given her.

'D'you live in Hastings?' the man asked as he upturned a chair on top of a table.

'No.'

'On holiday, then?'

'Martin!' exclaimed the woman. 'Leave the girl in peace.'

'I'm not on holiday,' Jane said. 'I'm . . .' She stopped.

'Oh,' said Martin.

Jane didn't look at either of them but she knew she had caught their interest. She stared down at the checked tablecloth. The yellow and white squares melted into a blur before her eyes.

'Don't mind me asking, but are you all right?' asked the woman concernedly.

'What?' Jane let her voice fade. 'Yes, I suppose I am.' She shook her head, as though gathering her wits. 'Someone said Hastings is a cheap place to stay. I need a bedsit. D'you know of anywhere good?'

'There are lots of places but I don't know I'd recommend any.'

'Oh.' Jane packed a lot into that one word: disappointment, resignation, hopelessness. She caught a fleeting exchange of looks by the Fellowshippers.

'If you like,' the woman said carefully, 'you could stay the night at our community.'

'Community?' Jane repeated.

'Yes. It's about half an hour from here, in a village.'

'What sort of community?' Jane asked suspiciously.

'Well, Christian, but don't let that put you off,' the woman said with a laugh. 'We're not Bible-bashers or anything, in fact, we don't go in much for Bible study. I take it you're not a church-goer, then?'

'No way.'

The woman said lightly, 'Well, it's up to you. If you'd like to come back with us, you're welcome. We'll drop you off here tomorrow morning, or you can stay with us longer if you like.'

It was one of the most laid-back evangelical approaches Jane had ever come across. She began to see why the Fellowship had never been designated an NRM. Was she wasting her time? Was the Scroll being fulfilled elsewhere? But she had her reasons for going there. She looked up. Martin and the woman were both watching her.

'All right,' she said with a show of slight reluctance. 'I'll come.'

'Great,' said Martin.

'How much is it?'

'It's free. I'm Abby, by the way,' and the woman offered her hand.

'Jane,' said Jane, remembering more of Sam's advice.

'We'll be another hour or so here and then we'll be on our way. Okay?'

'Okay. You want me to help you with the tables?'

'That's sweet of you, but don't worry. You look all-in.'

'I am a bit,' Jane admitted.

'Just you sit there, then.'

Jane did as she was told.

After Jane had gone, Sam had found a vantage-point in a shop doorway from where he could watch the café without being seen. He didn't know what he expected to see.

Time passed. Since Jane had gone in, he'd caught not a glimpse of her; merely people eating at the tables in the window and then, when they'd all left, a man in jeans and a denim shirt – a Fellowshipper, he realized – turning the sign on the door from 'Open' to 'Closed'.

Sam wondered what to do. He couldn't go and leave Jane there without knowing what was happening. During his wait, he had made short sorties to buy himself a sandwich and a newspaper but he didn't dare be away for long.

One or two passers-by glanced at him but he was well-dressed and not begging, and no one challenged him.

He'd had plenty of experience at 'doorstepping' – standing around outside people's homes, waiting to speak to them. It was generally exceptionally boring, but not this time, he found. Nervous energy sustained him.

The strength of his feelings for Jane had taken him by surprise. On meeting her the day before, he'd thought her attractive but his attention had been diverted by her extraordinary story. But the D-notice had made him angry, in a personal way, as if someone he cared for had been harmed. And then her kiss before leaving him.

The sweet smell of her, the softness of her lips, his desire for her, and his wish that she needn't put herself through this.

But he couldn't manacle her to him. And she was an expert, he reassured himself. No one could be better protected against a cult's pressures than Jane. She wasn't a kid like Kirsten.

But, like Kirsten, Jane knew nothing about being undercover. Her knowledge was academic, not practical. He agreed with what she was doing; he admired her for it. But if the Fellowship was responsible for child-murder, what would they do if they discovered an enemy in their midst? What had they done to Kirsten?

He looked at his watch. It was six o'clock. He'd been standing there for two hours; no wonder his legs ached. A movement caught his eye and he glanced up. The café's door was opening. A man and then two women emerged. One of the women was Jane.

Sam stepped back into the doorway but none of them looked in his direction. They walked off, Jane in the middle, towards the older part of town.

Sam stared after them until they disappeared. She was all right, he told himself. She was clearly not being forced to go with them, and she'd been talking to the other woman in what looked like a natural way. He felt useless and empty. Pulling out his mobile, he dialled the newsdesk.

He'd called in several times during the afternoon, with fictitious reports on the progress of his cult-special. This time he told Monica that the Deacon he needed to speak to would be away until the next day.

Monica was sympathetic but harassed. The paper had been inundated with Helen sightings from all over the country, she told him. They were running it big, with the new e-fit on the front page alongside the story about the dead child in Birmingham, and an exclusive interview with Helen's former landlady on page three.

'Looks like one pregnant women has miscarried and loads more are turning up at casualty departments. Maybe we should rename Helen, huh? Call her Listeria Liz?'

Sam winced.

'Why not call it a day?' Monica suggested.

'I'll do that.' Sam said, wishing he could. Cheerlessly, he returned to his car.

*

Normally, on Thursday evenings before supper one of the Fellowshippers washed David's feet – in the tradition of Mary Magdalene – but that evening when David was asked whose turn it was, he shook his head and took the bowl himself.

On this, the last Thursday, he considered it was right that he should perform the task. He knelt before a boy seated on a bench in the dining-hall and slipped off the deck-shoes that so many of them, like himself, wore.

'David, no! Let me.'

David removed the restraining hand. He washed each dirty, trembling foot and patted them dry with a towel, before moving on to the next person. He knew that every eye in that silent room was upon him, but they did not understand the significance of the ritual: that he was mirroring Christ Himself washing the disciples' feet at the Last Supper.

'I am become your servant,' he explained to the gathering, and watched them try to understand. It was no use, he told himself a little sadly. It was not their fault. Was it not he who had chosen to keep them in a state of Holy Innocence? Uncorrupted by potentially false readings of the Scriptures? He smiled, and they relaxed, happy children again, content that he should be their conduit to Jesus.

They were so precious to him, every one. All those present and the others, on their way home from work in the farm-shops and the café, and the special ones, that brave little band in America, so far away and yet, in his thoughts, so very near now.

He prayed to God that when the moment came they would obey Jordan, a good man and a useful one, made perfect by the Lord out of such unlikely earthly material. He prayed, too, that all would go well in South Carolina the next day.

He knelt before a girl. As he washed her small feet, he prayed for the daughter who was to go from the Fellowship in the morning, completing the final link of the triangle. At lunchtime, the Lord had at last revealed to him which of the two girls it was to be. 'Not that one, my son, but this. She looks rather like Ruth does now, don't you see?' As soon as the words were uttered by the Spirit, David had seen that, as always, the choice was perfect, the only one that could have been made.

Everything would go like clockwork: the last Scroll sign, and then the other three things.

'David?'

He opened his eyes and saw a worried face staring down at him. 'I'm fine, dear child.'

He moved along the pew. As he patted dry one more pair of feet, he looked up and saw that the boy was crying. With his thumb, David brushed away the tears. He smiled: there would be no tears in heaven.

The house was deep in the Vermont countryside, set well back from the road and hidden from it by trees. By the back porch, beside a pond, was an old-fashioned swing suspended from a heavy bough which was white with blossom. Jordan knew David would have loved it. He was only sorry that he wouldn't have a chance to show it to him.

He gazed at the dear faces of those before him – his ten followers, five men and five girls, whose joy on his return from South Carolina had warmed his heart.

They were good children, he thought, and smiled, realizing that he now regarded them in the way that David did: as children to be loved and guided, to be protected against too much harmful knowledge, to be given straightforward tasks, simple orders.

'Did you get the material?' he asked one of the girls.

'Yes, Jordan. It's out in the hall.'

They took him to look at it. Twenty rolls of purple cloth, twenty of black, and twelve of gold.

'Did they ask why you wanted it?' he asked.

'Yes. I said it was for a play.'

'Good girl. And the candles?'

They were stacked in boxes: two hundred of them.

'Excellent. We've got the whole house to do, so let's get started. If you girls will tackle the bedrooms at the back?'

He allocated three of the four reception rooms to the men. The fourth, at the back of the house, overlooking a small meadow, he reserved for himself. He knew where the long, low table was going to stand, where and how the others would sit, in a semi-circle, as David had suggested.

He closed the shutters at the windows, and turned on the light. He saw that it was 2 p.m., Eastern time. He took out the script David had given him, and read it into the small tape-recorder David had told him to buy. First thing in the morning, he would connect the recorder to the phone, pre-dialling the number David had given him, and setting the timer to ring that number the following afternoon. By then, Jordan thought, he and the others . . .

He stopped himself. He went out into the hall and fetched the gold cloth. Upstairs, the girls were singing as they hung their black drapery. Smiling, Jordan got down to his own refurbishment work.

CHAPTER SEVENTEEN

The Italian Adriatic coast was directly below Ryder's window in the jet when Broughton came on the line to tell him that Beck had arranged a conference call with senior ARIC personnel in ten minutes.

The call duly came. The other participants included the brigadier and the Number Ten representative, who again chaired the discussion. Their voices came through clearly on Ryder's headset.

Broughton was asked to supply the latest information, most of which he had faxed to Ryder within the previous half-hour.

'There are six female names beginning with the letter R in the Bible: Rachel, Ruth, Rebecca, Rhoda, Rahab and Rizbah. Computer records show that we have one Rachel, who's the leader of the Devon-based Christian Solstice group.'

'Is it her?' demanded the brigadier.

'It looks unlikely,' Broughton said diplomatically. 'Her group consists of her brother and sister-in-law.'

'Why the hell mention her, then?' the man growled.

Wisely Broughton let that pass. 'Membership lists show that we have twenty-nine Rachels; forty-one Ruths; thirty-five Rebeccas and eight Rhodas in one hundred and four NRMs. No Rahabs or Rizbahs.'

No one commented.

Ryder said, 'I take it those are the current names only, Jack?'

Broughton concurred.

'So, we haven't started going backwards yet,' Ryder went on, 'and we have to bear in mind also that many of the cults don't record membership details on principle.'

'That is good news,' said Beck drily. 'What about the groups we've got under guard, Broughton? Are any of these women in them?'

'There's a Rachel and a Rebecca in the first, and two Ruths in the second,' said Broughton.

'Each of them had better be re-interviewed, just in case,' Ryder told him.

Broughton said it would be done.

'So if she exists,' the chairwoman said slowly, 'you think it's more likely she's in one of the remaining cults?'

'More likely, yes,' Ryder admitted cautiously.

'But not necessarily,' put in Beck. 'She and her fellow accomplice could be a one-off, nothing to do with an NRM at all. Or perhaps they were stealing to order, or they were religious mercenaries.'

There was silence on the lines.

'I don't think we can risk going down that route,' said chairwoman decisively, and Ryder blessed her.

'We've got to work on the premise that this is the couple we're looking for until it's proved otherwise. Don't you agree, Mr Ryder?'

'I do,' Ryder said.

'What about the man?' interjected Beck.

Once more, Broughton supplied the data: 'We've fed his approximate age into the databases and it appears there are only thirty-seven males between the ages of fifty-five and seventy in our cults, five of whom are members of groups which also contain a Rachel or a Ruth.'

'That sounds more hopeful,' commented the chairwoman.

'I understand those groups are being looked at now?' Ryder prompted, and Broughton agreed.

'How long will that take?' she asked.

'It depends on what comes up,' Ryder said reasonably.

'Yes, of course.' She paused. 'I don't think I can overestimate the seriousness of our position. We are facing huge external pressure, both from the Bridegroom organization and from other govern-ments to find this group, or persons responsible, fast, in case whatever they are planning has global impact.'

Ryder tentatively supplied his own worst solution: 'We could detain every cult we have.'

'We could,' she agreed. 'But the logistics of doing so, as well as the implications regarding infringements of civil liberty, would be an enormous problem.'

Ryder perceived that such an idea had been mooted and had not met with Cabinet approval. He was glad.

'I was wondering if now might be the time to spread our net wider, as regards religious groups?' he said.

'What d'you mean?' asked the chairwoman, and Beck echoed her question.

Ryder thought fast – the idea had only just occurred to him. 'Only that nothing seems to be coming up on our known cults. Because we are so short of time, potentially, I wondered if we could ask the various churches for some discreet help? Without telling them why, of course. And local police collators? Clearly, anything major would have come to our attention by now, but perhaps a church-goer has caused concern locally with his views.'

'Good idea,' said the chairwoman.

'You're asking a lot of the churches not to say anything,' warned Beck. 'Nosey lot, vicars and their congregations.'

'It could be done tactfully, as Mr Ryder suggested,' the chairwoman insisted. 'Could the Bridegroom office activate both suggestions, Mr Ryder?'

More work for his team, Ryder thought. Aloud, he said it would be done.

'The public is responding extremely well to the Helen appeal,' she went on. 'Nearly twenty-five thousand calls at the last reckoning, I understand.'

'But they're not leading anywhere are they?' slid in Beck.

'It's a little too early to make such a statement, I believe,' she said frostily.

'I thought we didn't have much time,' retorted Beck.

She didn't rise to the bait again.

Via Broughton, Ryder had already sent a briefing fax on his interview with the janitor. 'We could issue a third e-fit of Helen,' he proposed now, carefully. 'One showing her with a fuller face.'

'I think that might be too confusing,' said the chairwoman

worriedly. 'The new e-fit only went out today, and it's provoked such a huge response. I think it might be better to leave it one more day.'

'I agree,' said Beck instantly.

'At least this Helen hunt is keeping the public occupied,' said the brigadier. 'No one seems aware of the Global.' He sounded slightly disappointed, Ryder thought.

'No, thank God,' said the chairwoman. 'The public, and more importantly the media, seem not to have noticed.'

'What about the baby-food contamination in the States?' inquired the Brigadier.

Ryder jumped in nimbly: 'I really don't think we can let that put us off our stroke. Apart from the janitor's evidence, I suggest there's just too much going on at home – for instance the listeria contamination, a perfect fulfilment of the until now unfulfilled part of the fourth sign in the Scroll – for us not to believe that the cult is ours.'

There was silence as that sank in.

'No news of your lost academic, I take it, Ryder?' Beck asked brightly.

Silently, Ryder cursed him. He didn't want to divulge Burroughs's suspicions of Carlucci's link to a journalist. Ferryman had not reappeared all day. 'I'm afraid not,' he replied regretfully.

'It's most unfortunate she's still at large,' said the chairwoman. 'Let's just hope she turns up or stays quiet.'

Ryder hoped so too. There were a few more comments and the call came to an end.

Ryder leant back against his head-rest. He was desperately tired.

'Didn't go too badly,' said Broughton – Ryder hadn't realized he was still on the line.

Guardedly, he agreed.

'Just before it, I took a call from the Boston groom office. They think the group's theirs.'

'Why?' Ryder frowned. 'Because of the baby-food stuff?'

'That and the California fires. Hundreds evacuated. People fleeing in terror. Fulfilment of sign . . .' he hesitated.

'Six,' supplied Ryder. He sighed. 'The Yanks know about the janitor saying the thieves were English?'

'Yup. It went out on the grapevine round about the time you

heard it, I would say. Boston says an old Palestinian man might not be able to distinguish between English and American.'

'He said the suspect spoke like a British army officer,' Ryder said. 'But, hey, if the group's American, I'm not complaining. Have they got any suspects?'

'Hundreds.'

'Yes, they would.' He cut Broughton off and abruptly fell asleep.

Werner Lindroth liked to think of himself as a mercenary. He felt the name had romantic and exciting connotations – 'soldier of fortune', 'gun for hire' – that it masked the grimmer aspects of his work. In thinking that, he was referring not to the results of his handiwork – dead and maimed people, wrecked lives – but to the tedium and often downright unpleasantness associated with some of the roles he had to assume.

He'd been a lavatory-cleaner, a waiter, a bodyguard. Sometimes, when the bomb went off, his first thought had been not of having successfully eliminated the client's target, but of having killed a vicious supervisor, a petty colleague, a sneering boss. His second thought was always the money.

As a freelance bomber, Lindroth earned a great deal of money, which in a twenty-five-year career, had enabled him to buy several hideaways in friendly states and, twice, his freedom. He had always evaded capture in the West, however. There, not only would it be far more difficult to buy himself out of trouble, but in many countries, he was now a wanted man. There were loose ends that might trip him up. The risks of working in Europe again were too great.

And then, six months before, he'd been contacted. The money was the most he'd ever been offered, but the target was in Europe: Vienna.

Lindroth had debated within himself. He knew the risks, but he also knew he was a professional at the height of his powers; he wouldn't get caught. And the money. With that amount, he could afford to retire. He was nearly fifty, and he'd always said that was when a wise man stopped, when he tidied up any loose ends.

He'd been in Vienna, undetected, for three months now. His job as a catering assistant was menial in the extreme; his supervisor a mean-spirited fellow, who unfortunately would be off-duty that night.

It was 20.21. Lindroth wheeled the supper trolley out of the kitchens towards the main meeting-hall at the rear of the building. When he arrived, he saw the delegates emerging for the break which allowed the caterers to bring in their supper.

Inside the room, Lindroth worked quickly, throwing a large white cloth over a side-table, setting out plates and cutlery, platters of sandwiches and pastries, with an extra box of the latter because they were so popular. His trolley empty, he left the room and hurried back to the kitchens; he was just in time to catch a lift back into the city with the rest of his shift.

As the last security barrier was lowered behind him, he glanced at his watch: it was 20.35.

In the meeting-room some of the hungrier delegates began to surge back for their supper. They noticed with greedy pleasure that tonight there was an extra box of pastries on the table.

The sun was shining out of a perfectly blue evening sky as the minibus carrying Jane pulled up the hill into the Moor.

There was a beautiful Elizabethan manor house, criss-crossed with ancient timbers; a duckpond with fat white ducks upon it, and thatched cottages grouped round a village green. It was picture-postcard perfect, she thought. Near the manor there was a medieval sandstone church with a square clock tower. It was ten past eight.

A door opened in a building next to the church, and a tide of Fellowshippers surged out.

'That's early supper over,' said Abby. 'We have a barbecue later on.'

'The best,' added Martin, who was driving.

Jane smiled wanly. Throughout the journey, she'd kept communication to a minimum. She wanted to appear subdued, and neither Martin or Abby had pressed her to be otherwise.

They parked in front of a cottage. Even the white picket fence that ran round it looked freshly painted, Jane thought, as she slid out after Abby. She felt as if she was stepping into a film-set.

They walked back towards the green. A lot of Fellowshippers stood chatting there, or lay sprawling on the grass. Several were barefoot, holding their shoes. She did a rough count: about ninety. They looked relaxed and carefree. No immediate evidence of brain-washing or coercion, Jane thought, or guilty consciences.

Heads turned as they passed, and several people smiled, but no one stared at her, an obvious stranger in their midst.

'I'll take you over to my cottage. We've got a spare room there,' Abby volunteered.

'Thank you,' Jane said. As she walked, she searched casually for a glimpse of the red-haired nineteen-year-old Kirsten that Sam had described. She could see no such person; no sign either, she told herself, of a woman looking like the e-fit picture of Helen that she'd seen. In fact, no one fitted Helen's age-range. Most people seemed in their late teens and twenties.

'Abby!' A woman came up eagerly. 'You missed David washing – Who's this?'

Abby made the introductions. Jane learnt that the woman's name was Mary.

She caught Jane's hands in her own. 'Jane, I'm so pleased to meet you,' and from the joyfulness of her expression, indeed she seemed to be. A classic example of love-bombing, Jane told herself, when a newcomer was saturated with love and attention to make her feel important and special to the group. Or was she being unfair? Was she imposing her suspicions on a friendly greeting?

'You are staying?' Mary asked hopefully.

'For the night,' Abby said firmly. 'We'll probably be taking her back to Hastings in the morning.'

'Oh, but . . .' Mary's eyes moved past Jane. Following her gaze, Jane saw a white-haired man approaching.

David Norton, she thought, and her heart jumped into her mouth.

She guessed him to be about sixty, a tall man who moved with the lithe grace of a much younger person. His face was deeply lined but tanned and vigorous. With his short white hair and in his blue denim, he looked American.

He made straight for her. 'Hullo,' he said, and held out his hand.

He had the most amazing eyes. They were a soft aquamarine blue. They compelled her to look at him, and as she looked they became misty. She experienced the oddest sensation: that he knew her; who she was and why she was there. She shook herself. If she was right about him, he was a clever, evil man who had been responsible for killing children.

'Hullo,' she said cautiously, and took his hand. It was dry and cold, with very long, thin fingers.

'You're staying with us?' he asked, smiling.

'I . . .'

'We'd very much like you to,' he said warmly. 'If you want to, that is. We're not into kidnapping people.' His eyes twinkled.

Jane smiled hesitantly back.

'Have you come far?' he asked.

'London.'

'You've brought no overnight things? No bag or suitcase?'

'I didn't have time to pack.'

'All right. Don't worry.' He gazed at her and again she had the unnerving sensation that he was reading her. Mentally, she ringed herself round with a barrier of steel.

'I don't want to hurt you,' he said softly. 'You've already been hurt, haven't you?'

It was a fair assumption that the majority of newcomers would say yes to that, she thought. She said nothing.

'You're so afraid,' Norton went on, his eyes shining. 'But no one's going to get you here. You're safe with us.'

She felt his pull, and within herself, in spite of all she knew, and suspected, she felt an answering tug. She had never encountered such charisma before.

'And you're not going to let me in, are you?' A corner of his mouth turned up.

She frowned.

'That's all right,' Norton said. 'Why should you? We've only just met. Why don't we talk again tomorrow? Abby' – he looked across at her – 'will you make sure Jane gets whatever she needs?'

'Sure,' said Abby.

Norton looked back at Jane and then down at her hands. 'Don't do that,' he whispered and she saw that, unaware, she had balled them into tight fists.

'You'll hurt yourself,' he said, and to her surprise his eyes filled with tears.

'See you later,' he said with a final, lingering smile and sauntered off.

Could he really be the Keeper? she wondered. A man like that, apparently so full of love for others? But also a man who expected people to yield to him, to bend to his will. Was he used to his Fellowshippers accepting without question any and every order he issued?

Abby said, 'All right?'

Jane nodded. She realized she had been standing staring after the departing figure of Norton. She felt drained. What chance, she thought, had Kirsten had?

'Come on, I'll take you over to the cottage,' said Abby and led the way.

For a long time, sitting in his car beneath the cliffs in Hastings, Sam had stared out to sea. If Jane called, it was important that he was within easy reach. On the other hand, he couldn't stay there all night and it was unlikely that she would call so soon.

The arrival of a group of bikers eventually moved him on.

He was half an hour outside Hastings when he saw a signpost for Hawkenhurst, the neighbouring village to the Moor. He took that road.

He knew from what Kirsten had told him that the Moor was up on the hill; Hawkenhurst was half a mile below in the valley. He entered the valley first. The village was a sprawling mixture of old and modern, and had two garages, a school, a long line of shops and a pub. Sam reckoned the pub would be his best bet.

Outside it was rustic, but inside, it had been 'done'. He bought a pint and stood at the bar, hoping someone would talk to him. But no one did, so after a while he said casually to the barman, 'The Moor's not far from here, is it?'

The barman continued polishing a glass. 'Just up the road,' he said.

'What's it like up there? I mean, the people? The Fellowship?'

The barman shrugged. 'They're all right. A bit clap-happy. Jesus loves them, you know? But they sell good veg at their farm-shops. Why d'you ask?'

Sam explained that he was intending to visit a friend who was a member. 'There's no hitting you over the head with a Bible as soon as you walk in?' he asked lightly.

'No, that's not their style. They pretty much keep to themselves round here. I think they go recruiting up in London.'

Sam looked interested.

'Look, the person you really want to speak to about them is over there,' and before Sam could inquire further, he called over to a man sitting near the window reading a paperback, 'Chap here asking about the Fellowship.'

Sam cringed, but no one else turned round.

'Oh yes?' said the man.

Sam went over, wondering who the man was. The answer came at once: the man introduced himself as the vicar.

'The vicar?' Sam repeated, eyeing the informal clothes.

'Yes,' said the man firmly. 'Off-duty, don't you know. And you are?'

Sam repeated his cover-story and his fears of being 'Bible-bashed'.

The vicar smiled. 'I don't think you've much to worry about. Their pastor, or leader or whatever he likes to call himself – the Keeper? Sam wondered – 'David Norton, is a nice chap, very gentle, you know? Not that I necessarily agree with him doctrinally. Bit too individualistic for my taste. Lets the spirit lead, know what I mean?'

'Sort of,' Sam said.

'Not a lot of emphasis on scripture, more to do with feelings. I've been to one of his services. He's very "free" – direct line to the Lord. But I'm not knocking him. He's worked wonders up there with some of those kids. Drug addicts, down-and-outs, including' – he lowered his voice discreetly – 'the Chief Constable's daughter.'

'Really?' said Sam, genuinely interested.

'Yes. Not long after Norton set up camp, so I believe – I wasn't here at the time – his recruiters picked her up down in Hastings. Heroin addict, she was. Shame.' The vicar took a swig of whisky. 'Her dad had given up on her. Tried private clinics, locking her up, the lot. Well, it was only a matter of time, wasn't it, before she wound up dead from an overdose.' He drained his glass. 'Norton saved her,' he said simply. 'Two weeks up there, and Mary was a different girl. She'd kicked the habit, on her own, no doctors, said it was all down to Norton.

'She's still up there, eight, nine years on. Okay, so she worships the ground Norton walks on – a lot of them do – but if someone had saved your life, wouldn't you?' The vicar smiled ruefully. 'I'd like to know how he does it, actually. Wouldn't mind a spot of his magic myself.'

Sam smiled distantly. The Fellowship had achieved perfect cover for itself, provided by the Chief Constable of Kent himself.

'I say,' said the vicar. 'I hope I haven't offended you. I'm not saying they're all drug addicts. Your friend probably isn't.'

Sam reassured him hastily. He went to the bar to buy the next round, and when he returned asked the vicar about rumours of coercion, of parents not being allowed to see their children.

The vicar shook his head. 'This isn't America, you know.'

'No, of course not.'

The vicar took another mouthful of scotch. 'Not that, when he first came here, folk weren't a bit concerned. Including my predecessor,' he said ruminatively.

'Oh?' Sam asked, careful not to show his interest.

'Yes. Well, you know, Jesus hippies invading the place, buying it up. People round here asked the old vicar to check him out.'

'Did he?' Sam waited.

The vicar nodded. 'He'd come from a church in London. That big, charismatic one where they bark like dogs. Pop stars went there.'

'In Knightsbridge?' Sam hazarded.

'That's the one. St Peter's, isn't it? Don't know if it's still going. Seems he had a row with them up there, so he turned up here to run his own show.'

Sam tried to keep his face impassive. Now he had a good lead. Now he could do some of his own checking into Norton. He'd find someone who knew him, follow a trail. 'How long ago would that be?' he asked.

'About ten years ago.'

'D'you know what the row was about?'

'No. You ask a lot of questions. You're not a reporter, are you?'

If the man had been wearing a dog-collar, Sam thought that he might have had a problem lying to him. 'No,' he lied easily.

'Good. Don't want anyone coming down here stirring things up, exposing people just because they're a bit different.'

In his shirt pocket, Sam's mobile started to ring. Jane, he thought instantly: she'd found something already.

'Excuse me,' he apologized. 'Hullo?'

'Is that Sam?' piped a girl's voice. It wasn't Jane's, but he knew he ought to recognize it.

'It's me, Kirsten. Remember me?'

'Kirsten. Yes.' He felt dazed. He kicked his mind into gear. 'How are you? Where are you?'

'I'm fine.' She laughed, and it struck him that she sounded very happy. 'I'm at the Fellowship.'

'The . . .'

The vicar was listening with interest. Sam mouthed his thanks and quickly left the pub.

'Are you really all right?' he asked Kirsten, as he crunched across the gravel of the car-park.

'Yes, fine. I'm sorry I didn't turn up on Monday. I hope you weren't worried.'

She didn't sound very contrite. 'I was bloody worried, as it happens.'

'Oh! You shouldn't swear. Swearing hurts . . .'

'What?' He wrenched his car door open.

'It doesn't matter. Anyway, I called to say I'm sorry. I lied to you about the trust-fund babes. There's only one girl like that here now, and she isn't being ripped off.' For the first time, she sounded remorseful.

'Why did you do it?' he asked.

'I wanted to get a job on a national. I'd read about other cults. I thought the Fellowship would be the same.'

'And it isn't?'

'Oh no! It's lovely here. I've given my life to Jesus.'

'You have?' He switched the phone to his other ear. 'So why didn't you ring me before?'

'I haven't had time. I only came to Jesus yesterday. I've been so busy. I rang you as soon as I could.'

She sounded genuine he thought, but then she always had.

'What about the brainwashing you told me about?' he asked. 'The high-starch diet? The forced all-night prayer sessions?'

'I lied,' she said in a small voice.

It was all too neat, Sam thought suddenly. A call designed to stop him snooping. 'Kirsten,' he said quietly, 'are you being forced to make this call?'

'Of course not!' She sounded indignant. 'I just wanted to explain what had happened to me, to stop you worrying.'

'I see.'

'And I needed to put right any wrongs I'd done, like lying to you.'

'So you're telling me the truth now?'

'Oh yes! I'm a Christian now. I don't lie.'

'Is anyone listening to what we're saying?'

'No.'

He decided to take the risk. 'Kirsten, is there anything happening at the Fellowship that frightens you?'

'Frightens me?' she echoed.

'Is there anyone who doesn't fit in?' He wasn't sure how to phrase it. 'Who's doing things you think are wrong?'

'No,' she said wonderingly.

This was hopeless, Sam thought. He decided to be bolder. 'Have you seen the stories about Botulism Helen?' he asked.

'No,' she replied simply. 'I haven't seen any stories about anything. We don't have newspapers or television or radio here.'

How convenient, Sam thought. 'She's a woman who's been poisoning children and pregnant women.'

'How horrible,' exclaimed Kirsten.

Sam closed his eyes. Again she sounded genuine. 'You don't know anything about it?'

'No, how could I? I just told you, we don't see the news here.'

Had she deliberately misinterpreted what he'd said? He tried one last time. 'Does David Norton ever call himself the Keeper?' As soon as the words were out of his mouth, he knew shouldn't have uttered them.

But Kirsten sounded merely mystified. 'No. He's just called David.'

There was no hesitation in her voice, no catch in her voice before she spoke. She was telling him the truth, as she knew it.

'Anyway, I'd really like it if you came down here,' Kirsten said, taking his breath away.

'Tomorrow, or at the weekend, or any time you like. My parents are coming on Sunday.'

She clearly didn't believe the group had anything to hide, Sam thought. But that meant nothing if she was brainwashed.

'Will you come?'

'I might just do that,' he said. And he might, he thought. If he hadn't heard from Jane by Saturday morning, he'd drive down again, ostensibly to visit Kirsten.

'You have forgiven me?' she pleaded.

'What? Yes, sure.'

'See you soon. Bye-bye.'

'Bye.'

Beyond letting him know that she was alive, the call had done nothing to reassure him. Jane might have successfully infiltrated a community of loving, addict-saving Christians or a cult bent on global destruction, with a Chief Constable and the local C of E on its side. Only time, and Jane's investigation, would tell.

Jane had said that six, or perhaps more, signs had been completed. Sombrely, Sam hoped it was not more. He turned the ignition key. As he left the village, he thought of Jane, on her own, in that place. She was an expert, he told himself. She'd be able to tell whether Kirsten was brainwashed or not; what was really going on there. He turned for London.

Thoughtfully, David replaced the extension on which he had listened to Kirsten's conversation with Sam.

It was much worse than he had feared. The journalist knew far, far too much: 'Does David Norton ever call himself the Keeper?'

Where had he got that from? Who had told him? Why had he, David, ever been stupid enough to call himself by that name, even briefly?

David put his head in his hands. 'Have you seen the stories about Botulism Helen?' He felt panic fluttering inside him, around his heart. This, coming now, he thought, within forty-eight hours of the Release.

It wasn't as if, being a journalist, Ferryman would keep his information to himself. He would have made notes; he'd have told his editor. What else did he know? David was agonized. Sweet Lord, was everything about to fall apart?

He took a deep breath. 'Jesus,' he began shakily, 'show me the way.'

He received his answer: Ferryman had to be stopped. By the time his colleagues noticed his disappearance, it would be too late.

David slipped his hand inside his shirt pocket and withdrew his slim mobile phone. First, he put in a call to free up adequate funds. Then he keyed in the twelve digits of a number he knew by heart, a number that would ultimately inform the man whose name he didn't know, and to whom, to his best knowledge, he had never spoken, that his services were required once more.

The number rang. It was answered by a female voice to whom he supplied the code, a simple sentence, and added one word: 'urgent'. The woman hung up. There would now be a short interval – very short, David hoped – before the return call requesting instructions.

And then Ferryman would cease to be a threat. The panic subsided. David felt light as air. He could hear Kirsten coming along the corridor. What a dear, innocent child she was! How eagerly had she seized upon his suggestion to call Ferryman and how willingly she had believed him when he said that it was to put the journalist's mind at rest, rather than to allay any concerns he might have about the Fellowship. No wonder Ferryman had believed her. Of course, David mused, she had been speaking the truth as she knew it.

She tapped on his door.

'Have you made your call, sweetheart?'

'Yes. I feel much better now, thank you, David.'

'Good, I'm glad. Is Sam going to come and see us?'

'He said he might. I do hope he does.'

'So do I,' David said sincerely. He closed the door. 'Why don't we pray for him?' he suggested.

The vicar took the empty glasses up to the bar.

'Who was he, then?' asked the barman.

'He didn't give his name. But the girl who rang called him Sam.' The vicar stared over at the window through which he'd watched Sam sitting in his car for a while before driving off. 'I think he might have been a journalist,' he said.

'What's he want to know about the Fellowship for then?'

'I don't know. But I wonder if I shouldn't warn David Norton about him?'

'Maybe you should.'

Still pondering, the vicar left the pub.

CHAPTER EIGHTEEN

The complex that made up the International Centre in Vienna had been built to withstand terrorist attack. It was one of the world's designated 'safe spots', where the most delicate of negotiations between governments and adversaries could take place in secret and without fear of reprisal. Rather than one tall building, which in the event of a bomb would collapse, scattering debris and causing further injury, there were eight semi-underground, single-storey structures.

In one of them, at 20.45, Werner Lindroth's bomb exploded. It killed eighteen people in the building and injured twenty-seven more. The victims were the negotiators of the Israeli–Syrian Peace Accord. Their injuries were terrible, not least because the bomb was composed of sharp metal shards that sliced through everything in their path.

Within three hours of the explosion, the media had christened it the 'Blade Bomb'. Sam Ferryman was among a posse of British journalists who left Heathrow shortly before midnight to fly to Vienna. At approximately the same time, Ivor Maitland, the man hired to kill him, left his Glasgow home and set off for London.

The Bridegroom office at Vauxhall was informed of the Vienna bomb within thirty minutes of its detonation. Ryder, still en route from Israel, was notified and, as soon as his plane landed, whisked by helicopter from the airfield to the office.

He then endured a series of calls with other grooms, Beck and assorted members of ARIC. Again and again, he agreed that Vienna was a perfect fulfilment of the second sign: 'False peace-makers shall be put to death; in their safest places, in their most secret council chambers, God shall cause them to be cut down.'

Cut down, Ryder thought, sliced to bits by that awful weapon. False peace-makers . . . many of the victims were regarded as traitors by their own side. The Scroll group was still completing the signs with ghastly attention to detail. The ARIC chairwoman had asked him whether that might not, in one sense, be good news. Might it not mean the group still had months of work ahead? Enough time in which to be caught? That was possible, Ryder thought. But the flurry of activity might just as easily signify a crossing of the last t and dotting of the last i.

At almost midnight, he left his own office for the main control room.

Fifty people were working there, and most were on the telephone, and yet the phones rang constantly. The hunt for the Scroll thieves was continuing. Three of the five cults that earlier in the evening had looked possible – they contained both an R-named female and a male of the right age – had now been ruled out. Helen calls were still coming in apace, but although names had been proferred none had checked out.

Carlucci still hadn't surfaced. Ferryman was on his way to Vienna.

Along one wall of the room crouched a bank of television screens, showing different versions of the bomb story. No one seemed to be listening or watching. Ryder went over to look.

He saw that the 'grandfather' of the Syrian negotiators had just succumbed to his injuries in a Viennese hospital. He swore savagely. That such a man should be killed in fulfilment of a fake document . . . He had met the old man several times and had been deeply impressed by him. His skills, honed by years of experience, were irreplaceable. Now there might never be an end to the conflict: already, each side was accusing the other of committing the atrocity.

Whereas the real perpetrators were a bunch of religious maniacs, Ryder thought, ticking off items on their Jobs-to-be-Done list.

Broughton came over. 'The Yanks still think it's one of theirs.'

'Good.' Ryder's call to the Austrian groom had been painful. Beneath the shock, unspoken but obvious, there had been blame. The groom, like so many, like Ryder himself, believed the group was British.

'No, wait,' Broughton went on. 'There's a group in upstate New York – fundamentalists, Christian Right – that's been issuing threats against the Syrian delegation for months. Calls them the "Great Traitors".'

Ryder frowned. '"The Great Traitor shall be assassinated",' he said. The third sign.

'It seems they're celebrating news of the bomb. With fireworks,' Broughton added. 'The groom's getting permission to go in.'

Was it possible the Americans were right? wondered Ryder. He could suspend everything, go home and sleep the sleep of an innocent man, one whose country was not harbouring such evil, who wasn't responsible for finding the cult before it was too late. He sighed. Until he heard that the Americans had seized the group and found the Scroll in its possession; that they had evidence linking the cult to Vienna, the Princes' murders, the swaddling-clothes theft, he had to go on believing the cult was his.

He got a cup of black coffee from the machine in the corner and returned to his office.

On his computer, via the Bridegroom link-up, he accessed the internal database of the Viennese Centre. As he had expected, there was already a plethora of files on the explosion. His eyes travelled down the index and stopped on the last entry. It read: 'Persons with access to Delta Unit in the twenty-four hours prior to explosion'.

Ryder tapped a key.

Thirty-eight people were named. They included the accredited delegates, their secretaries and bodyguards; the centre's security people, cleaners and caterers.

Ryder studied the list for some time. He knew the Austrian police would be examining it with the utmost care and, while giving polite ear to Bridegroom's theories, would also be looking into the possibility that one of the delegates or a member of their entourages had planted the bomb.

In Ryder's view, even discounting the Scroll, that was a waste of time. Although in the past both sides had resorted to dirty tricks, peaceful negotiation had become the style of the day, and the signing of the peace accord had been imminent.

The Centre's security checks were legendary. Visitors, no matter how high-ranking, and their belongings, were subjected to the most stringent of daily searches, which included explosives searches. Sniffer dogs checked all meeting-rooms at the start and end of each day, and often during the day as well. Which meant that the bomb must have been planted by someone who knew that routine and was himself or herself above suspicion.

A centre employee, then.

A security guard. Ryder had been involved in such scenarios before. He saw that four security personnel and two dog-handlers had had access to the room in the crucial hours.

He searched through their profiles, impressed by the depth and quality of the security, the number of references taken and followed up. As far as he could tell, nothing in any of the guards' backgrounds fitted the profile of a sleeper, but only further investigation by the Austrians could confirm that.

He moved down to the cleaners and caterers. Generally both categories were so poorly paid that staff turnover was high, and only the most security-conscious employers bothered to take up references. Not so in the case of the International Centre. The four cleaners and two caterers who had had access to the meeting-room in the pertinent hours had been as stringently vetted as their more highly paid colleagues. Each one had had to supply three referees who had known them for at least five years.

Ryder selected the first name and requested the man's full profile. He scanned through it but, as before, found nothing to excite his interest. He called up another profile, and then another. It was 2.30 a.m. and his eyelids were beginning to droop. Apart from catnaps, it was his second night without proper sleep. Why not leave it? he asked himself. Crash out for a couple of hours on the sofa? But he was locked into the task now; he had to finish it.

The next profile appeared on the screen: Werner Lindroth, aged forty-seven, from Linz. He had been employed as a contract cleaner at the centre for just two months. His referees were a priest, who had known him as a choirboy in Vienna, and two former employers, at a meat factory and a gas station.

Ryder was about to clear the screen and call up the final file when a phrase caught his eye. It came from the priest's glowing reference: 'When he was a chorister, his voice could have made the angels weep.'

Very distantly, at the back of Ryder's mind, a memory stirred. He had seen or heard something similar before – and in a context not unlike this one. The source, though, escaped him. He returned to his own database, to the hundreds of documents he kept on it because he hadn't got around to sorting through and discarding them.

He keyed in the last two words, 'angels weep', and asked the computer to find that phrase for him. It was a powerful machine which normally astounded him with its speed, but now it asked him to wait.

He looked out of the window. Below him the Thames swirled, lights glinting on the water. On the other side of the river, in the amber glow of street-lights, a few cars slid by on the empty roads. He turned back to his computer: it was still 'Searching'.

He went out into the corridor. The door to the communications room was open and inside he could see people still at their desks. He caught the snatch of a conversation about European mercenaries, but closed his ears to it. He didn't want to be waylaid.

He returned to his office. It was quite possible, he told himself, that his memory was playing him false. He was very tired and under extreme stress. He walked round to read his screen.

Halfway down it the cursor was flashing on a bit of text: 'He sang soprano; to hear him sing was to hear angels weep.'

Ryder's heart turned over. Swiftly he scanned the document. The sentence had been written by another priest, to secure a job for another menial worker, eight years before.

A bomb had exploded on a plane in mid-air, killing everyone on board. The German police had decided that Jules Vedrine, a forty-two-year-old Corsican, was responsible. He had been employed as a cleaner at Hamburg Airport, and had disappeared shortly after the explosion. Among the dead was the paymaster of a London-based revolutionary group; hence Ryder's interest and memory of that peculiarly poetic detail in the reference.

The priest had turned out to be a Corsican nationalist with suspected links to a terrorist group in which, presumably, the bomber had learnt his trade.

Ryder switched back to the data on Lindroth. The priests' names weren't the same, but he hadn't expected them to be. Lindroth wasn't the man's real name, any more than Vedrine had been the Corsican's. It would be one of a series of aliases. A photograph would have been nice, Ryder thought, but his old records didn't contain one. Perhaps Lindroth had taken a fancy to the description of his boyhood voice; perhaps the Austrian priest was a fake. Whatever, Ryder thought, Lindroth had made a mistake.

He checked the time. It was less than eight hours since the bomb. Lindroth might still be in Vienna, lying low at the address he had given on his Centre application form, confident that he had no need to flee, that his camouflage was perfect. For a moment, Ryder considered taking a British team over there, snatching the man, wresting the truth out of him. The British cleaning up their own mess. But it was only a fleeting notion. The Austrians would be rightly outraged. The most he could hope for was some involvement.

He went to his door and yelled for Broughton. Then he phoned the Austrian Bridegroom office. All senior personnel were in a meeting, he was told curtly. They could not be disturbed.

Ryder opened his mouth to argue, then realized he hadn't time for it. Leaving a message for the groom to call London, he slammed down the phone.

Broughton appeared in the doorway.

'Jack, where'll I find the number for the Austrian anti-terrorist squad?'

Broughton found it for him.

He dialled the number, and after a few minutes was put through to a senior detective who was still at the bomb scene. He spoke swiftly for several minutes.

'Jack,' he said, when he hung up. 'I need you to hold the fort. I'm going to Vienna.' Then he snatched up his laptop and ran.

Although she'd firmly intended to stay awake, Jane dozed. As dawn came up, she awoke. She experienced a moment of complete disorientation before remembering where she was: in Laurel Cottage at the Fellowship.

She was lying in a small white attic room under a sloping roof. She sat up. Against one wall was a dressing-table with an upright chair in front of it. On the chair was the pile of neatly folded clothes Abby had given her the night before. A blue denim shirt and jeans: the Fellowship uniform.

It seemed to be simplicity itself to 'join' the Fellowship, Jane thought. But if she was right about the group, there had to be layers of membership: those with some knowledge of what Norton was doing, and those who were entirely innocent. She had kept careful watch at the barbecue the night before. She had seen the way Norton moved from group to group, talking, listening, laughing, occasionally touching someone, giving someone else a hug. She had seen the way each group lit up in his presence, how adored he seemed to be by all.

But there was one group he hadn't visited. A group composed of two men and two women, later joined by Mary, the gushing woman who had greeted her. Senior people perhaps, Jane wondered, so close to Norton that they didn't need the reassurance of his attention. They had stood slightly apart, talking little amongst themselves. There was a watchful air about them, Jane thought. Once, when she glanced over, she had caught Mary's eyes upon her and for a moment had seen not the warm smile but a cool, appraising stare. It had lasted a second only. Jane had smiled falteringly, and Mary had come to herself, and beamed back.

Jane knew she must be very careful indeed. Mary slept in one of the rooms below. Guarding her? wondered Jane. Along with gentle Abby, Jane's so-called 'discipler'? She'd heard the word used last night. Was it innocuous, no more than the 'older member in Christ' looking after a newcomer, as in Abby's explanation? Or did it denote something more sinister? The word had unpleasant connotations: discipline, cruelty, jailor – keeper.

Was Abby her 'keeper' as Norton was keeper to them all? Who among them had been Kirsten's keeper?

In spite of a second, lengthy visual sweep the night before, Jane had seen no one who matched Sam's description of the girl. Was he right? Had Kirsten left? Or was she being kept there against her will?

Jane threw back the sheet that covered her, got up and dressed quietly in the uniform, transferring the contents of her pockets from her black jeans to the Fellowship blue ones. Her door creaked as she opened it, and she paused, cursing it, waiting for someone in the sleeping cottage to wake too.

But nothing stirred – it was four o'clock in the morning, she reminded herself. Abby and Mary must be deeply asleep in their beds.

Gingerly, she descended the stairs to their landing. Both women's doors were shut. The sound of snoring came from behind one. She went down the next flight, which led into the narrow hallway.

She glanced into the sitting-room. It looked comfortable and inviting, with a low table between two roomy sofas. There was a small bookcase in a corner. Jane went quietly over to it. It contained numerous novels, a dictionary, an encyclopedia, but no Bible, she saw in surprise. She would have expected at least that and some Christian books.

On a shelf beside the fireplace, there was a CD player. No television, and no sign of radio. She went into the kitchen, but there was no sign of either set there. Was the lack of external communication peculiar to Laurel Cottage? she wondered. Or was it Norton's policy? To keep the majority of his Fellowshippers in the dark about what a few of them did?

She unlatched the back door and stepped out into the garden, then went round to the front of the house. She climbed over the gate in the picket fence, rather than open and close it.

She made her way along in front of the women's cottages. All the curtains were drawn; there were no bars at any windows, no face peering out in the hope of rescue. Jane shivered. It was a cool morning, the sky greyish white, not yet warmed or coloured by the sun. Rabbits hopped out of her way as she progressed. She saw a silvery badger. On the green, she surveyed the Moor before her.

The main road up from Hawkenhurst passed through it, touching the green before descending in the other direction towards Rye. To her right was the beautiful manor house she had noticed on her arrival, then the row of cottages that included her own, a road, the church, the school-building, the men's cottages and, over to her left, the white wall and pillars, the dark trees beyond, that protected Norton's house from casual gaze. Abby had pointed it out to her the night before.

Jane wondered about going down its driveway but to be caught so obviously prowling would be foolish. At the moment, if challenged, she could simply say she was going for a walk. Not that such a challenge seemed likely, she admitted. The whole Fellowship seemed asleep.

She walked past the men's cottages. They seemed as peaceful as the women's. Well, what did she expect to find? she asked herself. A laboratory of blue-clad workers manufacturing listeria? Kirsten held under guard?

She reached the church and tried the doors, but they were locked. She tried the door of the old school-building that now served as the Fellowship canteen. It too was locked.

Jane turned into the small road. Just past the back of the cottages, it twisted and started to weave through a scanty copse of trees. Beyond them she saw fields, and beyond those, falling away into a dip, thick woods. She seemed to be leaving the Moor for open countryside, and she was about to turn back when she saw a gleam of red ahead: a phone box.

Sam, she thought at once. She knew it was twenty to five in the morning, but she also knew he wouldn't mind being woken up to hear from her.

She pulled open the weighty metal door, fished a coin out of her jeans pocket and ran through Sam's direct-line number in her head. She lifted the receiver. There was no sound. She depressed the cradle and tried again: the line was dead.

Her stomach dropped. Was it merely out of order or had it been disconnected? Now that she thought about it, she hadn't seen a telephone at Laurel Cottage. That was distinctly odd. No television and no radio could be explained away as an eccentricity, but no phone? And the only one within walking distance cut off?

Were the Fellowshippers marooned with Norton? Had such isolation from the outside world been imposed recently, in preparation for the Awful Horror, the mass suicide of the Fellowship that had always been one of her fears?

She stepped out of the box. A blackbird was singing sweetly not far off. She glanced back towards the Moor. It was about half a mile away, she judged. The disconnection of the telephone might have nothing to do with Norton. It was a public phone, on a public highway; it couldn't be owned by him.

The birdsong stopped. Suddenly, Jane heard another noise: a crash, then a cry, then muffled voices. They came from quite nearby. Keeping in against the side of the road, Jane rounded the next bend. Through the trees, she made out a low stone building and, parked in front of it, a jeep. Two people were standing in front of the jeep, another was coming out of the building. They were wearing the Fellowship uniform. If they looked round, Jane realized, they would see her. She retreated quickly back around the bend.

She heard a man crying, 'It fell on my foot!' and being shushed by someone.

What were they doing, Jane wondered, at that time in the morning? Had she found the laboratory? Were they loading fresh supplies for Helen? Was she about to discover the evidence she needed?

She stepped from the road into the copse of trees. She wished now that there were more trees to shield her, but she was approaching the building from the rear, and all the activity was at the front. Still, twigs snapped with alarming noise beneath her feet, brambles tore loudly at her clothing. She paused. All was quiet again. She went on, and reached the building.

The back wall was perhaps fifteen feet high. It had no window. Cautiously, she crept round the end furthest from the jeep. Halfway up the wall was a window, pushed open and held so by a string. She could hear voices again now: four or perhaps five of them – it was difficult to tell – at least one a woman's. One man had a soft, Irish accent. He seemed to be directing the others. Jane's head just reached the sill of the window. She needed something to stand on. She looked quickly about. There were no handy logs, only branches and a fallen tree, and she couldn't drag that along the ground on her own.

She inched round to the front of the building. The jeep was still there, its back flap open, a male Fellowshipper crawling out backwards holding a cardboard box.

'Load it in with the rest,' said the Irishman, and Jane saw that he stood in the doorway of the building, not ten feet from her. She presssed herself hard against the wall, her heart hammering.

His voice came again, close to her, through a window. He'd gone back inside. She peered round the corner once more. What she thought she might only have imagined was in fact there: a pile of wooden crates between herself and the jeep. If she was seen, if they were heavy and she stumbled . . . She gave herself no more time to think. She ran to the crates, seized hold of the nearest – it was heavy, but she could manage it, just – and ran with it back to her window.

'I'll start doing the cans now, shall I, Steve?' asked a woman's voice and the Irishman answered in the affirmative.

Jane got up on the crate. It gave her an extra eighteen inches, enough to see inside, but she kept her head below the window. If someone in there happened to look out just as she was looking in. . .

She raised her head by degrees. She saw what looked like a warehouse, with floor-to-ceiling shelves of tinned goods. More tins were being unloaded by two men. For a siege? Jane wondered. Was this the Fellowship's secret store to enable them to hold out against the authorities? Did the boxes being carried inside contain ammunition? Did the crates contain weapons?

She was standing on one of them. She could soon check. She got down. The lid was nailed on too tightly to prise open, but between the wooden slats she thought she could see something. She almost laughed in relief. She was standing on a crate of oranges.

She got back up. On one set of shelves against the far wall, a woman was stacking piles of sheets and blankets. Was the building simply a store-house?

She switched her gaze to the man the woman had called Steve. He had his back to her and was unloading something onto a table, although Jane could not see what. He turned, and she recognized him suddenly as one of Mary's élite group from the night before. A man quite a bit older than the rest, she remembered, dark-haired, saturnine.

'If you do that, Mike, you're going to drop it again,' he said, and moved off towards the open door. Jane stared at what he had left behind him on the table. Cartons and cartons of Lemsip, and other cold remedies, bottles of cough mixture, aspirins.

There looked to be sufficient for an army, Jane thought, staring. Were those ordinary, over-the-counter medicines about to be contaminated and put back on supermarket shelves, or had the Fellowship bought up huge supplies cheaply, in early preparation for the autumn's coughs and colds?

'Bring the oranges in now,' called Steve.

Jane froze. If they saw a crate was missing, they'd know there was someone about. They'd come looking for her. She lowered her head. Stealthily, praying that she wouldn't be heard, she got off the crate. From round the corner, came the sound of wood being dragged on concrete, the crates being hauled inside. Swiftly, as best she could, Jane covered hers with branches, then dived back into the trees. She kept as low to the ground as she could. If she was found now, running away, the crate there as evidence that she had been spying . . .

When she reached the road she was breathless from her flight, but she made herself start jogging back up to the Moor. She had to get as far from the warehouse as she could. She strained her ears as she ran. If she heard the jeep coming, she could plunge into one of the fields, hide among the trees, have a chance of getting away.

She heard no jeep. She rounded a bend and saw the back of the women's cottages, her own small, curtained window. She slowed. They weren't coming after her. They hadn't noticed the missing crate. Had she spied on nothing more sinister than the regular dawn arrival of food and other supplies for the Fellowship?

She was nearing the top of the road. It was almost half past five. She could be back in her room, apparently asleep, before either Mary or Abby stirred.

She heard a car coming and whipped round. But it wasn't the jeep; the road behind her was clear. The vehicle was coming from another direction, from the main road leading up from Hawkenhurst.

The nose of a blue van appeared. Jane crouched down beside a large rose-bush that overhung a garden wall. She was probably being over-cautious, she told herself, because of her earlier fright. She watched the van creep slowly through the still-sleeping Moor. She saw the man at the wheel. He wasn't in Fellowship blue. Without warning, he turned sharply into Norton's driveway.

It seemed extremely early for a visitor, Jane thought, emerging from her cover and staring towards Norton's house. Perhaps he too was delivering something? Newspapers, possibly, cancelling her earlier theory that the Fellowship was kept cut off from the rest of the world? She waited, but the van didn't reappear. She realized that, almost unknowingly, she had memorized the van's registration number. Before she forgot it, she took out the tiny pen she carried and wrote it down on a receipt she found in her pocket.

She reached Laurel Cottage. As before, she climbed over the fence. She glanced up at the house, and a movement caught her eye: a curtain falling back into place at a first-floor window, as if it had been raised and dropped again.

Mary's room. Jane felt ice in her stomach. Mary had been spying on her.

She must keep calm, she told herself. She had simply been out for a walk. She entered the cottage by the back door, half expecting Mary to be standing there. The kitchen was empty. She moved to the foot of the stairs. There was no noise from above.

Had she imagined the curtain moving?

She mounted the stairs softly. Both Mary and Abby's doors were shut fast. Perhaps Mary had seen her, but had thought nothing of a visitor taking an early morning walk?

She climbed on up to her own room. It looked exactly as she had left it. She sat down on the bed, trying to assess what she had seen. No one had been tampering with the goods. It was probably, as she had thought, a store-house. But it was a long way from the Moor, it was hidden in the trees, and why were Norton's élite shelf-stacking at that time in the morning?

She had found no laboratories, barbed-wire fencing, or signs of guards, and yet as she lay down again on her bed, she was certain that she had been right to come: that below the simple, open life of the Fellowship, another agenda was being played out, unknown to most of the members as well as to the outside world. Whether that agenda was linked to the Scroll, whether Norton was the Keeper, she had yet to find out.

She dozed once more.

She did not hear, thirty minutes later, the soft 'click' of the front door as it closed. Mary Wilson was on her way to David Norton's house to report the suspicious behaviour of the Fellowship's newest recruit.

CHAPTER NINETEEN

At 06.55 in Vienna, a team of armed anti-terrorist officers burst into the flat of the suspected 'Blade Bomber' in a tenement block in the north of the city.

The flat was in darkness, the curtains drawn, the bed unslept in. As the directional microphones had suggested, Werner Lindroth wasn't there; hadn't been there, according to his neighbours, for twenty-four hours or more.

Those details were relayed to Ryder upon his arrival at the scene. He swore softly. His journey had been a waste of time; his best lead yet was gone. It did not improve matters that en route he'd heard the Americans had mounted a full-scale assault on their New York fundamentalists and found them to be harmless. The group had offered no resistance. No weapons had been found, no plans for Armageddon, only boxes of extremist right-wing literature. Britain was again squarely and singly in the frame for harbouring the cult.

'We're circulating Lindroth's photograph and details but he probably left the country last night,' said Gerhard Fischer, head of the Austrian anti-terrorist squad.

He and Ryder were standing together in the kitchen of the empty flat. Their relationship had begun well with Ryder's tip-off. There had been no mention of the Austrian groom, and Ryder did not inquire after him now. He didn't want him to know about the failed raid. 'Does the priest who gave him the reference exist?' he asked.

'Yes. He's ninety-four years old. Very well respected in the city. How he comes to know a character like— Yes?' One of his men had appeared hurriedly in the doorway.

'Excuse me, sir. It's the referees.'

'What about them?'

'The gas-station manager was killed in a road accident three months ago. The second man, the meat-factory supervisor' – the policeman swallowed – 'has been missing since last weekend.'

'And the priest?' demanded Fischer.

'Lindroth called at his house last night but the old man was out, so he's expected there this morning, for breakfast.'

'*What?*'

It was already eight o'clock, and the priest lived on the other side of the city.

'Come on,' shouted Fischer, and Ryder raced out after him.

By driving through the night, Ivor Maitland had arrived in London at six o'clock, and by seven had already reconnoitred the only address he had for Sam Ferryman, the *Correspondent* building.

He had noted one obvious flaw, excellent for his purpose. He had noted, too, the two entrances: the front, manned by two security guards, for the white-collar staff and the public; and the side, where the auxiliary staff – the cleaners, canteen staff and warehousemen – entered and left. For Maitland, the latter was the better option.

He travelled in a smart camper-van. It might not be sleek or powerful, but it offered him what he needed most: privacy. He was parked in a quiet side street. Now he retired into the back of the camper, where his computer was booted-up and waiting, and called up a letter that he had used before in similar circumstances. He edited it, then changed the format on his screen and typed a briefer document. He printed both, and put them in an envelope.

He donned the white overalls of manual workers everywhere, and jammed a long-peaked cap on his head. Round his neck, he hung a laminated card identifying him as an employee of a well-known firm of heating and air-conditioning engineers. In his right hand he carried the envelope, in his left a toolbox.

He went to the *Correspondent*'s side-entrance and stuck his head round the door. As he had expected, a security guard sat there, bleary-eyed now at the end of his night-shift. There was a camera on a metal arm. Maitland ducked his head so that the peak of his cap hid his face.

'Can I help you?' the guard asked truculently.

Maitland proferred his envelope. 'Air-conditioning,' he said.

The guard frowned. 'What's wrong with it?'

Maitland could have said it was dripping into the street below, only feet away from where the guard sat, and it was that sight which had inspired him, but he forbore. 'The units are too noisy,' he intoned instead. 'Up on the third floor. In the newsroom.'

'No one ever said anything to me,' the guard said darkly. He opened the envelope. In it was what looked like a fax from the news-floor to the heating and air-conditioning company. It complained of the noise of the units, declared them faulty, a nuisance and a health hazard, and demanded they be urgently repaired, before the start of the next working day. It was signed by the news editor; the fax number was the right one. The accompanying letter identified Maitland as the company's technician assigned to the job.

'They're supposed to tell me if they're having any repairs done,' the guard complained.

Maitland shrugged apologetically. If he was refused, he'd simply bide his time, waiting for another opportunity, but there was a fifty per cent bonus if Ferryman was sorted before the next day, and Maitland was desperate for cash.

'They do seem a bit hot and bothered about it, don't they?' said the guard.

Maitland agreed.

The guard handed back the letters. 'Sign in,' he said, and swivelled round a visitor's book.

Maitland scrawled a name. By the time anyone thought to check it, he'd be long gone, the job complete.

'I'd better take you up there.' The guard heaved himself to his feet, his mouth turned down.

'I can find my own way if you like,' offered Maitland.

'Should really be accompanied at all times.' said the guard, although the look on his face said he'd like to be dissuaded.

Maitland shrugged again. 'I won't steal anything,' he said. 'You've got my company name there.'

'That's right.' Relieved, the guard sat down again. 'Straight ahead.' He nodded at the stairs. 'Third floor, you can't miss it.'

Maitland moved off quickly. On his way up, he passed cleaners coming down. On the third floor, one of them, leaving, held the door open for him.

He entered the newsroom. One last cleaner was vacuuming, but otherwise the place was empty. Desks were spaced out widely, and there was one long one running down the far wall. The computers had been left on all night.

Maitland saw an air-conditioning unit and walked purposefully towards it. He bent and took a screwdriver from his toolbox. He glanced over his shoulder. The cleaner had gone.

It was seven-thirty. Maitland didn't know what time the day-shift came on, but he assumed he didn't have long. Some of the side-offices had names on the doors. He checked them swiftly; there was no 'Ferryman'.

He started skimming the desks in the main part of the room. There was lots of paperwork lying about, letters from readers to journalists, bills brought in from home. That was all he wanted, Maitland thought: something that gave Ferryman's home address. He found Ferryman's desk, identifying it by a letter. Everything looked neat and tidy. Maitland leafed through it all, then tried the desk, but the drawers were locked. He straightened up and swore. There were no bills from home, nothing that gave the address. That meant a riskier approach. He would have to get Ferryman to meet him somewhere, which meant a greater chance of detection or failure, time wasted, his bonus in the balance.

He saw rows of pigeon-holes over by the newsdesk. It looked as if the post had already come, he thought distractedly. Desperation made him move to check Ferryman's pigeon-hole, but before he reached it, he paused. He stared. On the desk in front of him, beside a computer, lay a piece of paper under glass. It listed the home phone numbers and addresses of all newsroom staff.

Ferryman's was the eighth name on the list.

Maitland could have wept in relief. Instead, he wrote down the details. A phone on the newsdesk rang suddenly, making him jump, warning him that soon life on the paper would begin again, that he'd better be going.

He turned and, as he did so, saw what was on the computer screen in front of him. A slow grin moved over his plain features.

At the top of the screen was 'Night-log'. Directly underneath: 'Blade Bomb. Ferryman filed copy at 3.05, in time for last edition.'

Maitland read on, then fetched his toolbox and left the building.

'All fixed?' asked the security guard as Maitland passed.

'Yeah, no problem,' said Maitland, and he let the door bang behind him.

There were two Blade Bomb press conferences that morning: one at ten o'clock at the devastated International Centre; the other, twenty minutes later, at the hospital where the most seriously injured were being treated.

Sam opted for the first. He hoped that after it Monica would recall him to London. He wanted to pursue the lead on David Norton's old church, and he didn't like being so far away when Jane might ring at any time, possibly needing his help.

By nine o'clock, minibuses were waiting outside his hotel to ferry journalists out to the Centre. Sam got on board. The buses moved off on time, but almost at once hit a traffic jam on a ring-road south of the city. The driver apologized to the journalists. The delay was perhaps occasioned by the bomb, he said. In the light of that explanation, no one complained, and as if to lend credence, within a few minutes, sirens were heard in the distance.

Sam was seated by a window on the right of the bus. In the driver's wing mirror, he saw police outriders coming down the hard shoulder, their sirens wailing. He wondered sombrely if they were clearing the path for an ambulance, but as they drew closer he saw that behind them was a police jeep.

The outriders came abreast first.

The car in front of Sam's minibus suddenly, without warning, swung out into the path of the motorbikes.

'Shit!' exclaimed Sam and several others.

Brakes screeched. The bikes slewed, one rider fell off; the other only just managed to avoid being crushed by the jeep.

There was a second's silence, then the jeep driver jumped out and ran to see if anyone was injured. Most of the journalists moved forward to see better.

Sam sat staring into the window of the jeep, now alongside his own. He recognized the man sitting there. He wasn't an Austrian policeman – or hadn't been, Sam corrected himself, the last time he'd seen him. Four days ago that man had been in England, sitting in front of Sam at the Princes' inquest. He'd been a journalist then, or posing as one. Now he was sitting, grim-faced and very tense, in the back of an Austrian police jeep. Who the hell was he? And how did he connect to both events?

The fallen outrider remounted his bike. The driver ran back to the jeep. The sirens shrieked once more and the convoy moved off at speed.

'They were bloody lucky,' said the journalist next to Sam.

He mumbled a reply. In his head, he had just made a connection. He picked up his briefcase and opened it. There was a sheaf of papers lying inside. He found the one he wanted and read it. He felt a chill move through him.

'What's that?' asked his neighbour curiously.

'Nothing,' said Sam. He pocketed the paper. He should have realized earlier, he told himself. The supposed safety of the Centre was legendary.

Someone who believed he was following God's final instructions had killed those peace-delegates. Someone who perhaps had once called himself the Keeper and who ran an apparently innocuous little commune in the heart of Kent.

The traffic ahead began to move, and the minibus was soon speeding towards the Centre. Sam saw grey smoke still hanging in the sky, smelt the sickly sweet tang of burning rubber, saw the ugly remains of the bombed building. The first of several barriers halted their progress. Armed, unsmiling sentries took their passports.

Sam longed for the press conference to end quickly, so that he could get back to England to pursue his own investigations into David Norton, and to be there when Jane called.

After Mary had reported her suspicions and gone, David had sat meditatively for a while.

In the midst of the rejoicing that Ruth and Ross had arrived safely, another worry, another boulder in his path. Was Mary right? he wondered. Was Jane a spy, another reporter, like Kirsten? Were the three of them, Jane, Kirsten and Ferryman, linked?

Mary was the best of his scouts: his eyes and ears, he called her. It was she who had first suspected her own disciple, Kirsten; who had followed her to London, to her meeting with Ferryman, and who had found out who he was and where he worked. Mary, her father's daughter, had inherited his detection skills – and had a 'hunch' about Jane.

What should he do with her? he thought. What could he do? There was no time to spend days and nights turning her, as he had Kirsten. Jane's fate, like Ferryman's, would require a swifter resolution, and because she was there at the Fellowship, it would be that much easier. Steven could do it. Over the years, Steven had carried out most of the unpleasant tasks. David sighed: still, he hoped it wouldn't come to that.

From what Mary had told him, Jane had only gone a walk. True, it was a suspicious thing to be doing at that time of the morning, but might it not be that the girl was disturbed? At his brief meeting with her the night before, he'd sensed a great tension in her, but he'd also been aware of her intense interest in himself. Not a blatant, journalistic curiosity such as poor Kirsten had been unable to hide, but a fascination with who he was.

An intelligent girl, he surmised, one whose spirit, perhaps, recognized the Jesus in him. One whose spirit wouldn't let her sleep but moved within her restlessly until she came safely to haven, in his arms.

Besides, during her dawn walk what would she have seen? A sleeping, peaceful Fellowship. She might have seen Ross's van arrive – the timing would have been about right – but she wouldn't know who Ross was, and she couldn't have seen Ruth hidden in the back. The van itself would have meant nothing to her; it having, by the Lord's grace, escaped all media and public attention, and now being safely out of sight in the courtyard outside.

No, David decided. He didn't believe Jane had been sent by Ferryman. It would be as he had hoped: Jane would replace the girl he was about to lose. As the Lord had ensured success in Vienna, as He would ensure victory in Charleston and Vermont, so He would bring Jane to Himself.

There was a knock at the door: the others were ready.

David left his office, and went into another room. Ross was there, alone. A syringe lay in a white dish beside him.

The door opened again and Ruth ushered the girl into the room. The sleepy-eyed look that the latter had worn earlier was gone, replaced by apprehension. David didn't want her to be afraid. He smiled and held out his hand to her.

'Come, little one, sit by me.'

She came willingly and perched beside him on the settle. She was very small, he thought lovingly, like a bird. She glanced over at Ross, standing behind him, and then at Ruth.

'Look at me, darling,' David said.

At once her gaze came back to him. He washed her mind of fear and willed her to replace it with his love, to be wrapped up in it as a baby is wrapped in blankets, to let go. He watched the magic work: the warmth invade her, her lips turn falteringly upwards and then release into a full smile.

'Good girl. All right now?'

She gave a soft sigh of contentment. 'Yes, David.'

'As I told you, I'm sending you on a mission. The most special one there has ever been.'

Her eyes sparkled.

'I know you're going to do it perfectly, because Jesus has told me you are.'

She opened her mouth and tried to whisper something.

'What is it, sweetheart?'

She tried again. Eventually she managed, 'I hope I'm good enough.'

'Good enough!' He chuckled, and heard Ruth's gentle laughter behind him too. 'Oh yes, you're good enough. Think of it. Out of all the girls here, our Lord Jesus has chosen you.'

'Me,' repeated the girl in wonder.

'That's right, you.' He shared in her delight. It was a great joy to be able to bestow such grace upon a child whom the world had treated so badly. 'You're going on a plane for us, on a long journey, and at the other end someone who knows you're coming, who's been waiting a long time for you, is going to meet you.'

Ross snorted, but David didn't think the girl heard.

'Yes?' she breathed.

'Now, the place you're going to has got an epidemic of tuberculosis. You know that can be very dangerous, and we can't have anything happening to you, can we?'

'No, David.'

'So we're going to give you an injection, just a little jab in your arm.' As he spoke, he leant forward, unbuttoned the girl's cuff and rolled up her sleeve. She didn't resist, she was too far gone. She had nice veins, he saw, untouched, and remembered that she wasn't a drug addict like so many of them.

'Now,' he murmured.

Ross came forward with the hypodermic.

David held out the girl's arm. 'It won't hurt,' he told her. She flinched, but stoically held still as the needle penetrated her fragile skin. They all watched as the honey-coloured liquid went in.

Ross withdrew the needle, swabbed the puncture-mark with cotton wool and held her arm up to stop the flow of blood.

'I'll take it,' David said. He held her arm high and stared at her, but she simply continued to smile at him. There was no change. Ross had told him that it would be like that, that the recipient wouldn't fall down or start to foam at the mouth, that the serum wouldn't work for many hours yet, but nevertheless he found himself searching for a sign, thinking that there must be some physical reaction to the chemicals that had just entered her system.

The girl yawned.

'Are you all right?'

Her eyes widened slightly. 'Yes, David. Thank you.'

He recollected himself. 'Good.' He replaced her arm in her lap. 'So now that's done,' he went on, 'it's you and me for the airport.'

'You're taking me?'

Such an adorable child, he thought, with her bright, shining eyes full of love for him. He touched her cheek. 'Yes, I'm taking you. Ruth's already packed some things for your journey, so we can be on our way.' He got up and held out his hand to her. Shyly, she took it, and hand in hand they left the room.

By the time Ryder and Fischer reached the priest's house, the police marksmen had been in position around it for over an hour. It was ten o'clock, and Lindroth had not arrived.

Ryder and Fischer got into the communications van, which was parked two hundred yards from the priest's house in what Ryder thought was the quietest neighbourhood he had ever seen. The only sign of life was some building work on at a house further down the street. The area hadn't been cordoned off, in case it alerted Lindroth.

Ryder knew Fischer must be thinking the same as he: that

Lindroth had changed his mind about visiting the priest; that he was already in another country, under another name.

Ryder glanced at the array of small television screens mounted inside the van. One showed a photo of Lindroth, taken from his Centre security pass. He was smiling. On another screen a very thin, smartly-dressed old lady was walking her poodle, which seemed to pee on every lamppost. Ryder scanned the screens showing the rest of the street. There were three approaches to the priest's house, two from the front and one from a passage to the side. He knew that armed police were concealed within range of each approach; opposite the house there was a team on the roof, but Ryder could see no one.

Had Lindroth arrived earlier? Had he seen the teams taking up their positions? Or had he turned a corner, out of sight of the police cameras, sniffed the air and thought: no, leave the priest, run. How else, Ryder wondered, had he survived all those years on the run?

'We'll give him another hour,' Fischer said. A light on the console flashed red, and a technician handed him a telephone.

He listened for a moment, then hung up and told Ryder, 'That was the house. Nothing.'

'How's the priest?' Ryder asked.

'All right. Shocked, but co-operative. Seems he genuinely does know Lindroth, knew him as a choirboy forty years ago. Then, four months ago, Lindroth turned up and asked him for a reference, suggested most of it himself. His real name is—'

'Sir,' interrupted the technician.

He pointed at a screen. On it, walking quickly, was the figure of a man. The camera zoomed in closer. It was Lindroth.

Fischer whispered orders into a headset; Ryder kept his eyes glued to the screens. At a lamppost on the other side of the street, almost opposite them, Lindroth paused. Ryder saw him survey the scene, the almost empty street, the builders, then look over towards the van. It was very similar to the builders' vans – battered like one of theirs – but would it pass Lindroth's expert inspection? Ryder watched him narrow his eyes, thinking.

He was a good-looking man, slim, fair-haired, a smooth face, comparatively unlined, with a thin scar running down from one corner of his mouth. Without taking his eyes from whatever interested him, Lindroth reached into his jacket pocket.

'Wait,' breathed Fischer into his mouthpiece.

Lindroth withdrew a packet of cigarettes. He inserted one between his lips, slowly, and lit it, then threw the match down. All the while, his eyes remained fixed upon their van. Suddenly, he set off again, walking swiftly, out into the road, towards the end of the street where he would turn into in the passageway that led to the priest's house.

His jacket flapped open. There was nothing about his spare frame that suggested a concealed weapon. Perhaps he intended to use his bare hands on the old man – it wouldn't take much, Ryder thought; just a slight pressure.

There was a hiss of static, a disembodied voice on the radio. Fischer replied abruptly, and then a megaphone blared: 'Werner Lindroth, this is the police.'

Lindroth hit the ground.

'Stay where you are.'

Lindroth rolled under a builder's van.

'Freeze!'

A shot rang out. Over the radios, Ryder heard the marksmen moving out into the street. He saw them spilling out of the doorways on the other side of the road. They were wearing respirators.

Lindroth fired, and one man went down. His colleague crouched beside him, then moved forward.

'Throw out your weapon!'

The old lady with the poodle started to scream.

There was a volley of shots from beneath the van and the policeman crouching on the ground screamed. From a doorway came a burst of machine-gun fire.

'For Christ's sake, don't let them shoot him!' Ryder yelled.

There was a crack outside, and the old woman fell to the ground. White vapour filled the screen.

'We have him! Target is secure, repeat, target is secure.'

'Stun gas,' said Fischer matter-of-factly. 'It's against regulations to use it in civilian areas, but in circumstances like these . . .'

The gas was already clearing. From under the builders' van, Ryder saw Lindroth being dragged, feet first. He was quite limp.

'Its lasts for about thirty minutes,' said Fischer. 'Before you go outside, I advise you to put this on,' and he passed Ryder a mask such as the marksmen were wearing.

*

In Laurel Cottage, as Jane went quietly along the corridor towards the kitchen, she heard Mary and Abby talking softly.

'I'm sure you're wrong,' Abby protested.

'Maybe. But I've been right before.'

Jane paused in the shadows, listening.

'But if you could have seen her at the café, Mary. She was so desolate! So much in need.'

They were talking about her, Jane realized. She had been right: Mary had seen her coming back to the cottage that morning and was suspicious. But why? Something must be happening at the Fellowship to make Mary so wary of spies.

'Abby, sometimes you're so gullible.'

'And you're so—'

The kitchen door creaked, and the two women turned and saw her.

'There you are!' Mary exclaimed with the false heartiness of one who hopes she hasn't been overheard.

Jane gave a small smile. 'Am I too late for breakfast?' she asked.

'Not a bit of it. Come in, come in. How did you sleep?'

Jane caught Mary's eye. The woman hadn't meant to say that, she realized. 'Not very well,' Jane said. 'I went for a walk.'

'Oh, did you?' For a split second Mary looked taken aback. 'Did you see anything nice?'

'A badger,' Jane said truthfully.

Abby's smile was warm. 'Amazing. Wish I could get myself out of bed in time to see something like that. Would you like tea, coffee? There's some toast there.'

Jane asked for coffee, and sat down at the kitchen table. She hoped that her admission had deflected Mary's interest in her.

Over by the sink, Mary was stacking plates. She ran the hot water noisily. It was impossible to tell anything from a person's back, Jane thought.

Over her shoulder Mary said lightly, 'Have you decided whether you want to stay with us for a bit?'

Jane caught Abby's eye. Abby smiled hopefully at her.

'Yes,' Jane said. 'I mean, I'd like to, if that's all right?'

'Of course it is!' they chorused.

'I'm really pleased,' said Abby, and Jane saw that she meant it.

'So, then,' said Mary, wiping her hands on her jeans. 'You two had better be off pretty soon.'

'Off?' asked Jane.

'We're going to the farm-shop,' Abby explained. 'We've got to open it at ten.'

'But David wanted to see me this morning,' Jane said.

'He can see you at lunchtime. He's busy until then,' Mary said.

'That's why we're going to the farm-shop, not to the café,' Abby explained. 'The shop's only down the road.'

Jane would have liked more time on her own, particularly if Norton was absent. On her own, in daylight, she could wander 'innocently' down his driveway. 'Do I have to go to the shop?' she asked. 'I'm so tired. Couldn't I just stay here and wait for David?'

She caught a brief look from Mary to Abby.

'You'd get terribly bored,' Abby said easily. 'And it's much nicer serving at the shop when there's someone to talk to. Come with me.' She smiled winningly.

Were all new recruits under constant guard, Jane wondered, or was such treatment reserved for her, because she had already aroused suspicion? If she insisted on staying behind, it would only deepen Mary's doubts about her, and anyway it was unlikely that Mary would let her be alone.

She returned Abby's smile. 'Okay,' she said.

'You two be off, then,' Mary said brightly. 'I'll clear up here.'

For Alan Goodall, summoned to the hospital the previous evening with the news that his wife and baby son were both ill, it had been an awful night. Sally was beside herself with worry, and none of the medical staff seemed able, or willing, to tell them anything.

So he was glad when, in the morning, the consultant called him aside. They went into a small office at the front of the ward.

The consultant cleared his throat. Most people knew that the listeria microbe could cause miscarriages, he said gently.

Alan swallowed. He knew that. He managed a nod.

But it could also cause meningitis, the doctor continued.

Alan went white. 'You're saying Sally's going to get that?'

'It's possible.' He hesitated.

'And Ned?' Alan whispered.

The doctor felt terrible. 'He's not showing any symptoms yet,' he said hastily, 'and we're treating him early and aggressively with antibiotics – as we are Sally.'

'So they're both going to be all right?' Alan demanded.

The doctor looked away. Sally Goodall had just entered the second half of her pregnancy, which made her a prime candidate for miscarriage. However, the minimum incubation period for listeria was normally three days, and the bug, according to what Sally had told him, had been in her system for only five hours when she reached the hospital. Once there, as a matter of urgency she'd been given antibiotics, which ought to zap the bug – but already she'd reported cramping.

In Hereford, one woman had already lost her baby.

'Doctor?' begged Alan.

'We're doing the best we can for both of them,' the doctor promised. He watched helplessly as Alan broke down and cried.

CHAPTER TWENTY

In the ambulance, on the way to police headquarters, Lindroth was searched. A knife with a short, fat, scalpel-sharp blade was removed from the waistband of his trousers. Also found were a quantity of cash, a French passport, a mobile phone and a small key.

By the time they reached their destination, he had come round. He saw where he was, and a grey mask came down over his face, but he said nothing.

He was able to walk unaided, although hampered by the manacles on his wrists and ankles. He hobbled along the corridor and down the stone steps, past the many officers who had came out to look at him, but he kept his eyes low, trained like a searchlight on the floor in front of him.

He was taken to a medical room and examined by a doctor, who passed him fit for interrogation. Only then was he brought into the room where Fischer and Ryder were waiting. If he was nervous, there was no sign of it. Rather, he had a look of stoic resignation. They knew his real name now: Ernst Bulat.

The prisoner returned Ryder's stare unblinkingly and then, as if bored, looked away. He asked quietly if he might have his handcuffs removed.

'No,' said Fischer equally quietly.

There were three armed policemen in the room and two more outside. Cameras and microphones recorded every sound and movement.

The spools of the tape-recorder on the table began to turn. Fischer had offered Ryder an interpreter, but he had a good working knowledge of German and had declined. It was vital that he took part in the interrogation, but he was keenly aware of his guest status.

'For whom are you working?' Fischer asked.

Bulat-Lindroth stared at the floor.

'What is the nationality of this group or individual?'

Again, no answer.

'How did you receive your orders?'

How was he paid? Had he carried out any other bombings on behalf of the group? Lindroth remained mute.

What did they expect? Ryder thought. The man was a professional. Breaking him might take days, time they might well not have. His own personal nightmare, as yet unexpressed, was that Lindroth's capture might trigger the group's final act. There was a media blackout on his arrest, but how long would it hold? And would Lindroth's paymasters be alerted by his failure to contact them at a specific time?

The prisoner glanced up at the clock on the wall and away again.

In his chest, Ryder's heart beat painfully.

'How do you make contact with your paymaster?' asked Fischer. 'Or other members of the group?'

Overnight, Lucy-Ann had had someone check Ferryman's desk at his office but nothing relating to either Carlucci or the Scroll had been found.

She herself, acting on a sudden impulse that Carlucci might be hiding in his flat, had driven there at one o'clock in the morning, only to find the place in darkness, the curtains open: obviously no one was at home.

The wretched woman had to be somewhere, she thought. A person couldn't simply vanish, and yet that was what Carlucci seemed to have done. She hadn't gone abroad. She was staying with no known friend or acquaintance. She hadn't used a credit card to book into a hotel; she hadn't withdrawn any cash since Monday. So where was she? Who was harbouring her?

After an uncomfortable few hours on a camp-bed in the makeshift dormitory, Lucy-Ann was glad to get back to her desk at seven o'clock. A copy of Ferryman's paper lay before her. On the front page was his account of the Vienna bombing, with his picture by-line.

Lucy-Ann scoured it. It seemed to be a straightforward report. Was it possible that he knew nothing of the Scroll, or the identity of the Keeper? That he'd been in contact with Carlucci about another matter entirely?

Such thoughts chilled her. Ryder was expecting a lead to come out of Ferryman; they were desperately in need of a breakthrough.

No couple resembling the scanty descriptions of the Scroll thieves had been located in the country's cults. Some Rachels and six more Rebeccas still had to be ruled out, but their groups did not fit the image of Armageddon cults. During the night, a sixty-five-year-old former army captain from Leeds had briefly excited attention, but his 'worrying movement' (the words of the local bishop) turned out to be a group of twelve- to sixteen-year-olds whose exuberant acts of worship were looked down upon by other vicars. A lot of church people seemed to take the request to report any 'worrying or eccentric' member or parishioner as an invitation to get even.

Of course, Lucy-Ann knew, the vagueness of the request didn't help, but it couldn't be more specific, for fear of giving away Bridegroom's interest. At least the police collators supplying similar data were largely impartial, although the problem there was that they'd gathered so much information that time was wasted wading through it.

The Helen calls from members of the public were still coming in, and Lucy-Ann dealt with her share of them. By half past ten, over twenty names had been given to the police. Sometimes a woman was named more than once, but in every case questioning of the callers had resulted in no further action being taken. At worst, people were motivated by maliciousness; at best, they wanted to do all they could to help, like the elderly lady Lucy-Ann was now talking to, who had been logged by the *Crimewatch* team as needing a call-back.

'She's terribly like my little Ruthie, you know, dear.'

At the mention of the name Ruthie, Lucy-Ann sat bolt upright. 'I'm sorry. Who is?'

The woman tutted. 'The girl you're showing on the television set.

The thin one, this Helen. She's the spitting image of my Ruthie.'

'Your Ruthie?' Lucy-Ann repeated carefully. A mother shopping her daughter? Such things did happen. An old lady motivated by hearing that one of the listeria mothers had miscarried, that a baby might develop meningitis . . .

'I was her nanny thirty years ago. Lovely little thing, but when her mummy and daddy died, it really hit her. She stopped eating, got ever so thin.'

Lucy-Ann sighed quietly. The woman was reminiscing about a child. They were hunting for a woman. Why hadn't the *Crimewatch* team weeded her out? 'Do you still see Ruth now?' she asked.

'Oh no, dear. She went to live in Australia years ago. And then she died.'

'She died,' Lucy-Ann said flatly.

'Yes. Ever so sad. In the bush, it was. Malaria in the mission-house, the letter said.'

Politely Lucy-Ann expressed her regret before ending the call.

'How's it going?' Jack Broughton asked, looking in through the door.

'Oh, you know,' she said.

'When's Ferryman due back?'

Lucy-Ann had called the *Correspondent* newsdesk at ten o'clock. 'Some time this afternoon. How's Ryder's prisoner?'

'The silent type, it seems. Fingers crossed for Ferryman, then, eh?'

Lucy-Ann smiled wanly. Her phone rang yet again. It was the police collator from central Manchester with a list of three hundred and sixty-eight names of individuals and groups, thirty-six of which he rated as 'worth a look'. 'But I'll fax you the lot, shall I?' he suggested cheerfully.

'That'd be just lovely,' said Lucy-Ann bitterly.

In Ashford, the police collator for West Kent had his assistant compile the list for London.

When she asked what it was for, he shrugged. 'Ours not to reason why. Just do it, will you?'

'Everyone we've got data on?' she queried.

'Well, not everyone,' he said in some exasperation. 'It says: "any person or group with religious connections that currently or in the past has aroused police interest". So all our religious nutters, okay?'

She nodded hesitantly.

'Do it,' the collator said between his teeth. 'Then show it to me.'

She returned two hours later, looking proud of her handiwork. The collator ran his eyes down the list, grunting. He stopped at a name near the end.

'Have you entirely taken leave of your senses?' he asked pleasantly.

'What do you mean?' she said.

'You've put the Fellowship down here.'

'Well, they're religious,' she said defensively.

'Yes, they are. But who's their most important member?'

'Sir?'

'I can't believe you've forgotten.' The collator paused for dramatic effect. 'Only Mary Wilson. Name ring a bell, does it? Only our old man's daughter.'

He saw light dawn. 'Oh,' said his assistant.

'Yes, bloody "Oh". The Fellowship saved little Mary, remember? So, the old man loves the Fellowship. The Fellowship can do no wrong. What d'you think would happen to me if he saw this?'

'Sir,' she said weakly.

The collator picked up his pen and ruled a fat black line through the name. 'Delete it on your screen and send it up there,' he said in disgust.

The house was ready. Following David's advice, Jordan had waited until dark before he and the others covered the windows at the front of the house.

On the first floor, the bedrooms were draped in black; purple covered the walls on the ground floor, in every room save that for which Jordan had been responsible.

He had set his alarm for 5.30 a.m. When it shrilled, he was awake at once. He felt as though he was on automatic pilot. He went down to the hallway phone and connected the tape-recorder to it. He dialled the number David had given him and set the timer for one o'clock that afternoon.

Then he went back upstairs to the men's bedrooms, shook each of them by the shoulder; went on to the girls' rooms and knocked on the doors.

'It's time.'

They dressed as he had asked them to, in plain black sweatshirts and jogging pants, and silver Nike trainers. They followed him downstairs to the shrine room.

As they entered they gasped, and he couldn't help grinning; the room did look splendid. It was sheathed in gold: the walls, the ceiling, the floor, even the windows were covered. Only the altar stood out, gloriously draped in purple.

There were four objects on it: a Bible, a golden cross, a notebook and the document David had given Jordan before he left England.

David had asked him not to read it and he hadn't. But when he'd unfurled it to lay it on the altar, he hadn't been able to help seeing that it was very old, and was written in a foreign language.

Everyone was present now, awaiting his orders. They must have some inkling, he thought, and yet there was no sign of fear. He was glad of that; he didn't want them to be afraid.

He closed the door, and said 'Please will you all sit down in a semi-circle.'

They did as he asked, in two rows, the girls in front of the men.

He moved over to the altar. Beneath it, covered by the purple cloth, were the two bags of chemicals that he had to prime later. From the box on the altar, he took out the small plastic container David had given him. He opened it. There were eleven little white pills inside. He would be taking his later, once his last tasks were complete.

He went over to the first of the girls and put a tablet to her mouth. 'For David,' he said softly.

'For David,' she whispered, swallowing it.

CHAPTER TWENTY-ONE

The farm-shop stood in a lay-by beside the main London road. It was a simple wooden hut, lit by fluorescent strip-lights, with the produce displayed in the window. Jane realized that she and Sam must have driven straight past it the day before.

She wondered what he was doing, if he was getting anxious that she hadn't called, if any more had happened on the listeria story, whether Helen had struck again.

She longed for a newspaper or a radio or, best of all, a phone, but there was no sign of any of them in the shop, and she dared not risk arousing Abby's concern by asking. Judging by what she'd overheard, Abby was on her side. Jane needed to keep her there.

Abby wedged the shop door open.

'We'll have them queuing up in a moment, ' she said with a smile. 'We're very popular round here.'

'Have you been at the Fellowship long?' Jane asked.

'About a year. I got recruited up at Waterloo. I was a right old mess.'

'Oh?' Jane said.

'The booze. I was an alcoholic.'

Jane looked in surprise at Abby's fresh face.

'I know. I'm all right now. I got dried out. Well, David got me dried out.'

She told Jane of her sad childhood – children's homes, foster care, homelessness, her 'escape' to London, which had turned out to be anything but, her rescue by the Fellowship. 'I don't know what your life's been like,' she concluded, 'and don't feel you have to tell me if you don't want to. All I'm saying is, if Jesus can help me, He can help you too.'

Jane heard in her words the ring of truth. Abby was a good person, she thought, definitely in the innocent category at the Fellowship. Norton might be the Keeper, he might be responsible for committing terrible deeds, but, like many of the notorious NRM leaders she'd studied, he had clearly helped people like Abby. That was where the confusion lay: how 'good' people could also be capable of terrible evil. From Jane's work, she knew it to be true.

'Here's our first customer,' Abby said.

A string of others followed. As at the café, many of them were clearly regulars, who knew Abby and liked her.

'It's really nice having someone else here,' Abby said when the shop had emptied. 'It makes the time go so much faster.'

'Why not get a radio?' Jane suggested. 'That'd be company.'

Abby looked momentarily flustered. 'Well, yes, I suppose it would. Oh look, the boys in blue.'

'What?' Jane started.

'The police. They're paying us a call.'

The police car stopped in the lay-by, and two uniformed men got out. Jane's heart turned over. They'd tracked her down, she thought. They'd make her talk, although she had no evidence. If Norton was the Keeper, they'd panic him, force his hand. She froze where she stood.

'What's wrong?' Abby said sharply.

There was no time to think of an explanation.

'Quick, get in under here, under the till,' Abby hissed. 'They won't see you.'

For a split second Jane couldn't move, then she dived under the counter. There was just room. She tucked her legs under her, and buried her face against her knees, making herself as small as possible.

'Hello there,' said a man's voice.

Abby returned a cheerful greeting. 'What would you like today?' she asked brightly.

'I'll have some cherries, please,' said the man.

'You choose your own, then,' said Abby firmly, and Jane realized she wasn't going to leave her post in case it revealed her hideout. 'Then it can't be said I gave you any dud ones,' Abby added.

'As if you would, my dear.'

'How's things going up at the Moor?' asked the second officer.

'Fine, thank you. And at the station?' Abby replied perkily.

'Pandemonium, seeing as how you ask.'

He chatted on about overtime and his wife's grumbles that she never saw him these days.

It was all right, Jane thought, they weren't after her. They genuinely wanted fruit and vegetables. At last they went out.

When the sound of their car had died away, Abby bent down. 'It's all right, Jane, you can come out now,' she said quietly.

Jane emerged, dusting herself down. 'Thanks very much,' she said.

'Don't mention it,' Abby said.

'I thought they were looking for me.'

'Yes, I realize that.'

Jane felt she owed Abby at least a token explanation. 'I haven't done anything wrong,' she said.

The faraway expression left Abby's eyes. 'It wouldn't matter if you had, love. We'd protect you.'

Jane saw that she meant it. She wished she could question Abby outright, ask her about Kirsten, about the lack of telephones and televisions, but one wrong question might make her change sides and report Jane to Mary, or even to Norton.

'Feel safe,' Abby urged.

'Thanks,' Jane said with a smile. 'I will.'

Without a word, with only a look of blissful happiness, the girl accepted the items David gave her: a pink sweatshirt to go over her denim blouse, sunglasses, a handbag and a capacious suitcase with her name and New York address on its label.

In their new garb – his a dark jumper and old golf cap – they entered the airport. In the main concourse, he handed over her ticket and passport and directed her to the appropriate check-in.

Originally, he'd wanted to go with her, to handle the paperwork himself, but Ruth had pointed out the risk involved in that, of someone remembering him.

He watched the girl go forward on her own. He knew, deep down, that she had no mistakes to make: with every step that she took from now on, the Lord would be there in front of her.

He leant against a pillar. No one was watching her, or him. She came back towards him, her face alight with life.

'All done, angel?' he queried.

'Yes. . .' she hesitated, then said with a shy smile, 'Grandpa.'

She was changed. She was truly like his granddaughter, he thought, as they made their way to a coffee-shop. With deep joy, he listened to her animated chatter about New York. No trace now of the lost down-and-out, the most tremulous, the most fearful, of his children. He had only needed to say the word. He'd seen it happen many times before, yet each time was a miracle. Take an idea inspired by Jesus, add to it the power of the Holy Spirit, and see how gloriously everything was made new.

He let her talk on. It was good, he reminded himself, not simply for camouflage but for her own sake. If she sincerely believed, her sincerity would shine forth before others, and would shield her against any doubts Satan might seek to sow when she was on her own.

He checked the time. As if the airline had too, over the loud-speakers came the announcement calling her flight.

'I wish you were coming too,' she said in a small voice, suddenly a little too much like her old voice for comfort.

'You know I can't. Sweetheart, look at me.'

Unwillingly, her eyes came up. They were swimming with tears.

He felt her dread at leaving him. 'We won't be parted for long,' he promised.

'No?' The tears hovered.

'No.' He smiled. 'You believe me, don't you?'

She gave a small frown, and the tears rolled away. She nodded vigorously.

'Good. Now, we mustn't forget your tablets,' he said, and produced the packet from his pocket. They were an ordinary over-the-counter prescription for hay fever. 'We can't have you sneezing all the way to New York. Take four now,' he murmured, unpopping them from their plastic cover, 'and another two in five hours. Take a sip of water with them.'

Obediently, she put them in her mouth and swallowed.

He did stare then, just for a moment, but again it was as Ross had told him: no visible sign.

She got up and shouldered her bag. She seemed refreshed, stronger than he had ever seen her before. He knew it was Jesus' work, strengthening her for what lay ahead, breathing his Holy breath into her.

She wanted to hold his hand and he let her. They walked in silence, but when he looked down she was looking up at him, not smiling but absorbing him carefully. As if she knew, he thought, marvelling.

They reached the barrier beyond which he could not go. He could feel tears in his own eyes as he bent to kiss her, but she returned his embrace lightly, and as her boarding-pass was inspected she turned and waved him a bright goodbye.

There was nothing more he could do for her. She was in the Lord's hands now; the Lord would look after her: He would not let anyone tamper with the contents of her bag.

David walked back into the concourse. There was a bank of television screens there, and he glanced at them, but there was no news of Vermont, or Charleston, and nor should there be, yet. There was, though, fresh news about the listeria cases.

He turned away. He didn't like watching such things in public, for fear of giving himself away. He returned to his car.

A mile from the airport, he dialled a mobile number. It was answered on the second ring.

'What's new?' David asked cheerfully.

'Jane didn't want to go to the farm-shop. She wanted to stay behind here on her own.'

That didn't strike him as particularly ominous.

'She seems keen to meet you again.'

David smiled. He was right about her.

'And Daddy rang.'

Daddy was Chief Constable Edward Wilson, Mary's father. 'What did he want?' David asked, and his voice rasped a bit.

'Only to say he's coming on Sunday,' said Mary, and he breathed easily again.

'The vicar rang, too,' she added.

David screwed up his face. 'The vicar?'

'He asked if you'd call him back.'

David frowned. It couldn't be important. But he believed in treating the authorities, even the Church of England variety, with respect. He pulled onto the hard shoulder and scribbled down the number. Traffic screamed by. What did the vicar want? he wondered, dialling the number.

The vicar's wife answered. She put her husband on.

'David!' His hearty voice boomed in David's ear. 'Good of you to call back. Just wanted to let you know I think you may be going to get some unwelcome media attention.'

Thump-thump-thump went David's heart. 'Why's that?' he said.

He listened, aghast, as the vicar described his encounter with the man in the pub. Another journalist, David thought, trembling. Sweet Jesus, how many more were there going to be? Why was the Lord allowing it? What did He want him to do?

'What?' he interrupted suddenly. 'What did you say his name was?'

'Well, he didn't say. But the girl who called him asked for "Sam".'

'Sam?' repeated David, and rivers of relief flowed from him.

'That's right, and I think he called her Kirsty. Something like that.'

The vicar ran on but David ceased to listen. He was chuckling with Jesus. The vicar was reporting Kirsten's call to Ferryman, the one that had sealed Ferryman's fate. Indeed, David thought, he was expecting at any minute to hear news on that very topic.

'And you,' David said when the vicar eventually stopped, 'are you busy?' Vicars, in his experience, were always busy, but they liked to be asked.

'Very.' A sigh. 'And the bishop's just rung to ask me for the names of any parishioners whose views I find worrying or eccentric. I ask you!'

David froze. Why should the bishop ask that? It could only be that the authorities were looking for him. He remembered the alert that had frightened Ross. They must be desperate to risk involving the churches. Was that, he wondered, his stomach churning, the real reason why the vicar had phoned? To tell David he was about to shop him?

'Well, I could write a book on it,' exclaimed the vicar.

'I'm sorry?' David whispered. He could make another call, he told himself frantically, he could hire another professional, but that would take time. Perhaps Steven could be called upon? If he lured the vicar up to the Moor? Invited him for lunch?

'But there's no way I'm going to do it,' said the vicar.

'What?' David said inelegantly.

'Tell tales to the bishop. I'm sorry, but to my mind it's just not Christian.'

David's hand was sweaty. He almost dropped the mobile.

'Don't you agree?' the vicar said.

David found his voice. 'Yes. My goodness, yes! You're absolutely right. Not Christian in the least. ' He was babbling, he realized. 'It's Jesus who must judge, not us,' he said more soberly.

'You're so right. I might tell the bishop that.'

'Do that,' David said generously. 'Don't mention my name, though.'

'No? Why?' The vicar broke off, hee-hawing with laughter. 'You mean he might think I'm worried about you?'

He laughed some more. David joined in.

'You could always report me,' the vicar suggested.

'I might just do that!'

They ended the conversation with mutual best wishes. For a while, David sat staring at the traffic racing past on the motorway. The authorities were closing in. He'd known it would happen, particularly with Ruth's work being performed so close to the end. But that was how the Lord had willed it, everything coming together to tie in with Vienna. The Lord would see them through – and the diversions, of course, were about to be begin. Soon the authorities would be looking in an entirely different place.

He started the engine and moved out quickly into the fast lane. He was in a hurry to get back to Jane, to get Jesus' reading on her.

There was a day-care centre on the first floor of the Veerholt Institute in Charleston. Parents began dropping off their children at seven-thirty in the morning; some spent a few minutes first in the play-park opposite.

At seven-thirty that morning, six children were using the park; five of them were content with the slide and the swings, but the sixth, a little boy, insisted on playing in the bushes.

'Jonah, will you come out of there?' called his exasperated mother.

There had been reports of a man lurking around the area. 'Jonah!'

Reluctantly, the little boy emerged. His mother grabbed him painfully by the arm. 'You've made me late,' she said crossly.

'There was a box,' he wailed.

'Yeah?' She was going to be late for the second time in a week. Another black mark against her, and her productivity levels were lagging. She jerked Jonah along.

He tried again. 'It was tied up with black tape.'

They were outside the park now, waiting to cross the road.

'Mm, hmm,' she said.

'But I didn't open it, ' he said, peering up, seeking redemption.

'There's a good boy,' said his mother, seeing a break in the traffic and illegally running for it.

It was many months since Ross had seen Ruth and Norton together and he'd forgotten – or perhaps had never properly appreciated – how much it hurt.

Ruth changed when she was with Norton. He couldn't now imagine her selling poisoned toffee-apples or spiking maternity meals. She had become soft and much more religious; a curious light radiated from her eyes; she had become, if possible, he thought wistfully, more lovely. But she no longer saw him. She saw only Norton.

She and Norton shone in each other's presence, and their glow obliterated all else. They finished each other's sentences; sometimes they didn't even need words. When Norton said, 'Jesus made me laugh so much last night!' Ruth didn't snicker as Ross did, as any normal person would. No, she pealed with laughter. It was that joy that ground away at him, like grit in his eye, causing him agony.

Their love for each other – and, yes, he had to admit it, for their weird, off-the-wall joint-projection of God – transcended Ruth's love for him, Ross. It transcended sex and everything he had to offer her. Beside her feelings for Norton, those for him were nothing. When they'd arrived at the Fellowship, Ruth had left him sitting in the van while she jumped out and ran into Norton's outstretched arms. 'Darling,' she'd cried. 'My precious love.'

Ross came back to the present and saw that Ruth was watching him.

'Are you all right?' she asked.

'Fine.'

They were in the chapel at the back of Norton's house. On the floor in front of the altar was the container they had brought from Wales. Norton had wanted it there – 'God's new instruments', he'd called its contents – beside the casket with the ancient Scroll and the swaddling-clothes.

'I wonder if she's gone through yet?' said Ruth anxiously.

Ross didn't reply, although he knew that Ruth wanted to talk, that she was nervous and looking for reassurance.

'I'm sure they won't have found anything,' she said.

He glanced down at her.

'In her bag,' she faltered, and in spite of himself, his heart melted a little to see her thus.

'I'm sure they won't,' he said, although actually he'd been amusing himself with the picture of Norton being caught red-handed, spreadeagled on the floor with SAS men jumping on him.

'How long before anything, you know, happens?'

'Five hours,' he said. She already knew that.

Then, 'I hope you don't feel left out, Ross,' she went on in a rush. 'It's just that being back here' – her face filled with light – 'among these holy things . . . You know I love you, Ross.'

He whipped round in hope.

'But it's just that David and I' – he dropped his eyes – 'we're like two halves coming together again.'

But that was how it was for him, he wanted to cry. 'You don't have to explain,' he said hoarsely.

'Oh, Ross, I'm so pleased to hear you say that!'

And she did look pleased, light and free and heedless, like a happy child, of those she hurt.

'David should be calling any minute,' she said. 'Shall we go into the office in case we don't hear the phone from here?'

She went on ahead. Briefly he contemplated the container at his feet, what he could do there and then with its contents. The thought was tempting. He could destroy Norton's end-game, the years of planning, the timing of his other operations – but the end would be the same, Ross thought sourly. Norton would still win.

There would be another time, another way.

The interrogation had been under way for two hours, but to Ryder it seemed that he had been sitting forever in that drab, grey cell in

Vienna, with Gerhard Fischer beside him, and in front of him the sprawling, hateful figure of Werner Lindroth.

Lindroth was wanted in connection with eleven bombings in six European countries. He belonged to no known ideological group, although it was thought that in the past he'd worked for both the Iraqi and the Kuwaiti secret services. He had never before been caught in the West.

Ryder had watched Lindroth assess them. At first, he'd been watchful and alert, but when he'd realized the style of the interrogation: the quiet, almost respectful voice of Fischer urging him to tell the truth, to supply them, please, with the answers to their questions, he had relaxed. He'd grown as insolent as a chained prisoner could: he'd yawned and stretched and gazed about him and generally made a great display of his boredom.

Ryder was boiling with frustration. Lindroth might be the missing piece he sought, and Lindroth should, by rights, be his. Beck and one or two others in London certainly thought so, and were growing increasingly curt in the face of Ryder's failure, as they saw it, to get answers. If he'd been on his own with Lindroth, Ryder thought, he'd have had those answers by now. The prisoner wouldn't be sitting there, rocking gently to an inaudible beat. He'd have spilled his guts.

As it was, Ryder had been forced to play the silent partner, and to his prejudiced eye, it seemed that Lindroth knew that. Whenever Ryder looked at him, he smiled back, as if mocking him for his emasculated presence at the feeblest, most risible of interrogations.

'I said, shall we take a break?' Fischer asked.

'I'm sorry. Yes, indeed.'

They went to the adjoining room where a two-way mirror and listening devices allowed them to see and hear the prisoner. Ryder turned his back. He'd had enough of looking at Lindroth.

'A most unpleasant fellow,' Fischer said mildly.

'He is that.'

'Completely uncooperative.' Fischer took a bite of his sandwich. 'I think it's time to change tactics.'

Ryder paused, his coffee cup halfway to his lips.

'You agree?' Fischer asked.

'Absolutely I do.'

'So.' Fischer swallowed the rest of his sandwich whole. 'Are you ready?'

Ryder followed him out into the corridor. At the cell doorway, Fischer called the guards out and dismissed them. As the last one left, he put out a hand and took his rifle.

He and Ryder re-entered the room.

By the set of Lindroth's head, Ryder saw that they had won his attention.

'You talk to him,' Fischer said, and Ryder went forward.

There was a sheen of sweat on Lindroth's face that hadn't been there before.

'On whose orders did you plant the bomb?' Ryder asked.

Lindroth stared straight ahead.

'Did you hear what my colleague said?' asked Fischer, who'd taken up station behind him.

Lindroth said nothing but a nervous tic began in his cheek. Fischer released the rifle's safety catch. In that quiet room, the sound clicked round the walls. Lindroth swallowed.

'Who gave you your orders?' asked Ryder, going close up.

Lindroth dropped his head.

'Answer the question,' said Ryder.

The head dropped further.

Ryder caught the movement out of the corner of his eye: Fischer's rifle swinging back and up, then coming down fast, the steel connecting with Lindroth's unprotected arm. Ryder heard a bone snap.

Lindroth screamed. He rolled off the chair onto the floor. Ryder knew he should feel shocked, but he thought of the dead and maimed at the Peace Centre and felt only pleasure.

He stood over the man and asked, 'Are you going to talk to us now?'

Lindroth kept moving, trying to protect his broken arm.

Ryder kept pace. 'Lindroth?' he said.

Lindroth reached the wall. He turned his face into it.

Ryder caught Fischer's eye. He kicked Lindroth in the kidneys.

He screamed again.

Ryder glanced at the two-way mirror. Senior officers and the doctor would be watching. He didn't know how much more they would allow.

Lindroth vomited. The smell turned Ryder's stomach.

Fischer came up. 'You want some more?' he asked softly.

'No!' croaked Lindroth.

'So talk.'

Lindroth raised his eyes. He looked terrible.

Ryder squatted beside him. 'Who told you to bomb the Centre?' he asked.

A shudder shook Lindroth. 'He'll kill me,' he whispered.

'Or we will,' promised Fischer.

Lindroth's mouth worked. 'I don't know his name.'

'Come on,' growled Fischer.

'I promise. I've never met him. He contacted me.'

'Nationality?' asked Ryder.

'I don't know. French? Italian? He's got an accent.' Lindroth was doing his best to be helpful now. 'It had to be the Centre. It had to be peace talks. The rest was up to me.'

'How did he contact you? How were you going to be paid?'

The bloodless lips worked. 'He called me. On my mobile.'

'This one?' said Fischer, picking it up from the table.

The prisoner nodded.

Calls made to that number could be traced, Ryder knew, but to what end? It was unlikely that Lindroth's paymaster would still be in the same place.

'How did he pay you?' he asked. Money left trails too.

Lindroth looked up. 'Can we do a deal?' he pleaded.

Ryder looked at Fischer.

'Maybe,' said Fischer.

'He pays cash. A third up front, the rest after. Leaves it in a mailbox. Different places, countries, I don't know where.'

Ryder remembered the small key found when Lindroth was searched. 'Has he contacted you about your last instalment yet?' he demanded.

Lindroth shook his head. The movement seemed to jar him. 'My arm,' he groaned, closing his eyes.

Don't faint yet, Ryder prayed. 'When's he calling you?'

'Four o'clock.'

It was two o'clock now.

'Something for the pain,' begged Lindroth.

Fischer glanced towards the two-way mirror. 'Send in a doctor,' he ordered. 'We'll get you dosed with painkillers,' he told Lindroth. 'You'll be fine by four.'

'But I can't speak to him! He'll know!'
'He'll know nothing unless you tell him.'
The cell door opened and a white-faced doctor entered.

CHAPTER TWENTY-TWO

Promptly at one o'clock, Abby shut up the farm-shop and drove Jane back to the Fellowship.

'There's nothing to be nervous about,' she said, as they entered the driveway to Norton's house.

'I know.' Jane smiled briefly. But she was nervous. If she was right about Norton, he was clever and dangerous, and she was about to enter his kingdom, alone, to question him.

She knew what she was doing, she told herself. She could handle him.

The jeep brushed against the overhanging cedar trees. They rounded a bend and a square, white house stood there, its gleaming windows reflecting little light.

To the right, by some shrubs, there was a high brick wall with a black metal door in the middle. To the left, a double garage, being closed by a man in Fellowship uniform. She caught a glimpse of a white vehicle inside, but there was no sign of the blue van she had seen at dawn.

Abby parked by the steps to the front door. 'I'll take you in,' she said kindly.

They climbed the steps and went in.

The first thing that struck Jane was the smell of polish, and then flowers, a great bowl of roses on a round table in the hall. Everything gleamed with cleanliness. Ahead of her, a flight of stairs ran straight up to the first floor. Standard lamps cast a soft, creamy glow. It was very quiet and very welcoming, she thought, like the rest of the Moor.

'Hullo.' A man's head came round a doorway. He smiled. 'David's just coming.'

He and Abby looked towards the back of the house. Jane did likewise. Running along the side of the staircase was a narrow corridor leading to a baize-covered door. On the wall beside it was a brass grille: an intercom system. There was a buzzzing sound then the door opened.

'I'll just have a quick word,' Abby said, darting out, and taking Jane by surprise. She watched the door close behind them.

Was Abby reporting on her? wondered Jane, her pulse racing. In spite of her carefulness, had she aroused Abby's suspicions as well as Mary's? Had Mary already told Norton about her dawn walk?

She strained her ears in the direction of the door but she could hear nothing.

'Does David live down there?' she asked the man.

'Kind of. Those are his private rooms.'

Jane looked thoughtfully at the door. His private rooms, cut off from the rest of the house. Why the need for locks and intercoms? Were there secret laboratories down there?

The door swung open and Abby came out, with Norton behind her.

'Jane, my dear,' he said, his face folding into a smile. 'I'm sorry to have kept you waiting.'

He was looking at her with the same intensity of expression as he had the night before. His 'loving' look, she thought.

'Let's go in here,' he suggested, opening a door on his left.

'See you later,' murmured Abby, passing by.

Jane entered the room. It had the same comfortable, welcoming aura as the hall. There was an open fireplace with a sofa and two fat armchairs placed at angles to it. The colour scheme was blue and gold. There were books on the shelves, flowers on a table by the window.

'Like it?' said Norton, still smiling.

She turned quickly. 'Yes,' she said. 'It's nice.'

'Do take a seat,' he murmured.

She went to one of the chairs. Norton took the other. He crossed his legs slowly. For a full minute, he said nothing, merely sat, his fingers steepled, looking thoughtfully at her.

If that was his approach with all newcomers, she thought, she could imagine how intimidating some would find it. She didn't attempt to stare him out, but after a second or two dropped her eyes.

'Abby tells me you're afraid of the police?' he inquired in the most gentle fashion.

She was right; Abby had reported on her. 'Yes,' she admitted.

'Why is that?'

She'd had time by now to think of an explanation. 'My boyfriend's a policeman,' she said in a low voice. 'He beats me up.'

'Really.'

He didn't believe her, she thought. She resisted the urge to protest it was the truth.

'I'm very sorry to hear that,' he said eventually.

'I'm just scared of the police now, you see.'

'I see, yes.' Norton's eyes bored into hers. She had a sudden image of herself being sucked along in a fast river, trying to get a hand-hold to withstand the current. She saw how easy it would be to give in.

She bit her lip. 'You won't phone the police, will you, David?' she begged.

He smiled thinly. 'Be assured I shall not. We shan't let the police get you.'

Her heart turned over. Was that a threat? He knew, or suspected, far too much. How long would it be before Sam grew sufficiently concerned to come looking for her? The next day? Or next week?

Norton leant forward in his chair. 'Set your mind at rest, dear child. If we receive any police inquiries about you, we shall deflect them.'

She stared at him. He looked genuine now. Had she misread him? Did he believe her?

'This is your sanctuary now, Jane, and, if you like, your home.' He smiled, apparently with warmth. 'What lies ahead of you is a new life. A new world, if only you will open your eyes and see it.'

That was roughly Christian doctrine, Jane thought. He couldn't suspect her if he was trying to convert to her.

'"Behold I stand at the door and knock,"' he said.

A quotation from Revelation, the Apocalyptic book of the Bible. The book most loved by the Armageddon sects.

'"If any man or woman hears my voice, and opens the door, I shall come in."'

It was more of the same verse.

'That's Jesus speaking,' said Norton softly. 'Jesus knocking on the door of your heart, waiting to be admitted.'

He was being extremely direct, Jane thought. Most evangelists did a warm-up first, explored a recruit's life, looking for a toe-hold, in order not to frighten them off. What was his hurry?

He sat back. 'Your mind is full of questions, isn't it?' There was more of a challenge in his voice than before.

'I'm sorry. I was listening, only . . .'

'Only?' He picked up instantly.

'I think I've been afraid for so long that I find it difficult to relax. To believe that I can be safe anywhere.'

He studied her for a long moment. He might not believe her, she thought, but he wanted to. 'Can I ask you something?' he said, and she noted the paternalistic tone was absent.

She nodded cautiously.

'Are you a reporter?'

For a moment, time stopped. Her watch ticked loudly. He thought she was another Kirsten, she realized. She thanked God that she didn't blush easily. 'No,' she said firmly.

'No, of course you're not.' His relief was obvious.

'Why should I be?' she asked, doing her best to sound bewildered.

'No reason, none at all. Forget I asked. Will you do that?' He fixed her with his look.

Jane nodded. His ego was so big that he was actually quite easy to deceive, at least on one level.

'Good girl. In time you'll come to understand that Jesus can answer all your questions. You have only to ask Him.'

'Really?'

'Really,' he smiled. 'Fire away.'

'Why does He let people suffer? You know, innocent people? Like those children who ate the toffee-apples and were poisoned?'

He stared at her. It took all her courage to keep looking at him, the small frown intact upon her face. Was he guilty? she wondered, her heart hammering? Or was he merely trying to think of an answer to her question?

'I don't know,' he said slowly. 'Suffering is very difficult to understand, isn't it?'

She nodded. Were they both acting?

'One could ask why God lets Jane suffer at the hands of her boyfriend.'

'Yes,' she said, glad of the diversion.

His face lit up. 'To bring you here to me, that's why. There's a plan for everything and everyone on this earth. Do you believe that?'

'Maybe.' She looked confused. 'I don't know. Can I think about it?'

'Of course you can.' He looked at her fondly. If that expression was genuine, she thought, she'd passed his test.

'And will you also think about what I've said, about Jesus knocking?'

'Yes.' She nodded again. It was important for him to believe that she was going to convert. 'Yes, I will.'

'Good. Why not have Abby show you around this afternoon?'

'That'd be nice.' Jane hesitated. She needed to make contact with Sam. 'Or I might go for a walk. To think.'

Norton stood up. 'As long as you're back for the church service tonight. I think you'll find it . . . interesting,' he smiled.

She smiled back.

'Abby's waiting for you outside,' he said.

Her dismissal. 'Thank you,' she said awkwardly, getting up.

'God bless,' he said and, resuming his seat, closed his eyes, she presumed in prayer. She left the room, quietly shutting the door behind her. Outside in the corridor, she heard Abby talking to someone in the office off the hall.

She glanced behind her, then stared. The baize door to Norton's private rooms wasn't properly shut.

She felt as if she had swallowed ice. This might be the only chance she'd get to see what he was so careful to conceal. His laboratories? His prison? But if she was caught, what explanation could she give?

If she hesitated any longer, she wouldn't do it. She pushed open the door. She half expected an alarm to sound, but none did.

She eased herself through, pushing the door almost shut behind her. In front of her ran a long, narrow passageway with doors on either side. At the far end was a bolted stable-door. A single fluorescent striplight glowed dimly overhead. Voices came from one room. She froze, then realized it was the sound of a television set; the news. So Norton was in touch with world events; it was only his Fellowshippers who were kept in ignorance.

She went forward, her trainers silent on the stone floor.

'An eighth member of the Syrian peace team has succumbed to injuries inflicted by the Blade Bomb last night,' said the news-reader.

The door on Jane's right was open. A flickering light came from within. Her heart in her mouth, she went over and looked inside. The room was empty, lit by candlelight.

It was a chapel: at the front, there was an altar on which were a simple wooden cross and a box. On the floor were three wine-red velvet kneelers and beside them a small cubical container that looked a bit like a fridge.

Jane bent down, then saw the combination lock. She paused. The sound of the television suddenly seemed to get louder, but then the volume dropped again. She turned her attention back to the box on the altar. She put her hands on its lid, expecting it to be locked, but it lifted to her touch.

She felt rather than saw someone watching her. She whipped round and saw, or thought she saw, a figure in the doorway, but it moved so quickly that she wasn't sure. She raced across the chapel. There was no one in the passageway, but she heard footsteps very near by.

She ran to the baize door, pushed it open and pulled it shut behind her.

'Jane?' Abby was calling, out of sight.

Jane's heart was beating so fast that she didn't think she could speak.

Abby appeared at the top of the corridor. 'Are you all right?' she asked, concerned. 'You look dazed or something.'

'I . . . I've been thinking about what David said to me.'

The door of the blue and gold sitting-room opened, and Norton appeared. 'What's going on?' he asked sharply.

'"Behold I stand at the door and knock,"' said Jane in a faraway voice. 'I can see Jesus doing it.'

They both stared at her: Abby curiously, Norton suspiciously.

'Can you?' he asked.

'Yes,' she murmured.

There was a pause.

'What does He look like?' Norton asked.

'Oh, He's . . .' She bit her lip. 'He's golden,' she whispered.

She heard Norton's intake of breath. 'He is, isn't He?' he said softly. 'Abby,' he went on after a moment, 'take Jane for a walk, will you?'

Abby took her arm and Jane let herself be led away.

She could feel Norton's eyes on her as she went. Had she deceived him? She thought she probably had. But was it all about to be undone by the person who'd seen her in the chapel?

'What does He look like?' asked Abby softly.

Jane turned to her. She hadn't meant Abby to be deceived. 'I can't really describe Him,' she said.

'Oh. You are lucky, having a vision like that.'

In silence, they descended the steps outside together.

It was by simple good fortune that he'd seen her, Ross thought exultantly.

He'd been on his way to his room, leaving Ruth watching the news, when he'd seen the shadow on the chapel wall, the snooper's shadow cast by the candlelight. He'd seen her at the box, her face in profile, her dark shiny hair, and had got away just before she saw him.

Sitting on his bed, he hugged himself in excitement. Who was she? The police? Special Branch? MI5? Another journalist? She'd seen the Scroll. Norton would have a heart attack.

Should he tell him? But then the game would be over. He'd have nothing left to do but watch Norton and Ruth bill and coo over each other. Whereas now Ross could watch the girl, see what she was up to and, if he liked what he saw, decide whether to help her.

Ruth had deserted him. But the girl needed him.

Ross sucked the knuckles of his hand. The power had at last returned to him. He, not Norton, was in control now.

Was Jane who she claimed to be? wondered David. A battered runaway? She certainly had the hallmarks of a fearful person – jumpy, careful – and her description of the Lord . . . David himself always saw Jesus in a golden light.

Why should she not have a vision? In the last days, it said in the gospels, old people would dream dreams, young people would see wonders.

And yet . . . In spite of the vision, in spite of Abby's report on how Jane had reacted to the police, and in spite of his own careful examination, he could not quite dismiss a certain unease about her. She'd asked him about the toffee-apple children. Was that a mere coincidence – as he'd decided at the time – or had Mary been right about her all along?

Was she a spy? If so, for whom? She certainly wasn't a journalist. If she had lied to him about that, he'd have known instantly. Nor did he believe she was a private detective hired by a Fellowshipper's parents, or a policewoman, his two other main concerns. She wasn't professional enough and, anyway, as to the latter, Mary's father would never allow such a thing. There was always the possibility, of course, that she came from outside Wilson's jurisdiction, from Scotland Yard or MI5. He pondered that idea for a moment.

Had the swaddling-clothes thief had been arrested? Had he talked, had the trail led back, somehow, to himself? But no, if that were so they'd never have sent Jane, a mere girl, on her own. Men would have come in with guns blazing.

If that happened, everything would be lost, which was why they wouldn't come; the Lord would not allow it, not now when they were so close to the end.

David stared out of the window. In the courtyard sat Ruth and Ross's van. No point in taking chances. One slip now could still cost him dearly, could still ruin the Lord's plan.

He made up his mind. Jane might be innocent, a visionary sent to him as a last gift, a replacement daughter, in which case she would come forward at the church service that night, to give her life to Jesus.

If she did not, he would know she was not from the Lord, but a wolf, sent by Satan into the fold of his lambs. Steven would deal with her.

In the meantime, she would not be allowed to leave them. Every move she made would be monitored. She had mentioned a walk. She would not be on her own. Everywhere she went, the Shepherds would be watching. He would give them special instructions.

He glanced at the time. It was almost eighteen hours since he had given special instructions regarding Ferryman. Surely a dead journalist would be reported on the news? And yet there had been nothing.

He took out his mobile phone and looked at it. He wished he could ring for an update, but it was too risky. He must wait, he must have faith.

He dialled Mary's number.

With a quiet sigh of satisfaction, Maitland hung up. He had just been informed by a laconic man on the newsdesk that Ferryman was due back in the office later that afternoon.

'D'you have a precise time?' Maitland had queried.

'About four,' the man said, slamming down the phone.

They were very impolite on the newsdesk, Maitland thought. It was his second call of the day. From the first, he had learnt that Ferryman was only in Vienna for the morning. He looked at the time. Two hours to go.

He was bored with the camper-van; he'd slept all he needed to. Changing into dark trousers and a shirt, he left the car-park and went to explore the pedestrian precinct before it was time to report to the *Correspondent*'s front hall.

In her softest voice, Lucy-Ann asked to speak to Sam Ferryman.

'I'm afraid he's not yet back, but he will be soon,' said Monica. She paused, not wanting to frighten off Sam's contact.

'You called before, didn't you?' she asked quietly.

'Yes,' Lucy-Ann admitted, a trifle worried. But it was all right she told herself. The woman she was speaking to couldn't trace the call, and if she dialled 1471 she'd be told that the caller had withheld their number.

'Is there anything I can help you with?' Monica went on. 'You're not in trouble, are you?'

'Trouble?' said Lucy-Ann. 'No, nothing like that.'

'Good.' Monica paused. She wondered if the girl felt too intimidated to talk to her. 'I know who you are,' she added.

Lucy-Ann froze.

'I mean, I know you're working for Sam on the cult.'

'Ah,' said Lucy-Ann, her heart leaping. She longed to ask which one, but knew she couldn't. She waited, hoping that the other woman would say more.

On the other end of the line, Monica was hoping the same thing. Eventually she said. 'He'll be back by four. Why not call him then?'

'I'll do that,' promised Lucy-Ann, and rang off. She looked at her watch: only two hours to wait.

She'd be glad to get out of the room. It was hot and very noisy, and the pressure and exhaustion were getting to everyone. As if that weren't enough, the air-conditioning had packed up, and big, whirring fans had been brought in to do an inadequate job.

Her phone rang. She stared at it, hating it. She picked it up. A member of the *Crimewatch* brigade told her that a tourist from Manchester had some photographs he thought they ought to see.

'Why?' asked Lucy-Ann cautiously.

'He was in Covent Garden two Sundays ago. Took pictures of everything, including the Foodie Lanes.'

'Oh yes?' said Lucy-Ann, interested now.

'He says he's got a picture of a white Bedford van, with a young chap taking a baker's tray out of the back.'

'A man?

'Yup. But there's a woman in the picture too.'

Lucy-Ann closed her eyes and prayed. They so needed a clear head-shot of Botulism Helen.

'I'm afraid you can't see much of her. She was walking away.'

Her spirits slumped.

'Funny thing is,' the constable went on, 'the van number plate's different from the one we've got.'

A real plate, thought Lucy-Ann, her heart leaping again. 'Have you run a check on it yet?' she asked.

'No, I thought I'd let you know straight away.'

Lucy-Ann thanked the gods that he'd come through to her. She took down the new number and keyed it into her computer.

At the hospital it was ward-round time. The consultant and a team of medical students were clustered round Sally's bed. She wished now that she hadn't given permission for them to be there: so many eyes staring at her, secretly judging her a bad mother, a lazy cow who'd endangered her babies' lives because she couldn't be bothered to cook properly.

She could feel herself getting worked up, the very thing they'd told her she mustn't do. She took that to mean that they weren't fully confident in the treatment they were giving her; that if she didn't keep calm she might miscarry.

Ned, in the babies' ward, was doing fine, they'd told her, and Alan had reassured her on that point. But if he was doing so well, she'd demanded, why couldn't he go home?

No one had answered that one. There were things they weren't telling her; things they knew that would only panic her.

Her womb contracted painfully and she cried out.

'Mrs Goodall?' exclaimed the consultant in concern.

She could feel the baby move; she could feel his pain.

'Alan!' she screamed.

CHAPTER TWENTY-THREE

The drugs administered to Lindroth had numbed his arm without dulling his senses. To Ryder, he appeared hyper. The paymaster would know there was something amiss and would instantly be gone.

On the cell wall, the minute hand of the clock jumped. Lindroth, sitting opposite Fischer and next to Ryder, broke the silence. 'How long do I have to keep him talking?' he asked.

He knew that, thought Ryder. The bug installed in his mobile needed only fifteen seconds to work but Ryder was worried because, according to Lindroth, the caller was always very abrupt.

It was one minute to four. The caller was relentlessly punctual, Lindroth said.

Ryder could smell the man's sweat; he could see it forming on him.

Four o'clock. Five past. Ryder watched the seconds tick away. The mobile remained silent.

'He's not going to call,' Lindroth said, and there was relief in his voice.

'Shut up,' said Fischer.

If he didn't call, thought Ryder, they were lost again, back sifting through a haystack. There was no good news from London. A new number for Helen's van had turned out to be another false plate.

The country's police forces and clergyman had supplied thousands of new leads but no evidence: Bridegroom's staff were drowning in data. It wouldn't be long before desperate measures would cease to seem desperate, and in their taking lay the greatest danger.

The mobile rang.

'I can't do it.' Lindroth's voice shook.

'Do it,' said Fischer.

Lindroth picked up the phone. 'Yes?' he muttered.

Through Ryder's earpiece came a guttural mid-European voice. 'Amsterdam. The Red Post Box at 110 Rembrandtplein.'

'At Rembrandtplein,' repeated Lindroth dully.

'Correct. The number is 0126679. Got that?'

'Yes – No, wait.'

Fischer was making stretching signs with his hands.

'I'm not sure,' said Lindroth. 'I'm sorry. Can you repeat it?'

Ryder closed his eyes. The caller would know. Through his earpiece, he heard the number being repeated impatiently.

'Fine, okay, I've got it now, 'said Lindroth. 'Thank you.'

The line went dead.

'Well?' said Fischer, staring at the unseen faces beyond the mirror.

The call had lasted fifteen point two seconds. It would be enough, Ryder thought, so long as the caller hadn't been alerted by Lindroth's tone.

'Paris!' shouted Fischer. He pulled out his earpiece. Ryder did likewise.

'Hey, what about my deal?' demanded Lindroth as they made for the door.

Fischer paused. 'There is no deal,' he said.

Lindroth went white. 'You fucking bastard! You. . .'

'I know.' Fischer shut the door.

In the yard, a helicopter was waiting. An assault team was being scrambled and would meet them at the airport. They would be in Paris in ninety minutes.

The apartment, in a street off Paris's rue de Rivoli, was similar to hundreds that Mikhail Severin had rented over the years. It was in a quiet, prosperous area popular with tourists, so paying cash for two days' rent only had seemed nothing out of the ordinary to the landlord.

Severin believed he had stayed free – had stayed alive – so long because his security requirements were so exacting. They had been ingrained in him by his original Bulgarian masters and honed by his own long years of self-employment. He never spoke directly to a client, but both received and issued his orders through a system of cut-outs. The clients contacted them on mobile phones, and then called him in turn on a mobile. He changed his own number regularly. Mobile phones, though not untraceable, were far safer than land-lines.

He thought of himself as a man with extra eyes and ears. He prided himself on doing the unexpected. As well, he was superstitious, increasingly so with age: more and more, he believed in warnings, in gut-feelings, and believed in heeding them, which was why he had moved so abruptly the previous day, and why, the next morning, he would move on again.

On and off, since the Saudi boys, he'd had presentiments: a sense of the hunters being after him, a face in the crowd, footsteps, a sudden coldness in the nape of his neck. In the past seven weeks, he'd travelled extensively: Rome, Caracas, the Philippines, Austria (his favourite country), but nowhere had he been able to shake off entirely that foreboding. Occasionally, especially recently, he had suspected he was being watched. There had been a couple of dead calls on the mobile. Two days before, in Rotterdam, there had been a car, two men sitting in a side street.

It couldn't be true, he told himself: if it were, he'd have been caught by now. He was getting old, he was starting to imagine things, like the way in which the Vienna bomber had spoken to him just then: stilted, nervous-sounding as if someone had been listening in – and why, Severin worried, hadn't he got the address down straight away? He knew the score, how important it was not to talk too long, particularly when he, Severin, had been using a land-line. Not that the bomber would have known that, he admitted grudgingly.

Had the bomber been caught? Was he even now leading the cops to Paris?

The apartment was on the fifth floor of an old building; it looked down into the tree-lined street. Severin looked out cautiously both ways. There were two old men walking, arms clasped behind their backs, some parked cars but no one in them. It was safe down there; no one was coming.

All he knew of the bomber was that he was Austrian. The Austrians were a race who could be trusted, and their country was one where he'd have liked to live himself. He didn't know if after a job the bomber was jumpier than before. It took some people that way. He himself was always elated; the trickier the job, the greater the buzz.

Take those Saudi boys. His orders had been precise. First, he had to choose them from four sets of brothers, all Arabs. And then that peculiar detail had to be satisfied; the mode of their death, struck down – by an axe, by a car, by a blow, it hadn't mattered. It had been up to him, which had pleased him. He liked being given a free hand.

They'd been an easy target. He'd lured them away from their schoolmates by saying he'd lost his puppy in the woods. They'd run to look, one either side of the path, and a quick karate chop each was all that was needed. The client had reportedly been delighted.

He was an unusual client, Severin mused: the Saudi twins, then the bomb and now this latest order, the English journalist. Knowing a good man in Britain, Severin had been able to see to that matter quickly. He'd just heard that Maitland was already in position in the journalist's office. The call had come through on his mobile, as he was about to dial the bomber's number, which had delayed him not just by the duration of the call, but afterwards. He had a rule that once a job was in progress, the mobile was off-limits for any other use, in case there was a problem, or the client changed his mind. And so he'd had to go looking for the apartment phone, which was out in the hall, by the door.

A light came on in Severin's head. He had been late in calling the bomber, perhaps by five or more minutes, he estimated. He was getting old, forgetting that. At one time his memory had been excellent, now he was having to write numbers down. The delay would explain the bomber's nervousness. He felt a wave of relief; he would be able to concentrate now on the matter in hand instead of worrying over problems that did not exist.

Jane had hoped that when she left Norton's house she would be able to shake Abby off and make her way down to the village. She wanted to call Sam and tell him everything she'd seen. She wanted a second opinion on whether being 'seen' twice – by Mary and by the spy in the chapel – meant she couldn't hope to remain undetected much longer.

'I'd really like to be on my own,' Jane said as they reached to the village green.

Abby looked troubled. 'I think David wanted me to be with you,' she said.

'Why? I'm not going to run away.'

Abby smiled at her. 'That's good to hear.'

'So I'll see you later then?' She turned to go.

Abby caught her arm. 'Please. Let me come with you.'

There was real pleading in her voice. Had she been ordered not to let Jane out of her sight? Jane gave in; she didn't want a confrontation with the only Fellowshipper she felt might be a friend.

They walked round the Moor. There were few Fellowshippers about: Mary waved to them from the garden of Laurel Cottage. The clock on the church tower chimed three-thirty.

Jane's mind was racing. Had she been mistaken about the spy in the chapel? Was it her own nervousness that had made her feel she was being watched? Surely whoever had seen her would have reported her by now, and they would have come for her? She must have imagined the shadow.

Two male Fellowshippers were approaching them, one in dark glasses.

'Great day,' he said.

'Want a lift down to Hawkenhurst?' offered the other.

'Jane?' asked Abby.

Jane thought fast. She might have a chance of escaping from Abby, but not from three of them. 'I'm really enjoying just walking about,' she said.

'Fine,' said Abby.

The men left them.

'Why don't we go down the lane?' Abby suggested.

'Okay,' said Jane, and they set off along the road she had taken that morning.

She saw the defunct phone box up ahead. It would be a shame to leave now, she thought, before she had hard proof of Norton's guilt. The signs were there. He was an enormously egotistical and charismatic figure, hero-worshipped by his followers, among whom there was an inner circle. There was the warehouse and Norton's hidden annexe, his monitoring of world events while the majority of his Fellowshippers knew nothing.

If life at the Fellowship had always been like that, Norton would have come to her attention long before now. Recruits would have left, and their stories would have reached her. Did that mean, she wondered suddenly, that Norton was taking chances now, because he was in the very last stages of his own plan? That his final act was imminent?

If only she'd had another few minutes in the chapel, if only she'd seen what lay inside that box. Or been able to find out what or who was behind those other doors.

'You can always use the phone up at the house,' Abby said, breaking in on her thoughts.

'I'm sorry?'

'It's just you've been staring at that phone box. It doesn't work.'

Jane hadn't realized she'd been staring. She must be more careful. 'D'you mean there's a phone at Laurel Cottage?' she asked.

'No, at David's house. We're free to use it whenever we like.'

And be listened into, Jane thought drily. 'Don't you miss having a television?' she asked casually.

'Not really. We used to have one, but we hardly ever watched it.'

'Why not?'

'Well, most evenings there are activities and so much of what's on television is depressing.'

'D'you think so?' queried Jane.

'Yes, I do really. So much violence, and so on. David talked to us about it once, a few months ago. He said that, as so many of us found the programmes depressing, perhaps it would be a demonstration of love by the rest to do without TV. So we gave them away.'

So that was how he had done it.

Abby smiled at her. 'Don't worry, you soon get used to doing without it, you know. And newspapers. In fact, it's quite refreshing.'

Jane stared at her: she seemed to believe it. Again, Jane wished she could question her more, but she dared not probe further.

They rounded the bend in the road. Through the trees, Jane made out the low shape of the warehouse. 'D' you know what that is?' she asked.

Abby peered at it. 'No idea,' she said, and Jane was sure she was telling the truth. 'If we keep going on this road, it sweeps round to Hawkenhurst,' Abby went on. 'D'you want to go there?'

Jane nodded. The walk took half an hour. As they entered the high street, Jane saw the bright poppy-red of a phone box a little way ahead. But how to get rid of Abby?

She also saw, on the other side of the street, the two men who'd offered them a lift.

'Are you hungry?' Abby asked. 'We kind of missed lunch, didn't we?'

At her suggestion, they made for a tea-room. It was an old-fashioned place, half full of local people. Several looked round when they went in, glanced briefly at the uniforms, and then looked away again. Another indication, Jane thought, of the integrated nature of the Fellowship, of Norton's skill at creating no ripples.

A waitress came over and took their order. At another table, a woman hailed her.

'Is your telephone working today?' she called out.

It was, the waitress replied.

Jane watched the customer rise to her feet and go to the back of the shop, to a corridor where, according to the signs, the lavatories also were.

The waitress brought their food.

Jane toyed with it. The other customer returned. As soon as Jane could, she excused herself.

'Are you OK?' Abby was immediately full of concern.

'I'll be fine. I won't be long.'

She made her way to the back of the restaurant and the corridor. In an alcove under the staircase, the phone hung on the wall. She lifted the receiver and dialled Sam's direct line.

'Sam, it's me,' she said eagerly. It was so good to be talking to him, she thought, to be touching base with reality.

'Hi.'

'I've met Norton,' she said, keeping her voice low. 'I really think he could be a candidate.'

'I see.'

That wasn't quite the reception she had expected. 'Are you OK?' she asked him.

'Actually, I've got a visitor at the moment.'

A visitor? she thought. Wasn't talking to her more important? 'I don't know when I'll be able to get away again,' she told him urgently.

'Really?'

He sounded almost uninterested, she thought in exasperation.

'Can you call me later? There is someone here.'

Suddenly, she heard the strain in his voice. He couldn't speak openly, and what was more he was trying to shut her up. Who was the 'someone' with him? Had the security services traced their calls? Were they monitoring her now?

'I'll try to call you late tonight,' she muttered, and put the phone down. She was scared. Had she said too much? Had she spoken for too long, not just implicating Sam but leading them to her at what could be the wrong time – the critical time?

She stepped out of the alcove. Abby was standing there.

'I came to see if you were all right,' she said blankly.

Oh God, thought Jane. How much had she heard? Everything? 'Oh, thanks,' she stammered, 'I, er, felt better and saw the phone, and, er . . .'

Abby said nothing. Jane tried to read her expression: was it simple puzzlement, or was it betrayal?

Jane cleared her throat and tried again. 'I needed to make a call.'

'Oh.' Abby's worried eyes searched her face. A part of her wanted to believe her, Jane realized, was at war with the rest. 'But I told you you could use David's,' Abby said.

'Yes. It was a spur-of-the-moment thing.'

'Oh.' Abby said again. 'Who were you calling?'

Jane blinked. 'I'd rather not say,' she croaked.

'Not your boyfriend?'

What a godsend, Jane thought, lowering her eyes.

'Oh, Jane, you're crazy! Did you tell him where you were?'

'No.'

'Well, thank God for that, anyway.'

'You won't tell anyone?' Jane begged. 'Please don't. I feel so stupid.'

She could tell that Abbey was torn between helping Jane and doing what she was supposed to do. 'All right,' Abby said eventually. 'I won't tell anyone.'

'Oh, thank you,' Jane said sincerely.

'Come on, you, let's go and pay.'

*

As soon as Sam had walked in to the office at four o'clock, Monica told him his 'cult girl' had been on the phone, asking for him. Their conversation had been cut short by reception calling up to say there was a female in reception to see Sam, but she wouldn't give her name.

Either Jane or Kirsten, Sam had thought, racing to meet the lift. Then the doors had opened and Miss Burroughs stepped out.

She claimed to be from the Home Office department overseeing GUIDE, but Sam didn't think so. He thought she was a spook, like the man he'd seen in Vienna. He guessed they'd traced his calls to Jane's lines. He guessed, too, that one of the reasons she was there was to find out, if she could, where Jane was. He had no intention of telling her.

He had been playing her along nicely, he considered, giving an excellent performance of believing her cover-story, when Jane phoned.

He tried to get rid of her as quickly as he could without giving anything away, but when he replaced the receiver, Miss Burroughs was watching him closely. She couldn't have identified Jane's voice, could she? he thought anxiously.

'Who was that?' she asked.

'Our stringer in Vienna. I've just got back from covering the bomb story.'

'Oh yes. A terrible business.' Her eyes hadn't left his face. 'Peacemakers cut down like that.'

He realized immediately that she was referring to the Eighth Scroll.

She was still watching him like a hawk. 'Awful carnage,' he murmured. 'You never get used to it.'

'No. What did your contact say?'

For a moment, he was flummoxed. 'He's got a possible lead on who might have done it.'

'Oh?'

'But he's not very reliable,' Sam added quickly, not wanting to be detained over a lie.

'I see. Did you meet Jane Carlucci?'

The starkness of her question took him aback. Prior to the call, she'd been all concern, claiming to be there on a 'damage-limitation exercise' caused by Jane's illness: perhaps Sam had read the D-notice about her? They were anxious to trace all journalists she'd spoken to; Sam's name was in her notebook.

'Yes, I met her,' he said indifferently. 'She came in for lunch a couple of days ago.'

'Did she?' Burroughs's eyes gleamed and Sam hoped he had been right to tell the truth. But to have lied would have been risky: too many people had seen them together.

'And how did she seem?' Burroughs went on. 'Stressed?'

He shook his head. 'Not particularly, but then I hardly know her.'

'No?'

'I've only spoken to her a couple of times.'

'What about?'

He was starting to feel breathless. 'An NRM up in Hampstead that I'm investigating.'

'Oh?' she said. 'May I ask why?'

He saw an opportunity and seized it. 'I'm still doing the story,' he said reluctantly.

She chuckled. 'I won't tell anyone.'

I bet, he thought. 'They're stealing people's trust funds,' he confided. He could tell she wasn't convinced. 'My information is they're also into mind-control.'

'Are they?' she said softly. 'Was Jane able to help you much?'

'No, that was the problem. I knew more about them than she did.'

'I see.'

'Yes, she thought they were absolutely above board.'

'And yet you say you spoke to her twice about them?'

He took a breath. 'I invited her to lunch. People often say things face to face that they won't over the phone.'

He watched her unwillingly acknowledge that. 'Did she talk to you over lunch about any other groups?' she asked.

'Nope.'

She paused. 'Did she mention the Keeper?'

His throat constricted. 'No. Who's that?'

She said lightly, 'Oh, no one, probably. She's been making wild allegations about a number of people, giving them nicknames, alleging goodness knows what.' She rolled her eyes and Sam smiled.

For the first time since Jane had called, he thought about what she'd said. She believed Norton was a candidate, and in Vienna, he'd seen at first hand the result of the Keeper's carnage. But only 'a candidate'. Not 'guilty', so she couldn't yet have found any evidence.

'Jane didn't mention any particular fears?' Burroughs continued, her eyes boring into him. 'She didn't mention any old prophecies, in particular?'

'Prophecies?' She must be truly desperate to take the risk of asking that. 'What sort of prophecies?'

'Oh, you know, the end of the world is nigh. Your Hampstead group isn't into that sort of thing, I suppose?' she asked casually.

'Not that I know of. I think they're very much into having their cake here on earth.'

'They are.' She held his gaze. 'Do you know where Jane is, Mr Ferryman?'

He felt his heart thud. 'No, I don't,' he said.

She stared at him a fraction longer, then looked away. 'Well, thank you very much for seeing me.'

'Not at all.'

He escorted her back to the lift. 'Here's my card.' She gave him a Home Office one. It looked genuine, but then he would have expected it to.

'If Jane contacts you, you'll bear in mind that we are extremely anxious to locate her, for her own sake?' she asked.

'Sure. But I shouldn't think she will.'

They shook hands and she got into the lift.

As the doors closed on her, he leant back against the wall, feeling drained. He thought he'd convinced her, but he couldn't be sure. Apart from letting her desperation show, she'd been good. If the security services were prepared to go to the risk of questioning a journalist so closely, they must believe that Jane's knowledge was crucial to their investigations. He guessed that if he'd been anything other than a journalist, he'd have endured a far more rigorous interrogation, probably in less pleasant surroundings than his office.

Like Jane, though for different reasons, Sam had little faith in the authorities' ability to launch a successful assault on a dangerous cult. He'd investigated too many occasions when they'd made fatal mistakes and then attempted a cover-up. He recalled a raid on a 'bomb factory' in Leeds when two young children had been killed; innocent men forced to admit to crimes they hadn't committed; an embassy siege that had ended in a bloodbath.

Suppose, he thought, the Fellowship was guilty and it had a nuclear weapon? A botched assault could not just cause another Waco but a global holocaust.

Jane thought that about six signs had been completed. Vienna made it seven, which still gave them time – for Jane to get her evidence, for him to find out what he could about Norton. If they found something concrete, if they found what 'Awful Horror' Norton had in mind, that would be the time to alert the authorities: to present them with all the facts, so that mistakes couldn't be made. And, once it was over, he would be able to write the definitive backgrounder without risk of a D-notice.

He considered Jane's call. He'd scarcely given her a chance to speak, but he'd detected no panic or fear in her voice. If she thought Norton a candidate, as she said, she was in a dangerous place. But he believed her when she said she could look after herself.

If she failed to call him that night he would take up Kirsten's offer, and drive down to 'visit' her and Jane the next day. Either Kirsten had entirely misread the situation, or she had been lying to him. He rather thought it was the former.

He returned to his desk. He knew his phone was safe because of the loop, but even so, just in case Jane rang back sooner than she'd said, he used a neighbour's empty desk and lines.

The religious-affairs specialist came by. 'How's Hampstead coming along?' he asked.

'Not bad. I'd better get cracking with it, actually.'

He picked up his borrowed phone, and dialled St Peter's Church in Knightsbridge.

The doorbell rang. Severin had been dozing in front of the television, but instantly he was awake, on guard. He tiptoed out into the narrow hallway, unclipping his shoulder-holster and removing the small automatic.

Through the spyhole he saw an Algerian maid holding a pile of laundry. These were serviced apartments. She rang again.

'Towels and turn-down,' she called.

He opened the door on its chain. 'You're early,' he said.

'I'll come back later, Monsieur,' she offered with a shrug.

He had heard such offers before; they never came back. He was a fastidious man. He put away his gun and unlocked the door.

'Come in,' he said shortly.

When the flight attendant passed the girl a meal-tray she took it, but she didn't unwrap or eat anything. She was feeling rather sick and she had pins and needles in her hands and feet. Not having flown before, she didn't know whether those were symptoms of air-sickness or the effects of the drugs administered to her. David had warned her that her tuberculosis jab might make her feel slightly unwell.

In her hands she held the packet of hay-fever tablets. She had read the instructions and knew that he'd already given her twice the recommended dose. Yet he'd told her to repeat that dosage now, five hours later. She wondered why, especially when she didn't suffer from hay-fever in the first place, but she wasn't worried. David must know she needed them. Her lips formed a gentle smile: David wouldn't let any harm befall her. She was his special child. He loved her.

To her it was a miracle that he did, that he should have chosen her, her who had been so reviled and hateful all her life. But since coming to the Fellowship and meeting him, she had met Jesus too and her eyes had been opened to her sins. She had asked for, and received, forgiveness, and much more besides: love such as she had never had before. Now that she was loved, she was able to give love in return. She loved the fat man sitting next to her, the whiny toddler in the row in front. She loved everyone with the love of God that David had given her, she could feel it course through her body, warming her. In return for such love, she would have done much more for David than what he'd asked of her; she would have given everything she had, she would have laid down her life for him.

She frowned: there was something the matter with her eyes. The weave of the blue cloth of the seat in front kept swimming out of focus, like the game of lazy mirrors at funfairs. David was right, she thought groggily, she did need some more of those tablets. She pushed them out of their silver foil and put them in her mouth, and then, because her eyes still seemed to be playing tricks with her, and her feet were numb, she leant back against her head-rest, closed her eyes and fell asleep.

Within an hour of the call to Lindroth, French commandos had stormed apartment 14 in the building off the rue de Rivoli.

Forty minutes later, Ryder and Fischer arrived. The target was on the fifth floor; there was a lift, but the doors had been jammed open upstairs by the police, so they took the stairs.

A commando in a black flak-jacket was waiting for them. He escorted them down the dark corridor and through a door that hung off its hinges.

The body lay on the carpet, face upturned, the eyes fixed and staring. Blood was still oozing from a massive throat wound. The man's head was almost off. Ryder had seen many violent deaths, but for a moment nausea seized him and he had to turn away.

'He hasn't been dead long,' commented Fischer, crouching by the body. 'He's still warm.'

The dead man was wearing a white shirt. There was a shoulder holster, but no weapon. Fischer pulled it from a trouser pocket.

Why, Ryder wondered, had a professional killer not tried to defend himself? There were no signs of a struggle in the flat. Had the man had admitted his killers? Had he been taken unawares?

Ryder knelt down on the dead man's other side, and saw a piece of paper sticking out of his pocket. 'May I?' he asked Fischer, out of courtesy.

'Of course. You want some gloves?'

Ryder pulled them on. The paper was pinned to the pocket lining with a dressmaker's pin. He extracted it carefully. It was folded in four. Ryder flattened it out and saw that it was ruled with faint blue ink, the sort of paper found in an exercise book. In spidery black ink, there was a short line in Arabic script. Written below in English was 'There will be no hiding-place. Vengeance is mine.'

He closed his eyes. He heard Khalil al-Safr's voice after the inquest, reading out Prince Ibrahim's vow to avenge the murder of his sons.

'What is it?' demanded Fischer.

'I think I know who killed him.'

'Well?'

'It's not going to do us any good,' Ryder said bleakly. He suspected the trail would go cold long before it led back to the boys' father. And in context, in the hunt for the cult, it would be wasted effort. This killing had nothing to do with the Eighth Scroll, it was a personal matter.

A commando came in from the bedroom. 'This was by the bed,' he said, handing Fischer a small notebook.

Fischer flicked through it. 'Telephone numbers,' he said briefly to Ryder. 'No names, only initials.'

'Any of them in Britain?' Ryder asked.

'I don't know, most of them look like mobiles to me. Here you are,' Fischer said, giving it up. 'It's yours.'

'But surely it's your evidence?' Ryder protested.

'It's Bridegroom business now, and I don't like our groom.'

Ryder took the book. 'I'll get the contents scanned straight over to London,' he said.

CHAPTER TWENTY-FOUR

The newspaper was folded into a wire rack hanging outside the village store. Its headline was clearly visible: 'Peacemakers Cut to Death by Blade Bomb'.

Jane stared at it. She saw at once the connection to the second sign. She'd thought that sign had been fulfilled years ago; there had been an atrocity in Jerusalem that seemed to fit. The truth jumped before her eyes. Had Norton done it?

'Jane?' Abby had walked on ahead. Now she turned. 'Is there something you want to buy in there?'

Since the telephone call, and her promise to keep it a secret, Abby had been even sweeter and kinder to Jane than before, seeing her as a victim, Jane thought: someone in need of protection. Jane didn't like the deceit, but she needed Abby's sympathy.

'I can lend you the money,' Abby offered, coming back.

'It's not that.' Suddenly Jane wanted to test her. 'There's a terrible story about a bomb,' she said, 'about peace-makers being cut to death.'

'Oh, how horrible,' Abby said instantly. She glanced up at the paper rack, and away again, quickly. 'That's what I mean, Jane. D'you really want to get upset reading about such things?'

Jane was sure she knew nothing. How cleverly Norton had

achieved his purpose. Not by banning access to the media, but by offering instead a haven from the world, where no one knew anything about bombs, or violence, or babies dying, or mothers miscarrying. Where the majority of the Fellowshippers experienced only love and easy living, and didn't want to inquire further. Basic mind-control, but so subtly done that it had passed unnoticed.

They resumed their walk back along the high street. They'd already seen the local beauty-spot, a ruined abbey, and they agreed it was time to go back to the Fellowship. As they crossed the road, Jane saw a sign to the railway station.

A car pulled into the kerb beside them.

'Hi, there,' called a woman's voice, and glancing down Jane saw Mary in the passenger seat. There was a male Fellowshipper driving, and two other men in the back seat.

'Hi,' said Abby.

None of the men bothered to greet them, Jane noted.

'Where have you two been?' Mary asked, and to Jane it seemed there was more of a demand in her voice than a casual enquiry merited.

'Nowhere. I mean, we've just been here,' said Abby. 'I took Jane along to see the ruins after we had some lunch.'

'Oh.'

'Were you looking for us?' Abby asked.

'No, no,' Mary replied quickly. There was a pause. 'But you must be awfully tired by now. Would you like a lift back?'

'We're fine,' said Jane.

'Abby, you look tired,' said Mary firmly.

'Well, I . . .' Abby was flustered.

'There isn't any room,' Jane pointed out.

'Oh, the chaps won't mind walking, will you?' Mary asked, swinging round on the two in the back seat.

They got out. Jane recognized one of them from the village green earlier on, and she realized she'd seen him in Hawkenhurst that afternoon. They must have been following her and Abby, she thought with a chill. When they had left the café they'd used a side door that led on to a footpath to the ruins. To their watchers, they had gone 'missing'.

The man was holding open the nearside door.

'I suppose we might as well,' said Abby. 'Jane?'

'I'll walk back up on my own,' Jane said.

They all looked at her. They couldn't manhandle her into the car, she thought, in daylight, in the middle of the village. Already one or two people were looking over at them.

'But Jane you must be tired after your dawn walk,' said Mary, and again Jane detected steel in her voice.

'Come on, Jane,' murmured Abby, taking her gently by the elbow.

If she resisted, if she caused a scene, they'd abandon her there, Jane thought, and then she wouldn't be able to return to the Moor to continue her investigation. If she considered she was really in danger, that was precisely what she ought to do. But she remembered that headline; she still needed proof. She got into the car and Abby got in beside her.

The door slammed shut, and the car moved off.

Coming in the opposite direction was another car with two male Fellowshippers in front, two women in the back.

Jane recognized Steven at the wheel. He was talking into a mobile. A search party had been sent to look for her and Abby. She wondered now whether her decision to return to the Moor had been the right one.

'Isn't it nice to get the weight off your feet?' asked Mary.

Abby agreed quietly.

Jane glanced back. Steven's car had done a U-turn in the pub car-park and was following them back up the hill.

She was being herded in, she thought with a stab of panic, and the gates would be locked behind her.

Replacing the telephone receiver, David offered up a quick prayer of thanks. Jane had been found.

There still remained, however, the matter of Sam Ferryman. David stared at the newspaper story on his computer screen. Ferryman knew about the Scroll. Ferryman was showing off.

'Peacemakers Cut to Death by Blade Bomb'.

The other papers talked of the Blade Bomb, talked of the victims being cut to shreds, but only Ferryman had used the word 'Peacemakers'. His headline stood out, as he had intended it should, sending a message to David.

Ferryman ought to have gone on, David thought wrathfully; he ought to have transcribed the whole sign – but no, he wanted only to tease.

David's eyes narrowed. That was a dangerous game to play. Very dangerous, if Jane was part of the game, and was there at the Moor on her own. If he found that was the case, she wouldn't be playing much longer, and neither would Ferryman.

He supposed the journalist's trip to Vienna to report the bomb would have delayed the hitman a bit. But hitmen could travel, couldn't they? Certainly for the sort of money David was paying, they could. By that night, or assuredly by the next morning, Ferryman would cease to be a problem. Jane too if she didn't convert. The Lord would see that it was done, according to His plan.

David glanced at the time. It was almost five o'clock; noon in Vermont, New York and Charleston.

The Lord's plans were all under way. The plane first, then the house, then the bomb. He felt a thrill of excitement. He could stay there, in front of CNN and watch each one unfold.

He sobered. He was needed in the chapel. Ruth was already in there, praying. He went to join her.

It was good news, they told Alan Goodall. Sally had not miscarried; her pain had been caused by sudden, severe cramping, the most likely cause of which was stress.

She had been given a mild sedative.

'But the baby,' Alan cried.

It was designed specifically for pregnant women. It wouldn't harm the baby, the houseman assured him.

Alan nodded. In truth, after that afternoon, he was too drained to feel much.

Sally was asleep now, the doctor said, would probably sleep until early morning. Why didn't Alan go home and get some rest himself?

Alan shook his head. He couldn't do that: go home to an empty house, without Ned, without Sally.

He went up to the children's ward.

They'd put Ned in a little cubicle on his own. There was a nurse with him, playing peek-a-boo behind her hands. Ned was chortling gleefully.

'Oh, Mr Goodall,' she looked up. 'You've got a gorgeous little boy.'

'Yes,' said Alan. 'Yes I have.'

He picked Ned up. He held him close, smelt his special baby smell. 'Please God,' he prayed, 'if you have to take one of the babies, take the one I don't know. Leave Ned.'

'I'll leave you together,' said the nurse, discreetly withdrawing.

At an early stage of his enquiries, Sam learnt that Norton's old church had undergone what were described as two 'revolutions' – complete changes of leadership, and therefore largely of congregation – in the previous ten years. Tracking down someone who remembered Norton was proving frustratingly hard.

After an hour, he located a deaconess with an old address book. She gave him eight names. In the next forty minutes, Sam discovered that one had died, three had moved away and one was at a bridge tournament. On the answering-machines of the remaining three, he left messages.

Monica came over, asking how the 'special' was coming along, what his undercover woman had said, when he thought he'd be able to start writing.

Sam answered evasively, saying he was planning to start work on it properly that weekend.

'Good man. Don't work too hard. See *Crimewatch* is running another Helen special tonight?'

Sam said he hadn't.

'They've got a second number plate for her – false again, but they're hoping someone will have spotted it.' Monica paused, uncharacteristically pensive. 'She's really thought it out, hasn't she? I mean, she must have planned it for months. Makes you wonder why she's doing it.'

Sam said nothing.

'Anyway,' she went on more robustly, 'it makes great copy. We've got "A Psychologist Writes" for tomorrow's paper. See you Sunday?'

Sam nodded. When she'd gone, he checked on the latest about the botulism and listeria cases. All the botulism children had recovered sufficiently to be sent home. The listeria news wasn't so good: a second woman had miscarried and the condition of a third, the mother whose ten-month-old son was also in hospital, was 'giving some cause for concern'.

Sam felt sombre, and in some way, because of his secret

knowledge, responsible. If later, when Jane called, she was able to supply one iota of evidence linking the Fellowship to Helen, they must act at once.

It was almost seven o'clock. He diverted all incoming calls to his home number, and left the newsfloor.

In the lobby, Maitland glanced at the time: two minutes to seven. He'd been sitting in the *Correspondent* lobby for three and a half hours. He had seen that day's paper, he had seen Ferryman's photograph on the front page, so there'd be no problem identifying him. But there'd been no sign of him.

Maitland had positioned himself as close to the reception desk as he could, so he had the best possible chance of overhearing what people said. Once, right at the beginning, a woman had come in, asked for Ferryman, and been admitted. He had waited on tenterhooks for them both to appear, but after half an hour she had emerged alone.

How long did journalists work? Maitland wondered. And how long could he sit there unchallenged? The lobby, crowded until now, was beginning to thin out. He watched the night security staff arrive; soon someone would want to know who he was and why he was there.

Maitland stood up. He leant over the reception desk and asked for Sam Ferryman.

'And you are?' the receptionist enquired.

Maitland gave a fictitious name. 'It's about a story,' he said, inspired.

The receptionist gave him a blank look, before picking up a handset. 'He's gone,' she told Maitland a minute later.

'But I've been sitting here,' he exclaimed.

The receptionist shrugged.

'Did he know you were waiting?' one of the security men asked.

'No, well, not precisely.' Maitland saw the man regarding him curiously. 'I dropped in on the off-chance,' he said with dignity.

The other security man, less suspicious, said, 'He's one of the journalists isn't he? He'll have gone straight down to the basement to get his car, I should think, and gone home.'

'Oh,' said Maitland, knowing he should have thought of that.

'Next time, ask for him,' suggested the pleasanter guard.

Maitland gave a brief nod, as if in thanks. He was in a hurry now to leave.

After her meeting with Ferryman, Lucy-Ann immediately called Vauxhall from her car and asked Jack Broughton for a 'likelihood' check on any Hampstead NRMs.

The answer came back quickly. There were only two in that area, one Buddhist, the other Baptist with a lot of wealthy young people in its congregation. GUIDE had recent files on them and there was nothing to suggest 'Keeper' status, but did she want the members of either or both detained?

Lucy-Ann considered. The Hampstead group appeared to fit in perfectly with the information Ferryman had given her. She knew that trust-fund scandals were in the news, but on the other hand she suspected Ferryman had been lying.

During the alleged Vienna call, he'd been eager to get rid of the person on the other end. Lucy-Ann had had a fleeting notion that the caller was Carlucci. Ferryman had covered up well, but then journalists were practised liars. She was almost convinced that the Hampstead NRM was a red herring, but she couldn't afford to take chances.

'Have someone pay them a visit.'

'Tonight?' Broughton asked.

'Yes.'

'What're you going to do about Ferryman?' he asked.

'Continue to monitor him,' she said.

'You could lift him,' he sugggested.

Ryder had sanctioned it, saying the decision was hers. She suspected, however, that such an action could prove counterproductive: that Ferryman, with his anti-establishment bias, would resist interrogation. Of course, he'd crack eventually, but there were all the problems associated with detaining a journalist. Lucy-Ann felt she could obtain the information she wanted, and was nearly sure he had, more quickly and less painfully by monitoring his home line, and keeping a watch on his flat.

She'd have to do it herself – the acute staff shortage meant there was no one else available, and there might not be, Broughton warned her, until the following morning. Additionally, she might have to be recalled.

Lucy-Ann didn't mind. Sitting in the car-park in Battersea Park would be pleasant compared to Vauxhall.

For once, the roads weren't clogged and she was able to make good time. Twenty minutes after she arrived, she saw Ferryman park his car and let himself in to his mansion flat opposite. She even saw him, briefly, in the bay window on the second floor.

Watching for Carlucci, perhaps? Or waiting for her call? It was Friday night and he wasn't due in at his office again until Sunday. Before then, if she was right, they would be in contact, and she'd be the first to know.

A camper-van rolled past and parked a few spaces away. Lucy-Ann paid it no heed.

There seemed little point to Ryder in staying in Paris. The contents of the dead man's notebook were being analysed at Vauxhall, and he knew that, whatever was found, he'd have to report to ARIC before the end of the night.

He hoped something would come out of that notebook. It was the sole lead the flat had yielded. The phone had been used only once, to call Lindroth's mobile. Oddly, there had been no sign of a mobile phone. Ryder suspected that the killer had taken it – having used it to locate the target, and then removed it to eradicate evidence.

When he said he was returning to London, Fischer asked to come along. Ryder readily agreed. He liked the man; they worked well together. Consequently, at eight o'clock that evening, Ryder's jet having deposited them at Heathrow, they were on the M25, being driven back to Vauxhall.

Ryder's mobile rang. One of his grooms had found something.

'Fourteen of the fifteen numbers listed are mobile phones, and one of them's British.'

Ryder's stomach tightened.

'We're putting tracers on it now. But the fifteenth isn't a mobile; it's the number of a bank account.'

'Is it indeed?' Ryder said softly. 'Swiss?'

'No, Austrian. In the name of Mikhail Severin.'

'What's the name of the bank?' Ryder demanded. He wrote it down, and the account details, and passed them to Fischer.

For the next half-hour, as the Mercedes crept along the hot tarmac of a contraflow system, Fischer made calls. At twenty to nine, when they entered the suburbs of London, his mobile rang.

'Ja?' he said eagerly.

Faintly, Ryder heard the voice at the other end of the line. It seemed to be talking a lot. Fischer made notes. When he ended the call, his eyes were bright.

'Six big payments into Severin's account in the last year. Five from the same Swiss bank account since January. The last one went in today.'

'You've got details of that account?' Ryder interrupted.

'Only the number,' Fischer said, looking worried. 'I don't have any contacts with Swiss banks.'

'Ah, but I have,' said Ryder. Several years before, one of the smaller Swiss banks had unwittingly financed a Libyan assassination attempt on a British cabinet minister. The authorities had wanted to prosecute the chairman, Jurgen Altmeyer, but Ryder had persuaded them not to. Altmeyer was now regarded as one of the most influential figures in the banking world. 'He'll give us whatever help we need,' said Ryder. He leant forward to speak to the driver, then turned back to Fischer. 'You want to come?'

'Try to stop me.'

The driver did an illegal U-turn and headed back to Heathrow.

Since her escorted return to the Moor, Mary hadn't once let Jane out of her sight. She had insisted on accompanying Jane and Abby to the old schoolhouse for a communal supper and had followed them out of the building afterwards.

Glancing back as they crossed the green, Jane saw the two men from the village walking a few paces behind them. Their shadowing of her, she thought, their paranoia, was her greatest indication yet that they had something to hide; precisely what it was, remained unclear.

It was nine o'clock. They were heading for the church, for the service that Norton had mentioned to her earlier.

In the clear evening light, the old building of yellow stone and flint, surrounded by its beautifully tended graveyard, looked serene and inviting. The great doors stood open, and the Fellowshippers filed in.

The church was plainly furnished, with its original pews, stone steps leading up to an altar covered by a white and gold cloth. A silver cross stood upon it, gleaming. On either side, an intricately carved rood-screen concealed choir-stalls. Looking up, Jane saw that the roof was spectacular, its dark wooden beams exposed like the skeleton of a ship against the white ceiling. From hooks, great iron candelabra hung down, their candles alight and steadily burning, and coloured lights, pinks and blues and golds, filtered in through a stained glass window depicting Jesus surrounded by lambs.

The pews were filling quickly and, guided by Abby, Jane entered one on the left, and sat down beside a boy with a terrible stammer whom she had met at supper. She looked around. Mary had gone to the front and was talking to Steven on the altar steps.

They seemed worried about something, Jane thought, or was it her imagination?

Mary raised her hand and conversations dwindled away.

'There is going to be a delay tonight, I'm afraid, people.'

The Fellowship sighed in disappointment.

'David would like us all to remain here, however, singing and praying quietly.'

What had caused the delay? Jane wondered.

'What are we praying for?' someone called out.

Mary stared for a moment, then said, 'For God's will to be done.'

'Amen,' said Steven sombrely beside her.

Jane frowned. What did they mean by that?

'All right?' asked Abby softly beside her.

She nodded.

Mary said, 'Let us pray. "Our Father, who art in heaven, Hallowed be thy name. Thy will be done on earth . . .'

'As it is in heaven,' breathed Abby fervently, eyes closed. On Jane's other side, the boy with the stammer was mouthing the words.

Where was David? And what was he doing? She caught Steven watching her. She bowed her head and prayed too.

CHAPTER TWENTY-FIVE

The voice was male, British, quiet. It said, 'Flight VS104, inbound from London to JFK New York, is carrying enough of the nerve agent sarin to wipe out Manhattan.'

'Yeah?' the operator said uninterestedly but she had already pressed the Record button on the tape machine.

'There are four canisters in a suitcase in the cargo-hold, and one more in the handbag of passenger Nancy Andrews, sitting in seat 53A.'

The security chief leant over to switch off the tape. The call had come in ninety minutes before; he already knew it by heart but to the others, including the two FBI agents on duty at the airport, it was new.

They looked at him, waiting on his words. 'We've had a steward go check,' he said. 'She's there, asleep. There's a bag on her lap.'

'Can't risk a snatch mid-air,' one of the FBI said instantly.

'No. And she might be wired.'

The decision to treat the call seriously had been taken almost at once. Sarin, a poison gas much deadlier than cyanide, was developed by the Nazis during the Second World War to wipe out huge numbers of allied troops. It choked its victims, sent them into violent spasms. A single canister released into the New York subway would cause hundreds of deaths, many caused by panic.

Nancy Andrews, shown on the flight manifest as an American citizen, had boarded the aircraft in London at one o'clock, UK time that afternoon. Who she was, whom she was working for, why one of her comrades had chosen to betray her, no one knew; no one, at that juncture, cared.

Everyone agreed that nothing must be attempted while the plane was in the air. Three hundred and sixty two dying people, and an aircraft out of control, plunging to earth, into Manhattan or Harlem or the Bronx, with an unknown quantity of nerve gas on board . . . And who knew what else besides? Who could ever trust the word of a terrorist?

The airport was being closed. The runway furthest from the main terminal had been cleared. Down on the apron, out of sight, the assault teams waited. On the flight-deck of the aircraft, new orders were being given to the captain.

'How's the evacuation going?' demanded an FBI man of an underling.

'Still in progress.'

'Let's speed it up, come on.'

Everyone was horribly conscious of the dangers of making even a small mistake.

Overhead came the sound of an aircraft. People looked up then away again. Flight VS104 was not due to land for another thirteen minutes. The overhead aircraft, forbidden to land, whined away into the blue sky.

The electrician had been called the evening before and asked to come to the house that afternoon but 'absolutely not' before four o'clock, as no one would be home until then.

Arriving at quarter past four, he recognized the truck of the local plumber and, pulling up behind him, the car of a real-estate dealer. The people must be having the house fixed up before moving on, the electrician thought. The caller had been English; he guessed they were going back home.

He turned to look up at the house: white clapboard, very old Vermont, and then he saw the black drapes at the windows and he was suddenly glad that he was not alone there.

He waited for the real-estate dealer to get out of her car. He was about to ask her how business was, when he heard a scream from the house. They looked at each other.

'Wait here,' he said, and started for the steps.

The front door was open. He could hear someone gasping and moaning inside. There was a strange smell in the air, a mixture of burning plastic and marzipan. He stepped into the dark hall. He saw black cloth hanging down. He made out the writhing figure of a man on the floor: the plumber.

'You all right?' he cried, kneeling.

The plumber was red in the face, gasping for air. Behind him, the electrician saw a room of gold. He pushed the door fractionally. He saw bodies on the floor, stuff on the altar, two fat plastic bags with smoke coming from them. The fumes threatened to overcome him.

Retching, he dragged the plumber out on to the porch.

'Freeze!' someone yelled.

The electrician saw blue and white flashing lights, a fleet of police cars coming up the drive, the real-estate dealer spread-eagled against a bonnet, and the gun of an FBI man trained at his head. The anonymous call to the New York airport had been traced and the siege team had arrived.

Minutes later, the semi-conscious plumber and electrician were taken away by ambulance.

The siege team, having seen the bodies and the leaking gas, retreated to the top of the drive. The Boston groom, alerted by the sarin/NRM link, arrived, but she was barred from entering the house until it had been checked by chemical warfare experts.

The bomb exploded at four o'clock local time in Charleston. At first, its target seemed horribly evident: the toddlers from the daycare centre had been using the children's playground and it was they who took the full brunt of the blast.

But within minutes, as the smoke began to disperse and the eerie silence gave way to screams, it was seen that the Veerholt Institute had been damaged too. Most of the windows at the front of the seven-storey structure had been blown out. The revolving doors at the entrance had been blasted flat. As horrified onlookers stared, the building began to fall, cocksided, from the middle, one floor crashing down into that beneath. A woman fell out of a hole in the wall on the second floor.

Sirens were coming. The first ambulances and fire crews, desperate to get to the children, were on the scene too early to be aware of their own danger, but their back-ups, when they arrived, were wearing biohazard suits and carrying emergency supplies for their colleagues.

The Veerholt Institute, a private company, held one of the largest collections of bacteria in the country. It sold samples to hospitals and universities all over the States. It was too soon to tell how much of the collection had been damaged in the blast or, yet worse, released into the air.

With the help of the local militia, preparations began to seal off an area five miles in radius. The city hospitals, bracing themselves for the arrival of dead and injured children, were warned to expect potentially the greatest medical emergency ever to hit the United States.

The plane was three minutes from landing. The captain reported that the terrorist woman was still asleep. The passengers, to the best of his knowledge, were unaware that anything was wrong.

In their jeeps in the hangar at the far end of the runway, the assault teams, the fleets of fire-engines and ambulances, waited. The plane's engines were heard in the sky, and then it broke through the clouds.

In the control tower, the crisis co-ordinator murmured, 'Ready?' into his microphone.

The captain replied grimly, 'Ready,' and prepared to do a manoeuvre he had not done since training school. He let the wheels touch down, then brought them up again. The aircraft bounced. He did it again. Some of the passengers began screaming.

He made an immediate announcement: 'There is no cause for alarm, ladies and gentlemen. There is simply a small problem with one of our wheels. It will not affect our ability to come to a safe stop, I assure you.'

As he spoke, he brought the plane juddering to a standstill at the very edge of the runway. None of the passengers could see the hangar, or the assault jeeps racing towards them.

From the main cabin came a collective sigh of relief.

'However, in the interests of your safety,' the captain continued in his English drawl, 'we shall be asking you to disembark from the aircraft here, by means of the chutes which will now be deployed by the cabin crew.'

A few people cried out. They were quickly calmed by the cabin crew.

The aircraft doors opened. The emergency chutes spewed down on to the hot runway. The crew began to assemble the passengers for disembarkation, reminding them to cross their arms over their chests to prevent injury and assuring them that airport staff would be waiting outside to help them.

Indeed, some passengers by the windows could see them: several men in dark overalls already standing at the bottom of the chutes.

The procedure began.

In the control tower, the crisis coordinator sweated. Each scenario he and his team had considered had contained high risks; the current option had seemed the safest, and it also offered the greatest chance for the greatest number of passengers to get out of that aircraft alive. If the girl released the gas, at least the aircraft's doors would be open, at least the gas wouldn't be released into a confined space.

On the other hand, the 'emergency' might panic her into action. As the seconds passed, however, and nothing happened, that looked less likely.

Disembarkation was completed in fifteen minutes. The aircraft, reported the commando in charge, was empty except for one passenger: the terrorist. According to the flight engineer, the last to leave, she hadn't moved from her seat.

Did that mean she was waiting for them? That at the first sign of attack she would detonate her bomb if she had one attached to, or separate from, her canister?

A ladder was put up to the fuselage. The team donned their gas-masks and went in through the flightdeck.

A message to Nancy Andrews was relayed over the captain's address system. She didn't move.

A second team appeared from the rear of the aircraft. Two commandos, one from either end, approached her aisle, breathing heavily in their masks.

The man coming from the front was nearer. He saw the fair-haired head on the seat, tilted over towards the window. He kept his gun trained on her. He leant between the seats and touched her arm. It was still warm. It still lay protectively upon the bag in her lap.

He felt for a pulse: there was none.

He stood back and let the specialists get to her. They worked swiftly: detecting no wiring mechanism within the bag, they removed it. A recent needle-mark on her arm was noted before her body was taken away for post-mortem.

Her suitcase was easily identified, being clearly labelled, within the hold and transported to a military establishment on the far side of the airport. A total of five aerosol tins, purporting to be a variety of different hair products, were removed from her suitcase and bag. Technically, no aerosols were supposed to be carried in hand luggage but everyone did it, as everyone knew. So the girl, in carrying one with her, had taken only a slight risk of being discovered.

What she had been intending to do with her cargo no one knew, but there were awful clues in the Bible found in her handbag. It was heavily scored at Apocalyptic passages. The book of Revelation was almost obliterated by red ink but some phrases in the margins stood out. Beside a graphic description of plagues were 'They're getting what they deserve' and 'The Awful Horror is upon them'.

Her diary, in context, was fearful. One month before was the entry: 'I am to be The One! The Last Angel. Jordan says the Lord's told him so!'

The Boston groom, who by then had been given a gas-mask and allowed into the house in Vermont, was informed. The information fitted perfectly with what she had found. On the altar, in the room where the bodies were, lay what appeared to be the original Eighth Scroll itself, and beside it a pile of dirty bandages. They puzzled her at first; then she realized that they were the stolen swaddling-clothes.

Resting upon them, in an exercise book, was a translation of the Scroll, with notes, in neat, black-ink capital letters, detailing the fulfilment of each sign. After the first: '14 April 2000. Bodiam Castle, England. Princes Harry and Michael al-Amlah struck down.'

The groom removed her booty to one of the FBI cars outside. Her eyes travelled down the paper, noting the Blade Bomb reference, the claims for outbreaks of food-poisoning in Atlanta and across Europe.

The last sentence was 'And then the End, the Awful Horror of the Ungodly, shall come.' It was ringed in red, and to it had been added that day's date and, in the same neat capitals,

'The Veerholt Institute, Charleston' and 'Flight VS104'.

With the verification from the airport that the Andrews girl's aerosols contained atomized sarin, there could be no room for doubt. Children had died in Charleston, more people might fall sick there, and twelve cultists lay dead, presumably by their own hand. But it could have been much, much worse.

Although one of the 'significant' Charleston laboratories had been damaged, it looked as no lethal agents had escaped. The flasks in which the anthrax, bubonic plague and yellow-fever cultures were stored, had done what they were supposed to: they had withstood the bomb blast. The first air-sampling, the groom had just been informed, read clear.

Why a British cult had chosen to include America in its diabolical plans, Vermont as its exit from the world, she could not begin to guess. Perhaps they had feared the British authorities were on to them? She presumed that in the mass of documentation in the house there would be an answer. For now, she could only feel relief.

She telephoned first her own office and then the state governor's to tell them that it was all over. And then she broke down in tears.

CNN was showing a clip of the scene at the Vermont house. Smiling through his tears, David counted the covered stretchers being loaded into the ambulances.

Jordan and the children were at rest now, he thought: beyond capture and betrayal, which he admitted now had always been a vague worry to him. They were out of harm's way, with the Lord in Paradise. Their tasks were completed.

As was the sarin girl's. She had died quietly, without causing a fuss or calling for a doctor. They were calling her 'The sweet-faced killer from Kansas', and speculating about a connection between her and the Charleston bomb.

'Two terrorist attacks within an hour,' said CNN's presenter edgily, 'one planned to wipe out New York City, the other leaving at least forty dead, twenty-one of them pre-schoolers; a mass suicide at a cult headquarters. Professor, what is going on?'

The professor cleared his throat. 'Well—'

He was cut off as the studio switched back to Vermont. Two people were coming out of the house. One, a woman, was carrying a document case, holding it out in front of her as if it itself contained a bomb.

David watched her progress. Clearly, someone had realized the significance of the things laid on the altar. He estimated that it would be twenty-four hours at least before an expert could confidently declare them fakes. That was ample time for his purposes, more than he needed. In the interim, let them speculate, let them discover that the papers on the bodies were fakes, let them count their dead.

There was a tap on his door and Ruth entered, her expression tense.

'Like bees to a honeypot,' he told her.

Her face relaxed. 'The power of your prayer.'

'And yours.'

They smiled at each other.

'Shall we go?' The Fellowship was waiting for its service; Jesus was waiting outside the door of Jane's heart. Admittance and life everlasting, David wondered, or a hard heart, the devil's heart that needed to be cast out from the midst of his lambs? By the light in her eyes, he would know her.

Ruth pulled up the hood of her cloak and together they stepped out into the corridor.

The first news from America reached Ryder before he and Fischer took off for Zurich. At first, seeing it on television in the departure suite at Heathrow, it seemed tragic but nothing to do with him. A bomb in a playground in Charleston; no religious motive mentioned, and none imagined by Ryder.

But once airborne, he heard about the sarin girl. Sarin, instantly a worry, the parallel with Aum Shinrikyo. And then Vermont, and with that flood of data, an e-mail from Jack Broughton: did Ryder agree that there was a resemblance between the dead terrorist girl, Nancy Andrews, and Botulism Helen?

Ryder saw a likeness. For a moment, he believed it; he was exhausted and desperate. Could this be it? Was the hunt over? On the surface, at least, it all fitted.

While they was still in mid-air, the second emergency ARIC conference call that night was convened.

The ARIC chairwoman said, 'I suppose what we're asking you, Mr Ryder, is this. Are the Americans are right? Are all the Keeper cultists, including Helen dead? Can we afford to down tools?'

'I think not,' Ryder said, after a pause.

There were a few groans.

He continued, undeterred: 'This girl, Andrews, if that's her real name, is between eighteen and twenty years of age. Helen has never been put at less than "in her early thirties". That's quite an age difference. And the dead girl is small, about five feet one, whereas Helen's always been described as "of medium height". I think it's no more than a coincidence that she resembles our "thin Helen" e-fit.'

He took a deep breath. 'I think it's highly likely that Helen is still alive in the UK.'

'Why hasn't she done anything since Wednesday, then?' put in the brigadier.

'Perhaps she's accomplished all she needed to,' Ryder replied quietly. 'I believe we must continue our hunt for her. There could well be a rump of the cult in the UK – or it could be the main group, for all we know. Vermont might have been an offshoot.'

'Well, if all that this second group here is likely to do is top themselves, like their chums in Vermont, who cares?' asked the brigadier.

'We do,' said the chairwoman, 'because second time around, they might not top just themselves. Isn't that your thinking, Mr Ryder?'

'It is.' He paused again. 'I think maybe they hoped Vermont was going to put us off the scent. That's why Jordan took the blame for all the signs, and left the "evidence" lying there for us to find. Identification papers on all the bodies, even a membership list, in case we wondered whether they were all dead.'

The chairwoman said, 'Make us think it was all over, like the Americans?'

'Exactly.'

'Whereas it's anything but over. For us,' she said.

There was silence for a while, then Beck said, 'God, I wish it was over.'

'As do we all,' said the chairwoman wearily. She asked for the latest information on the Helen hunt.

The second *Crimewatch Special* had gone out earlier in the evening. Calls were still being analysed; sightings of the white Bedford with its new false number plate had been reported at a total of one hundred and ninety-seven places around the country.

Another deluge of data, probably all worthless, to swamp his team still more, Ryder thought resignedly. He heard Fischer tapping away on his keyboard behind him, and reminded himself, thankfully, of his other lead. They'd be landing in a few minutes. It was nearly 2 a.m. He hoped the banker, whom he had called before leaving London, had kept his promise to wait up for them.

Broughton concluded his report with a summary of the Scroll thieves inquiry: no British man or woman answering the old janitor's description had been found. Information from police collators and local priests was still coming in.

'Anything?' asked the chairwoman.

'Not so far, ma'am,' answered Broughton.

The chairwoman brought the call to an end, and wished Ryder good luck in Zurich.

'Hope you're right, Ryder,' said Beck heavily when only he was left on the line.

'Yes,' said Ryder.

'Everyone else will be calling off the Alert.'

'I know, sir, but I don't think we can risk it.'

'No. Well . . .' He left the sentence unfinished and hung up.

As the plane rolled to a halt on the runway, Fischer, who had been sitting behind Ryder, working on his laptop, came forward.

'Pressure?' he said.

'Lots of it,' Ryder agreed. 'We'd better be on our way.'

'Before we do, there's something else.' Fischer sat down in the seat next to his. 'While you were on the phone, I was looking again at the data we got on Severin's bank account.'

'Oh yes?' Ryder didn't want to be rude, but he thought of that waiting banker.

Fischer opened his laptop. 'Severin received five payments from the Swiss account. The first in January this year, the second in February, then the third, a much larger amount on April 15 – that's the day after the Princes were murdered, isn't it?'

Ryder nodded. He was interested now.

'You remember Lindroth saying he was paid in instalments: one-third before, two-thirds after?'

Ryder nodded again.

'It looks as if Severin was paid the same way: two instalments for the Princes' murders and two for Vienna. The big payment that went in this morning we presume is the second Vienna instalment. But there's another one, a smaller one, which went in on Thursday evening. You see?'

'May I?' Ryder took the laptop. The monies were in Austrian schillings. He saw the smaller amount Fischer referred to. It had gone into Severin's account at 22.00 on Thursday.

'So there's a spare first instalment?'

Fischer nodded.

Ryder's heart raced. 'Severin was booked to do something else.'

'Looks like it.'

'We've no way of knowing, now, whether he's done it, was planning to do it, or had subcontracted it to someone else like Lindroth.'

'Correct,' said Fischer. 'It suggests, maybe, that Vermont isn't as tidy as it appears. That there's a loose end.'

Another unfulfilled sign? Ryder's stomach turned over. He thought of calling Beck back, but decided to wait until he knew more.

He returned the laptop to Fischer. 'Let's go,' he said.

CHAPTER TWENTY-SIX

The church doors shut with a bang, making Jane jump. Around the great stone walls, the candles flickered. It was one o'clock in the morning.

For four hours, the Fellowship had been waiting for the service to start. The prayers and the chorus singing, which they had been told Norton wanted, had dwindled; some people had even fallen asleep. Beside Jane, Abby was dozing, and very briefly Jane had entertained the idea of trying to slip away down to the village to call Sam, but Mary, Steven and some of the others were positioned around the church like sentries, and always, it seemed, at least one of them was watching her.

People were waking up. There was expectancy in the air.

'Here he comes now,' said Abby, sitting up.

Jane followed her gaze to the front of the church, and saw a number of people moving behind the rood-screen. They entered the choir stalls on the right.

Then David Norton emerged, alone. He came forward, stepped round the altar table and halted, dead centre, on the chancel steps.

He stretched out his arms. He bowed his white head.

Christ on the cross, Jane thought.

He raised his head, and she saw that his face shone with light. She felt a quickening inside her.

'Have you missed me, my children?' he called softly.

'Yes,' they whispered, their sibilance passing like a breeze.

His smile deepened. He brought his fingers to his lips, and kissed them and blew kisses out like bubbles. Chuckling, they made pretence of catching them and blowing them back, and he caught them too and then blew them up to the ceiling, to God.

It was a pretty display, Jane thought, a guru and his children in perfect harmony. They were as one with him; they would do any-thing for him. But which one, she wondered, gazing at the happy, almost childlike people around her, had spiked those maternity meals? Which one had sold poisoned toffee-apples to children?

Norton held up his hands and there was instant silence, a tension as they waited for him to speak.

'Would you like to know what I've been doing?' he asked teasingly.

'Yes, David,' came the eager chorus.

'Well, I can't tell you exactly . . .'

There was a general moan.

'I'm sorry, but it's a secret. I can tell you it's to do with a mission, a mission that I want every one of you here to go on with me.'

There was a buzz of excitement. Did 'mission' mean, Jane wondered, a sign fulfilment? Was he responsible for the Blade Bomb?

'Yes, every single one of you,' he repeated deliberately, and his eyes roamed the congregation before coming to rest on Jane.

She didn't move; she didn't look away. She knew he believed he was pulling her in, and it was important that he thought he was winning.

His scrutiny lasted several seconds. She could hear the hush in the church, the watchfulness of Abby beside her. David smiled and moved on. She breathed again.

'Your mission, my children, is going to be the biggest, the most important, ever.'

Jane's pulse quickened.

'How many times have I told you that the last shall be first? Ten times? A hundred times?'

'Yes, David,' cried the throng.

He smiled, suddenly mischievous. 'Now what d'you think this great mission could possibly be?'

'An outreach camp?' called a voice.

'Building another church?'

'Knocking down this one?' There was a roll of laughter.

'No, none of those,' Norton said. 'All I'm going to tell you is that we're going on a journey.'

That, Jane thought, could mean anything. A day trip, a relocation of the Fellowship, anything. She saw Norton looking at her again, and cut away to study the rood-screen, behind which sat the people who had come in with him. She could see only one of them clearly, a man who in profile looked rather handsome. He was much older than the Fellowshippers, nearer to Norton's age. He turned suddenly and in the glow of candlelight Jane saw his face: not friendly like a Fellowshipper's. In fact, he looked rather menacing. She looked away.

'Please don't go too far away tomorrow,' Norton was saying. 'I'd like everyone to stick around the Moor.'

Tomorrow, Jane thought in dismay. That gave her almost no time to find out more.

'Let us pray.'

'We thank you from the depths of our hearts, O Father, for sending your beloved Son to die for us.'

'Yes, Lord.'

'And we ask that those among us who have not yet committed themselves to You, haven't yet met Jesus, and known the height and width and depth of His love for them may be brought to Him tonight, Amen.'

'Amen,' said Abby, with meaning.

'And now, dear Lord, on this special night, the eve before our mission, I ask in faith for a miracle.'

Miracle? Jane asked herself. What was Norton thinking of? Such a demand could not be his usual custom, or she'd have heard about it long before. Then she remembered Christ's prophecy: miracles would be a trademark of the Last Days. What was Norton trying to prove?

'. . . for a sign that You are with us, a sign so definite, so over-powering, that the unbeliever, who stands apart in judgement . . .'

Jane met Norton's eye.

'. . . the lost lamb will be convinced,' he said, smiling at her, 'and come forward tonight to give her life to Jesus.'

Should she play along with him? Would she find herself with more freedom or less if she converted? As a new convert, might she not find every moment of her time taken up with Fellowship duties; her behaviour more curtailed as befitting a true member of the community?

'A miracle, sweet Jesus. Come, children, add your voices. Sweet Jesus. Jesus.'

'Jesus, Jesus,' they took up the cry. Softly, and then the sound increased in volume. Out of the corner of her eye, Jane saw hands being raised. She felt Abby sway, and looked along the pew: everyone but herself was swaying and humming, their eyes closed, their hands in the air. She didn't like it. People going out of control, egging each other on. Soon they'd be barking like dogs and falling down, slain in the spirit.

'The Lord has given me the sign,' David called and the babble hushed, and the worshippers' arms fell back to their sides.

Norton closed his eyes. 'Mm,' he murmured, 'Yes, Lord,' and now, no one echoed him. He opened them again, and Jane thought he was looking at her, then realized he was staring at the boy beside her.

'Philip,' he said.

Philip trembled.

'Come to me.' Norton held out a hand but Philip didn't move. Jane saw how badly he was shaking. She wanted suddenly to help him, to tell him he didn't have to do what Norton said, but she would be stepping outside her role.

Norton came towards them, down the centre aisle. He stopped at the end of the pew and held out his hand again.

'Philip,' he said, and there was a touch of reproach in his voice. 'Come on,' he said softly. 'Don't be afraid.'

The boy's head jerked round. Jane saw he was bright red and sweating. He tried to speak but his mouth worked uselessly.

David reached in past Abby and held out his hand. The boy took it and let himself be pulled out.

'There, my child,' crooned David. 'There's a good boy.' With his arm around his shoulders, he walked Philip back up to the front, and turned him to face the congregation. The boy looked terrified, and Jane felt frightened for him.

'Philip is going to say a prayer for us, aren't you, Philip?'

'I . . . I . . . I.' The boy's eyes bulged. He looked round frantically for help.

'"Gentle Jesus, meek and mild." Come on Philip, you can do it. I'm telling you to speak clearly.'

'Gen . . . ge . . .' The broken words echoed from the stone walls.

'Stop stammering!'

Jane couldn't bear it. She closed her eyes. If she could, she would have closed her ears too. What a sadist Norton was to subject the boy to such public humiliation, for nothing, for a cheap stunt that wouldn't work. She knew how such charlatans worked: when he failed, he'd blame Philip for not having sufficient faith. Why didn't the Fellowshippers, witnessing the boy's distress, cry out, 'Enough!' Why, come to that, didn't she?

'All right. Sssh, it's all right.' Norton touched Philip's arm. 'I haven't been able to heal you, have I, my child?'

'N . . . n . . . n . . .' Philip began to cry.

'Sssh. I can't. But Jesus can.'

Oh no! thought Jane. Don't prolong the agony.

Norton tilted his head back and the light above the altar caught his white hair, making it glow. For a moment, he looked like an angel.

'Jesus. Our Jesus,' Norton called, raising his hands, palms upwards.

'Jesus,' came the chant again. 'Jesus, Jesus,' like a threat.

'Touch these my hands with Your Spirit. Make our brother whole.'

The rhythm pounded in Jane's head. She felt pure dread for Philip. What were they going to do to him when he failed to be healed?

Norton put his index finger on Philip's lips. The church grew absolutely still.

'Jesus, heal this child,' Norton said simply.

Philip stopped shaking. His eyes widened in surprise. Jane felt how hard her own heart was beating. Suddenly, she desperately wanted Philip to be cured.

'Now,' said Norton firmly, taking Philip by the shoulders. 'In the name of Jesus, speak.'

'I . . . I . . .'

Oh no, thought Jane, oh, sweet God, no.

'I—' Philip's eyes shot open even wider. A look of sheer delight lit his face. 'I can!'

'Yes!' Norton punched the air.

'Yes!' erupted the Fellowship. Thunderous clapping broke out.

'Gentle Jesus, meek and mild,' cried Philip in ecstasy.

Jane's mouth went dry. She had just witnessed a miracle, or something very like one: over supper, Philip's stammer had rendered him almost incomprehensible.

Abby squeezed her arm. 'Isn't it wonderful?' she said, tears running down her cheeks.

But Jane couldn't respond. She stared at Philip, who was dancing at the front, and at Norton laughing beside him. Had she been wrong about Norton? Was he special?

He caught her eye once more, and winked. 'Enough?' he mouthed at her.

She stared back at him.

'Praise God,' he said, turning back to the Fellowship.

'Praise His Name!'

Norton clapped his hands. 'Jesus is with us as we prepare for our mission. Thank Jesus!'

'Thank Him!'

Norton smiled hugely. 'Some of you are going to be the leaders of this mission. Children,' he called. He gestured to the people in the choir-stalls, and they began to emerge. Six men and then a young woman. Jane stared. The woman had startlingly red hair.

The seven of them lined up at the top of the chancel steps.

Norton called out their names, and as he did so each Fellow-shipper came down to where he stood, and he embraced them. He came to the last person, the girl.

'Kirsten,' he cried, and he led another round of applause.

To Jane, it sounded even louder than before. She gazed at Kirsten, enwrapped in Norton's arms. Had the girl been at the Fellowship all the time? Jane had looked so carefully for her, and not seen her. Where had she been?

'Oh thank goodness,' breathed Abby beside her.

'What d'you mean?' asked Jane.

'Kirsten was at our cottage last week. I thought she'd left.'

So where had she been in the interim? And why hadn't she called Sam? Jane's heart caught in her throat. By the look of Kirsten, she had genuinely converted. Had she told Norton about Sam? Was Sam in danger?

Kirsten and Norton were holding hands. They stepped down together on to the floor of the church. Kirsten was laughing delightedly. Beside her, on the steps, stood Philip, cured of his stammer. They looked so happy, Jane thought, so full of love – she broke off. The man she'd seen in the choir-stalls was craning round to get a better look at the scene. He wore the same sneering look on his face as he had before. He saw Jane looking at him. He smiled.

Norton raised both hands.

'We're short of a girl for the team,' he crooned.

Abby straightened up. She wanted to be picked, Jane realized.

'Jesus is telling me He wants a newly committed daughter, a sister for Kirsten.' Norton's eyes came to rest on Jane. He wanted her. 'She has seen the miracle tonight.'

Jane glanced at Philip. She didn't believe he had been a 'plant'. She'd heard how bad his stammer had been. But she also knew that stammering often has a psychological cause. Philip believed so strongly in Norton that he'd been cured. It was a miracle, of sorts.

'She has heard Jesus knocking at the door of her heart all evening.'

If she 'converted', she'd become a mission leader; she'd be more likely to gain knowledge of what his plans were. On the other hand, she might find herself hidden away where Kirsten had been, unable to phone Sam.

'Will she let Him in?'

Norton was looking straight at her; everyone was looking at her.

'Open her eyes, sweet Jesus. Breathe on her your own Spirit. Yes, Jesus.'

'Yes,' urged the gathering.

'Yes?' Norton mouthed at her.

It was a risk she had to take, Jane decided. She looked Norton straight in the eye and nodded.

'Thank you, Jesus!' he cried.

'Thank you, Jesus!'

'Oh, Jane,' breathed Abby, touching her arm as she squeezed past.

Jane began walking up the aisle. Over to her right, Mary was staring at her. Jane kept her eyes on Norton. The Fellowship began to sing: 'Make me a channel of Your love.'

Love radiated from Norton's face. The candlelight flickered above his head. As Jane reached him, he dropped Kirsten's hand and took both her own. He drew her to him, his turquoise eyes delving into her, seeking the truth.

She was afraid to meet his eyes.

'Look at me, baby,' he breathed.

She looked. His eyes were swimming with tears. He didn't really see her, she realized. His own belief stood in his eyes.

'Do you take Jesus as your personal saviour?'

'I do.'

'To have and hold Your Love for evermore,' sang the Fellow-shippers.

Norton hugged her close. She felt the heat of him. She felt his lips upon her hair. He held her away and pulled Kirsten to him, then joined their hands together.

'You're sisters now,' he told them, the tears running down his face.

Kirsten smiled delightedly at Jane.

'United together on this special morning, as Jesus wanted it to be,' said Norton. 'Hallelujah!'

'Hallelujah!' echoed Jane and Kirsten.

'Hallelujah!' cried the throng.

CHAPTER TWENTY-SEVEN

When Ryder and Fischer arrived at Jürgen Altmeyer's flat at 02.40, he was waiting for them. He was brief, but helpful. He'd contacted senior people at the bank where Mikhail Severin's account was held and had applied pressure, stressing that it was an international emergency. He had obtained the information Ryder wanted.

The bank account in question was operated by a trust, run by a firm of lawyers in Zurich.

'Will they co-operate?' Ryder asked immediately.

Altmeyer raised his eyebrows. 'I don't know. But under our law trustees have to know, or be able to know in the future, the identity of the trust's beneficiary.'

Ryder and Fischer exchanged a glance.

'You need to know now?' Altmeyer asked, looking at the time.

'If possible.'

'If you'll wait here please, gentlemen?'

They heard him on the telephone, arguing. He made another call, then he emerged. 'Let's go,' he said.

Twenty minutes later, they arrived at the offices of a legal firm, as a police car was also drawing up. Two shocked-looking lawyers were escorted inside.

Ryder, Fischer and Altmeyer were shown into a large office on the first floor. The senior partner, a man in his seventies, was ensconced behind an imposing desk, while his young colleague stood beside him. The old man spoke with barely controlled anger. There had been no need for the police, he said.

Altmeyer made a perfunctory apology. 'As I explained on the telephone, this matter concerns international security.'

'This matter concerns the confidentiality of my client,' shot back the lawyer. 'And yours too, Herr Altmeyer.'

Altmeyer said stonily, 'You do not seem to appreciate the seriousness of the situation.'

'Really?' snapped the lawyer. His fingers tapped on his desk.

'Which is that if you fail to divulge the information we seek, the special relationship between our bank and this firm will be terminated forthwith. Moreover,' he went on more loudly, as the lawyer tried to interrupt, 'I shall ensure that the banking community understands why.'

The lawyer's face hardened. 'Following your outrageous breach of client confidentiality tonight, Herr Altmeyer, I cannot imagine that the community will be in the least interested in anything you have to say to them.'

There was a stale silence. It was all very well, Ryder thought, Altmeyer taking up cudgels on their behalf, but they needed results. He glanced at Fischer and realized he was of the same mind.

'Can you be more specific about the sort of crisis we're facing, gentlemen?' Altmeyer asked, turning to them.

Ryder thought quickly. 'There's been a spate of reported terrorist attacks in America.'

The lawyer snorted.

Fischer went on quietly, 'We believe the group could be targeting Europe next. Specifically, Switzerland. They're using sarin gas. It was devised by the Nazis.'

There was a strangled sound from the younger lawyer. (Ryder later learned he represented a company being sued by Holocaust victims for manufacturing the gas used in the Nazi concentration camps.)

'Who's behind the trust?' Fischer asked baldly.

'There's a bank account in Antigua—' the man began.

'For God's sake,' his partner exploded, but the other man didn't look at him.

'The account there is run by a company called World Image of the Windward Isles,' he said.

Ryder knew instantly, as surely as if he had the information in front of him, that behind World Image would be another registered name-only company, and behind it another, and so on. It could take weeks to find the true owner, and if he was right, if there was another Keeper movement in the UK, they might not have weeks, they might not even have days. And then there was the 'loose end' Fischer had found; the fulfilment of another Scroll sign might already be in progress.

'How about the beneficiary of the trust?' he asked.

'I . . . er . . .' The lawyer shot a distraught look at his colleague but there was no help there. 'I'm afraid I can't . . .'

'We can sit here for the rest of the night,' Altmeyer pointed out reasonably. 'If necessary, we can have you charged with endangering state security.'

'There's a letter,' blurted the younger lawyer.

'You bloody fool!' thundered his partner.

'Where is it?' demanded Ryder.

'It's not to be opened until 2010.' The lawyer swallowed. 'We're bound by ethical considerations.'

'You're bound by shit,' spat Altmeyer, making everyone jump. He picked up a silver-framed photograph from the desk in front of him. Judging by the older lawyer's reaction, Ryder reckoned it belonged to him. It showed a family skiing party, everyone grinning into the camera.

'Nice,' said Altmeyer. 'Fine children. Your grandchildren, are they? The sarin gas that this group's using will choke them to death, won't it, Herr Ryder?'

'For Christ's sake!' The lawyer snatched back the picture. The room went very quiet.

'All right, all right, God damn you.' The old man pushed his chair back and stood up. He took a key out of a drawer and with it unlocked another drawer in a cupboard. He removed a metal box from which he extracted another key marked with a white cardboard tag.

'Come with me,' he growled.

He led them down a maze of corridors and stopped before a heavy steel door. He worked the combination lock until the door clicked open, revealing a narrow, vault-like room lined with safety deposit boxes.

He went inside, Ryder, Fischer and Altmeyer squeezing in single file after him. One of the policemen waited outside.

The lawyer went to the far end. He ran his eyes up and down the dull silver boxes, then knelt and shakily inserted his key. He opened the box and lifted out a slim white envelope, which he passed up over his head.

'Here, take it,' he said.

Ryder did. On the front of the envelope, printed in English, were the words, 'Not to be opened until 2010.'

He tore open the seal. Inside was a single sheet of paper. On it, also in English, was written: 'In the event of the Trust being wound up, all remaining monies are to be paid to Ross Edgecombe, of The Old Manor House, Pentridge, Dorset, England.'

Ryder's mouth went dry. He turned to Fischer. 'We've got him,' he said.

When Battersea Park closed at dusk, Maitland had to leave and find a parking space in the road outside. At first, there had not been a place available within view of Ferryman's flat, but as the hours passed, cars moved off, and after midnight he was able to take his pick.

He considered himself perfectly positioned now, across the road from Ferryman's flat, able to see Ferryman's windows, and with the best line of fire for the flat's only entrance. When the journalist eventually emerged, it would be a piece of cake.

It being Friday night, Maitland had expected him to go out during the evening, but he hadn't. Maitland had seen him twice in the window on the second floor, and then the glow of a television, getting brighter as darkness had fallen; and yet the flat had remained unlit.

Ferryman had fallen asleep on the sofa in front of the box, Maitland reckoned. It was ten to three in the morning. He'd probably stay there all night, but Maitland wasn't prepared to take the risk of falling asleep himself. Although he was in the back of his van, he didn't lie down on the mattress there, but remained sitting, his eyes level with his spy-hole. He knew Ferryman might appear at any time. When he did, Maitland consoled himself, yawning, he would have him.

*

In her car, parked on the same side of the road as Ferryman's block of flats, but a little distance from the main entrance so that she could see his window, Lucy-Ann alternately dozed and kept watch.

Various people had entered and left the block that night, the door closing each time with a convenient slam, notifying her, but not Ferryman and not Carlucci.

Ferryman had received no phone calls at home, nor had he made any. The group he'd mentioned to her, Hampstead for Jesus, had apparently crumpled under the mildest of questioning and had revealed duplicity in their accounts. That was all. There was no indication whatsoever that they were the 'rump' movement Ryder feared still existed in the UK.

Was she right about Ferryman? Was she right, now, to continue her surveillance? She knew something was breaking in Switzerland – Broughton had made an elliptical reference to it in his last call. Ryder might already have the information he needed.

Was she wasting her time there? Were her suspicions regarding Ferryman based on her determination to find the girl? Was her crusade too personal, emanating from wounded professional pride? Was she sitting up all night to prove a point that didn't in fact exist? Was there no connection between Carlucci and Ferryman?

Lucy-Ann groaned quietly. She could not be wrong again, could she? But it was still important to find and detain Carlucci before the crisis was over, in case she talked and caused mass panic.

A couple wove their unsteady way down the pavement towards her. Earlier, Lucy-Ann had got out her identity card, ready to flash at the police in case anyone reported her, but no one had, and she doubted now that anyone would; it wasn't that sort of area.

She glanced over at the camper-van that had been in the park earlier. She couldn't see the driver; she presumed he had gone into one of the flats.

She looked up, yawning, at Ferryman's windows; the flickering light of a television set still reflected against the glass. No doubt he had fallen asleep, watching it, she thought, and settled herself for another light doze.

There had been no fresh coverage from America for the last half-hour. It was nearly three in the morning and Sam was bleary-eyed.

Jane wasn't going to call now; he ought to get to bed.

But it seemed that the Keeper had been found. A British cult, as Jane had said, which had decamped to America to carry out a few signs – fear of the air, he guessed, with the sarin gas and the bomb at the virus laboratories – and then kill itself.

He looked at the screen, at the gruesome image of the Keeper, Mark Jordan, and his followers wearing black clothes and silver trainers, lying fanned out in a semi-circle around a golden altar.

On that altar, the presenter said importantly, had been vital documents, which were now being examined by the FBI. They included the Eighth Scroll, and ancient Christian relics.

Sam suspected that was a reference to the stolen swaddling-clothes – so Jane had been right about that, even if not about a lot of other things. Not that it was her fault. She'd been led astray by his call about the Fellowship, and by the memory that had surfaced of Norton calling himself the Keeper.

It was a huge weight off his mind. She was safe. If it hadn't been so early in the morning, he'd have driven down to fetch her. As it was, he'd call her there, first thing, and then go to get her.

He'd only put on the television for company while he had waited for her call. He'd watched *Crimewatch* in a desultory fashion, and had the impression that the police were getting desperate in the hunt for Helen. They'd composed another e-fit, live in the studio, of a man allegedly seen driving her van.

'Is it possible that the dead terrorist on the plane was Botulism Helen?' the British presenter asked an American journalist, and the screen showed the e-fit alongside a passport photograph of the dead girl. Sam couldn't see much likeness between the two faces, beyond the colouring of hair and perhaps a similarity about the eyes. Helen looked at least ten years older than the girl.

And that, he told himself, meant that Helen was still at large, either working on her own or, as the television was suggesting – and he was inclined to agree – hiding somewhere in Britain, the last member of Mark Jordan's terrible sect. The hunt would intensify enormously now; she was bound to be caught in the next day or so, if she hadn't already killed herself as her comrades had.

'"Many shall suffer, particularly little children and pregnant women."' The signs and their fulfilments were being read out on the television. Sam had thought of them for so long as his and Jane's exclusive property, that it was strange to hear them made public.

The presenter gave the latest update: sixty-nine pregnant women had been admitted to hospital in the UK. Two had miscarried. The condition of a third, the pregnant mother of a ten-month-old baby, was still giving cause for concern. The rest of the women were under observation.

Sam sighed and got up from the sofa. He switched off the television set, and went to bed. As his head touched the pillow, he remembered the feel of Jane's mouth on his. In the morning, he'd see her again. With a smile on his lips, he fell asleep.

Within minutes of Ryder's request, his laptop's screen began to show the data on Ross Harold Edgecombe. The first section was his work record.

'Jesus Christ,' Ryder whispered as his eye ran down the screen, 'He's our man, all right.'

'Yes?' Fischer queried. They were speeding back to Zurich airport.

Ryder angled the laptop under the rear seat passenger light. 'He's part of the dirty tricks brigade at Porton Down – that's our chemical and biological place. They hatched up God knows what for the Gulf War, and some other places. He's a microbiologist, ex-army, investigated GulfWar syndrome. He could've done the botulism and listeria poisonings with his eyes—'

'Which cult is he with?' interrupted Fischer.

'No mention yet.' Ryder scrolled further down and came to the entry about Edgecombe's activities since 1993. He skimmed through it, then his eyes came to rest on one paragraph. He went cold. He reread the data frantically.

'What is it?' asked Fischer.

Ryder said tonelessly, 'Edgecombe was one of a group of scientists who tried to dig up the 1918 flu virus.'

'The Spanish flu?' Fischer asked, and Ryder saw that the Austrian was as afraid as he was.

'It killed fifty million back then,' Ryder continued, more to himself than Fischer. 'Scientists have been trying to unearth a sample of it for years, because if it ever comes back . . .'

'There's no effective treatment,' Fischer finished for him.

'That's right. Edgecombe was part of an Anglo-American expedition to Norway two years ago. They found some bodies but they were too decomposed. Edgecombe claimed he knew where to find intact ones, but no one believed him. He'd been their main scout. It was because of him that they'd spent weeks digging in the wrong place. Edgecombe went off the rails. Three months later, in August '98, he left Porton.'

'But it doesn't necessarily mean he's got the virus now,' said Fischer hopefully.

'No?' Ryder felt as if he was talking from far away. 'Don't you remember the hue and cry last year over graves being robbed up in the Arctic Circle?'

'Not really.'

Ryder frowned. He was dazed with tiredness. 'Maybe it wasn't publicized, I don't know. Someone drilled holes in a flu corpse. Looked as if they'd got some samples out. I was asked to look at it in case any of the bad boys had done it.'

'But they hadn't?'

'It didn't look that way. None of our groups had the know-how.' Ryder's words caught in his throat. 'We thought. The investigation was a real mess, a double-hander between us and the Yanks. They suspected us of sending our own team of scientists for one last try, and we suspected them. As far as I know, that remains the status quo.'

'Edgecombe was never suspected?'

Ryder shook his head. 'No. There weren't any real suspects on the British team.' He shook off his lethargy. Edgecombe had to be found, fast. He moved on to the next page. 'Where's the bastard now? What the . . . ?' The page was blank.

What he had must be only part of Edgecombe's history. He requested the next file.

'Please wait,' said the screen.

As he did so, he ran the cursor back up the page. He read the last entry, a security note on Edgecombe, a parting shot at the end of the man's MOD career. Edgecombe was judged unstable, a depressive, prone to violent mood-changes. Ryder swore. Why had a man like that ever been allowed within a hundred miles of the flu search? What the hell had Porton been thinking of? Didn't they, of all people, know what that virus could do if it fell into the wrong hands?

Why had he, Ryder, ever agreed to be the extra pair of ears for the inquiry?

He'd reached the beginning of the file again. There was a photograph of Edgecombe that he'd only glanced at before. He saw now that he was a handsome man, dark-haired, with chiselled features. He read his full name, his date and place of birth, and the other crucial fact that, in his earlier haste, he had missed.

His jaw dropped. He couldn't believe it. 'Oh thank God,' he muttered.

'What?'

For a moment, speech deserted him. 'He's dead,' he croaked at Fischer. 'In a road smash. He died before the grave was robbed.'

'You're sure?'

'Sure I'm sure.' Sudden relief made him light-headed. 'Take a look.' He angled the machine towards Fischer. 'He died in December 1998, five or six months before someone dug up that grave.'

'But he was the beneficiary of the trust,' Fischer reminded him.

'I know. Obviously he was heavily involved with the group. It must have been he who advised them how to carry out the food-poisoning.' Ryder remembered the boy who had worked briefly at the Colindale health laboratories. 'He could well have meant to get hold of the flu virus for them, but died before he could do it.'

'You don't think he could have told them how to do it?' asked Fischer.

'And then they could have done it themselves?' Ryder unwillingly toyed with that idea. 'Unless they were scientists themselves with intricate, specialized knowledge in the field, as well as all the right paraphernalia, I doubt it very much.'

Fischer nodded. 'Fine. I mean, if international teams have been trying for years, and failing, a bunch of religious fanatics aren't going to succeed, are they?'

'No.' But Ryder was worrying again. They'd carried out the British botulism and listeria poisonings without Edgecombe's help; the Vermont group had killed themselves with a cocktail of lethal chemicals; Nancy Andrews had overdosed on a bizarre combination of drugs; and then there was the sarin gas itself. Unless Edgecombe had done a lot of pre-planning before his death, someone with scientific knowledge very similar to his been lending them that expertise.

'How – exactly – did he die?' Fischer asked meditatively.

'In a road crash,' Ryder answered promptly, then he saw what the other man was getting at. On his laptop, he requested additional information on Edgecombe's death; it came through quickly. The crash had happened on the night of 17 December. Edgecombe's body had been found in the burnt-out remains of his sports car at the bottom of a gulley in the Pennines. He was so badly burnt that he could not even be identified through his dental records.

Ryder frowned. A former colleague had identified him by the watch he'd been wearing – his left forearm was the least badly damaged part of his body. He'd been cremated – Ryder winced at the destruction of evidence – near his home in Devon.

'And I said Vermont was stage-managed,' Ryder muttered.

'Sorry?'

'I said I think you're right. I don't think Edgecombe's dead at all. Look at this.' He passed over the laptop.

'D'you think it was him, then, last year, robbing that grave?'

'It fits, doesn't it?'

'So he's got the virus?'

Ryder felt his stomach knot. 'I've got to assume so.'

'What do you do next?'

'Panic,' said Ryder, with gallows-humour. 'We'll just have to find him before it's too late, won't we?' he went on.

A few moments later, they arrived at Zurich airport. Ryder e-mailed Broughton in Vauxhall; he put in a call to Beck, then he bade farewell to Fischer.

'Good luck,' Fischer said.

'I'm going to need it,' Ryder replied. He turned and boarded the waiting jet.

CHAPTER TWENTY-EIGHT

3.30 a.m., England

Jane sat, fully clothed, on the edge of her bed. Laurel Cottage was quiet at last. Its occupants, who now included Kirsten, had retired to their beds half an hour before; by now, she hoped everyone would be asleep.

The service had ended ninety minutes before. Jane and the other seven 'missionaries' had not been called into the church sacristy to hear details of their mission, nor been led off to be kept apart from the rest of the Fellowship, possibly under lock and key, until the mission started.

Everyone had been free to disperse. Kirsten, clinging to Jane's arm, had begged to return to her 'old room' at Laurel Cottage, and Mary, her former discipler, had fairly gushed in response.

Kirsten had insisted upon sitting up to talk, saying she was too excited even to think of sleep. She'd done most of the talking, mainly about herself: her 'old' life, and her 'new', her devotion to Norton.

Sam's name hadn't been mentioned, nor had any reference to Kirsten's role as a reporter. Jane wondered whether the omissions were Kirsten's own, or whether the information had been extracted and expunged from her memory by Norton. Kirsten said she'd spent the previous week under Norton's special care up at the house, but now on the eve of the mission – she giggled – she was deemed fit for release.

Jane wasn't sure how fit she really was. There was something brittle about her. Her eyes were overbright, she talked too much, she seemed childishly anxious for other people's approval.

'I've always longed for a sister,' she told Jane at least half a dozen times. 'Now I've got one, I don't ever want to let you go.'

Kirsten's bedroom was next to Jane's. 'In the morning,' she'd said eagerly, 'we'll have time for a proper chat. It's late now, and there's still so much to tell you.'

Jane doubted it would be anything useful. Norton would never have entrusted important details to Kirsten. In fact, having Kirsten around seemed likely to be a distinct hindrance. Mary might be less of a problem after Jane's 'conversion' – certainly, she no longer watched her so closely, and down in the kitchen she had seemed wholly absorbed in Kirsten. But if Kirsten carried on being limpet-like the next day, it would be impossible for Jane to get away on her own, if there was time before the mission started.

Jane needed to phone Sam right now. She knew it was risky, but she was relying on her new status as a fully fledged Fellowshipper to protect her if she was caught. She rose from the bed and went to the door. On the landing, a floorboard creaked. She stood stock still and waited for Kirsten to call out, but she didn't.

She crept quickly down the stairs, not even pausing on Mary and Abby's landing, let herself out the back door, and pulled it silently shut behind her. The sky looked purple, and towards Norton's house the shadows of the trees loomed darkly.

She glanced up sharply but no figure stood at Mary's window, no curtain was raised. No one was watching her. She climbed over the fence and made for the road to Hawkenhurst.

With his ear to the closed door of the chapel, Ross listened to Norton and Ruth.

'I am my Beloved's and He is mine,' sang Ruth sweetly.

'And His banner over me is love,' answered Norton's beautiful baritone.

Of course Norton *would* have a good voice, Ross thought bitterly, while his own was flat and dull.

'You're not tired, my angel? It's very late.'

'I'm never tired when I'm with you, Beloved.'

Sand in his eyes, Ross thought, razor blades in his guts. Those were lovers' words. Did they think him a fool? He turned away. Why torture himself? Why listen to them? Better to gloat over what he knew and they did not: that they harboured a spy, Jane, in their midst. How delicious that Norton wanted her so badly as a 'missionary'! That he had got what he wanted at that service when Jane had 'converted'.

Ross had seen that she was dissembling, but clearly Norton had not. Watching her go up to the altar, Ross had wanted to laugh out loud, but that would have given her away, which was the last thing he wanted to do at the moment. He wanted to take it much closer to the edge, to make them think it was all going to happen according to their precious, well-laid plans.

All they – Ruth – had ever done was use him. Even when she'd first approached him two and a half years before. He remembered his incredulity at his good fortune. Sexy, adorable Ruthie Grant, whom Ross had always loved, actually returning his love – which had always been a bit of a family joke. Pretty, popular Ruth, twenty years his junior, and himself such a loner, a misfit, and yet she said she loved him.

He'd never forget that first weekend, at his home. She'd seemed like an angel, full of affection, wanting to know all about him, about what he did with himself, about his work at Porton, his forthcoming expedition to Norway, news of which had just been publicized in the media; about his knowledge of the 'flu virus.

After the expedition's failure, she was cool with him until he mentioned the other possibility; the second site.

'You're sure, Ross?'

She'd believed him when no one else did. Was it any wonder that he'd fallen even more deeply in love with her? That he'd told her how much she meant to him? That he'd agreed to do as she asked? He'd found it exciting, a challenge, to prove his love – and a professional challenge too.

Even when she told him about the Scroll and about how the virus was to be used, even when he'd realized that Norton, not Ruth, was the mastermind, he hadn't let her down. He'd picked the fight at Porton, he'd got the sack. He had even arranged his own death. And how had she repaid him? By choosing another man. By flaunting her preference for Norton.

Ross straightened up and eased his shoulders. He had Jane to think of now. He'd help her get the information she needed without alerting the others. To do so, he'd have to keep up the pretence of going along with them. He laughed silently. It would be vastly more entertaining to fool them than to fight them! To aid the serpent in their midst. And she was a pretty serpent, dark, shiny hair, beautiful eyes.

Groans came from behind the chapel door. They were at it again. Ross's stomach twisted in pain. He walked to the end of the corridor, unbolted the door and let himself out into the night.

Neither he or Ruth was supposed to leave the building again until the mission. With satisfaction, Ross unlatched the garden gate and emerged on to the driveway.

At the top, he turned left towards the other dwellings. He saw someone come round the corner of one of the cottages, and climb over the front fence. A Fellowshipper on the run? he wondered. Another headache for Norton? And then he saw who it was. Smiling, he followed Jane down the hill.

Dew glistened in the cottage gardens as Jane made her way along the high street. By the yellow glow in the sky, she could tell that dawn was not far off. It was possible Norton would summon his mission team early. She quickened her steps.

She saw a car coming and stepped into a shop doorway until its lights disappeared round the bend. She hurried towards the phone box.

Please God, she prayed, let it be working.

She lifted the receiver and heard the dialling tone. She dialled Sam's direct number at work. It rang and rang. Had he forgotten to divert it, as he'd said he would? She wouldn't get another chance to call him before the mission. She clenched the receiver tightly: he *had* to be there.

'Hullo?' It was his voice, stunned with sleep.

'Sam. I'm really sorry to call you so late. It's me, Jane.'

'Jane?' He seemed suddenly wide awake. 'Hi. What's the time? Are you all right?'

'Yes. I'm sorry,' she repeated. 'I had to call you now. It was the only chance I had to get away. It's okay to talk, is it?' she asked, suddenly anxious. 'I mean, when I called you yesterday . . . ?'

'I had MI5 with me.'

'Oh God.' Had she talked too much already? 'I'd better go. Bye—'

'No, wait,' he cried. 'They can't be monitoring this call, even if they are bugging my flat.'

'Why not?' she asked. 'You're at home aren't you?'

'Because I diverted my work number through to an unlisted number here. My burglar-alarm line. Nobody knows about it.'

'Oh.'

'Anyway, we're hardly their priority now.'

'What d'you mean?'

'It looks like the Keeper's been found.'

'What?' She couldn't believe it. 'Where?'

Her mind reeled as he talked. It couldn't be true – could it? She'd been so sure Norton was implicated. And yet Sam said the Scroll and the swaddling-clothes had been found. The Vermont leader had called himself the Keeper, had signed himself as such. The mass suicide sounded like textbook stuff. What more evidence did she want?

'What about Botulism Helen?' she asked. 'Has she been found as well?'

'Not as far as I know. There was some talk of her being the dead terrorist girl on the plane, but I think it's just wishful thinking.'

'Well, then, perhaps she's part of the British end of things.'

'That's what I think,' he answered promptly. 'Any sign of her at the Fellowship?'

'No,' Jane admitted. 'But I still feel there's something going on here. Maybe not the Scroll, but something.'

'Why?' He stifled a yawn.

'There's a mission planned for tomorrow. Norton called it the "biggest ever" but he hasn't given any details.'

'Perhaps he likes being mysterious.'

'Perhaps. Anyway, I've got myself on to the team that's leading it. My co-partner's Kirsten.' She paused, expecting an exclamation of surprise. 'Kirsten's here,' she repeated. 'She's okay, sort of.'

'Yes, she called me.'

'She called you?' Jane echoed. Sam seemed to be ahead of her on every score.

'Yesterday evening, about nine.'

When Kirsten was still incarcerated in Norton's house, Jane thought. 'What did she say?' she demanded.

'That she was a happy Christian.'

'I'll bet Norton was listening in. If he was, he'll know your number and who you are. Did you say anything incriminating?'

'Yes-no. I don't know. It doesn't matter now, does it?'

She hesitated. 'Not if you're right about Vermont.'

'I haven't imagined it.' There was an edge to his voice she hadn't heard before. 'It's on all the news channels.'

'Yes. I'm sorry. I'm sure it is. I'm jumpy. But look, I've got more news.' She told him everything she could remember about the stockpiles in the warehouse, Norton's secret chapel, and his monitoring of the news, about how she'd almost been forcibly escorted back from the village to the Moor.

'Right,' said Sam decisively, 'I'm coming down to get you right now.'

'Don't do that,' she said instantly.

'For God's sake, Jane! You tell me all this stuff, then you expect me to do nothing about it?'

'I want to find out what this mission is.'

He groaned. 'You're wasting your time.'

'Maybe I am.' She paused. There was dead silence at Sam's end. 'But I still think Norton could be dangerous.'

'Well, then!' he exclaimed.

'I can't leave without knowing what he's up to.'

'You're mad.'

'I probably am.' A milk-float trundled past, which reminded her of something else. 'Sam, can you trace registration numbers?'

'Maybe.' He sounded reluctant. 'Why?'

She took out the receipt on which she'd scribbled the number of the blue van. 'Norton had a very early visitor yesterday morning.'

'Jane . . .'

'Please?'

He sighed. 'Go on, then.'

She heard the scratch of a pen as he wrote down the number. She smiled into the receiver. 'Thank you,' she said.

'Oh, any time. Four o'clock in the morning, whenever. How much longer do you want to stay down there?'

'Another day?' she hazarded.

'Will you call me tomorrow?'

'If I can.' The receipt fluttered to the floor and she made a mental note to retrieve it.

'Please look after yourself. I've been worried. I still am, a bit.'

'You're sweet.'

'And you're bloody-minded.'

She grinned. 'Sleep well,' she told him, and she rang off and left the kiosk. Outside, the sky was definitely lightening. Was Sam right, she wondered? Was she wasting her time? If the Keeper was already dead in Vermont, what could Norton be guilty of? For a moment she saw him as he'd been in the church: the inspiring, loving guru, curing a boy of his stammer.

There was a white van parked up ahead. She was sure it hadn't been there before she made her call.

She heard a sound behind her and turned. There was nothing and nobody there. Her heart hammered. She was imagining things, she told herself. She heard a burst of static, then footsteps. She looked back again. A man had just crossed the road behind her.

She quickened her pace. He did too. She started to jog and heard him break into a run. She veered into the road away from the van and heard its back door crash open. She ran. A hand seized her arm. She tried to wrench herself free and, twisting, fell to the ground. A hand slapped round her face and in terror she bit it.

'Bitch!'

'Hush, it's all right now. Enough,' said a quiet, male voice.

Two men hoisted her upright. She was half dragged, half carried to the van. Another man helped haul her inside.

'I told you she was up to something when I saw her coming out of the cottage,' he said excitedly.

'Yes,' said the quiet man. 'We won't talk now.' Jane detected the faint brogue in his voice and knew that it was Steven.

A hood came down over her head, her hands were tied behind her. She felt the hotness of her own breath. Whatever happened, she thought, she must not pass out; she must remain fully alert if she was to have any chance of escape, of talking her way free.

She was laid, not ungently, on the hard, carpeted floor. A blanket was placed over her. A hand touched her hair, and she froze.

'Don't be a trouble now,' Steven said. The door slammed and the van moved off.

*

5.30 a.m.

By the time Ryder entered the communications room at Vauxhall, six of his staff, including Broughton, had been hunting for a trace of Edgecombe in all available records for over an hour.

They had found nothing. Since the night of his supposed death, Edgecombe had ceased to use a bank account or credit card, to visit a doctor or a dentist, to be in contact with his few friends and fewer relations. He had disappeared.

A grain of doubt entered Ryder's mind. Was he wasting valuable resources in a hunt for a dead man? Alarming Beck and the rest of ARIC for no good reason? He reread the details of the car crash. He might be wrong; Edgecombe might have died that night. But what could he do except follow through the inquiries he'd set in motion? The consequences of doing otherwise were too horrendous to think of.

Well, he thought sourly, what had he expected? The hunt to be easy? Edgecombe traced within the hour? Hardly! To the people who'd planned the Keeper operation and carried it out so meticulously – latterly in two continents – Edgecombe's death and concealment would be child's play. The Keeper cult had had luck over Helen, too. The whole country had been hunting for her all week; she'd been seen, and yet escaped; surveillance pictures of her had failed to produce one clear image. The devil was on their side – and the devil was winning.

He gazed round at his dishevelled team; their white, strained faces; the half-eaten sandwiches and plastic cups of filmed coffee that strewed their desks. The air they breathed was stale; the air-conditioning had failed. They all were exhausted, and they were getting nowhere.

He devoutly hoped he was wrong about Edgecombe.

He walked over to the far wall, where the bank of television screens played silently to the unheeding room. Ryder recognized the site of the Charleston bomb on one, Vermont on another. He increased the volume on the former.

'Thankfully, it appears that no lethal toxins escaped into the environment,' the presenter said. 'People are now returning to their homes.'

Ryder turned up the sound on the Vermont report.

A presenter was interrogating a woman in a white laboratory coat. 'So, what are you saying?' he asked.

'The bandages had been dipped in tea to make them look old.'

'But they were in fact new?'

She smiled wryly. 'They were in fact from K-Mart. There was a piece of the packaging still stuck to one of them.'

Ryder kicked the wall. Hard. He was right: Vermont had been a dummy – false swaddling-clothes, no doubt a false Scroll too, whereas the real ones were here, in Britain, with the real culprits. Finding them was his responsibility.

Where the *hell* were they? According to Beck, the government was panicking. No bloody wonder, in Ryder's opinion. The knowledge that a madman capable of launching a full-scale biological attack was at large in the country, and that no trace of him could be found, was pretty well guaranteed to make people panic. And if the news got out, and the public started to panic as well . . . He pushed the thought away.

The grass-roots investigation of religious groups and individuals had provided no strong leads. What was he to do now? Investigate the churches; pull in the vicars, the curates, the Sunday-school teachers?

He glanced back at the television screens. Two of them showed the face of Ross Edgecombe.

'Jack?' he called out, puzzled. 'I didn't know we'd released Edgecombe's picture yet?'

'What?' From a few desks away, Broughton looked up with a frown. 'We haven't.'

'What's this, then?' Ryder demanded, but the faces had gone. He turned up the volume. A newsreader said, 'Police searching for Botulism Helen are now looking for a second person, a man, seen driving a vehicle with part of her registration plate in the early hours of Friday morning.'

Edgecombe's face reappeared. Before it could disappear again, Ryder pressed the 'freeze' button. It was an e-fit, he saw, not a photograph, but the similarity was there; he was easily recognizable.

'Why the hell wasn't I told about this?' he demanded.

'What?' Broughton appeared alongside him. 'That's one of the *Crimewatch* e-fits. They were getting desperate by the end of the programme. They did some e-fits live in the studio, based on callers' descriptions.'

'But this is bloody Edgecombe, don't you see?' Ryder swore.

Other people in the room were staring at him.

'Where's that photograph of him?' Ryder demanded. 'It's at the top of his personal file.'

Broughton called it up on his computer screen.

Ryder's eyes cut between it and the television screen. 'Don't you see it?' he asked.

Broughton gnawed at his lower lip. 'There's a bit of a resemblance,' he said cautiously.

'Christ, it's more than that! Look at the eyes and the mouth.'

'The mouth's different,' said another officer solidly, crowding to look.

'Well, it hit me between the eyes,' Ryder retorted. 'I want every scrap of information there is on this e-fit, who gave the description, where the subject was, what he was driving . . .'

Two officers instantly set to work, pulling down the data from the *Crimewatch* files. Within minutes, they were done, and had passed Ryder a print-out.

The subject had been seen at a service station on the M25 near Redhill in Surrey at 03.55 on Friday morning. CCTV footage had shown a blue Bedford van, with the first two letters of the new false Helen registration number, J8.

Reading over his shoulder, Broughton said: 'You can see why we didn't think it was a priority. It wasn't even a white van.'

'So they sprayed it,' snapped Ryder. He carried on reading.

The rest of the plate had been obscured, and there was no shot of the driver, but the manager remembered him: he'd been short with him, nervy, and he'd paid in cash. The manager had told the *Crimewatch* producer that he was confident his description was accurate.

Which it was, Ryder thought: it was excellent. The e-fit had been put out as the programme ended. Almost three thousand fresh calls had been received.

'Anyone checked these calls?'

No one had. Broughton explained again that it had not been considered a priority. Much more promising data had been occupying the team, and then of course there had been Ryder's emergency call regarding Edgecombe.

Ryder nodded briefly. 'Okay, but let's get on to it now.' He called out to the room at large, 'Right, everyone. We want any and all callers who responded to the *Crimewatch* e-fit of Edgecombe.' He saw

Broughton's expression, and added 'I'll take some too.'

He sat down at the nearest free desk. The information was all there, on the *Crimewatch* database. Over half the calls referred to the e-fit of the man described as Helen's driver. Ryder took the last eighty of them.

At first, he worked methodically. The sightings had come in from all over the country but they were virtually the same. A man seen on his own, or sometimes with a woman like Helen, speeding down the M2, parked in a cul-de-sac in Tunbridge Wells, in a motel car-park in Chelmsford.

The wall clock ticked on. It was ten past six. In two hours, he was supposed to be presenting his action plan to ARIC. The adrenalin rush caused by the e-fit began to fade. He'd been awake for the best part of three days and nights. The transcripts merged before his eyes. He began skimming, looking for mentions of the van only, before moving on.

He paused. Then he went back to the start of a transcript. The witness was a soldier. It wasn't the military background that caught Ryder's attention, it was the difference between his account and all the others.

The soldier had described a car, not a van. It was the e-fit that had interested him. He'd twice seen a man resembling it, in a grey Renault estate car outside his barracks. The first sighting had been six weeks before; the second just three days earlier, on Wednesday afternoon. It was the car the soldier recognized that time. On the first occasion, the driver had merely sat in a layby – but for a long time, which was why the soldier had noticed him. On the Wednesday, however, the man had walked the barracks' perimeter. The soldier had been fully occupied with 'special duties' or else he'd have challenged him; as it was, he'd kept an eye on him on the circuit cameras.

'Jesus,' swore Ryder softly.

'You've got something?' Broughton asked.

'Maybe.' He saw that the soldier hadn't yet been interviewed by the police, probably because of the sheer volume of calls and the apparent discrepancy between his statement and the rest.

He dialled the number in Gwent and got the duty sergeant. He gave the code-name of his department and was patched through to the commanding officer, who quickly absorbed the seriousness of the situation. Orders were given for the soldier to be fetched immediately.

When he came on the line, he sounded young but self-confident. He said that as soon as he saw the e-fit he'd recognized Wednesday's weirdo.

'He was talking to himself, sir. A real loonie, if you ask me, sir.'

Ryder asked him about the surveillance cameras.

'Yes, sir, we've got him all right. I offered to send a still up to *Crimewatch*' – Ryder's hand tightened on the receiver – 'but they said maybe in the morning. They didn't sounded that interested, to tell you the truth, sir.'

Ryder swallowed. 'Would you send it up to me? Now?'

'I'll do that, sir. And I took down the car registration, if you'd like that?'

'Yes,' Ryder said with careful non-emphasis, 'I'd like that very much.' He took the numbers: it was a full plate. He thanked the soldier for his help and commended him for his vigilance, then rang off.

He gave the registration number to Broughton to trace. He made a copy of Edgecombe's photograph from the file on his own laptop, and then went over to the scanner to wait for the soldier's photo to come through. It didn't take long.

It was a good, clear picture, showing the subject in semi-profile. With a shaking hand, Ryder placed it beside the first photograph. He was vaguely aware of Broughton looking at them over his shoulder.

'Well, Jack, what d'you say now?'

'I'd say you were right.'

'You would?' Ryder turned to him gratefully.

'Yes, sir. I've just got the details on the car. It belongs to a company called Beyond the Bounds in the Brecon Beacons.'

Ryder's mind snapped back into gear. 'Scramble SARS,' he ordered. The Seize and Render Secure team was a dedicated military unit trained to deal with terrorist attacks involving chemical and biological weapons. 'Full NBC precautions,' Ryder added. 'Advice on the wing from Porton.'

'You going down yourself?'

'No time.' He picked up his phone to call Beck.

CHAPTER TWENTY-NINE

Jane sat perfectly still. She thought she was alone in the room, but she couldn't be sure. She was still hooded, her hands still tied together behind her back. Her fingers just reached the wall.

She was sitting on a bed. The journey in the van had lasted minutes only. Prone on the floor, she'd felt the van tilt as it climbed a hill, heard the soft crunch of twigs beneath its wheels, a metallic clanking as automatic gates opened, then closed behind them.

Steven had helped her out, across cobbles, up three steps and in through a narrow doorway. His apparent solicitude had made her hope for one wild moment that he might help her, but he'd brought her into the room, lifted her on to the bed, and having removed her watch – again, gently – left her to her thoughts.

She knew, as certainly as if she could see, that she was in Norton's private quarters, where Kirsten had been kept, where she herself had come snooping. Would the person who had seen her in the chapel come forward now, and denounce her?

Jane thought of Sam, of his offer to come and get her. She'd refused, confident that she had outwitted Norton and his agents. Meanwhile they had been waiting for her outside the phone box. She'd walked straight into their trap.

Would they kill her because of what she knew? Possibly (she felt curiously light-headed about that thought). Why else, she asked herself distantly, the executioner's hood, the tied hands, the cell? And the silence. She'd wondered why Steven bothered to take away her watch – after all, she couldn't see it to tell the time – but now she understood: its quiet ticking would have broken the silence that engulfed her. The room must be sound-proofed: try as she might, she could detect no noise but that of her own quick breathing. Was this what they had done to Kirsten, day after day, night after night, for a week? No wonder she was brittle, hyper, desperate for human contact, for a sister.

The hood was so thick that she could not tell whether the room was lit or in darkness. It was already becoming difficult to be sure of the time – though it must surely still be the same morning. She touched the wall, and a piece of paint flaked off into her cupped hand. She held on to it. She was still in contact with the outside world. She was still the person she had always been.

She supposed she could tell Norton who she really was, and offer to mediate between him and the authorities. That had always been her plan. But she couldn't make the offer as she was now, his helpless prisoner: he'd never take her seriously. She sucked in air, felt the fibres of the nylon hood in her mouth, pushed it back out. No, better to keep her identity secret. She had only made a telephone call. They couldn't kill her for that.

There was a sound behind her, and she moved her head sharply in its direction. A key turned, and the door opened.

Several people came in. She heard the scrape of furniture being set down. Hands lifted her forward on the bed so that her feet touched the floor. Her hood was pulled off and she blinked in the sudden glare of light. Norton was staring down at her.

He put out his hand and she flinched, thinking he was going to hit her. Instead, he stroked her cheek. 'What have you been up to?' he asked, his voice a mixture of sorrow and curiosity.

'I was only—'

'Ssh.' He placed a finger on her lips. 'Not now.' He stepped back.

She saw that she was in a small, square, windowless room. It was crowded. Two male Fellowshippers were setting three chairs in a row in front of her. A third stood next to Norton, watching her intently. He smiled, and she recognized the man from the choir-stalls the night before. He wasn't in Fellowship uniform but wore khaki trousers and a white shirt. Beside him was a thin woman with fair, wispy hair; something about her was vaguely familiar. Over by the door, his hands behind his back, his face expressionless, stood Steven.

Norton untied her hands.

'Bring in the witnesses,' he said over his shoulder and one of the Fellowshippers went out.

Witnesses, thought Jane. This was a court-room.

'This is Ruth.' Norton indicated the woman and man with him. 'And Ross. You've a right to know your judges.'

The three of them sat down. She felt terribly exposed before their gaze. Ross kept darting quick, gleeful glances at her – Jane wondered if he was mad – while the woman, Ruth, was frankly staring at her, unblinking. Jane lowered her own eyes. Ruth's face was familiar. She wished she could remember where she had seen her before.

More people entered the room. Jane looked up. She saw Mary, Abby, Kirsten, and three men, two of whom she recognized as part of Mary's team in the village.

Jane met Kirsten's eyes and saw terror in them, but also sympathy. The girl's pale hands were twisting convulsively. Jane wondered if the same thing had been done to her.

Kirsten took her place with the others in the row behind Norton's. The door clanged shut. Steven resumed his position in front of it.

'Shall we begin?' said Norton pleasantly enough.

One of the male Fellowshippers rose. Ross had seen a woman had leaving Laurel Cottage at 03.40 that morning.

Jane glanced up. Ross was smirking at her. She lowered her gaze, feeling sick.

Ross had followed her, the Fellowshipper continued, and when stopped himself by one of the Shepherds had divulged his suspicions about her. From his description, the Shepherd had recognized Jane. In accordance with David's orders, she'd been lifted upon leaving the telephone box.

Jane bit her lip. She'd been fatally overconfident, so sure that she had escaped Mary's attention that she'd been careless. But she could explain away that telephone call, and then what evidence did they have against her? Oh God, the receipt! The one she'd written the van's number on. Had she left it in the box? She saw it in her mind's eye, lying on the plastic ledge by the telephone. She'd meant to pick it up, but she'd forgotten. They'd know she'd been spying on them. They had the evidence they needed.

'The telephone box was examined,' the man went on.

Jane found it difficult to breathe.

'Nothing was found.'

She fought to keep her face blank. Had the receipt fluttered to the floor? Had someone seen it, but overlooked it?

'The redial button was pressed and the number which came up was . . .'

She thought her heart would stop. She hadn't seen a redial button on the phone; she didn't know there was one. She didn't often use public telephones.

Sam's number was read out.

There was a pause.

Would Kirsten know that number? If she did, would she say so? Or would her sympathy for Jane keep her silent? Jane didn't dare look at her.

'Whose number was it, Jane? Norton asked reasonably.

Was it a test? she wondered. Did he already know?

'Jane? His voice hardened.

'David, may I? said someone else timidly. It was Abby.

'Later, my dear,' said Norton, with a small frown.

'But I really think I know and Jane can't speak,' Abby insisted.

'Of course she can speak,' Norton growled.

Abby said resolutely, 'I think she phoned the same person when she was with me.' Then she closed her eyes.

There was a pause. 'I don't think I remember you mentioning that,' Norton said, and there was steel in his voice.

'No,' Abby said nervously. 'Jane was so upset – I promised I wouldn't tell a soul. She phoned her boyfriend, the abusive one, when we were in the café. She can't break free of him. She feels she has to talk to him. It's a sickness, isn't it, Jane?' she appealed.

Jane felt a thrill of hope. She'd been planning to use that excuse herself to explain away her call, but it sounded much more authentic coming from Abby. 'Yes,' she whispered, dropping her eyes.

'Is that who you were phoning?' intoned Norton. 'Look at me, Jane.'

Slowly, she raised her eyes. He had to believe her. She nodded.

'Challenge,' said Mary, and she stood up.

'Yes?' said Norton, looking round at her.

Mary looked straight at Jane, her dislike evident in her face. 'You've been aware of my suspicions from the start, David. I suggest she be made to call the number now, on the speaker phone so we all can hear her.'

Norton shook his head. 'We can't risk it, Mary. She might use some sort of alert code.'

'Then why don't we call the number ourselves?' suggested Mary.

Jane bit her lip again. Mary was determined to get her.

Norton frowned. 'The person is unlikely to identify himself to us, and if he is as you suspect he might trace the call. We might try the number later, from one of the mobiles, if we've time.'

He turned back to Jane. 'I'd like to believe you,' he said musingly.

Fiercely, Jane told herself to remember who he was. He believed he had special powers. He was surrounded by people who fed that belief. He thought he'd converted her. He thought God had spoken to him when he chose her as one of the 'missionaries'. He had no evidence against her. If he believed Abby's story, he might still believe in her.

'Is Jesus your personal saviour?' he asked.

'He is,' Jane said with emphasis. 'I'm sorry if I've done anything wrong, David. I couldn't sleep and I knew he'd be up because he's working nights this week and—'

'Of course, he's a policeman,' interrupted Norton smoothly.

Jane's missed a beat. Was her cover story to be her downfall?

'Does he know where you are?' David asked casually.

'No. He wasn't interested. He just said I'd better go home if I knew what was good for me . . .' She made her voice die away.

They were all watching her closely, judging her.

'What does everyone else think?' Norton asked. 'Do we believe her?'

'I do.' Kirsten got to her feet. 'I think she's telling the truth.'

'Do you, little one?' Norton smiled round at her.

'Yes.' Kirsten swallowed nervously. 'I know Jane's been a bit unwise. Maybe she should have asked permission to phone, but she's only new, she didn't know. I don't think she's done anything wrong. She's just asked Jesus into her life.'

Norton's smile widened. 'And she's your sister,' he pointed out.

'Yes.' Kirsten reddened. 'She's my sister in the Life, and I know what she's going through being judged by everyone like this. It's horrible. I deserved it, but she doesn't.'

Norton raised an eyebrow. 'Thank you, Kirsten. Mary?'

Mary rose once more, a notebook in her hand. As she read from it, in a clear, emotionless voice, Jane went cold. It wasn't her dawn walk the previous morning that had first made Mary suspicious; she had been monitored since she arrived at the Fellowship. At the barbecue Mary had noted how watchful she was.

'Although allegedly a stranger in our midst, she appeared to be looking for someone,' Mary said.

Jane caught the gaze of the woman beside Norton. The one he had introduced as Ruth. She knew suddenly of whom she reminded her: Botulism Helen.

Ruth returned her stare, and Jane swiftly looked down. Did Ruth realize she'd been recognized? Did this mean there were two Keepers, Norton and the man in Vermont? Was Norton also planning a mass suicide? Was that what his great mission amounted to?

She could feel Norton's eyes on her, and kept her head bowed. Her fists were clenched tightly in her lap: deliberately she uncurled her fingers. If she was to have any chance of getting away, of alerting the authorities, she had to get out of that locked cell. She had to convince Norton she was harmless. Over her head, Mary was describing seeing Jane's return to the cottage the previous dawn.

Jane looked up with a distressed expression. 'I couldn't sleep, I—'

'Hush,' said Norton.

Mary's monologue continued. Jane's request to remain alone at the Moor had been noted as had her reluctance to accompany Mary in the car back from the village. Jane kept frowning and shaking her head. She didn't know if she was overdoing it, and she subsided into giving helpless little shrugs.

She heard that the previous afternoon, a full-scale discreet surveillance operation had swung into action. Her room and later, while she was at supper, her handbag had been searched. Silently she thanked Sam for making her empty her bag of anything incriminating.

'I remained unsure following Jane's conversion.'

Norton nodded.

'But on David's orders I and the team suspended our surveillance duties last night, when the four Shepherds were appointed to take over watch of the Moor. They didn't see Jane leave the cottage, and might have missed her altogether, had it not been for Ross—'

'Who was placed there by Jesus,' Norton murmured, and he gave Ross a loving look. Ross smirked again at Jane.

Mary sat down.

'Anyone else?' asked Norton.

Over at the door, Steven moved. 'There's just one thing, David,' he said quietly. 'Did Jane, on her dawn patrol yesterday, notice a crate of oranges lying anywhere about?' He spoke lightly, and Norton and one or two of the others smiled.

'Oranges?' repeated Norton.

'Yes. A crate of them went missing yesterday.'

Was this another Fellowship game? wondered Jane. Had Steven found her crate by the store-house window? If he asked the question, he must suspect her, so why was he toying with her?

'Jane?' Still smiling, Norton turned to her. 'D'you know anything about these oranges?'

She shook her head. 'No, David,' she said wonderingly.

'You didn't take them back to your room for a little early breakfast?'

'No.'

Norton was treating it as a joke, she saw, but Steven wasn't. If he'd found her crate, he'd have said so, so he was suspicious only. But he was obviously important, probably one of Norton's lieutenants. To have him suspicious of her as well as Mary, who was clearly the chief of Norton's police . . .'

'I think we can say Jane is innocent of orange theft,' Norton said, and several people laughed.

'Anyone else?' he asked.

Now it would come, she thought. Right at the end, when she was nearly clear, whoever it was who'd seen her in the chapel would speak out.

The room was quiet. No one spoke. Almost incredulously, Jane realized there were no other witnesses. She had been reprieved.

'Time is short,' Norton began – Jane suddenly remembered the mission. Was the systemic killing of the Fellowshippers about to begin? Was she, as one of the mission leaders, supposed to hand out lethal drugs? – 'so we'd better come to a decision. Mary, if you'd take the others out?'

The Fellowshippers departed. At the door, Kirsten gave Jane a quick, brief smile, then she too was gone.

Four people remained in the room with Jane: Norton, Ross, Ruth and, by the door, Steven.

'What do we think?' asked Norton.

'Kill her,' said Ruth.

Jane heard the sentence but her mind refused to believe it. They'd just been laughing about oranges, she thought distantly.

She saw Steven looking at her. The look struck her as predatory. Was he her executioner?

'Why do you say that, Ruth?' Norton asked mildly.

'We can't afford the risk,' she said succinctly.

'It is a risk,' he agreed. 'But if we kill her, and she is connected outside, and they come looking for her in the next hour or two, before we start, wouldn't it be better to be able to produce her, alive, to show them her claims were false?'

'But we're talking of such little time,' Ruth muttered.

'Every moment counts,' Norton reminded her. 'Anyway, I'd rather not kill her,' he went on, wrinkling up his nose playfully. 'My suggestion is she remains here in this room, out of harm's way, and that she then accompanies us on our mission as planned.'

Ruth gave an audible sigh.

'Or there is Ruth's suggestion. Shall we put it to the vote?' suggested Norton. 'Those in favour of my proposal?'

Jane felt completely outside herself, disconnected from what was going on. Only David's hand rose. One against three: she was going to die.

'Those in favour of Ruth's?'

Ruth's hand went up and so did Steven's. Ross hesitated, then, with a wink at Jane, he slowly raised his hand.

She wondered how and when they would do it, whether she would be brave, or would she beg for her life.

'Jane,' said Norton teasingly, 'you haven't voted. Do you vote to live?'

Shakily her hand rose into the air.

'That's two against three.' Norton rubbed his chin ruminatively. 'And then of course, there's Jesus's vote. Jesus wants Jane to live,' he said simply. 'And in a tie, I do have the extra casting vote.'

Jane caught a quick look of annoyance on Ruth's face, then it was gone. She understood how little life mattered to her.

'We should leave Jane on her own,' Norton said, standing up.

Jane didn't care now whether he put back the hood, and retied her hands. She'd been saved.

Norton stooped to her level. 'You will pray?' he asked.

'I will,' she said.

The door closed behind the four of them, and she heard the key turn in the lock. She waited, staring straight ahead, scarcely daring to breathe. She had been spared – but for how long? She still needed a miracle: she still had to get out of there.

The helicopters flew in low over the hills, landing in a dip between them, half a mile from the target. Forty-six figures emerged and ran, a difficult task given the terrain and the weight of their gear: the multi-layered, rubberized NBC kit, the heavy respirators, guns.

They surrounded the house. Through a loudhailer, the SARS captain advised any occupants to show themselves. No one did. He gave the order for the team to go in.

They were working the buddy system. They checked each other's breathing apparatus, and then they advanced, running again, keeping close to the ground, flinging themselves down as they came within ten feet of the house, going forward on their bellies up to the walls. They stuck explosives on the doors, and retreated to wait for the 'boom' and the covering smoke, and then entered.

They checked the hall first, then spread out through the ground floor and up. They radioed back: no one at home.

The two scientists with the team advanced. They carried devices that looked like metal detectors, but these monitored levels of chemical compounds in the air. In a room next to the kitchen, they found laboratory equipment and their monitors began to emit low 'beeping'. Nitrates had been used in that room, the scientists concluded. Nitrates were used in the manufacture of bombs. But it looked as if the laboratory had been used for other purposes as well.

Against the far wall was a large, metal container with a plastic hose coming out of the top. The end of the hose had been fed into a hole in the wall and sealed. The scientists recognized it as an air-filtering unit. There was also a rubber seal round the door. Attempts had been made to turn that room into a Level Three Plus laboratory where highly hazardous substances could be safely contained.

The scientists knew what they might have to deal with. It was in here, they judged, that Edgecombe had grown his bugs and, if he truly had it, resurrected the Spanish flu virus.

They took air samples, they scraped benches for minute particles and deposited them in their bio-boxes for analysis back at their own laboratories. Then they followed the SARS captain down a corridor to a curious room that his soldiers had found. The door had been sealed with red biohazard tape such as they themselves might use.

'Ours?' mouthed the senior scientist, speaking with difficulty through his gas mask.

The captain shook his head. 'It was already here,' his voice boomed back, then he left them to answer a summons from his team outside.

The scientists cut the tape and cautiously entered the room. It was at least thirty feet long. A window high in the wall had been recently bricked up. The room looked as if at one time it had been used for storage, but now at one end there were four single beds; at the other, behind a screen, a lavatory and shower. There was a makeshift kitchen, sofas and a ping-pong table.

These were evidently in living-quarters, but why the suction-sealed door, the biohazard tape, the air-filtration system against the far wall? The scientists went outside. They found the place in the wall where the window had been but no sign of the air-system's exhaust pipe. There wasn't one, which meant that any air in that room would be filtered straight back in.

They looked at each other. The room had been an isolation unit, its inhabitants human laboratory rats.

'He tested the flu virus on them?' asked one incredulously.

'Looks that way, doesn't it?' muttered his colleague. A horrid thought hit him. 'If they were infected with it, if they left here . . .' He let his words die away.

'We're too late,' said his colleague.

Both men thought of their own families, of the possibility that perhaps they could still escape, could get far enough away.

'We don't know if he actually got the virus,' the first man pointed out.

'Or if it worked,' said the other, clutching at the hope.

They walked away from the house. They saw one of the SARS team coming rapidly down the hill towards them. It was only when he reached them they recognized the captain through his mask.

'There are graves up on the hill,' he said.

The two men experienced pure dread. 'How many?' asked one.

The captain held up four fingers.

'No one's tampered with them?'

The captain shook his head.

'We must seal the site,' ordered one scientist. 'Anyone with flu symptoms in the neighbouring area must be isolated immediately.'

Through the fish-eyes of his mask, the captain goggled. 'You think it's got out?'

'We can't be sure. We've got to assume the worst. We've got to get lung samples out of those bodies.'

The captain nodded. Through his earpiece came the voice of another of his officers: a car had been found in one of the out-buildings. A grey Renault.

The captain scowled. He'd hoped it would be the van. If it had been, they'd have stood a chance of finding Edgecombe through the car's traceable number plates. Now, all they knew was that he was out there somewhere, probably with his virus. And he knew the virus worked.

The captain rang Ryder with the news.

08.50

Most of the ARIC members were too busy with their own crisis meetings to spare the time to meet in person. Once again, therefore, Ryder had set up a conference call. At least this time he was speaking to them from his office.

Not many were present. Besides the chairwoman, Beck, Ryder and the brigadier, there there was a biological/chemical warfare expert from Porton Down. When the SARS captain came on the line, he was co-opted into the call.

There was dead silence as his news sank in. The Porton Down expert left the call temporarily to question the two scientists.

When he came back on the line, he said, 'Our problem is, there's a limit to what we can do.'

'What d'you mean?' demanded the chairwoman. 'Surely, in light of what we've just been told, we must have a national shutdown until this man's caught?'

The brigadier said, 'There's never been a shutdown such as you describe, ma'am, for the very good reason that it would cause mass panic and anyway be impossible to enforce. We haven't got the manpower.'

'But if the public were informed of the risk?' she argued.

'Panic,' interrupted several voices.

'There isn't a vaccine,' the Porton expert reminded everyone. 'Nor is there likely to be in the foreseeable future.'

There was a silence.

'What's the incubation period for this flu?' asked Beck.

'Short, usually one to three days,' said the Porton man.

'And it will spread?'

'Oh, yes. To Europe first and then on – more quickly than you can imagine. In 1918, it killed most of its fifty million victims in just six months.'

There was another taut silence.

'We must quarantine ourselves to the best of our ability,' said the chairwoman gravely.

'But if it's airborne,' said Beck, 'how can we?"

'We can stop international travel. Seal the airports, the Chunnel, railway stations.'

'If we're infected, yes,' said the brigadier. 'But there's still a chance, isn't there, that we'll catch this bastard?'

Ryder's lips twisted: not much of a chance.

'It's going to be bloody difficult,' said Beck. 'And we don't know if he's already released it.'

'Is it at all possible,' the chairwoman said tentatively, 'that Edgecombe's out of the picture?'

'You mean, dead?' asked Ryder.

'Yes.'

Ryder sighed. 'It's possible, of course, but I don't think so. I think he's alive and his end-game's up and running.'

'I agree,' said the brigadier gloomily. 'He's put too much into it to top himself before his big moment. He's a clever bastard. Look how he killed that girl on the plane.'

The results had just come in, from New York, of the early analysis of her blood and tissue samples. She had been injected with a massive dose of a compound drug known as PPR, a triple serum administered to front-line troops during the Gulf War to give them some protection against chemical attack. Her stomach contents revealed she had also heavily overdosed on antihistamine tablets. The correlation between antihistamine – at normal dosage – PPR and cases of Gulf War syndrome, had been quietly established by

British and American military scientists investigating the syndrome in the mid-1990s, though the link had never been made public. Edgecombe's file revealed that he had been one of the handful of scientists involved in the PPR project.

'God knows what scheme he's dreamt up for this bloody flu release,' the brigadier continued. 'Pity Porton didn't detect him as a loon a bit earlier.'

'There's no reason to suppose he'll need any sort of intricate device,' the Porton man said stiffly.

'That's comforting,' murmured the chairwoman. 'You mean, he can just let it go, take the stopper off his test-tube and that'll do the trick?'

'It would. But to be more effective, to ensure a greater dispersal amongst first-strike targets, he could spray it from a light aircraft – a crop-duster, say – or aerosolize it.'

'Sounds easy,' said Beck.

'Oh it is, if you know how,' said the Porton man.

'And Edgecombe does.'

No one said anything.

'Are we still looking for a cult working with Edgecombe?" the chairwoman asked after a moment.

'We are,' said Ryder. 'Although I'm afraid that we have no likely candidates, and as far as we know Edgecombe had no religious affiliations up to the time of his supposed death.'

'Bloody needle in a haystack again, isn't it?' grunted the brigadier.

Ryder told them that every NRM, or religious group or even individual, that had come to Bridegroom's attention during the course of its inquiries would now be placed under military or police guard.

'Think what the media's going to make of that,' commented the brigadier.

'Who bloody cares?' snapped the chairwoman.

In addition, Ryder went on, the photograph and e-fit of Edgecombe, and both e-fits of Helen were being posted at every port, airport, railway station, military base and police station in the land. They had no idea where the virus might be released – it could be Stonehenge, the Millennium Dome or a remote hilltop.

Edgecombe's photograph had already been released to the media and at any moment the first in a series of public appeals to find the pair would be broadcast on television and radio.

'Mightn't that spook them into releasing the virus?' asked the brigadier.

'They're beyond spooking,' Ryder said. 'They've got their own timetable; unless detained, they'll release it according to that.'

'Terrific,' muttered Beck.

There would be both overt and covert military presence at all airports, ports and stations but, Ryder pointed out, it was impossible to stop and search every person passing through an airport, or using the London underground or the Channel ferries. There would be random checks and, of course, detention on sight of any suspicious individual or group.

'If Edgecombe's with a group, won't they be quite easy to spot?' asked the Porton man.

'I doubt very much that they're going to make it easy for us,' said Beck crushingly.

Without being told of the nature of the emergency, Ryder added, every hospital in the country was to be put on crisis standby.

Finally, the voices quietened. No one had anything else to say. One by one, they wished each other luck. Ryder, exchanging the last greeting, tried to dislodge the sense that it was all too late.

He returned to the communications room.

An estate agent in Hereford had called his local police station, Broughton informed him, deadpan, to report that he'd leased a property to a man and woman he thought looked 'a lot like' Edgecombe and Helen.

'What's the address?' barked Ryder.

'That's why I didn't interrupt your meeting. An outdoor leisure centre in the Brecon Beacons.'

'The same one?'

Broughton nodded.

'Where the hell's this estate-agent been all week?' Ryder demanded.

'On holiday. He got back last night.'

Ryder closed his eyes. 'I see.'

He turned to gaze at the photograph of Edgecombe, now on the wall beside Helen. Where were those bastards? Then his anger turned to prayer.

CHAPTER THIRTY

9 a.m.

Plastic, garish, economy-size, the four yellow bottles stood upon the altar – like skittles, Ross thought. He picked one up. It claimed to offer maximum protection against the sun's harmful rays, which he found amusing.

He weighed the bottle in his hand and scrutinized its pop-up lid. It looked perfect. There was nothing to suggest it was but what the label said it was: a leading brand of suntan lotion. He raised it above his head. Only there, under the concave base, was there anything out of the ordinary, and to the untrained eye it would merely look like a tiny plastic knob, a design quirk, perhaps. There was nothing to say 'timing device', nothing to indicate than when twisted anti-clockwise it would activate the mechanism that would spring the lid and release the aerosolized spores.

A similar device had been used in the Gulf War. At Porton, Ross had worked on a prototype. In Wales, he'd adapted that design to meet Norton's requirements: a device that would appear innocuous, that would pass metallic security checks, that could be activated easily by an amateur.

He had met every specification, and more. If, by ill-chance, anyone tampered with it, flipped open the lid, say, to check the contents, he would automatically activate the aerosol and would inhale not the sickly smell of suntan lotion but the odourless, deadly flu virus itself.

Inside each container were enough microdroplets to infect up to a thousand people. They would be unaware that they were infected. They would go about their business, breathing in and out, clearing their throats, kissing, touching, talking, feeling perfectly well for twenty-four or forty-eight hours until the virus hit. By then, many thousands more would have been infected. Each person was his or her own walking biological weapon.

Before, when Ross had loved Ruth, when he had conditioned his mind to death with her, a little part of him – an ignoble part, he'd told himself – had thought it a pity that he'd receive no acclaim for the two greatest achievements of his life, the resurrection of the virus and the perfection of its release. Now, however – he set the container back on the altar, beside the things Norton had put there, 'for Jesus' blessing' – now, if he was not mistaken, there was the possibility of both life and glory.

He took out of his trouser pocket the receipt he'd found in the phone box. Curiosity had prompted him to follow Jane; shock at being apprehended by a Shepherd and then self-preservation had prompted him to betray her. It had been easy then to ask to accompany Steven, to be part of the kidnap team, to search the phone box first.

The receipt, with his own van's untraceable plate number scribbled on the back, had been lying on the floor for all to see.

Jane, Jane! Ross shook his head. How careless she'd been, how utterly she owed her life to him. If he had produced that piece of evidence at her trial, there'd have been no vote. Jane would now be lying out in one of the stables, dead.

He turned the receipt in his hands. Who was she? An operative from a dedicated unit, sent in to get the definitive evidence for the SAS? Probably something like that. He was going to supply her with that evidence; he was going to get her out of there, ensure she made contact with her people.

And in return, she – no, they, the government – they were going to reward him with something better than 'The Lord has given you such gifts' and 'Praised be God for using you as His channel.' He'd return to Porton not as a vilified employee but in triumph, as an esteemed visitor: Ross Edgecombe who had turned the deadliest bug the world had ever known into the best-ever biological weapon. He'd travel the world, lecturing. At peace ceremonies, he and Jane would mount the podium together; together, they'd accept the Nobel Peace Prize.

'My dear,' he murmured. At her trial she'd looked so pretty, so delicate, so defenceless. She'd got herself into hot water, and he'd saved her. He'd voted for her death so that he himself would remain above suspicion. And the ruse had worked. After a dreary 'final blessing' session in the chapel with Norton and Ruth, Ross had asked to be left on his own there to pray – Ross snorted – over his canisters, and Norton had gladly agreed. In fact, Ross meant to stay close to Jane, so that as soon as the coast was clear he could act.

He went to the door now, and peeked out. David's office door was closed. He must be in there, preparing, and Ruth by now would be in her room, right at the end of the other corridor. Jane's room was nearly opposite the chapel, the key in the lock awaiting Norton's return.

Two strides and he was there. Quietly, he turned the key. He would quickly show her the canisters, tell her about the flu and the other details of the mission, then smuggle her out the back way.

'Ross?'

He whipped round. Norton was coming down the corridor.

'Just checking on her,' Ross said. He flicked the eye-hole cover on the door.

'Good man.'

For a second Ross thought Norton looked sad, but then the expression was gone.

'Ruth's buzzed me to ask if we'd go along to her room. Said there's something important she needs to talk to us about.' Norton smiled disarmingly. 'She wouldn't tell me what it is.'

Ross frowned. A change of heart in Ruth? Or a further demand on him? A flexing of the power she still believed was hers?

'She said it was urgent.'

He could hardly go ahead with his plan while Norton stood there, watching. He'd have to come back later. He set off with Norton towards Ruth's room.

At first, hearing the key in the lock, Jane assumed they were coming to get her, that time had run out and the mission was about to start, but nothing happened.

Very faintly, she could hear voices outside the door but she couldn't tell whether they were male or female. Then silence fell again. Had they forgotten about her, or had they merely moved away down the corridor to see what she would do?

Telling herself she had probably been imagining the sound of the key turning, the eye-hole cover being lifted, she slid off the bed and went to the door. She put her ear to it and listened. Silence. She turned the knob; the door opened. She listened again. Still silence.

She risked a look. The passageway was empty. At either end, both doors were closed. By the door to the rest of the house, she saw an entry-pad fixed to the wall, but it would be a waste of time to try it: she didn't know the code. And she mustn't be found there, trying different combinations.

She turned and ran soft-footed down the corridor. Another corridor kinked off to her left. She reached the stable-door, saw its bolts, top and bottom, and two locks. It was useless, she thought. She couldn't get out. She was still trapped. The realization brought her close to despair. She had been let out for no purpose. Then she thought about whoever had unlocked her door. Soon they would remember doing so and would come back to check. She had to be where they had left her.

She headed quickly back to her room. She had almost reached it when she saw that the door opposite, the chapel door, stood ajar. In her haste to escape, she hadn't noticed it before. She listened intently but she could hear no sound from within. She gave the door a gentle push.

As before, the candles were lit on the altar. The box still stood there, but it was no longer alone. Beside it were bottles of suntan lotion – suntan lotion? she must be going mad – and some other things she couldn't see properly.

Jane closed the door silently behind her and went over to the altar. The other things were airline tickets, fanned out as if on display.

She lifted the lid of the box. What looked like brittle wafers were packed inside. She picked one up. It was feather-light: a narrow strip, about five inches long, holed, and stained brown and black in places. A fragment flaked off and fell to dust. She set it gingerly aside and felt inside the box. Her fingers closed on a piece of soft leather.

She drew it out. It looked like a jewellery roll. She undid the tie and unrolled it. The parchment lay curled in her hands.

She shivered. Sam was wrong. The Keeper wasn't dead in Vermont. He was alive, here in England. The parchment was the Scroll; the strange wafers were the remnants of the swaddling-clothes. She turned over the Scroll. There, on the back, was the Greek script: 'And then the End, the Awful Horror of the Ungodly shall come.'

Vermont hadn't fulfilled that prophecy, she saw that now. Vermont had been the slaying of the godly – in the cult's eyes – by their own hands. From the Moor, in a few hours' time, Norton was going to launch the Awful Horror: what he had called the 'greatest mission' there had ever been.

She snatched up the airline tickets. There were six; two each to Lima, Tokyo and San Francisco. They were in six men's names, none of which she recognized, and none of them Norton's.

What did it mean? she wondered desperately. If she and Kirsten were involved in the mission, where were their tickets? And why the bottles of suntan lotion, placed on the altar for blessing?

She picked one up. What was really in it? Her fingers moved to the pop-up lid . . .

She heard two distant 'whumps'. To her ears, they sounded like gun-shots. If she was found there, they would surely kill her. They mustn't know she'd been tampering. She set the bottle down, put the scroll and the bandages back in the box and shut the lid.

She eased the chapel door open. Footsteps were coming – from the direction of the other corridor. She fled to her cell and eased the door to. She had barely made it inside when the footsteps turned into her corridor. She didn't dare close the door properly in case the sound gave her away.

The footsteps paused outside. Oh God, whoever it was, was bound to see that it wasn't properly shut. Then she caught the sound of a stifled sob. The chapel door opened and closed and then all was quiet again. She shut her door and sank down on to her bed, trying to make sense of what she had seen, trying to convince herself that she could still stop Norton.

In the chapel, David fell to his knees.

He couldn't see Jesus; he could see only the blood. Another sob shook him. He wished he hadn't gone into the room, hadn't looked. But, waiting out in the corridor, he'd heard two shots and had panicked. Why two? Ruth was already dead.

Steven explained that Ross had turned at just the wrong moment, so he'd needed that second bullet. When David went in, he saw Ross lying face down on the floor on one side of the bed, Ruth over on the other side. Their blood was seeping into the carpet, a deep, rich red, staining the sisal. And the look on Ruth's face, the sheer terror, the knowledge of betrayal.

'But it was what You wanted, wasn't it, Lord?' David asked piteously. 'It was what You always said. That Ruth and Ross, having performed their duties, should precede me into Paradise?'

He knew the Lord was right. To have had them on the mission would have been too great a risk. Out in the world they had been seen too often. As if in confirmation of the Lord's desire, in his office after the Last Blessing, David had seen the public appeal. They knew who Ross was, knew he wasn't dead. They had named him, and had shown his photograph as well as the e-fit of Ruth. The hand of every man, woman and child in the country would have been turned against them. Of course they couldn't come on the mission!

Neither could they be left behind at the Moor; it might take days – weeks even – for them to catch the virus, and the SAS would track them down, perhaps soon, torture them, make them talk, make them inadvertently ruin everything at that late stage.

No, Ruth and Ross had served their purpose. They had served the Lord.

David took comfort from the fact that they had not suffered; there hadn't been time, Steven had assured him. They had only gone ahead a little earlier to Jesus' house. Very soon it would be his turn; he could shed his weary load, he could rest in the Saviour's arms.

He rose from his knees. Everything was ready, or almost. At any moment, he expected to hear about Sam Ferryman. He placed the suntan lotions in their special carrying case, pocketed the airline tickets and left the chapel.

He paused in front of Jane's door, and flicked back the spy-hole. He saw – dear child! – that she was praying.

How right he'd been not to heed the others' suspicions about her! With a light heart, he set off to shed his Fellowship clothes.

*

10 a.m.

After Jane's dawn telephone call, it had taken Sam a while to fall asleep again. He woke at seven, realized it was Saturday, remembered that Jane had wanted to stay another day down at the Fellowship, rolled over and slept again.

At ten o'clock he roused himself, put on his dressing-gown and went to fetch his newspapers from his pigeon-hole down in the entrance-hall. Back upstairs, he ground some coffee-beans and turned on the television.

'In an unusual step, police have issued a photograph of a man wanted in connection with the Botulism Helen poisonings.' The man was dark-complexioned with strong features, dark hair, just going grey.

So there were two rogue members of Jordan's sect in Britain, Sam thought. The police must be pretty confident if they were naming the man, and issuing his photograph.

'The public is being warned not to approach the pair, who could be dangerous.'

Sam turned down the sound and spread out a newspaper. E-fits of Helen and her male accomplice dominated the front page, and there was a rag-out of their van's registration numbers.

'WHY CAN'T THE POLICE FIND THEM?' the headline demanded, and the article below began, 'They know what she looks like. They have two number plates. There have been thousands of sightings of her this week. And yet, thirteen days after she struck down her first child victims, she is still at large.'

But surely not for much longer, Sam judged, with the saturation coverage she and her companion were receiving.

He picked up another newspaper. It had splashed on the Vermont cult, as had the *Correspondent*. The Eighth Scroll ran in full on an inside page. Again, it was strange to see it publicly displayed. That thought led at once to thoughts of Jane. He wondered if she'd found out any more about the 'mission', whether she'd want to stay down at the Fellowship all weekend, if she had yet satisfied herself as to Norton's danger or non-dangerous status.

The phone rang. He went to answer it, but when he picked up the receiver he heard the dialling tone, and the ringing continued. He was confused for a second, then he realized it was his other line.

Jane, he thought, dashing to answer it.

'Hullo? Is that Sam Ferryman?' It was a female voice but none that he recognized.

'Yes?' he said cautiously.

'You rang me last night about David Norton,' she prompted.

He remembered then. His caller must be one of Norton's former associates.

'I was out playing bridge. This is the *Correspondent* I'm talking to?' the woman asked, a trifle shortly, annoyed by his lack of response.

'Yes, I'm sorry, it is.' His own intense interest in Norton had dwindled away but he recalled Jane's.

'So, what d'you want to know about him?'

Sam said that he was researching community NRMs and so was interested in the Fellowship.

'I've never heard of it,' she said forthrightly.

Sam briefly explained.

'So that's what happened to David, is it?' Her voice had softened. 'He always had leadership qualities, I thought.'

'You haven't seen him for some time, then?' Sam asked.

'No. It must be a good twelve or thirteen years, now. Just after the the big row.'

'Oh?' Sam asked politely. He saw that, true to his journalistic training, he'd made notes on Jane's call.

'Yes. It was a storm in a tea-cup, or would have been if old Jolyon – he was our minister – hadn't over-reacted.' She paused. 'Look, are you planning to publish this?'

Sam assured her that it was for background purposes only.

'That's all right, then. I wouldn't like David to think I'd been blabbing behind his back.'

'What was the row about?'

She hesitated. 'It may sound daft to you. He thought he'd had a vision.'

'I see,' Sam said. He wondered if that would be of interest to Jane.

'He thought God was talking to him directly. Well, we'd all like to think that, wouldn't we?'

Sam made a noncommittal sound.

'David was very enthusiastic, very keen. It happens that way with some older converts. He thought God was talking to him about the end of the world.'

Sam's heart skipped a beat. 'The end of the world?'

'Hardly surprising, really.' The woman went on. 'They were very into Armageddon at the church back then, interpreting the scriptures for the Last Days. What did they expect with impressionable new converts?'

Sam hunched closer over the phone. 'Can you remember any details of his vision?' he asked.

'Well, some of them.' She hesitated again. 'Like I said, this may sound daft.'

'Oh no, please, go on.'

'He thought God was speaking to him through the Dead Sea Scrolls,' she said in a rush.

The word 'Scrolls' pounded in Sam's head.

'I know it sounds a bit odd but—'

'Are you sure you don't mean the Eighth Scroll?' he said hoarsely.

'Of course, that was it,' the woman exclaimed. 'That's what Jolyon got so upset about. How could God possibly be talking through a fake?'

Her voice continued but Sam didn't hear. Norton was the Keeper. Vermont had only been part one. And Jane was going on the 'biggest ever' Fellowship mission.

He came back to reality and heard the woman say, 'David should have hung around. Jolyon dropped dead six months after David and his girlfriend walked out.'

'What was she called?' Sam butted in.

'Ah, now what was it? Ruth? Yes, that's right.'

Sam thanked her, said he had to go. His hand was unsteady as he put the receiver down. Who to call to ensure the right response? Not the police. By the time he'd convinced them, by the time they got their act together, it might be too late.

Burroughs, he thought. He found her card in his jacket pocket and dialled the number of the mobile. A voice calmly informed him that his caller was aware he was waiting.

'For God's sake,' he moaned.

'Please wait,' said the impassive voice.

He stared down at his notebook, at what he had written down during Jane's call. He ran for the newspaper he'd been reading and the rag-out of the second false number plate: 'J898 SPC', it said, the same number that Jane had given him.

The van had arrived at the Fellowship at dawn, she'd told him. Yes, but delivering what?

He snatched up the phone again. 'Please wait,' purred the voice.

He slammed down the receiver, and ran to get dressed. He would try Burroughs or, failing that, the police from his car.

Lucy-Ann Burroughs received the summons to go to the office: everyone was needed in the hunt for Edgecombe. She was going to obey that summons; but first she intended to find out who besides herself was spying on Sam Ferryman, and why.

An hour earlier, to wake herself up, she'd gone for a walk in the park, a circular walk, to ensure that she didn't lose sight of Ferryman's flat. On her way back, as she was checking the road for traffic, she'd seen a flash of sunlight on glass; it came from the camper-van she'd noticed last night. There was a man in the driver's seat, and he was looking at something through binoculars, so intent on his quarry that he didn't notice her.

Lucy-Ann followed his line of sight: it was the same as her own.

She returned to her car by a roundabout route, lest the man see her, and called Records with his registration number. They were extremely busy, she was informed snappily. Was it an emergency?

It was, she confirmed.

They put her on hold.

She saw the man was apparently reading a newspaper, with the same attention he'd been giving to Ferryman's flat, but she wasn't fooled.

While she waited, she kept getting messages that a caller was waiting, she was sure it would only be Broughton chasing her, and if she broke off to speak to him, she'd lose Records.

The Records man came back on the line. 'Your lot are already looking for him,' he said bluntly.

'What?'

'As of yesterday evening, Ryder's order, there've been tracers out on his mobile but he hasn't used it.'

The evening before? Lucy-Ann racked her brains. Ryder had been in Paris, he'd found the hitman dead.

'Ivor Maitland,' Records read out, 'from Glasgow. Suspected of involvement in at least two gangland murders.'

Ferryman was being cased by a hitman with a Keeper connection.

Lucy-Ann was pressing the code to call the office, when she saw Ferryman emerge on to the street and walk quickly along the pavement, away from her, away from Maitland.

She jumped out of the car. She saw – although she hardly believed it, in broad daylight, with witnesses about – Maitland running, with a gun in his hand.

'Ferryman,' she screamed, and the journalist spun round 'Down!' she yelled, but he stood there, frozen.

She heard the bullet's passage through the air and Ferryman fell. She couldn't see if he was hit.

Maitland was aiming at her. She flung herself down and rolled under a car. She heard a scream and the slam of brakes, footsteps running. She peered out: Maitland had gone; a second later, she saw his van pass at speed.

She crawled out. Ferryman was surrounded by a gaggle of people. She pushed her way through. His eyes were closed and there was blood on his face from a wound on his right temple.

She knelt beside him. His eyes flickered.

She pressed the emergency code on her mobile and quietly gave her whereabouts. 'Help is on its way,' she told the bystanders.

The key turned in the lock and back again. The door opened and Norton came in. He was alone, Jane saw, and was no longer wearing the Fellowship uniform. Instead, he wore dark trousers, a white shirt and a sober tie.

He looked perplexed. 'The door wasn't locked.'

She swallowed. 'Wasn't it, David?' she said.

His face cleared. 'Well, no matter. Will you come with me now?' He extended a hand and she knew she had no option but to take it.

It felt papery dry in hers, the hand of an old man.

He drew her up close to him. He was smiling. He caught a piece of her hair and tucked it behind her ear. She wanted to flinch away. 'Don't be afraid, little one,' he said softly. 'I only want you to get changed.'

He led her out into the passage and up to the entry-box. He pressed the code – one, two, three, four, she saw – and the door clicked open. They emerged into the main part of the house.

The front door was partially open. She heard the sound of many voices outside.

'You run upstairs now,' Norton murmured, his eyes on that door. 'Kirsten's in the second bedroom on the left. She'll tell you what to do.'

He left her at the foot of the broad staircase, and advanced to the front door, flinging it wide with a dramatic gesture. There was an immediate tumult of noise, then Norton said, 'My children,' and hush descended.

'What's this? A mutiny?' he cried and there was a roar of laughter. 'Or my Jesus army, awaiting their orders?'

There was another roar. The door closed behind him. His voice grew muffled.

At last! thought Jane. She was alone. The office with the telephones was on her right.

'Upstairs on the left,' came a soft voice. Wheeling round, she saw Steven on the other side of the staircase. Thank God she hadn't moved.

She went quickly up the stairs and tapped on the door. Kirsten opened it.

'Oh, Jane, thank goodness!' She pulled her into the room. 'I was so scared for you, but at least you weren't in that place for long.'

She spoke with genuine relief. Jane remembered how she had stood up for her at the trial, and wondered if she could be turned. After all, she'd had only been at the Fellowship a short time, and she'd been a journalist before.

She smiled at her. 'It was horrible,' she agreed. 'You were in there for nearly a week?'

Kirsten nodded.

Jane gave an authentic shudder. 'Did David talk to you about the Second Coming?' She made it sound as if he had to her.

Kirsten shook her head. 'No. What's that?'

'When Jesus comes again and the world comes to an end?'

'No, nothing like that.'

'Or about certain "signs" that have to happen before He comes?'

'No.' Kirsten looked worried.

It was too great a risk, Jane decided. Kirsten was too fragile, too liable to run to David with the strange things Jane had been telling her. Jane was on her own. The best she could hope for from Kirsten was camouflage.

'Has David said what our mission is?' Jane asked brightly.

'No,' Kirsten said more happily. 'Only that the eight of us are to get changed up here and meet him outside in ten minutes.' She glanced at her watch. 'Hey, you'd better be quick. Your clothes are over there.'

For the first time, Jane realized that, like Norton, Kirsten was no longer in Fellowship uniform. She wore a white cotton skirt and dark shirt. Her own new clothes seemed to be the pink shirt and black jeans, hanging on the back of a chair. Quickly, she changed into them.

As she did so she looked around the room. Apart from the bed, there was a small cabinet, a dressing table and chair, which Kirsten was sitting on, applying make-up. Doing up her shirt, Jane crossed to a window on the far wall. The dark cedar trees of Norton's wood were only feet away, and they stole most of the daylight. Below and to her right, she could just see the top of the high brick wall that divided the front of the house from the rear. They were in the front part, Jane realized. The fall was perhaps thirty feet, easily survivable. She released the window catch.

'What are you doing?' Kirsten asked.

'Just getting some air.' She could scarcely jump out with Kirsten in the room.

'D'you want any make-up? There's a bag of it here.'

'I'm fine, thanks.'

'Listen to that.' Kirsten paused. 'Isn't it beautiful?'

Through the open window came the sound of the Fellowship singing an old spiritual. Had Norton's last orders been given? Jane wondered. Was that their mission song?

A hasty knock came on the door, and a voice said, 'Kirsten? Jane? Downstairs, please.'

'Just coming.' Kirsten turned. 'Jane?'

'You go on. I won't be a moment.'

She expected Kirsten to argue, to insist on waiting for her, but she did not. She was clearly eager to get down to Norton. As soon as she'd gone, Jane opened the window wide and hoisted herself up on to the sill.

Quiet voices came from below.

'It seems so weird not to be wearing blue,' exclaimed a woman.

'I think you look lovely,' a man assured her.

Jane looked down. The couple were directly below her; she could see the tops of their heads. At any moment they might look up and see her.

She jumped softly back into the room. What else could she do? Whatever it was, she'd have to do it soon. Once the mission was under way, it would be too late. She had no way of alerting the authorities. She did a final sweep of the room: there was nothing, it was useless.

Her eyes veered back to the dressing table, to the make-up Kirsten had left lying there, to a lipstick with its cap off. She ran over and snatched it up. With a shaky hand, she tried to write on the mirror.

Another knock, louder this time. 'Jane?'

Whoever it was, must not enter, must not see, but someone was already coming in. Mary's head came around the door.

The emergency response team reached Lucy-Ann within fourteen minutes of her call. Sam Ferryman was lifted into the back of a low, white van with blacked-out windows and a green light on its roof. To the casual glance it looked like an ambulance.

It moved off with its light flashing and reached the yard at Vauxhall six minutes later. A doctor examined Sam's wound and declared it not much more than a graze.

As soon as Sam came round, Ryder got into the van and looked down at him grimly. Sam was deathly pale, the colour of the field bandage that been applied to his wound, but Ryder merely demanded 'Where's Jane Carlucci?'

Sam didn't prevaricate. 'The Fellowship. Hawkenhurst, Kent. Norton's the Keeper.'

On her laptop, Lucy-Ann entered a data-search on the group.

Sam tried to sit up. 'The van you're looking for – Botulism Helen's – is there. Jane said there's a mission today. The biggest ever, Norton said. She's one of the eight leaders.'

Ryder's and Lucy-Ann exchanged glances.

She said, 'All we've got is that it's a Christian drug-rehabilitation community in Kent. Zero security rating. There's no other recorded data.'

'There are about a hundred members,' Sam volunteered. 'They wear blue denim. Jane said there's a secret warehouse.'

'Where?' said Ryder.

'I don't know. They're stockpiling tins, she said, and cold remedies.'

It made awful sense to Ryder. 'Did she give you a time for this mission today?' he asked.

Sam shook his head, then winced at the movement.

Ryder thought fast. The local police could seal the area, set up road-blocks, let no one leave the Moor; begin an immediate evacuation of the surrounding area. But every one of those procedures risked alerting Norton to the fact they were on to them. That might provoke him into releasing the virus straight away, when he might not intend doing so for hours or even days yet. Although, if Carlucci was right, the 'biggest mission' was due to start that day.

There was no time to confer with anyone else.

On his mobile, he ordered SARS to go in. The south-of-England unit was still in Wales; the northern one was based near Manchester and said it would take them an estimated ninety minutes to reach the Moor. He told them to move at once. He and Burroughs would join them there.

'I'd like to come,' said Sam, sitting up on his gurney.

'Sorry,' Ryder said curtly.

Lucy-Ann got out of the van.

'But if there's a siege, I could help,' Sam said desperately. 'I know Jane and another girl in there. I could be the go-between.'

With a bullet graze in his head, Ryder thought. Then he reconsidered. Ferryman's link to Carlucci might be useful if she was one of the 'leaders' of the mission. And if there was a siege, as Ferryman said both sides would need the media. Better a journalist working with SARS than against it, Ryder thought, and anyway, he owed Ferryman.

'You feeling okay?' he asked brusquely.

'Fine.'

'Come on then.'

By a headlong dash, almost a collision, Jane had succeeded in preventing Mary from entering far enough into the room to see the mirror.

'Everyone's waiting,' Mary said coldly, taking a step back.

'I'm sorry, I was just doing my hair.'

'This isn't a beauty contest, you know.'

They descended the stairs in silence. In the hall, Norton was standing with Kirsten and the six male 'missionaries'. A little to one side, were the group of minders, the Shepherds.

Norton turned with a smile to welcome her.

'Let us pray,' he said softly.

Jane didn't hear a word, although she murmured 'Amen' and 'Yes, Jesus' along with the others.

Her thoughts were on Steven and three of the male Shepherds, who had retired to the Fellowship office. She heard the repetitive sound of a machine at work. A shredder, could it be? Were they destroying all evidence of the group's membership? Would they, as part of their final leave-taking, check every room, and find what she had written on the mirror?

'And now, I think our brothers and sisters are waiting,' Norton said pleasantly. 'Jane?'

She started.

'Don't you look pretty in pink, my dear? If you'll take my hand?'

She obeyed.

'And Kirsten, my other hand?'

Kirsten did so, smilingly.

'Boys?' he murmured.

The male missionaries fell in behind them. With Jane on one side, Kirsten on the other, Norton led them forward through the open doorway on to the top step of the house.

A great cheer went up.

Before her, Jane saw a sea of upturned, adoring faces; she thought suddenly of the Hitler rallies. The whole Fellowship seemed to be gathered there, and none of them was in uniform any longer. Their ordinary clothes made them strangers. Then she saw Abby standing at the front, and Philip in a grey sweatshirt nearby. Were they all going to die?

'God's blessing on our brothers and sisters as they lead our mission,' Norton called.

'God's blessing!'

'Praise His name!'

'Praise Him!'

Norton grinned hugely. 'To your vehicles!' he cried, and like a great ship turning, they wheeled and began to surge away.

Norton turned to the Shepherds in the hallway.

'Mary?'

She came out. She was wearing a pale-green linen dress, a scarf at the neck and dark glasses. She looked cool and efficient.

'You'll take your group to the station in Tunbridge Wells.'

She nodded and was gone.

He called another name. Another Shepherd came forward and was instructed to take his group to London, and then proceed by Tube to 'the destination'.

Five more minders were given direction for travel by road.

Of course, thought Jane. There'd would be no convoy travelling along the motorway, attracting public and perhaps police interest. The Fellowshippers would arrive at their destination by ones and twos, by rail, road and Tube. They looked like everyone else now; they would merge with the crowds.

Norton led the way to the back of the house, past her cell, past the chapel and out into the courtyard. She saw a small blue van parked up against a wall. She recognized it. Would Sam check the registration number she'd given him? she wondered dully. Even if he did, where would it lead him? What good would it do?

There was a people-carrier with a yellow TAXI sign on its roof. Its doors were open and at Norton's prompting, they got in. Jane took the seat indicated for her, next to Kirsten. The other missionaries climbed in, Norton coming last. He was carrying a small green nylon bag, which he laid carefully, horizontally, on his lap.

Jane suddenly realized there'd been no sign of Ruth or Ross. She hadn't seen them at the rally or in the house. Were they searching the house? Would they see the mirror and denounce her?

Steven came out of the house, crossed the cobbles and climbed into the driver's seat.

'All right?' asked Norton.

She held her breath.

'Fine,' said Steven.

The engine started, the van crept forward, the automatic gates clanged open and then shut behind them as they went slowly out into the drive. They were on their way.

The morning was warm and overcast with a light breeze: perfect weather, Ryder had been informed en route, for the release of a biological weapon.

The cloud cover meant that the virus wouldn't be exposed to much sunlight, and would therefore survive longer. The breeze would aid its dispersal.

The Moor was within visual range. Ryder's helicopter hung back in the sky; the SARS team, nine shiny black helicopters, whirred on ahead.

Ryder and his passengers would not form part of the assault; they would only get in the way. They must observe only. He looked down, and saw a patchwork of fields, a fête being held in the main village, people looking up at the helicopters. He saw the spire of the church at the Moor.

'No sign of activity,' reported the SARS commander over his head-set, but that meant nothing: Norton and the rest could be anywhere – in the church for instance, for a last prayer before releasing the virus.

'Going in,' came the commander's voice and at once, like beetles, the helicopters began dropping from the sky.

Ryder's remained hovering.

He saw the teams out and running. He saw them circle the church, while another group entered the manor-house. His glance took in the immediate surroundings; the two roads that led away from the Moor, one going down into Hawkenhurst village, the other winding away like a thin snake between fields.

He saw a double-decker bus toiling up the hill from the village; a jam of vehicles by the traffic lights. Was Norton in one of them?

SARS deployed, his own helicopter dropped onto the Moor, landing a little way from the rest on the village green. Its engine cut, the rotator blades slowed, but no one was allowed to get out. The Moor might be booby-trapped; Norton and his followers might be armed and were certainly dangerous. Until the 'all clear' was given, they had to remain as they were: strapped in, gas-masks on, listening and watching only.

Ryder peered through his mask. He could see no civilians, no blue-clad Fellowshippers, no cars parked on the verges. Where were they all? Was SARS about to find a mass of bodies?

'Church clear. Manor house ground floor clear. School clear.' The commandos' voices came over his earpiece.

'White house entered. Front room clear. Rear room clear. Secondary passage door locked. Attaching explosive.'

There was a soft 'boom' over the earpiece.

'Going in. Two, three doors, all locked, another passageway to the left.'

More explosives were attached, doors blown.

'An office: clear. Chapel: clear.'

Ryder longed to know what else was in the chapel.

'Bedroom: clear. Bedroom: clear. Bedroom: Bodies found.'

Ryder stiffened. So too, he noticed, did Ferryman.

'Man and woman. No pulse . . . Going on.'

'Wait,' ordered Ryder. 'The woman. Description?'

'Light build.'

'Age? Colouring?'

'Difficult to tell. Late thirties. Blonde probably.'

Ryder turned to Ferryman, who shook his head clumsily in his mask, to indicate that it wasn't Jane.

He faced front again. How many more bodies would they find?

There was another 'boom' as another door was blown. 'Stable-yard,' said a commando's voice. 'Outbuildings. Three. Clear. Clear. Clear. Blue Bedford van, registration number . . .'

Botulism Helen's van, Ryder realized: Ferryman had said it would be there. How had Norton done it? How had he, Ryder, allowed such a thing to be hatched on his own soil? It must have taken years. Why hadn't he known about it?

'Returning to the main house. Upstairs. Bedroom: clear . . . Bedroom: message on the mirror.'

Ryder tensed. 'Well?' he said sharply.

'Heathrow'.

The release of a biological weapon into the world's busiest international airport, Ryder thought. And it was a bank holiday weekend, the place would be packed.

Not only would those inside the terminals be infected, but passengers would board planes, would spread the virus around the globe. Unless they were stopped, unless the airport was sealed.

'Awaiting your command,' said the SARS captain.

Was the message genuine or a hoax, Ryder wondered in agony? Designed, like Vermont, to deliberately lead them astray while the true release happened elsewhere?

What option did he have?

'Heathrow,' he commanded, buckling himself back in.

His helicopter rose with the others. In fan convoy, they headed for the airport.

CHAPTER THIRTY-ONE

By the grace of God, David thought, and in the nick of His Holy time, had he and the children made it away from the Moor.

As the people-carrier travelled up the M25, he'd seen helicopters suddenly rise up over the horizon, nine black ones, their underbellies gleaming as they passed overhead before dipping south-east. David knew where they were going as surely as if they had broadcast it by loudspeaker.

But he'd felt no panic. They wouldn't know where to look. They'd find no clues at the Moor; no paperwork: no means of tracing them by their vehicles – each one had been bought for cash by a Fellowshipper using his home address; the Fellowshippers no longer even looked like Fellowshippers. Very soon it would be too late, anyway. There had been no hold-ups on the back-roads or the motorways, the journey had been easy and quick: they were already on the approach-road to Heathrow.

Now there was no time to launch another public appeal; no time for more memories to be jogged. The authorities had run out of time. But then the authorities were not working to the Lord's perfect timetable.

At the roundabout Steven took the Terminal Two turn-off.

Butterflies jumped in David's stomach. The long-awaited

moment was upon him. The Awful Horror, and then Jesus coming in glory, the clouds dividing, the trumpets sounding and the gathering of the faithful into His arms. David trembled in holy awe.

And also, he admitted, with a little fear. Ross had described the details of the killer flu so graphically. His fever was going to be terrible; his throat on fire, his lungs would grow heavy and dense. His feet, perhaps his face too, would turn black. A peculiar stench arose from many patients. He would begin to gasp for breath; bloody fluid would froth at his mouth, then finally he would become delirious, and death would follow from suffocation. Eight hours after his death, when rigor mortis set in, bloody fluid would gush from his mouth and nostrils.

Truly, a horrific way to die. And he would watch many succumb before he did himself: the virus spectacularly targeted the young. His plan had been to return with the children to the Moor, there to nurse them as long as he could, but he couldn't do that now: the SAS was there.

Steven headed up the ramp to Terminal Two Departures. The airport was extremely busy, David noticed with approval.

He saw an army jeep pull up outside the terminal.

'There's a space now,' Steven said softly and he pulled into a drop-off bay.

David glanced back at the jeep. Two officers had gone inside the terminal, leaving a third at the wheel. It could be anything, he told himself: a terrorist incident, a yet another security alert. Nevertheless, he'd be quick.

He called the first two boys forward and gave them their tickets – first-class, as an extra shield, because first-class passengers were less likely to be stopped than others. He unzipped his bag, took out their canister, and told them what to do.

'Do it an hour before you land,' he said.

The elder boy put it in his flight bag.

It would be all right, David told himself, anxiously: Ross had promised it wouldn't self-detonate 'unless you chuck it against a wall'. Dear Ross! David already missed his mordant sense of fun.

The boys got out of the vehicle. They took their suitcases from the boot, the executive ones with their names and fake business addresses on the labels, and headed for the terminal. He watched the doors open and shut behind them: two young high-flyers off to a conference in San Francisco. The doors opened again, and the two soldiers came out and jumped back into their jeep. It screeched off, honking its horn to clear a path. They were in a hurry, David thought.

In the near distance, he heard sirens. He didn't like that very much. If pushed, he could set the canisters there, all three together. But the Lord had always told him it would be North, South, East and West, the four corners of the earth, or approximations of them. San Francisco was West; if the other three canisters were all North – but no, the Lord wouldn't let that happen. He must have faith.

'Terminal Three?' Steven asked.

David considered. If they were looking for him, the longer the missionaries remained with him, the greater their danger of being taken. He told Steven to drive to the nearest bus-stop. Shuttle buses left every few minutes for the other terminals. He called the four male missionaries forward and gave them their instructions and their canisters, and they were dropped at the bus-stop.

'Terminal One,' he told Steven.

Most of the Fellowship, by their various routes, would be inside it by now. It didn't matter if some were late. The air in that cool, air-conditioned environment, once contaminated, would remain so for many hours to come.

He had to go inside to breathe it himself but he wouldn't be holding the girls' hands. No one would connect them to him.

He turned to look at them, sitting three rows back, side by side.

Kirsten immediately smiled back at him, but Jane was looking out of the window. Her jaw was tightly clenched. She was a nervous girl. He'd give the canister to Kirsten.

The van bounced over the hump at the entrance to Terminal One's short-term car-park.

Two miles from Heathrow, Ryder was informed that as a precaution, the Cabinet and other prominent persons were being evacuated to places of safety.

It had not yet been decided whether to close the airport. To do so with an Armageddon cult inside – if it was still there, if it hadn't already taken to the skies – would be an act of mass murder. But better to kill ten thousand, some ARIC members argued, than to wipe out millions around the world; and it was possible, Porton argued, that a vaccine might be found in time to save at least some of the airport victims. A vaccine engineered from the DNA of the dead.

The decision might already have been taken out of their hands. Norton had over an hour's start on them, according to an eye-witness in Hawkenhurst. If the bio-experts being flown in detected the virus in the air, the decision would be made for them: the airport would be sealed, turned into a vast isolation hospital – or, more truthfully, Ryder thought, a morgue. It was a scenario too awful to contemplate.

His only hope lay in finding Norton before it was too late, in talking him down from his Last Battle stand. It was a slim hope, and he knew it. The bodies at the Moor had been identified as those of Edgecombe and Botulism Helen. If Norton was killing his most faithful servants, he was not going to be dissuaded by anyone or anything.

Burroughs and Ferryman were with him, because Burroughs was familiar with Carlucci's photograph and Ferryman with the woman herself. In addition, a photograph of Carlucci was being circulated to staff, police and army personnel at the airport. Extensive efforts were under way to track down photographs of the other known cultists: Norton, Kirsten Cooper and Mary Wilson, the Chief Constable's daughter. But there was so little time.

Any one of the hundred or so Fellowshippers could be carrying the biological weapon – or they all could be in effect, weapons, if they had been exposed at the Moor. They weren't wearing uniform any more, according to the Hawkenhurst witness. The troops were still at the airport from the global Alert, but there weren't enough of them to stop and check every individual, even if that had been advisable, which it wasn't. Flight lists were being checked, but thus far none of the known names had come up. That didn't mean much, Ryder knew. The contaminated Fellowship could be about to take the skies en masse.

He looked down. Heathrow lay below him. From the air, it looked like a toy model, with miniature planes and trucks and people. Something for a child to play with.

The helicopter dipped on its final descent. SARS was splitting into four, one group for each terminal. Four terminals, the four horse-men of the Apocalypse. Ryder had to decide which one for himself, Ferryman and Burroughs.

'One,' he called out and the helicopter instantly keeled in that direction.

From the motorway, Jane too had seen the black helicopters, had prayed they were headed for the Moor, that they'd find her message. But if they had, surely the vehicle would have been stopped by now? They must have been going somewhere else; she had entertained false hope.

Steven pulled up in Terminal One's car-park.

Once she was inside the terminal, Jane would only have Kirsten with her; she could escape with the canister, get to a policeman or an airport official, warn them what was happening.

Norton turned to her and Kirsten with a smile.

'Come, girls,' he said.

He was about to hand over their canister. Jane had watched each previous procedure. He always gave the bottle to the older Fellow-shipper. He gave theirs to Kirsten: 'You're senior to Jane in the spirit. You don't mind, do you, Jane, my little one?'

She blinked. She could still make a run for it, she thought. Identify Kirsten to the police. . .

'Under here,' Norton said quietly, holding the canister up so they could see, 'is a little plastic wheel. Turn it anti-clockwise as far as it will go. Then leave it. All right?'

Kirsten nodded.

'Jane?'

She nodded too.

'Just hold the bottle upright in your hand. Casually, my angel, that's it. Now, if anyone tries to stop you, anyone at all, a policeman for instance' – Surely Kirsten would query that, Jane thought? But Kirsten was simply smiling acquiesence – 'just flick the lid open. Got that?'

'Yes, David.'

It must contain a bomb, Jane thought. Once in the terminal, she could scream, 'Bomb!' but wouldn't that cause panic? If Kirsten panicked too, she might activate it. Jane could wrench it from her, but again that might set it off. She'd have to make her own escape and get help.

Norton said he had no air-tickets to give them, that their mission would take place there in the terminal. He told them exactly where, outside a café on the first floor.

'You're enacting a parable, the meaning of which I'll explain to you later.'

'Yes, David,' beamed Kirsten.

'If you see any of the others, give no sign. All right?'

Kirsten nodded. Others? thought Jane. The rest of the Fellowship? She hadn't factored them into her escape plan, but there would be hundreds of people inside that building; she could still get away.

On their foreheads, Norton was tracing the sign of the cross. 'Go forth, then, my children,' he said softly. 'I won't be far behind.'

It didn't matter, Jane told herself. He wouldn't be holding her hand.

They got out of the van, Kirsten holding her bottle carefully. Steven got out too.

'Steven will go with you,' said Norton.

Jane's mind whirled. What chance did she have now?

The three of them started walking towards the terminal building.

By the car-park ticket machines, Mary and four male Shepherds were waiting. They fell in behind them.

They went into the terminal, stepped on to the moving walkway. Steven led, then came Jane and Kirsten, and right behind them were Mary and the men.

It was estimated there were six thousand people in Terminal One.

A SARS unit was searching it for Jane Carlucci, and police, customs and army personnel were also trying to pick her out from the throng. She was supposed to be a 'leader' of a mission. But what did that mean? That she was carrying the virus, or a Bible?

A photograph of Norton had been found, culled from a nineteen-year-old passport application form. It was due to be wired through to the airport at any moment.

Sam, as he knew Jane and Kirsten, had two SARS officers with him. They wore plain clothes with, on their chests and backs, identification patches concealed by tear-off strips. Their weapons were also concealed. There had been no question of anyone wearing protective clothing or masks; it would have caused public panic.

Sam looked round the check-in hall, craning to see over people's heads: endless snaking lines of people, one solid block of confusion.

The noise was deafening. An announcement that a flight would be delayed came over the tannoy system and at once the pandemonium increased.

Sam stared from face to face. People, or most of them, were basically good-hearted. They didn't deserve to die the terrible death he'd heard described in the helicopter. A bio-medic had explained over the radio to Ryder what would happen if the virus was released into the terminal. There would be too many dying people for the overstretched medical teams to deal with. But there was a simple way to tell if someone merited treatment. If their feet were already black, there was no point in wasting resources, because the patient would be dead within the hour. The virus struck the young first.

Sam knew that he would die, and Jane too, if that virus was released. He couldn't see how it was to be prevented. He couldn't see that Norton, having spent so long fulfilling the Scroll, would allow his Armageddon to be stopped.

'Nothing?' muttered one of SARS men in his ear.

Sam shook his head.

They had completed their square; Terminal One, like the other three, had been divided into eight roughly equal parts, four airside, four public. They climbed the stairs to the next floor. Just ahead of them was Ryder with his own discreet contingent.

There they split once more: Ryder to the right, Sam to the left where the shops and the restaurants were.

A heaviness was seeping through Jane's limbs, stealing into her brain like a sleeping-pill, making it an effort to continue walking.

Steven kept his hand on her elbow, guiding her and Kirsten forward.

There were hundreds of people milling about, and, Jane thought, more policeman than usual, but none of them was looking at her. Steven moved them towards the escalator up to the next floor.

Kirsten was holding her canister upright, awkwardly, like a beacon in front of her, but no one seemed to notice it. People were too busy going on holiday.

Jane saw a policeman looking at her. She stared back imploringly, willing him to stop her, but he moved on.

Behind her, Mary was walking with one hand inside her bag; the man with her held his right arm stiffly by his side, probably concealing a weapon, Jane reckoned. There were two other Shepherds over to the left, and not far back was Norton, in a panama hat and glasses and pulling along a small case on wheels. He was almost unrecognizable: older, muted, ordinary.

A hand came down on her shoulder. Steven's fingers wormed in hard under her collar-bone. She gasped.

'All right, Jane?' he asked.

At the least excuse, she knew, he'd kill her.

They reached the top of the escalator, and Mary and her partner walked away a little way.

Steven turned to Jane and Kirsten. 'You know what to do,' he said. 'I'll be right behind you.'

The two walked on. The coffee-shop Norton had described to them was dead ahead. It was packed with people, their suitcases bulging out on to the concourse. There was a big, black floor fan squatting near the entrance, just as Norton had said. In front of it, also squatting, was a small girl of perhaps three years, her eyes blissfully closed, her hands outstretched into the cool air.

Jane glanced back. Steven had stopped, but he was watching them intently.

'Kirsten?' she muttered.

'Mm?'

'You mustn't set that thing. It's dangerous. It'll kill people.' She was guessing, but with good cause.

'What?' said Kirsten, dreamily.

'Hundreds of people. Us. That little girl.'

Kirsten frowned. 'Oh no,' she said. 'David wouldn't do anything bad.'

'Yes. David's sick. He thinks God wants him to do it, to bring about the end of the world, but he's wrong.'

Out of the corner of her eye, Jane saw Norton standing by a bank of telephones, watching them. Norton on one side, Steven on the other, and the armed Shepherds in between.

'Give me the bottle, Kirsten, and I'll get help,' she begged.

'What?'

'Or else, just pretend to do it. Pretend to set the device.'

'The others . . .' said Kirsten uncertainly.

'They won't know.'

Kirsten said nothing. They had reached the fan. The little girl looked up at them and scowled.

Kirsten's hand moved towards the base of the suntan bottle. 'It's only a parable,' she said in a thread of a voice. 'Don't worry, Jane.' Her fingers fumbled with the screw beneath the bottle.

Time stopped. Jane looked down upon herself and saw Kirsten standing there, and the child, and Steven staring, and David, and all the Shepherds, watching. There were so many things she had wanted to do with her life. She remembered how she had longed to change her name, but she hadn't done it because it would have hurt her father too much. She remembered crying in her father's arms for the moon and that he had promised to get it for her.

She need never have worried about Eccles, about her future, she thought mistily. She would never have a career . . . She wished she'd met Sam earlier. She wished they had had some time together.

She saw him standing by a pillar, a few feet from Norton. There was a bandage round his head.

She blinked hard, then looked back again; he was still there. Beside him were several men, all staring at her. She recognized Paul Ryder.

Kirsten was bending down with the bottle in her hand.

The little girl reached up to take it.

'Give me that!' Jane grabbed the bottle.

There was a shot and people screamed. She didn't know if she'd been hit. She ran towards Sam but Norton was coming at her and she swerved to the left, dodging people, clutching the bottle tightly, trying to keep it upright. Her hands were slippery with sweat – she *mustn't* drop it.

How long did she have? How long before the device activated?

There were two more shots. People were hitting the floor all around her. She risked a glimpse over her shoulder: Steven was coming after her, a gun in his hand, and there were other men with guns.

In front of her was a door marked 'No Entry'. She crashed through it and leapt up the stairs.

The door banged back against its hinges. She heard men's boots on the stairs behind her.

She kept going. She had to get away.

The door banged again.

'Halt!'

She took the next three steps in one. She landed badly, and felt herself falling. The bottle fell from her grasp.

In slow motion, it tumbled through the air. It bounced once on a step, then up into the air again. A gunman on the steps below her reached out and caught it.

His gun clattered down the stairwell.

'Freeze,' yelled another gunman, pointing his weapon at her.

Jane didn't move. She saw the yellow letters on their chests, and realized who they must be.

'It's been activated,' she shouted. 'I don't know how long we've got left.'

'It's a popper!' shouted the first man, descending the stairs with care.

There were other men at the bottom, and they cleared a path for him. As they moved away, Jane saw Sam.

'Sam!' she yelled.

'I told you! Don't move,' shouted the SARS man, still aiming at her.

'It's OK,' Sam said urgently. 'She's with us.'

'And who the hell are you?' snapped the gunman, not altering his aim.

'They're both on our side,' came Paul Ryder's voice.

The man lowered his rifle.

Sam squeezed past him up to Jane. He put his arms round her and held her tight. 'Are you all right?' he whispered.

'Are you?' She touched his bandage.

She heard the airport's tannoy system appealing for calm. She felt suddenly light-headed. 'There are others,' she croaked.

'Others? Where?' demanded Ryder.

'Getting on planes to San Francisco, Tokyo and Lima.'

Ryder went white. Did she know the names of those passengers? he asked.

She'd seen them once, fleetingly. She couldn't remember. She described the six male missionaries as best she could.

Ryder barked fresh instructions into his mobile.

Twelve minutes later, eight SARS officers in plain clothes, entered the VIP suite in Terminal Four. The flight to Tokyo was departing in forty minutes, but first- and business-class passengers had yet to be called.

The team combed the open-plan area. They were looking for two men in their middle to late twenties, one with fair hair, one with brown, both wearing dark business suits. The canister was in an attaché case carried by the older man.

The VIP suite was crowded with people, many of whom bore at least some resemblance to those descriptions. The team didn't know whether the men would be travelling separately or together, whether they would have swopped the attaché case for another bag.

'Would all first-class passengers please board now at Gate Number 17?' asked the suite manageress pleasantly, nothing in her voice betraying what she felt.

The team positioned themselves at strategic points about the lounge: two at the reception desk, two by the departure door, two by a fire-exit; two 'floaters' mingling with the passengers, watching for any tell-tale sign.

It was these last two who spotted the Fellowshippers. Seated over by a window, they were amongst the last to get to their feet. Neither man spoke to the other. The younger looked a little blank. The elder looked purposeful. He had an attaché case in his hand.

One floater murmured into his jacket lapel, then he and his colleague approached the pair.

'Excuse me,' said the floater, and the Fellowshippers stopped expectantly.

The first floater grabbed the case. The second produced an assault rifle from inside his jacket.

'Down!' he bellowed into the faces of the startled pair.

They dropped to the floor.

Passengers began screaming.

'Secure,' yelled the SARS commander a moment later into his mouthpiece.

In the observation room at the top of Terminal One, Ryder, Jane Carlucci, Sam Ferryman and Lucy-Ann Burroughs were keeping watch. Ryder passed on the commander's message.

Attempts had been made to stop the activation device on Jane's canister but it wasn't yet known if those attempts had been successful. Until it was, no one could leave the terminal building.

Steven had been shot dead. Down in the main concourse, attempts were still being made to quell the resulting pandemonium.

Norton and several other Fellowshippers were in custody.

The public-address system was asking anyone in David Norton's party to gather at a specified airline desk. It went on to say that following a security incident, doors had been locked automatically but that incident was now under control and the airport would soon be functioning normally.

Ryder hoped so. Bio-hazard experts were examining the canister now and sampling the air within the terminal. It was too soon to tell whether it was too late for everyone there. He chose not to share those thoughts.

He turned back to the phone, and told the ARIC chairwoman, 'Two more canisters to go.'

The flight to Peru was not due to depart for another hour and a half. Passenger lists were checked. There were seventeen young men travelling to Lima, of whom five had checked in at roughly the time suggested by Jane. Four of them had already gone through passport control. It was safe to assume that two were the Fellowshippers, but it was too great a risk to call their names.

They weren't in the first-class lounges, so they were most likely to be among the two thousand people currently airside. Their rucksacks had been checked in and Jane had been unable to remember any further details about them.

The airport staff agreed readily to Ryder's request, to set up a secondary scanning check, as sometimes happens, at the departure gate.

An early boarding-call was put out for the Peru flight.

The SARS team were wearing the airline jackets. Two of them manned the scanner, and others stood to one side, apparently gossiping. Still others, in plain clothes, waited in the departure pen. The passengers started to arrive: mixed couples, young women on their own, businessmen.

Two young men approached the desk together. They proferred their boarding-passes, they waited patiently in the short queue for the scanning machine.

An old lady was going through, fussing about X-ray damage to the film in her camera.

The first young man set down a plastic bag on the conveyer. SARS knew what they were looking for, but as the contents appeared on screen, they saw no bottle of suntan lotion, only chocolate.

Had they been mistaken? Were the Fellowshippers yet to come? Or had they been forewarned by a message from a comrade in Terminal One?

The second boy set down his flight bag, carefully upright. The way he did so was enough to bring the conversation of the watching commandos to a halt. They moved forward casually; the officers inside the departure lounge did likewise.

The bag entered the rubber flaps of the scanning machine. Its contents were revealed: paperback, sunglasses, wallet and suntan lotion wedged upright in one corner.

The SARS commando monitoring the screen stopped the scanner. He glanced up and nodded slightly. The boy and his partner were thrown to the ground and pinned there.

Other passengers, witnessing the incident, were too taken aback to scream.

'Secure,' reported the SARS commando, satisfaction in his voice.

There were two flights bound for San Francisco that morning, one direct, the other via Chicago. The first had completed boarding and was waiting to leave, but was held on the runway so that SARS could check the passengers. The two men Jane had described, one with straight golden hair, the other tall and thin with a short, goatee beard, were not on the aircraft.

'So what're you telling me?' rasped Ryder, although he knew.

'They're on the other flight. It's been airborne for thirty minutes.'

Ryder had a sudden mental picture of the people on board that aircraft. It was a 747: three hundred and eighty-one men, women and children on board. He imagined the two men sitting up in first class with the plague in their laps, and he felt hope die within him.

CHAPTER THIRTY-TWO

The young man with dead-straight golden hair accepted a second glass of champagne from the air-stewardess. He sipped it and closed his eyes in pleasure. When he opened them again, he caught a disapproving glare from his colleague, sitting beside him.

'I won't have any more,' he promised.

'No.'

He took the role of senior Fellowshipper a little too seriously, the younger man thought. He too felt the honour of the mission; he too would not dream of questioning David's orders. But why, if they were not mean to enjoy themselves a little, had David bought them first-class tickets? Hadn't he intended them to eat, drink and be a bit merry, and to smile at the pretty stewardess? It wasn't as if he had taken one of the newspapers offered.

'Ladies and gentlemen,' the captain's voice came over the loud-speaker system. 'My sincere apologies and there is absolutely no cause for alarm, but I am afraid we shall have to return to Heathrow.'

A groan of disbelief ran down the aircraft.

'The second-in-command is unwell and flight regulations state that we must have two fully operational pilots at all times. Once again, I can only apologize' – the disappointment was more muted now that illness had been mentioned – 'and tell you that it is for your safety that such regulations are in place.'

The announcement ended.

'What a nuisance,' murmured the senior Fellowshipper.

The young man said nothing. When the stewardess came down the aisle again with her tray of champagne flutes, he did not take a third glass, although it wasn't out of deference to the senior man. He was deep in thought. God used every sense, David often said, including the sixth, to communicate His purpose to mankind. He felt he was receiving such a communication right now. The mission was in jeopardy. David or the Lord – they were interchangeable in the young man's mind – needed him to act urgently.

He leant over the arm-rest. 'We must activate the device,' he said softly.

'What're you talking about?' his partner asked.

'It's what David wants us to do.'

'He does not.'

'I'm telling you, he does. I've had a prophecy.'

The other man's face hardened. 'Don't talk rubbish.'

The younger man remembered too late his colleague's jealousy. Having so few spiritual fruits himself, he envied others theirs. The canister was in the flight-bag by the window. The younger man made a lunge for it.

'Stop it!' The senior man hand seized his wrist painfully. 'You're disobeying David,' he hissed.

A stewardess was staring; the younger man withdrew his arm.

'David ordered us to set it an hour before we land,' the senior Fellowshipper said, regaining control.

'David's orders have changed.'

'That's blasphemy!'

Wait, whispered Jesus.

The plane began its descent. As its wheels touched down on the runway, the captain announced that regrettably, owing to crew shortage, it would be some time before the plane could resume its journey. Would all passengers therefore kindly disembark?

The first-class cabin emptied first, the passengers descending on to the tarmac, where several limousines stood waiting.

'Classy,' crowed the younger man.

The first limousine took on four passengers. The Fellowshippers were directed by polite ground-staff towards the second vehicle.

Inside the terminal building, said Jesus.

The senior Fellowshipper got into the blacked-out car. The younger man bowed his head to enter. He saw his colleague on the floor, a man sitting on him, another man backing out of the other side of the car, holding the flight-bag.

The young man cried out, but the sound was muffled, as he was hit from behind, then shovelled into the car. The doors slammed, the car took off at speed across the tarmac.

In the detention room, two men in black tracksuits were watching David.

He could feel their hatred of him, their bottled-up desire to hurt him. They still didn't know if their world was safe. Until they did, he guessed, they'd leave him alone. But David had every confidence that the Lord would prevail, that at least one of the canisters would make it through.

They'd tear him limb from limb, they'd take turns at torturing him. David could bear that. Hadn't Jesus died on the cross for him? As long as he knew the virus was out there, working, that the Awful Horror might be delayed a fraction but would still come to pass. The attempt by Jane, daughter of Satan, to destroy the Lord's work had failed.

Jane, whom he had harboured to his breast.

He felt bile rise in his throat. He would not dwell on her any longer. He would return to the strange half-dream he'd been having, almost a vision in its clarity – and yet he knew it could only be a dream – the two boys bound for San Francisco, coming back to Heathrow, himself telling the golden angel what to do.

He saw them somewhere dark, face-down. The angel's mouth was cut, he was crying. Satan's agents were fingering the canister, harming it. David took a sharp intake of breath. It was really happening. As for the other canisters . . .

His mouth fell open at the pictures he saw: the four other male missionaries were in rooms similar to his own; the canisters had been taken from them, de-activated. The virus would die. The Lord's work was ruined. His, David's, years of devotion, of hardship, brought to nought. Not for him Paradise, where Ruth and Ross waited so longingly for him. . .

He checked himself. He'd forgotten. Of course, Paradise still beckoned! Had not Ross, at his insistence, supplied him with an escape route? An ejector seat, Ross had called it.

The SARS men had body-searched David, but they hadn't checked every tooth in his mouth, tapping each one to see if it was genuine. That would come later, David thought, when they'd branded him insane and locked him away forever in an lunatic asylum.

With his tongue, he worked at the space where once a molar had been, where, before leaving the Moor, he had removed the capped tooth, and inserted instead the tablet that Ross had promised would take him away within ten seconds.

He loosened it, although the act of doing so had attracted the notice of one of the guards who was coming for him now.

David bit down hard.

The guard's hands were on him, grabbing at his mouth, wrenching his jaws open.

'. . . seven, eight, nine . . .' David felt himself drift free. He saw Jesus, holding out His hands to his good and faithful servant.

News that the fourth canister had been seized and made safe brought a cheer to the observation room. The SARS, army and police commanders, taciturn until then, became effusive in their praise of each other and of each other's officers. The noise level grew.

Jane felt suddenly limp.

'Thank God,' said Sam, taking her hand. He brought it to his lips and kissed her fingers.

She smiled at him. She hardly dared believe the nightmare was over.

Behind her, she heard Ryder say, 'How long before we know?' She turned and saw him on the phone.

Others seemed to notice at the same time. The room went quiet again. When Ryder looked up, it was as if all the blood had been drained from his face.

He spoke tonelessly. 'The device of the canister in this terminal wasn't activated.'

'But that's excellent news,' exclaimed someone.

Kirsten hadn't done it, Jane thought. She'd done what she had suggested: pretended only. Then she saw the dead look in Ryder's eyes.

'But Porton says the lid of the canister popped,' Ryder said.

When it fell on the steps, Jane thought. When she dropped it. She heard, distantly, that Porton experts were taking it apart, to see if the spike in the lid had penetrated. It would be another hour, at least, before they knew.

'I'm afraid we're sealing the building,' said Ryder quietly.

There was absolute silence.

Forty minutes passed. On the top floor of the terminal, a sick-bay was discreetly set up. Ryder was informed that massive doses of antibiotics would be flown in, and anything else they needed. The outside world would do anything it could for them – save let itself be contaminated.

Inside the terminal, calm announcements continued to be made about the earlier security incident, in which a man had been shot, and the ensuing safety procedures. For the time being, the sealing was blamed on the unknown terrorists/drug cartel/serious criminals who had now been apprehended.

Journalists started phoning in, not just to the airport's PR department, schooled in what to say, but to the terminal building itself. They began talking to members of the public. The phones were cut.

Ryder waited by the phone. If the news was bad, only six thousand people would die, rather than fifty million. He tried to be glad about that, but he felt only numb.

He heard the first announcement over the public address system, inviting anyone who felt unwell, to report to the sick-bay.

There was one patient already, in a guarded room: Norton, under sedation after he had realized that his 'cyanide' pill was harmless: it would later prove to be a vitamin tablet, encapsulated in a white coating to look like a tooth.

In the observation room, someone sneezed. All eyes turned towards Sam Ferryman. Of course, Ryder thought, he had been one of the nearest to the canister when the lid came off.

Ryder's phone rang. He felt the silence close in on him as he picked up the receiver. 'Yes?' he said, and his voice was a croak. 'I see,' he said a second later.

He replaced the phone. He looked up at the strained faces and found that he couldn't speak. 'The canister,' he began. 'The spike didn't penetrate the interior. The virus didn't escape.'

The room erupted in cheers.

A nurse drew the curtains around Sally Goodall's bed.

Thanks to the sedative, Sally had slept well. She felt better altogether, and the cramping had gone, but the news that the consultant was coming to see her made her tense again.

'Don't worry, love,' Alan begged her, squeezing her hand.

'No,' she promised. If she worried, she'd have another panic attack. This time she might not be so lucky, she might lose the baby.

The curtains swished back. The consultant entered, again with a bevy of his students behind him. He smiled down at Sally and Alan.

'I've got good news for you two,' he said.

'The antibiotics have worked?' Alan blurted.

The consultant beamed; the students did too.

'Well, they haven't done any harm, let's put it that way,' he said.

'What d'you mean?' demanded Sally.

'They were never necessary, Mrs Goodall. The final lab tests are back on you and Ned, and what you ate. It wasn't contaminated.'

'What?' whispered Sally.

'Not all the packets were.'

Sally stared at him, and then at Alan.

'Oh God,' she whispered. 'I can go home?'

'You and Ned, both,' he said.

Sally broke down in grateful tears.

EPILOGUE

David Norton was ordered to be detained for life at Broadmoor Hospital.

Ruth Grant was buried on her family's estate in Scotland.

No one claimed Ross Edgecombe's body and it was eventually cremated in Hastings. He never received the credit for perfectly recreating the 1918 influenza bug.

The British government never admitted to having the flu virus – but then neither did any other government. A quantity of it resided, under conditions of utmost security, in a laboratory at Porton Down. A safeguard, said the few who knew about it; the most powerful biological weapon ever invented, said others.

Paul Ryder was asked to be the new chairman of the Bridegroom organization, an honour, he told his fellow grooms, that he regretfully declined.

Most of the Fellowshippers, after counselling, were able to return to normal lives, although a few were always drawn to other NRMs. Kirsten Cooper went to drama school.

Jane wrote an academic paper on the phenomenon of Armageddon NRMs, with special reference to Norton's Fellowship. The paper became a book, and eventually a film. She was offered a professorship at London University and took it. Within a year, she had eclipsed Eccles in the NRM world.

Her book was serialized in the *Correspondent*.

By that time, she and Sam were living together, having found that they liked each other very much.

The Eighth Scroll, which was found in Norton's baggage at Heathrow, was never seen again, although of course copies of it were. Sam and other journalists suggested that the original been destroyed by a nervous security service, but in fact it was kept in an airtight case in the vault of a building off Vauxhall.

No one ever went to look at it, except, in an occasional reflective moment, Paul Ryder. He would think what might have happened that day, and then he'd lock it up again and go about his business, thanking God, sincerely, that Armageddon had been averted.

The two leaders had read every word of *Thy Will be Done: Inside the Fellowship*, by Jane Carlucci.

Although it was written by an unbeliever, it gave them many valuable insights into David's mind, a mind they had come to revere as that of the Lord's penultimate prophet on earth. David had spoken the truth. He had shown them the error of their previous beliefs.

They had left the Church they ran and set up another, much smaller group, like David's attracting no attention.

Donald was the last prophet, and his wife, Esther, the last prophetess. It had taken them a while to grasp that: that, after David's imprisonment, the Lord was calling them to put on his mantle: to enact the last prophecy of the Eighth Scroll.

David's attempt with the flu virus had been not a failure but a smoke-screen. As part of the smoke-screen they themselves had been under suspicion. They had been interrogated by Paul Ryder, and the members of their Pilgrim Community Church imprisoned. They were now above suspicion, dismissed by MI5 as harmless religious cranks.

In the two years that had passed since Heathrow, they had worked hard. They had read avidly the newspaper articles telling how to buy deadly germs over the Internet. They had quietly expanded their Church; they had enrolled scientists. The Lord had made it easy for them.

In eighteen hours' time, when the four young people in America stood upon that point on the Earth's surface known as Four Corners, He would ensure that everything went perfectly. Four vials of anthrax spores released into the atmosphere, carried through the air, breathed in, breathed out.

The Lord would bring it to pass. He would keep His word: He would rain down the Awful Horror upon the Ungodly, and when enough of them were dead He'd come again.

Esther and Donald joined hands. 'The Lord is my Keeper,' they chanted.